Serendipity of Fate

Becky Banks

Ha'ikū
Press

Published by:

Maui, Hawaiʻi | Portland, Oregon
haiku-press.com

Cover design by James T. Egan of Bookfly Design.

beckybanksbooks.com

2nd Edition

ISBN: 978-0-9882614-6-4

eISBN: 978-0-9882614-2-6

This book is dedicated to every soul who has laid their life on the line for honor, duty, and freedom.

Preface

Two years ago.

Cason had been expecting the punch to his face. After all, Ryan had found out that Cason was fantasizing about his sister. And it was a hot day, perfect for trouble.

The sun was relentless. After an insurgent attack that morning, the heat had been particularly punishing. So the afternoon quiet felt less like a reprieve and more like the windup for a pitch or, well, a punch. Something more was coming. This was but a break.

Most of the men lay sprawled, shirts off, in the red dirt of their makeshift base on the hill. The valley, with its craggy rocks and gnarled green-tipped trees, spread out wide below before tucking steeply into the *V* up the mountain. The very air felt parched; with the war, sun, and formidable earth, all life was being sucked from the place.

Cason had taken shelter in his sleeping bunker. In the partial darkness, he held her photo. Savannah Sparling, Savi, looked back up at him, her smile full and warm. It was shit here in this place, total shit. The memory of piping-hot fifty-caliber shells hitting the ground all around him gradually ceased its machine-gunning tattoo in his mind. The taps to his adrenaline seemed to be perpetually on, unless he was holding her photo. Then he was transported back to her, sitting in her mother's living room, listening to her laugh and watching her watch him. He loved her, of that he had no doubt, and when he got back, he'd make his fantasy real. He'd take her on a real date. He'd ask her to marry him.

"I knew it!" Ryan's voice interrupted Cason's thoughts.

Cason looked up as his childhood buddy—and the extremely protective older brother of the object of his desire—straightened up from ducking through the doorway, a smile cracking his face. He was still in his desert fatigues. The black of his hair matched the wraparound shades he'd shoved up on top of his head, revealing his raccoon tan.

"Shit," Cason said as Ryan reached to intercept the photo on its way back under the bed. Cason wasn't used to having to keep his daydreams a secret. Ryan was in a separate squad that had met up with them that morning for a surprise attack on the enemy the following morning.

"No way, man! Give it here. The guys tell me you've got one fine piece of ass and gonna tie the knot next R&R. Don't know why you can't tell me about it, but can I at least see her before I'm standing up there as best man?" Ryan laughed as he lunged again.

"No. Get off me!" Cason pushed him off with one hand and tucked the photo behind him. But Ryan had a long reach and determination, and soon he was shuffling backward in the tight quarters with the photo in hand.

Cason got up, and Ryan put his free hand out, keeping him back. "Now, let's get a good look the poor girl who'd let you fuck her." He took his first look at the photo.

Cason went cold.

"What the...?" Ryan flipped the picture over and back again, as though the movement would shake the image into something else. "What the fuck is this?"

Cason just stood there.

"Is this some kind of joke?"

"No." Cason flushed.

"No," Ryan said, his cheeks going blotchy. "No, no. *No!* No fucking way. Not with my sister!"

And that was when Ryan coldcocked him.

Cason let the punch land and felt that it was just. The things he'd thought about doing with Savannah...He should have punched the ideas right out of his own head.

"Not with my sister!" Ryan shouted at him again. "Not now. Not ever! Do you hear me? You stay the fuck away from her!" He jabbed Cason in the chest with his index finger for emphasis. "Don't go near her ever again!"

Cason stumbled back and really looked at the dusty, dark-haired man who stood shaking with rage in front of him. He and Ryan had changed. They had both grown up in different directions after enlisting. He wasn't the playboy Ryan surely remembered him as, and Ryan wasn't the impressionable friend he'd once known. As much as Ryan had once been his best friend, they were nearly strangers now.

"Fine," Cason said through dry lips.

"You'll promise me," Ryan hissed.

Cason knew the war did that to people. Every war throughout time, including these endless Middle East wars that called for them to leave home in six-month-to-yearlong deployments with little to no R&R in between. The seemingly ceaseless fighting twisted small things into the unbearable. It was as if life were a glass of water, the war drinking it up until there was just one drop left, and then it took that too, leaving nothing but emotionally parched soldiers.

"Right now, promise," Ryan said.

Cason gritted his teeth. "Fuck this." And then he turned, shoving his way out through the bunk's flapping doorway.

Gunshots rang out then. Dust puffed up as bullets hit the red dirt around the base. The men scrambled, and for the second time in as many days, hell broke loose from her tenuous leash. The mission was a bust.

It was only later, as he lay in a cold, sterile room of the US military hospital in Germany, IV dripping fluid into his harm, that Cason realized that bloody battle had claimed a life, which indelibly changed his. His life was now fate-shackled by a blood promise he had given to his best friend. A promise he never thought he'd have to make and a death he wished he'd never known.

Chapter One

Savannah stepped from the creamy leather interior of her pearlescent white SUV and hauled out a bag of groceries for her mother. The late Thursday afternoon was like every other toward the end of a New Orleans summer: hot, humid, and downright suffocating.

Bumping the car door shut with her hip, Savannah turned toward the house. It was a single-level blue bungalow that blended in with the other nondescript seventies bungalows around it. A postage-stamp front lawn, like the neighbors', separated it from the road. The various yards' details, the only apparent means of homeowner expression, ranged from untamed wilderness to fashion gardens to bright-green lawns trimmed to within an inch of their lives with military-like precision. Her mother's was the latter.

Savannah shoved the front door open. "Mama, I'm here," she said with a soft New Orleans drawl. She knocked the door closed with the sole of her high heel. Having come straight from work, Savannah still wore her designer skirt suit in fashionable black and layered strands of sterling-silver beads.

Shoving her sunglasses up onto her head, she carried the

groceries through the air-conditioned living room of her childhood home and into the kitchen. She heard her mother's footsteps down the hall before she emerged into the kitchen, wearing her spectacles and looking down at a crossword puzzle in her hand. Savannah dropped the bag of groceries onto the counter, and the noise got her mother's attention.

"Oh hi, hon. I thought I heard the front door." Helen took her spectacles off and smiled at her daughter. "Are those groceries for us?"

Us? Savannah had thought Cason would be moved out by now. Just a year, he had said; then it was another ten months, and then last month he finally had a place lined up. *He can't possibly still be here,* Savannah thought.

As if on cue, she heard the bathroom door open and the man in question step into the hallway toward the room that had once been her brother's. Before Ryan was killed in Afghanistan, where he was serving his last tour. Whose death was in part that man's fault. Each time she watched him walk into Ryan's room, the one her mama had given to him, she felt the grate of angry betrayal deep in her belly.

"Actually," Savannah said, putting her hand in the bag and pulling out a carton of milk and yanking the fridge open, "these are for *you.*"

Now able to see down the wood-paneled hallway, Savannah watched Cason pause in the bedroom doorway at the sound of her voice, his work clothes in his hand. He turned, looking over his shoulder, short sandy-brown hair still wet and spiky from his shower. His gaze went past her mother and made brief eye contact with her. As if acknowledging that, yes, he was still there, and no, he wasn't going anywhere. She gave him a hot glare back that said that it would be talked about.

Savannah continued with her mother. "Last time I was here, it was bare bones."

"Yes, well," Helen said, "Cason went shopping in the interim.

Now that we have double of everything, how about you stay for dinner?"

"No, Mama, you know I still have work."

"Savannah, it's after five. You have to eat sometime."

"Why don't we have dinner in the city, Mama? We can have some *alone* time to catch up."

"Savannah..." Her mother's tone was disapproving. "I know you weren't expecting Cason to stay longer," she said, diving into the thick of it.

At the mention of his name, he came to stand in the entry to the hall, silently crossing his arms over his chest.

Hand on the top of the fridge door, Savannah gathered her calm. "Yes." She gave her mother a soft smile and then Cason a hard look. "He said that he'd be moving out on the first. Today's the fifth. I'm pretty sure—"

"Your mother asked me to stay." His voice was low and deep; its masculine tone felt like an intruder in a house that had seen only women for so long. Savannah hated the way his definitiveness felt like law.

Savannah's mom looked over her shoulder at Cason, her demeanor warming. She moved to pat his arm. "You're home early—did you have a good day?"

The way she asked him, the way that she could just slip back to when they were all kids, when he and Ryan would come barreling in after school—it was as if Ryan hadn't died at all.

Savannah shoved the fridge door shut.

Cason gave Helen a quiet smile. "It was fine."

"Good," she said and gave him another pat before turning back to Savannah. "Really, Savannah, why don't you consider staying for dinner? Then we can all talk about this."

"Mama," Savannah said, taking the groceries off the green laminate counter, "both you and *Cason*"—now giving him a glare equal to the one he'd settled on her—"know how I feel about him staying here.

He needs to move on with his life, and you need to find a hobby other than saving strays."

Cason's eyes narrowed.

"Savannah Rae Sparling," Helen admonished.

"Mama, you don't need him here. You can manage without—"

"It has little to do with my capabilities. Savannah, after Ryan's death—"

Cason shrank back slightly, and Savannah said, "Don't, Mama."

"After Ryan's death, this house was empty. I prefer to have this house filled with life, and Cason can save his money until he has enough to buy a place of his own."

"Mama, you don't need companionship. You have me. I can come by more," Savannah said. "Wouldn't that be nice? And Cason can get on with his life. Meet a girl, get her knocked up, and start a family."

Cason's gaze went back to being icy. It was their preferred way—distant frost. Her mama could mother him, but he and Savannah sought a far more hostile interaction. They could accomplish that simply by standing quietly in the same room.

Helen smiled at her daughter. "Having you come by more would be nice, Savannah. How about we start to—"

Savannah's phone rang then. "Hold that thought," she said, putting up a finger to her mother. She let the grocery bag rest back on the counter and went to the wide front window. "This is Savannah," she said into the phone.

Helen turned and looked up at Cason as Savannah talked on her phone. "I'd believe she'd spend more time with me if she got rid of that thing," she said.

Cason gave her a reassuring smile, "Mrs. S., she'd likely spend more time with you if I weren't here."

"Nonsense. We've talked about this. You two were good friends when Ryan was alive—"

At the mention of Ryan, Cason looked away.

"She needs to remember that. And you need to lighten up some." She nodded as if that decided that.

"Yes, ma'am."

Cason watched as Mrs. S. looked over at her daughter, whose back was turned. Mrs. S. sighed. He knew what she was thinking; she'd said it more than once. Savannah was so successful: a nice condo by the country club, a fancy car, crisp suits—though those were a little too tight and her heels a little too high. She was a highly respected and sought-after interior designer. Too successful, maybe—barely had enough time for her own mother. Savannah, he could almost hear her mother say, was like her late father in the aggressive nature she had in business dealings. Unladylike. Helen sighed again. And Cason allowed himself to look at Savannah, from her straight brown hair, cropped at an angle to the tip of her chin, to the tight knee-length skirt. She was indeed all business.

"Slow down," he heard Savannah say to the person on the phone. "No, the damask was what was agreed upon...No, that will be the fourth change to the order; he must pay for this one. We're purchasing the bolts. Tell Charlot I'll not accept another change order—those bolts aren't cheap. I'll swing by and smooth things out. Give me ten minutes." Savannah hung up and turned back to her mother. "I have to go, sorry, Mama. Can we continue this conversation later?"

Savannah wasn't asking, though. She was down the porch steps before the door slammed shut behind her.

Helen shook her head. "This is what I mean." She gestured at the bag of groceries on the counter where Savannah had left them.

"I got it." Cason went to the bag and started to unload it.

"Why don't we wait on that, Cason. Just put the cold things away. I'll call her tomorrow to come pick them up at her lunch break. If I know my daughter like I do, she needs these in her cupboards more than we do—might as well use it for an excuse to have lunch with her." Helen added, "I noticed that hitch in your leg has gotten a little worse. You all right, hon? Maybe I can make a call to your doctor to see if we can't get you in tomorrow."

He turned back to face her. "I'm all right, ma'am. I'll let you know when it gets worse."

"Okay," she said, and as she looked back to the newspaper cross-word in her hand, she caught sight of her watch. "Oh my, it's well past five! You must be starved! I've been so distracted by this silly puzzler today." She dropped the crossword and her spectacles on the counter. "Why don't you do your physical therapy routine, and I'll call you when supper is ready."

"I can make supper if you have things to do, Mrs. S."

"No, no. You have your PT to do. Now, shoo. Let me get to work."

Chapter Two

S avannah pulled into the semicircle driveway that was ubiquitous in that section of town. Large trees lined the road; the stoic old homes set back from the street looked right out of colonial times. The home of Savannah's client, Phillip Nigel, was a two-story mansion with wood siding, cream trim, Doric columns, and navy shutters framing the eight front-facing windows. The old crushed-quartz gravel drive would soon be paved over with concrete, and the landscaping already bore no resemblance to its neighbors. No shrubbery, simply vivid-green golf-course-short grass. At the apex of the circular driveway was a single-story fountain, a tower of cherubs sitting and climbing on one other with water shooting from their mouths. From a short distance away, when you couldn't make out the individual cherubs, the fountain looked like a giant phallus. The meticulously clean driveway, save for stacks of lumber and a portable potty, held no other cars.

Savannah dug out her phone and called Charlot, the head designer assigned to her team, whom she'd put in charge that day.

"Savannah!" Charlot exclaimed, answering after only the first ring.

"Where are you? I told your intern I'd be right over."

"Yes, she told me. But it's a lost cause. We'll go back tomorrow. There's nothing you can do."

"Nothing I can do? Is this about the fabric?"

"The guy—"

"The client, Mr. Nigel."

"Yes—he threatened me, and when I said not to use all that negative energy with me, he said, 'I refuse to pay some filthy hippie to work in my home. This is a Nigel home!'" Charlot did do an excellent Phillip Nigel impression. "And then he started waving his hands around and saying everyone needed to leave. So I told everyone to leave."

"Okay...It's after five. It's all right that everyone left, but why—"

"Oh no. That was at three."

Savannah bit her lip to keep from sighing. Why was she just now hearing about this? "You left early and had everyone leave too?"

"Absolutely. Savannah, he seriously almost hit me."

Savannah felt her heart thump a little quicker. A serious accusation. One she didn't want to ignore but one she wanted to be cautious about. Phillip Nigel was a whiny creature she couldn't imagine risking damaging his manicure.

"And your intern?"

"She left with me. I don't know why she'd call you..."

Savannah knew why. The intern was one of the sharper tools in the tool shed. Charlot, however...How had she made it at Knight for so long? Her design skills alone, clearly. They were superb, that was true, but her other "talents" seemed to be louder, competing with her design skills.

"Okay," Savannah said. "I'm here now, so I'll take the lead back on this project and talk with him."

"No, Savannah, I really think you should just let him blow off steam, and I'll go back tomorrow and talk with him. I'm sure all that negative energy will have dissipated by then."

"Charlot," Savannah said and then stopped, unsure how to

explain that the economics of the situation overrode the energy of a client who had a lofty budget and expectations: fulfilling those expectations on time and not violating their own timeline were connected to payments that in turn helped pay all their salaries. "Let me see if a fresh face can't fix this."

"Don't say I didn't warn you. I had to go home and realign my chakras, he set me so far off balance."

Savannah sighed as she hung up. Then hoped Charlot didn't bill the Nigel project for her chakra time and made a mental note to check. She stepped out of her SUV into the warm air and headed to Phillip Nigel's front door.

She clanged the brass knocker and waited, looking back at the loudly splashing fountain. Savannah squinted. It seemed even larger than when she'd come to the house for the budgetary estimate meeting. The pile of cherubs seemed to hold strained expressions and grasp at each other in awkward, frenzied, sexual ways.

Savannah turned back as the door swung open and the home's AC sent out a welcome wintery breeze.

"Can I help you?" Phillip Nigel asked coolly, rubbing his hands together; the motion carried with it the smell of hand sanitizer.

Savannah noticed the older man's particular care with color, contrast, and coordination. Sandy chinos, a sky-blue button-down, and a nicely contrasting salmon long-sleeve that he had tied over his shoulders. He carried a slight paunch and had a reddened nose, but his tanned skin and nails were immaculate. Some would confuse his clothes, boutique leather shoes, and jeweled pinky ring with class, but Savannah had worked in the industry long enough to know that class was more than nice clothes and a big house.

She dug deep for her sugar and prayed she could pave the road straight. "Mr. Nigel, I'm Savannah Sparling with Knight Interiors. You might remember me from the initial budgetary meeting. I'm here to help sort out the problem we seem to have." She smiled like Miss America.

"Well, that was quick. No doubt that dirty hippie you have

working for you took offense at my high standards. So, can I trust that you will not tell me that I need to accept what fate has devised for my home renovations?"

Savannah tried to not let it show that she thought Charlot probably did put it like that, simply saying, "Why don't I come in, and you can you can tell me what happened."

His muddy-brown eyes just stared back at her.

Negative energy, she heard Charlot say.

"Ms. Sparling, it has been a trying day. I'm not interested in talking with more incompetent people. Come back later, when I'm feeling up to par."

Savannah kept her smile up. "Mr. Nigel, I assure you that Knight doesn't send me out to watch paint dry. When I show up on your doorstep, it means that we're about to move the moon and stars for you. Let's chat, shall we?"

His eyebrows arched slightly. "Fine," he said and opened the door wider. "Do come in."

"Thank you very much."

She stepped into the foyer and reached down for disposable booties. Slipping them on over her heels, Savannah took a quick glance around; as she did, she felt Phillip Nigel's eyes watching her every move.

The construction was going well; all surfaces were either covered fully with plastic or protected with cardboard. Rooms not under construction were sealed off with plastic zipper doors. The opulent hardwood staircase sweeping up to the second story was safe under cushioned cloth and cardboard. The open balcony had been zippered, and the high-ceilinged foyer held most of the scaffolding, tools, and drop cloths. It and the sitting room to the far left of the cavernous room were being repapered, and the built-ins were being replaced.

Savannah's heels hit quietly on the hardwoods as she moved to set her case down on the massive front work table that spanned the width of the room. Designs, documents, and the purchased bolts of fabric took up one end.

"Ms. Sparling. Let me dive in. This has all been a horrible experience for me." Phillip Nigel pointed to the thousands of dollars of fabric bolts that he had yet to pay for. "Knight assured me that I'd be getting top service, but I've been dealt nothing but idiots for the last three weeks. Frankly, you are the first person to put on those protective shoe coverings, and I've had enough of all the dust. I'm angry that it's taken so much time for someone of your caliber to notice. I went into this believing that I'd be respected, not treated like a commoner. The Nigel name still means something in this town."

Savannah had in fact checked on that very point after their design meeting, hoping to have caught a big fish with family connections. The Nigels had arrived from Texas within the last ten years and had no family to speak of in the area. His name meant nothing in this town.

Savannah answered, "Agreed, Mr. Nigel. I'll reinforce the bootie policy. And can you show me where the dust is getting in?"

"It's everywhere."

"Behind the zipper doors?"

"No!" he said heatedly. "Look around you!"

Savannah took a moment to look around the active construction zone and formulate her argument against insanity. "I see."

"This is intolerable."

"Mr. Nigel. This area is the active construction zone. There is a level of dust that will accumulate while they work. I will advise the crew, however, to clean thoroughly at the end of each day so that the dust doesn't travel any farther than this room."

"That will hardly help."

Savannah tried an understanding smile. "Mr. Nigel, I know living through a remodel can be quite difficult. We will be here for just a few more weeks; then you will have your home back, better than new. Is there somewhere you can—"

Mr. Nigel scoffed and crossed his arms. "Better than new? Not with these fabric choices."

For the next few minutes, Savannah went through each bolt, applauding the choice, and Mr. Nigel responded to each, telling her why it was the worst.

"Fine," he eventually said. "Do the damn damask. It is better than the rest, but the filth you have working for you brought in these other options."

"Excellent choice," she said, ignoring his rudeness one more time. "I'll have the crew back in here in the morning. Do you have somewhere else you could stay? It might ease the stress of living in a construction zo—"

"And have those people rob me blind? No, I'll stay here and monitor the progress." He then added, "And I'm not paying for these." He gestured at the bolts.

Savannah smiled blandly. "Those will be removed first thing in the morning."

"Good."

Savannah gathered her things and handed him a card from her silver card case. "Call me if anything else comes up, Mr. Nigel." As she spoke, she had a sinking feeling that she would deeply regret offering that.

He took her card. "I will."

"And remember, Mr. Nigel, this project will be over soon, and your house back to normal."

"I thought you said better than new."

"Exactly."

OUTSIDE IN HER SUV, Savannah phoned Charlot and the lead contractor for the job and debriefed them. She reiterated the bootie policy and that they needed to press forward. If Mr. Nigel got in the way, they were to either call her or have him call her. They were not to deal with him at all. She added that first thing in the morning the bolts of fabric they weren't using were to be picked up.

"How does his energy feel?" Charlot asked.

"Enlightened."

Chapter Three

The next morning Savannah's coffee hadn't even had a chance to cool in its to-go cup before she stood next to an angry Phillip Nigel, looking at a bolt of rich blue damask, the fabric he'd settled on the evening before.

"Ms. Sparling, you have underestimated me, and I have lost any trust in you with your obvious plot to deceive me in this banal case of bait and switch. I'll not be paying for this."

It was only 8:00 a.m., and she was already making a mental list of things she'd rather be doing than standing where she was. *Tightrope walking without a safety net, getting into a knife fight with pirates, driving her car off the levee...* Just the evening before, she had been confirming that very bolt of fabric with Phillip Nigel.

The wallpaper crew stood behind her while the other craftsmen kept their heads down, swiftly moving about their tasks.

"Why is that, Mr. Nigel?"

"Simply look at it—this isn't what I agreed to yesterday."

"It's a fine fabric. Original to many homes in the area and your first choice—"

"It's unnecessary to repeat yourself, Ms. Sparling. Your faux shock at my decision this morning makes me steadfast in my resolve. I know which fabric I chose yesterday, and this is not it."

Savannah made an acquiescing noise in the back of her throat and then added, "Mr. Nigel, this is the exact fabric you agreed to yesterday evening."

"No. It is obvious what you are trying to do, Ms. Sparling. The fabric yesterday was more opulent. I know what I saw, and this isn't it. Your people switched it out when they took the bolts an hour ago. They assumed I wouldn't notice, but I have, and what you've tried to pass off as antique damask is abominable. I am a Nigel, Ms. Sparling; I know quality."

"I see...So, to clarify, you feel that we took the original $100,000 roll of silk fabric that was here when you woke this morning, had a cheap knockoff made, and then switched them in a matter of moments while you weren't looking?"

Phillip Nigel's appearance was ruddy that morning, and his sweater was askew over his shoulders, as if he'd hastily dressed or done so drunk. He pointed at Savannah—ringed pinky finger also raised. "Don't play games with me, Ms. Sparling. Remember who's paying you."

Savannah took a sip of her coffee to keep her mouth busy. Its darkly bitter warmth infused her with caffeinated patience. Charlot stood to the side, chewing her nail.

Savannah said, "Mr. Nigel. I'm trying to be clear in order to prevent more miscommunication. I'm not trying to trick you, just trying to understand where you're coming from."

"This is the wrong fabric."

SEVERAL HOURS LATER, Savannah left to attend to another client, the Mathers family. Savannah had only dealt with Mrs. Mathers up to then, but she was happy and she assured Savannah that her husband was too. The hour appointment at their home soothed her nerves after her interaction with Phillip Nigel.

As she slid into the driver's seat afterward, her phone rang. She punched the answer button on her console. It was Knight, her boss. The company would purchase only one more bolt of fabric for the Nigel project, and then there would have to be a come-to-Jesus meeting with the man. His current bill was still unpaid, and Knight Interiors didn't run a charity.

His behavior now made a little sense. Clients that couldn't pay often played elaborate games to cover that fact. Or Phillip Nigel was a cat with a vast fortune, and the only thing he knew how to do with it was pay people to enter his home so he could bat them around like mice.

As soon as she hung up with work, her phone rang again.

"Savannah, hon! I'm glad I caught you."

"Hi, Mama." Savannah turned the key in the ignition.

"Remember those groceries from yesterday?"

"Ah, yes. I'll come get them after work. Or can you use them?"

"No, dear. They'll go bad before I get to them. Want to come by for lunch and pick them up?"

Savannah's stomach growled as if on cue. It was almost noon, and the only thing she'd put in her stomach all day was a twenty-ounce cup of coffee. "Yes, but I can't stay long."

AT THE HOUSE, Savannah dropped her purse on the couch and jabbed her thumb back over her shoulder. "Is Ms. Myrna getting a new driveway? Didn't she just get one?"

Helen came around the corner from the kitchen. "Hello, hon, yes. You know Myrna—she wants to support the troops as much as possible, even if that means getting her driveway redone every year." Helen turned back, and Savannah heard the telltale sounds of mixing emanating from the kitchen: clanks and scrapes of a metal spoon against a glass bowl.

Savannah went to the front windows to inspect the crew working at Myrna's. Up the block, two houses down and across the street, were the white work trucks of Miner's Concrete. The crew—made up mostly of military veterans—was currently jackhammering the so-called old driveway and hauling large slabs of it in wheelbarrows to a construction Dumpster. Savannah let her mind wander away from the demands of her design projects and over the sweaty, muscular physiques. No machines were required with that work crew. It was the company that the loathsome Cason worked for, but luckily his team only worked the big jobs.

"Mama," Savannah called, her mind succumbing to her day's tasks anyway, "do you know anything about the Nigels?"

"Hmmm," her mother responded from the other side of the kitchen/dining pass-through as she scooped tuna from cans and into a mixing bowl, "they're Myrna's favorite topic of gossip. They hire a lot of people but don't keep folks around. I think it's only the son now, though. I heard that early on, when they first moved here, the son ran out all the nurses who were watching his sick mother. She died of bone cancer, I hear, but some folks will tell you the son poisoned her. Not sure how much value I'd put on those opinions, but the bottom line is that they aren't nice folks. Boastful."

The way her mother said *boastful*, especially after talking about more serious issues like poor working conditions and murder, showed that if there was anything in Helen's community that you didn't want to get known as, it was boastful. It was ungentlemanly and unlady-like. The Nigels could consider themselves out of favor.

Her mother tapped the spoon clean on the edge of the mixing bowl. "Why do you ask?"

"He's a client of ours, and I'm having difficulty working with him. I thought if I knew some unconfirmed information about him, then I'd be able to work another angle. He is boastful, but there's something else that I can't put my finger on."

"I'd be careful with that one. I'm not inclined to believe the rumors, but Myrna tells several."

Savannah looked over her shoulder back toward her mother. "More than poisoning?"

"Her housekeeper's sister used to work for the Nigels when they first moved to town, and she said that the son threatened to beat her with the mop handle if the floors didn't shine."

Savannah shook her head. "That's terrible. Did she quit?"

"Yes, a week later. Myrna's housekeeper swore she saw bruises on her sister, but she never said anything."

Savannah's gut twisted, remembering his seemingly innocent hand waving and Charlot's statement. Savannah had thought he was an old grouch who came off as threatening but was actually a big chicken. She worried now that he might not be all that innocent.

She refocused on the workmen down the street. By this time of day, most of the men had taken off their shirts; the midday Louisiana sun was working its magic to slicken their bodies. Savannah's gaze caught on one of the men, the lifter. Wheelbarrows came to him, and he hefted massive concrete chunks out of the driveway rubble with gloved hands and dropped them systematically into the wheelbarrows. The chunks were then hauled off and unloaded into the Dumpster as another wheelbarrow rolled in to take its place. All the men moved at their own jobs, jackhammering, tossing concrete, and disposing, like one giant, well-oiled machine.

"You would think," Savannah murmured at the windowpane, "that hauling concrete chunks shirtless would tear up your skin."

"Mmmm," her mother said confirming her eagle-like hearing, "I guess they don't care."

"Yeah, I'm gathering as much."

Savannah watched the flex and bow of the lifter's back; his was a well-made example of sinewy muscle forming ropey ridges down his spine and over his shoulders. He stood again and, with an aggressive pitch of the broken slab of concrete, made his target, the waiting wheelbarrow. The wheelbarrow's minder, though, left to assist the man who was jackhammering. Savannah watched as her concrete tosser moved to take the wheelbarrow pusher's place. He turned in her direction and maneuvered over and around broken pieces. Her eyes hadn't left his torso; she drank in his private power play, enjoying the way he pulled and pressed the wheelbarrow across the torn-up ground.

"Exquisite," Savannah whispered as her eyes trailed from the sand-colored work boots and cargo pants to the black nylon belt to the man's taught abdomen. It was only when he was on the smooth, level road in front of the Dumpster that she realized he had a hitch in his step. Her eyes flew to his face in recognition. "Son of a bit—"

"Savannah Rae Sparling!" her mother admonished.

Savannah turned from the window in disgust. "I just realized the man I was admiring is Cason."

Helen's admonishment slid into a low laugh from the kitchen.

"Mama, that's not funny."

"You're right, dear, it's not funny. It's *very* funny. I've told you time and time again that he's a good man. Mind, I think you could learn more about him from that old adage that it's not what you say but what you do that's important."

"Mama, I'm not even sure what that means regarding him—"

"Then perhaps you just needed to appreciate certain particular qualities before seeing his other ones."

"You mean I need to admire his half-naked body doing hard labor so that I can find it in me somewhere to forgive him for his sins? I think you've misplaced your lady's sensibilities." Savannah joined her in the kitchen and opened the refrigerator.

"I've already got the pickles," her mother said.

"Oh." Closing the fridge, Savannah noticed the third plate on the counter. Then realized the trap. "Mama, why is there a third plate? Cason isn't joining us, is he?"

"I'm not sure if he's joining us; I set it out just in case, since he's working so close," Helen said, avoiding eye contact with her daughter. "Please bring the bowl of potato chips to the table."

Savannah sighed and sent up a small prayer that her day wasn't going to get worse. She put the old turquoise glass bowl down on the dining room table as her mother opened the refrigerator and pulled out a pitcher of iced tea.

"Would you like a glass?"

"Yes," Savannah said as the front door opened and a shirtless Cason walked in. She felt her grip on the back of the dining chair tighten.

CASON HAD JUST CROSSED the threshold when he started to put his shirt on, but he paused when he sensed someone looking at him. He met Savannah's glare. Her high-waisted, knee-length tight black skirt, white long-sleeve shirt, and heels made her look like something out of the movies. A horror movie, since her eyes were like chilly black pools.

"Savannah."

She made a point to rake her eyes slowly over his upper body. He grew even warmer and finished pulling on his shirt.

"What a pity." Savannah turned and walked into the kitchen, returning with a plate. She dropped the third plate with a loud thud on the oval oak dining table.

"Savannah..." Helen said as a warning to her daughter and then said to Cason, "What a great treat having you both with me for lunch!" It was as if she couldn't feel the blizzard brewing between them.

Cason undid his boots and toed them off. "Mrs. Sparling, I've got work dust on me. I'll take my lunch in the kitchen, if you don't mind." He moved to the table and reached past Savannah—inches from her body—to pick up the plate she dropped.

Savannah's head tilted to the side; his body heat and sweat were clearly not going unnoticed. Instead of stepping back, she whispered, "That's a great idea, Cason."

He could feel her chastising breath on his jaw, cooling the sweat that still lingered there. Starving and not enjoying the increasingly sharp pain his shrapnel hip was giving him, he turned his head to look her dead in the eye, close enough to see the gold flecks around her pupils. "I'm glad you think so, Savannah, but now that you mention it, it'd be rude to leave your mother alone at the table. I'll take my lunch here."

"I had no designs on helping you eat your sandwich in the kitchen."

"Neither did I. But about halfway through lunch, your phone will ring, and you'll leave. So, how about you save Mrs. S. the heartache and *you* eat in the kitchen."

Savannah's face flushed, and her wide mouth compressed into a thin line.

Helen spoke up. "Now, you two, nobody is eating in the kitchen. Let's sit down and enjoy the sandwiches before they get soggy."

Eyes still on Savannah, watching hers get to an even deeper black, the gold flecks vanishing, he stepped back and slid onto the wooden chair next to where she stood. There was a perverse joy in him because of their banter. She would think of a comeback, no doubt, and he'd be there waiting for it.

As SAVANNAH SAT, she turned, ignoring Cason, and put a smile on for her mother. "Mama, are you familiar with the new plastic surgeon in town, Dr. Mathers?"

Her mother had worked as a medical assistant to one of the town's pediatricians, Savannah's in fact, for years, but she was retired and out of that community—what Savannah knew was her mother enjoyed a good bit of gossip. Gained and given.

Grateful for a diversion, Helen dove in. "Yes! Nice folks, from what I hear."

"They've hired Knight Interiors to redo their entire bottom floor. It's a historic four-thousand-square-foot home, and they're ready to take that lower floor down to the studs."

"Wonderful! Will you be working on it?"

"As a matter of fact, I was just there." Savannah spoke casually, but her insides were on fire from Cason's accusation that she would leave lunch early. *The bastard,* she thought. Her job was demanding, and her mama knew that.

"Excellent! I can't wait to tell the Devereaux—they're neighbors to them, you know."

"The Devereaux?" Savannah asked. Why was her mother talking to her finicky socialite acquaintances again?

"You know Lucille and Theodore."

"Yes, Mama, I just didn't know you and Lucille were friendly right now."

Helen looked suitably aghast. "Lucille is attending tea tomorrow. She's bringing Theodore. You remember Theodore, don't you, Cason?"

Cason paused, sandwich midway to his mouth. "What?"

"Theodore, Lucille's son, you remember him?"

Savannah looked from her mother to Cason and smiled on the inside at seeing Cason on the defensive. "Yes, Cason, you remember Theodore—fantastic eye for men's fashion, gets hundred-dollar manicures, and starches his underpants. You remember him?"

"I remember him," Cason said, giving her a warning glance.

"Oh, excellent," Helen said. "I'd like both of you at tea tomorrow."

Savannah nearly laughed at the request. Was she a child with nothing else on her plate but to be at her mother's call? "Mama, your society meetings start at sunup and end at sundown. I won't be able to make it. I've got three clients I need to finalize proposals for. I need the weekend to do that."

"Tea is at ten, Savannah, and you only need to come by for a moment," Helen said. "I'd like you to be there, and you too, Cason. I think you and Theodore will hit it off. He could use a down-to-earth friend like you."

Savannah admired her mother's not-so-subtle social-elbow-rubbing setup. Cason looked askance at Helen. Theodore wore linen suits with matching paisley ascots and managed his family's investments. Savannah had known Cason since childhood and never in that time had she seen him wear a suit, much less a ruffled piece of silk about his neck, ever.

Savannah felt like a wolf when she smiled then. "Mama, did you just call Cason down-to-earth? You mean, salt of the earth or a down-and-dirty sort of man? I can see Theodore enjoying that immensely."

"Now, Savannah, I'm implying no such thing. Theodore and Cason need to make friends outside of their circles of friends, and this will be a good opportunity for them to branch out."

Cason's eyebrows rose even higher.

Savannah nearly clapped with glee.

"Pardon me, ma'am," Cason said, coming to life, "but I've come to like the friends I've got. I'm not sure how Theodore will—"

"I know you go to the bars with your military friends, but Theodore comes from a different view of the world. It'll be good for the both of you to hang out, as it were."

"Fantastic. Glad that's solved," Savannah said, mock toasting Cason with her iced tea. "Looks like you'll be Theodore's new best friend tomorrow."

Across the table, Cason's eyes slid back to hers, his face impassive. "I don't think your mom's done."

"Savannah, hon. As I said, I'd like you to be there. For just a bit. It's been a very long while since Lucille or any of the others have seen you."

Savannah's smile faded. "Mama, you can pass on my hellos for me."

Cason cut in. "How hard is it to drive here, get out of your car, say hi, eat, and then leave? Come on, Sparling, even you can manage that."

Savannah's lip curled into a sneer as Cason spoke. "Sorry? Did you say something directly to me?" She turned to look at her mother, managing a small smile. "Mama, I know you'd like me to be here, but for me your tea parties do last all day because I end up sauced on mimosas and talking with Ms. Myrna about turning her garage into a photo studio for male nude portraiture. I'm sorry I won't be able to go."

"Savannah, I've promised Lucille you'll be there—"

"Mama...why'd you promise her something like that?"

"What good is all that money you make if you can't spend time with your mom?" Cason said.

"What did you just say?" Savannah let the chill of her gaze settle back on Cason.

Helen interjected, "Now, Cason, I'm not saying—"

"You get promoted to veep status at Knight, and yet you—"

"I wasn't asking you to explain. I was hoping you'd hear the words you were saying and would think again about speaking to me. I realize, though, that for someone like you, it'd be hard to comprehend the virtues of financial stability."

"Savannah Rae—"

"I'm clarifying for you that you're putting money before family. And yeah, I don't know how to do that, you're right." Cason stood.

"How dare you," Savannah said.

"Now, you two—"

Cason grabbed his plate. "Thanks, Mrs. S. I've got to get back to work now."

Savannah snatched her plate, feeling her hunger vanish, and followed him into the kitchen. "You have no right. I work my ass off—"

"Doesn't change that you put making money over seeing your mom."

She tossed her plate on the counter as he rinsed his. "As an interloper in this house, you have no right to say—"

"Actually, I fought for the right to say what I just did. What have you done? Made buckets of money?"

Savannah laughed caustically. "You fought for American free speech? Is that what you were doing in Afghanistan?" She watched his countenance change, which she'd aimed her words to cause. He knocked the tap off as she added, "I didn't realize that your allegiance was that blind. Though—"

He got in her face. "Say what you want about me. I fought for my country, gladly would have given my life for it. Unlike you, who has a life worth living, and you're ditching it for the almighty dollar."

"Get the hell out of my mama's house."

"Show up tomorrow. Your mom deserves better."

"I'll not have you manipulate me into—"

"Then show up." His green eyes had gone satisfactorily dark.

"I think not, especially not now, at your beck and call."

"Fine. I'd hate for Lucille Devereaux to hear your happy news secondhand, though."

Savannah narrowed her eyes dangerously. "My happy news?"

Cason cocked his head. "What else? Your pregnancy."

"That's ridiculous. Gossip mongering at its finest." Savannah folded her arms over her chest. "You're so childish, Cason. I've not been seen with a man, much less gone out with one, in a year. You'll have to be cleverer."

"I'm sorry. Did I say it was your happy news? I meant it was mine. So glad you'll let me tell everyone you're pregnant with my kid." He saluted her then and stalked from kitchen and out the front door.

As his words hit home, an angry heat blossomed in Savannah's chest and bloomed up her neck. Her mind went blank with rage.

Helen came around the corner with her half-eaten sandwich. "It's a good thing I'm not hungry today—I'd be eating alone now!"

Savannah was still fuming. "I'll be right back."

Cason was halfway down the street by the time she was out the front door. She marched smartly past her car and into the street. Ahead, the crew had taken a break for lunch, sitting on broken concrete pieces in Ms. Myrna's drive. The heat of the sun and the humidity warmed her skin and moistened the air she breathed. With the fury she was feeling inside toward Cason, she was nearly at overload.

Cason paused up the street and reached his hand over his head, pulling off his shirt. He tucked it into his back pocket and stood still, naked back to her, as Savannah's heels clipped a pointed staccato up the street.

She barely registered that some of Cason's crew stopped to watch her progress; she was wholly focused on the shirtless man in front of her.

He turned and slid his hands into his front pockets; the effect— that pointed attention to the flat planes of his chest—would have been heart-stopping for any other hot-blooded female. However, Savannah didn't care.

Cason waited as she closed the distance, his face impassive, eyes focused on the horizon.

"Cason," she said crisply.

"Ma'am," he replied as she stepped up to him.

"Don't ma'am me—"

"You wouldn't like the other word I was going to use."

Her eyes narrowed; she barely noticed the sheen that his skin was starting to take on in the heat. Her blood got even hotter. "I don't care what you call me, but it'd be best if you and I agreed right now that threatening to tell lies to the Devereaux family tomorrow to manipulate me into being there will land you in a world of hurt."

His lips twitched. He took a step closer and slid his angry gaze to hers. "A world of hurt, huh?" he said, letting those words fall between them. "How will I ever survive it?"

They stood staring at each other, both thinking of real survival. As it always happened, Ryan, his death, the insurgent attack in that crimson valley came between them. The real ripping apart of their worlds.

Ryan had been more than Savannah's only sibling. He'd taken care of her as both a father and a brother after the death of their own father when they were kids. Cason had killed two men at once when he dared Ryan to join the army with him, then in Afghanistan left him to die. Those were Cason's own words. Pity was something she couldn't spare him.

The twist the conversation took landed them far from the Devereaux family by the time she spoke again. Savannah met the battle-green eyes in front of her. "I'll personally ensure that it's a new level of hell you feel."

"I doubt you know the level of hell that that would need to be."

"Really? You might want to rethink creating a personal vendetta from Ryan Sparling's sister. I can find people you don't want found. Especially since I hear your mama's been off the sauce for a while and is looking for you. I hear she's wanting some time with her baby boy."

"Don't."

"Trust me, Cason, when I say I know how deep that dagger is in your chest, and I have no problem shoving it deeper and twisting. I'm not an idle-threat maker, and I'm not in a position to have the man who led my brother to his death manipulate me into societal game playing. Do we understand each other?"

"I don't know how many times I have to tell you, Savannah, that I'm sorry Ryan died. And getting more pissed at me doesn't change the fact that he's never coming back."

"Says the man who stepped over his dying body to escape when a little shrapnel nicked his skin. He wouldn't have been in that godforsaken place if it hadn't been for you—so yeah, it'll take a whole lot more than just 'sorry' to erase those wounds. And as of the first of next month, you'll be out of my mama's house, or so help me god, I'll come for you like a hellhound seeking vengeance. That sandbox you left will look like a vacation."

He leaned in. "You don't get it, do you? It already does."

"Then go back." Savannah turned and slid her sunglasses on and started walking away.

Cason raised his voice. "Your brother died a damn hero, Savannah, and the sooner you realize that, the better."

She looked at him over her shoulder. The power of the man was undeniable, but he was a devil in combat boots. "And what are you— the pedestal his memory is supposed to sit on?"

His jaw clenched. "Fuck you."

"Fuck you too, McPherson." She stalked back to her car.

CASON'S BLOOD was on fire as he watched her leave. She knew just where jab at him, knew where the opening was to crawl under his skin and turn him into a human inferno. It was hard to believe that there had been a time when he thought she walked on water, a time when all the world stood still when he looked at her picture. She had never known it; he was grateful to the world for such small mercies.

Cason turned back toward his work crew, pulled his gloves from his back pocket, and shoved them on. He realized then that they all were staring at him, crooked grins on their faces.

One whistled low. "McPherson, you never told us you were datin' Mrs. S.'s daughter."

He smiled halfheartedly. *Here we go,* he thought.

Another said, "Datin'? Shoot, no. Makin' babies in the middle of the street, more like."

Cason chucked a piece of cement into the wheelbarrow. "If that's how you think babies are made, Alexander, that explains why you haven't been laid."

There was a low whistle and a hoot of laughter. "Hoo, Xander, he's got your number."

"Just sayin', a fine-looking woman like that putting her body up against me in the street? Shoot—she's not lookin' for a fight. She lookin' for some love."

Cason shook his head and went back to work. There was no need to explain any of what had just happened; his crew knew who Ryan Sparling was to Cason. Knew of that valley of death, each of them having his own version of a similar story.

Pouring concrete might not be as complicated as the tasks he undertook as Sergeant McPherson, but having a purpose and the brotherhood of his crew helped ease his transition back to civilian life. And in moments like that they helped to keep him grounded.

Chapter Four

At nine forty-five on Saturday morning, Savannah arrived at her mother's house, phone to her ear, Phillip Nigel on the other end. Talking to him then was like another session of attempting to smooth out the Blue Ridge Mountains. At least she thought so until she saw the Devereaux arrive and exit their sedan. Now, there was a real challenge. The weather had turned drippingly humid, and a thunderhead held promise on the horizon. Still, Theodore looked immaculate in his relaxed, white linen chinos, silk shirt, and cravat. His vintage couture alligator boots and matching belt cost as much, Savannah knew, as her luxury SUV.

Mrs. Devereaux waved her pink-manicured hand at Savannah in Savannah's side mirror. Savannah jumped as the woman pulled a fluffy white object with beady black eyes from her purse and thrust it at the car window. She made it wave with one of its front paws as it growled, before depositing it back into her purse. Savannah forgot Phillip Nigel's drone; tea had been raised to eye-twitch level with the arrival of Mrs. Devereaux's purse shark.

A rare pause in Phillip Nigel's tirade jolted Savannah back into the phone conversation. "Yes, Mr. Nigel. I completely understand.

We'll review the contract on Monday and see what can be done. Have a good weekend." She hung up. And by that she meant that she'd be firing him as a client on Monday. She'd cleared it with her boss that she could pull the plug—she hadn't even had to twist Knight's arm. She thought she'd give Mr. Nigel this one last conversation to calm down, but clearly nothing was going to change. And feeling her stress levels rise with the arrival of the Devereaux posse, Savannah knew that she'd have an ulcer before noon if she kept all the plates spinning in her life.

Savannah tossed her cell into her purse, slipped out of her SUV, and adjusted her flowing shirt and hip-hugging jean shorts. Her mother would tsk about the shorts; they were her small rebellion. She ran her fingers through her hair before shouldering her purse and slamming the car door shut.

Helen exclaimed a bright hello as her daughter stepped into the house. Savannah shoved the door shut with the heel of her pump as the delicious smell of coffee enveloped her. The front entryway became immediately cluttered with hugs and greetings. In addition to the Devereaux, Helen's neighbor and good friend, the one with a new driveway every year, Ms. Myrna Daria, was there. But where was Cason? *Oh, he better not be ditching this.*

Lucille Devereaux addressed Savannah. "I was just explaining to your mother and Ms. Daria that Miles is such a new addition to our house that we couldn't—just couldn't—leave him at home alone." The jeweled clip in her dyed auburn hair sparkled as she nuzzled the puffball in her arms. "Your mother is so sweet to let him stay. He's really a good boy."

Ms. Myrna swept in next, pulling Savannah into her bosom for a heavily perfumed hug and then held her out at arm's length. Ms. Myrna wore a black tent of a shirt over tights; her heavy-looking red cherry earrings matched the giant cherries printed on the silk shirt. "Well, now, just look at you. I'm so glad Ms. Big Shot could spend some time with us old biddies." She gave Savannah a long-lashed, heavily eye-shadowed wink.

"Big shot? Oh no, just paying the bills. I can't complain," Savannah said with a smile. "How do you like the new driveway?" she couldn't resist asking.

Ms. Myrna waggled her penciled-on eyebrows. "I love new driveways, but I love the construction more. If you know what I mean."

Savannah's mind flickered to the memory of Cason's shirtless body. She'd never felt so thankful for Theodore as she did right then. He stepped forward and, she hoped, distracted everyone from the blush creeping across her cheeks.

Theodore raised a slender hand in greeting, his smile nearly as iridescent as his pomade-slicked hair. "Savannah, sooo good to see you." He took her hand and kissed the space between her knuckles. "You look amazing—have you had something done? Your skin is positively glowing." He spoke excitedly.

Savannah wanted to say it was the glow of her golden nest egg. She smiled politely and lied, "Just a new skin care product—thanks for noticing." She then said, "You're looking well too."

"Yes, I could barely make it today with all the work I have to get done. But true duty calls!" he said with a mock-exasperated glance at his mother behind him.

Savannah held in her sigh. She looked well, and it must be lotions and potions; a man looked well, and the presumption was work was bustling. "You are too kind to escort your mother here this morning. I know we're all looking forward to catching up," she said, not mentioning that she'd never seen him without his mother. Savannah nodded down the hall. "I'm going to put my purse down. I'll be right back." *And locate that bastard Cason and drag his ass out here.*

She tossed her purse onto the striped purple comforter covering her mother's queen bed and quietly closed the door again behind her. Cason's door was shut, but she heard the distinct sounds of someone behind it.

Savannah wrapped her hand around the doorknob and slowly turned it. The door opened soundlessly, and she slipped into Cason's room. The room was well lit from the bank of windows facing the front lawn. Her brother's old bed was as he'd left it; next to it was a cot, as neatly made as a cot could be, with a shirt laid out on it. Under the cot was a wood trunk in military green with a lock and black stenciled letters that said, *C. McPherson.* The dresser had just six items on it: a stick of deodorant, three prescription bottles, a wallet, and keys. The walls were bare save for a Miner's Concrete calendar that had Cason's neat blocky handwriting on it. A small, tidy pile of laundry was behind the door next to the closet.

And in front of the closet, his shirt halfway on, his slacks resting open on his hips, was a man with a very surprised expression that was morphing into a very irritated one. "What the hell—are you trying to catch me without my clothes on?"

Moving her gaze up from his open slacks, Savannah adjusted her own look, transforming it from surprised to scathing. As he pulled his undershirt down over his abdomen and tucked it into his pants, she said, "No, this is my house. I'm allowed to go where I please without asking permission." It sounded childish even to her, but she didn't care. "Call me crazy, but I have a vested interest in your whereabouts. I'm wondering why you're dodging company. You should have been dressed an hour ago." She narrowed her eyes. "Speaking of which"— she went to the closet, pushing him aside, so she could get at its contents—"you need a better shirt."

"Yes, welcome. Make yourself at home."

"As I said, this is my home."

"*Was.*"

She flicked through his shirts.

"I have a shirt out," he said.

"The one on the bed? I saw. Theodore showed up in couture. I'm helping you, so shut up."

Cason grunted. "Couture? The UFC fighter?"

She turned her gaze back onto him. "The *what* fighter?"

"Never mind."

"Right." She continued to dig. "Is this all you have? Oh..." She stepped deeper into the closet to dig out something she'd glimpsed at its very back. "Oh yes."

"No. I'm not wearing that." His voice was calm and definitive.

"It'll be tight, for sure. But formfitting we can work with. Take off your undershirt." She pulled the pitch-black long-sleeve shirt off its hanger.

"No."

"Now."

"Screw you, Sparling."

"Tell me something you don't want to do. Now, take it off," she said, pointing to his white undershirt.

A warm flush of color spread across his cheeks. "Fine." He pulled it off and tossed it onto his cot, then snatched the black button-down out of her hand.

Before he buttoned it up, it was already obvious it would fit as if it were tailor-made for him. As he closed the peekaboo show with each button, Savannah noted the shoulder seams were set just right at the edges of his wide shoulders, and the sides fit slim against his skin. The black provided perfect contrast to the gray of his straight legged slacks.

"Where'd you get this?" Savannah asked as she leaned against the closet frame.

"What do you care?"

"Just want to know if you actually have taste, or if someone you know does."

He glared at her. "It was a gift."

"Girlfriend?"

His lips went to a thin line as if glued shut in reluctance to admit what he was about to: "My mother."

Savannah's brows rose. Envisioning the woman as someone who would purchase something other than hooch was hard. "That's weird."

"Yeah."

"Why did she buy it?"

"What's with the twenty questions?"

"I'm trying out a new technique. If I can't be polite, I ask questions."

"Do you even know how to be polite?"

Her smile was caustic. "Very funny. Why'd she buy it?"

Cason took his time with the two top buttons and with answering her questions. Eventually he said, "She probably traded a family heirloom for it, thinking she'd give it to my father—then remembered when she sobered up that he'd left her."

Savannah knew the story of his mother well and let it be. "Either way, the shirt fits you great. Leave the top two buttons open, and yeah, this belt will work." She held one out to him.

"Leave it open? No. I was instructed to wear a tie."

"Mama has old-fashioned sensibilities. I say leave it open."

He snatched the belt from Savannah. "Has she caught a look at you yet?" he said, giving her shorts a glance.

"Yes, not to say anything, though." As his hands were busy looping his belt, she yanked his top two buttons open.

He met her gaze. She was his height in her heels. "Really?"

"Open."

"No need to rip my goddamn shirt off."

"I *will* rip those off if you try to button them again," she said, pointing to the offending buttons.

Cason's eyes narrowed, creasing the skin on either side. "Ever think to say so nicely?"

She raised her eyebrows at him. "With you? No."

"Right," he said. "Your mother's gonna pull something like what you just did when she sees you. You might as well be in your pajamas." He buckled his belt.

"There are things girls can get away with that boys can't. Such as using shoes. Simply wearing tasteful heels with shorts makes them instantly upscale," she said and, stepping into his space, pulled gently at his tightly tucked shirt.

She wasn't sure why she did it, the adjusting. It was a habit. A kind of caregiving that she did in the homes she designed for clients. The constant fiddle and nudge of objects and fabric so that they looked just so, leaving her mark on them. She didn't have to do that with him, but she was just doing what felt right.

Cason cast her a dark look and then stepped out of her reach to fasten his cuffs. "Sounds like sexism."

Savannah made a sound at the back of her throat. "It's amazing that you, *a*, know that word and, *b*, used it properly."

"I'm here to amaze."

Savannah stepped back to get a better look at Cason.

"Why do I feel like a set of your client's drapes?" Cason mumbled.

Ignoring him, she said, "That must be very expensive Egyptian cotton, the way your shirt has a sheen like that. And the reason you don't need a tie is that we don't cover that bone structure," she said, coming around to reluctantly admire the work that hard labor and sun had done. His work replaced the gym and tanning beds celebrities worshiped. He naturally came by the collar bones that were playing peekaboo with his shirt's neckline. Sandy hair and sharp eyes and strong jaw...All of it made him look the part of ex-military Southern playboy.

"You going to stand there and eye-fuck me all day, or are we going out there?"

Savannah's gaze went to his as she debated what she really wanted to say, and whether or not admitting he was a fine specimen of human male genetics was wise. She broke his challenging but waiting gaze to turn for the door and said, "There's no need for you to be crass, Cason. I was just thinking that it's too bad I hate you. You really can wear poor man's linen like a god."

"Wow, Savannah," he said, following her, "that was almost nice of you to say."

"Today I'll try for almost nice because there are witnesses, but starting first thing tomorrow, I'll be back to trying to run you over with my car."

"Roger that."

Returning to the kitchen, Savannah helped her mother and Ms. Myrna bring out trays of petits fours and fruit, as well as porcelain pots of coffee, tea and teacups. She was retrieving a tray when she heard Cason greet the Devereaux. Savannah thought he had put on a different personality as well as shirt; the tray of fruit in her hand slipped slightly when she heard his voice, loud and cheerful, say, "Theodore, Mrs. Devereaux, you are both looking well. Ms. Myrna, good to see you again. Managing all right with your driveway in a construction zone?"

Savannah arrived in the living room in time to see Cason's grin of camaraderie, his firm handshake with Theodore, the way he gave Theodore's shoulder a double pat with his left hand. It was as if they'd been close friends for decades. The effect was obvious: Theodore was beaming, and his mother was tripping over herself to bathe next in Cason's towering light. There was that: as despicable as she found him, he was always polite to her mother and her friends. Even with that stacked in his corner, he owed her mother more than just pleasantries.

Savannah returned to the kitchen to pick up the last of the trays. As she turned with one of delicate crustless sandwiches, she nearly bumped into Helen, who took the tray from her. "I'm not sure I've seen a man as handsome as Cason. Have you? He sure has blossomed today, hasn't he?" Helen gave her daughter a once-over. "You know, you could take a page out of Cason's book on attire. What were you thinking, wearing shorts? And *jean* shorts of all things." Helen turned fully toward the living room. "Look at him." Cason was smiling, a grin that pleasantly narrowed his eyes so that they exuded sweet mischief. "He could be on the cover of one of those men's magazines. What's that famous one called, *Maxim*? Yes, he could be on the cover of *Maxim*."

Savannah raised an eyebrow at her mother. "I see that you haven't actually seen a copy of that magazine. You mean *GQ*."

"Yes, well. He's a cover model for sure," she said, looking over at her daughter. "Unlike how you look in this getup."

"Not everyone wears slacks and blouses with their best pearls to tea anymore, Mama." Savannah gave her mother's outfit a pointed study.

"Well, I don't care for the new look. It's all right, I suppose, since everyone else called in their regrets because of the foul weather expected this afternoon."

Savannah looked at the buffet, realizing that explained the extravagance. Why hadn't she thought of the weather as the perfect excuse? "I'll help get the mimosas going for those of us who kept our promises," Savannah said as her mother walked back to the living room, taking the tray with her. Savannah stood in the coolness of the open fridge. One glass and she'd go. *The weather and all.*

She set the champagne and orange juice on the counter and looked out the kitchen window at the blackening sky. She parted the lace café curtains for a better look. The sky along the horizon held a barge of dark clouds that was moving in, sucking away the blueness as it crept along.

Savannah was reaching for the champagne flutes as a deep rumble of thunder reverberated through the house. Miles the purse dog responded. His high-pitched yaps pierced the air in machine-gun repetition. Savannah cringed but stepped toward the doorway in time to see Lucille and Theodore rush to Miles in Lucille's purse.

Mrs. Devereaux got to him first. "Oh, hush now, Miles. Hush."

She picked him up out of her purse with one hand, but the little dog squirmed, and tea splashed out of her cup and onto the carpet.

"Oh no!" she exclaimed.

"Here, Mother, give him to me," Theodore said.

Lucille passed off the pooch and turned toward Helen. "Oh, Helen! I'm so sorry about the carpet!"

"Mother..." Theodore whined over the yapping.

Savannah rubbed her temple.

"No, that's okay," Helen shouted, putting a linen napkin on the spill. Her daughter knew that tone. It was not fine.

Cason and Ms. Myrna, on the far side of the couch, watched the commotion. Miles squiggled out of Theodore's grip and jumped down onto the couch.

"Oh, well, that's better then," Mrs. Devereaux said to the dog.

The ball of fur paced the couch, scratching the air with his high-pitched barks, and then stilled and wet the cushion.

"Oh no! No, bad Miles! Bad Miles!" Mrs. Devereaux said, picking him up under his front legs.

Cason headed into the kitchen. Ripping a handful of paper towels from the roll, he mumbled under his breath, "Fun times."

Savannah sighed and decided she couldn't let Cason do all the helping. She tore off more paper towels as she heard her mother say, "Oh no. Don't worry about that, Lucille. Theodore, no, it's okay, really—accidents happen."

In her medical career, Helen had seen many accidents, so this was no big deal, but they'd never had a pet because her mother was a firm believer that animals belonged outdoors in the wild. Not as entertainment pieces in the home.

Savannah passed more towels to Cason, who was leaning over the back of the couch easily blotting the cushion. Theodore was making soothing sounds at the barking Miles and rubbing his mother's back.

"Mrs. Devereaux," Savannah said over the hollering, "Miles would be fine in the garage. Do you want to put him out there?"

Lucille and Theodore turned their attention from the shouting fur ball in Lucille's arms to her. Theodore's expression was one of shock. "In the *garage?*" his mother gasped.

"Yes?" Savannah said, not sure what was atrocious about that option. "We can make him a little bed and give him a bowl of water."

"What on God's green earth would excuse me placing him in the garage and treating him in such an indelicate manner? Shall Theodore and I spend the afternoon there as well?"

Savannah looked at her mother and Cason; both had carefully blank expressions. "I thought, since Miles is not housebroken—"

"He is perfectly housebroken, I assure you!" Mrs. Devereaux exclaimed, clutching Miles harder to her chest. The dog's bark quieted to a growl under the pressure.

Savannah suddenly felt as if she were talking to Phillip Nigel. "My apologies. I assumed he had urinated on the couch." *Ten minutes.* "Let me get the mimosas now."

"I'll help," Cason said and followed her into the kitchen.

She paused before filling the glasses, hands braced on the counter as she took deep breaths. Out the window in front of her she watched the storm whip closer. Through her peripheral vision, she noticed Cason take a champagne flute, fill it to the brim with bubbly, and slide it across the counter to her before filling the rest of the glasses with a champagne–orange juice blend.

She was still at the sink when he left with the mimosas on a tray. Savannah looked down at the glass, then at her watch, then back up again as the rain started pounding against the pane. The large round drops sounded like tiny pebbles tapping against the glass.

"Mimosas!" she heard Helen exclaim needlessly, "Here, why don't I pass them out. Cason, will you help Savannah in the kitchen. I think she needs input on deciding which jams we should serve. Lucille, mimosa? Oh my, will you look outside."

"It sure is coming down out there! My, that reminds me of the storm we survived in '98..."

"I assume jam is code for something?" Cason's voice was too close for Savannah, but she didn't move.

"A polite suggestion that I not try to climb out the kitchen window to escape." Savannah slid her eyes to him. "This is why I don't attend these functions." She looked back out at the chaos kicking up in the backyard. The purse pooch accented the conversation inside and the storm outside with his periodic growl-barks.

"You haven't touched your champagne. Drink it, and you can't leave. Stay and—"

"I'll kill someone."

"Drink it. I'll drive you home."

"In ten minutes?"

"After we eat."

"That could be in an hour. We don't have enough booze for that."

"You could try to be—"

She turned then, putting her mutinous gaze fully on him. "What? Be nice?"

"I was going to say nonhomicidal."

She breathed out, looking down at her drink and then out to the front room. "Not after the week I just had."

"Want to talk about it?"

Savannah smiled wickedly and gave him a half laugh. "Do I want to talk about it? With you?"

He nodded. "It felt weird saying it too."

She gave him one last look and downed the contents of her glass. Savannah lowered her empty glass and coughed, gently dabbing her mouth with the back of her hand. She picked up the half-empty bottle on the counter and refilled her glass. After a sip of the second glass, the first glass warming her belly, she said, "Are you having sex with Ms. Myrna?"

Cason choked, his face going sour. "What?"

"She's pet your arm three times now, and those are the times I've seen. It's obvious she has a comfortable relationship with you—"

"That's just what Ms. Myrna does—"

"It's a blatant come-on Cason. Why not sleep with her? She *is* wealthy."

Cason watched her for a moment, crossed his arms over his chest, and then said, "I thought we had a truce for today."

"Truce? Hardly. Even in the middle of my mama's tea, I can't forget you leaving Ryan to die."

Savannah watched Cason's countenance go satisfyingly dark. The green of his eyes built thunderclouds of his own.

"Really? We're going to hash that out again? Now?"

"Why not? Would you rather discuss why you prefer cougars? Is it because the older they get, the fewer questions they ask?"

He took a step closer to her, lowering his voice. "Let's focus on you instead. Still single? Still torching relationships?"

"You know...that's true. It's because I have very high standards. Unlike you." Savannah couldn't stop the words. Being trapped at her mama's house toppled one of the many plates she had balanced in the air; she could feel it crash into others as it descended. Calling a truce with Cason was only bearable when there was a time limit; now it was looking like she would be there all day. Just as she had said she wouldn't be. She felt claustrophobic and distracted herself from the suffocating feeling by diverting her attention to the needle in her side that was the closest. "Why are you still here, basking in the fawning of old women? Maybe...maybe I've missed something. Why don't you date women your age? Is it because they want more from you, Cason? Hmmm? Like, say, oh, kids? You know younger women like to start families—is that why you steer clear of them? Can you even get a girl pregnant?" Savannah said, letting doubt seed the air.

His eyes narrowed at her in warning.

"You used to be such the playboy in high school. Any girl would suit you just fine. Maybe that shrapnel did more damage than just to your hip. Did it nick Little Cason too?"

A very low noise rumbled in his chest, and he slid in close, arms unfolding. "Only one way to find out."

"Really?" she said and tilted her chin, taking him on. "Now, in my mama's kitchen?"

"Afraid you might like what you see?" Cason was close enough that Savannah could see the individual lashes framing his eyes and the intent creased in the firmness of his mouth. She took a step back and felt the counter hard against her backside. Cason smiled at her small acquiescence to his frontal siege. It was one that pleasantly creased his face, but instead of happiness in his eyes, there was dark joy.

"Don't look so smug," Savannah said. "You look like a cat with a stolen milk bowl. I just don't want your whole body against mine."

It was his turn to tilt his head at her. "Funny," he whispered. "Did you purposefully leave room for me to offer a comeback? Such as...You don't want my whole body on yours, just a bit of it? And what bit exactly?" She noticed his fingertips glided over his belt buckle.

"Again, really?" she said, "How old are you, Cason?"

"Don't forget who started this pissing match."

Savannah was past using her logical mind, and with the aid of the champagne tossed another of her plates of care to the floor: the one labeled *sensibility*. She bit her lip and pushed against Cason, only mildly surprised that he didn't move an inch. Her body against his, she watched the question of what she was about to do cross his mind. His eyes rested on her mouth, the dark joy becoming curiously guarded.

"So, I shouldn't question your morals while you live in my mama's house?" she asked quietly, intimately, as if he were a lover.

His gaze returned to hers. "Morals? You mean, don't question you."

"So, ethics, is it? It's hard for you to take orders from a woman? We can't make money like men without seeming like we're materialistic bitches?"

"Oh, I see now."

Savannah barely noticed his body against hers anymore, barely felt the increasing warmth his gave off or that his hand was still on his belt buckle sandwiched between their combative bodies.

"Do you?"

"This is about what I said yesterday—"

"And every day before that. You still haven't answered me. You have a problem with women trying to make money, to be independent?"

"No. But we're talking about you, right? I got a problem with *you*.

You leave your mom with bags of groceries and no intention of eating them with her. Your mom isn't an invalid. She can do her own shopping. What she wants is to see her kid."

His comment gut-punched her. "Now I'm a horrible daughter because I bring groceries to my mama?"

Cason made a *tsk* sound and looked out the window before sliding his now angry gaze back to hers. "No, I'm saying to make some damn time for her."

"Get out, and I will."

Cason's eyes went to slits. "I'd buy that bullshit by the ton if I believed it."

"Then pay—"

"Shut up. Last month I was gone for two weeks on a job in Grand Isle. Did you come by? Did you even fucking know? No. You didn't. So I call bullshit."

Savannah's insides felt on fire. She really wanted to grab him by the collar and shove him through the wall. He knew just where her soft spots were and poked at them.

"Asshole" was what she managed instead. "You will not make me feel small for being a successful woman who's financially securing her and her mama's futures. You will not, in the house we grew up in, tear me down because I've chosen to honor my mama's goose-egg idea to invite you into this house like a stray dog—"

At Savannah's words, Cason flexed his fading patience and stepped into her, pressing her back against the counter.

Savannah's breath caught as Cason said, "You make me so damn mad. This isn't what your brother wanted. If you'd just take care of your mother, I'd leave—"

Savannah's fingers splayed across his chest with indecision: to shove him back or to grip his shirt front in anger? Her other gripped the edge of the counter for balance. "If you just tossed what Ryan would want in my face"—she swallowed, hard, blinked against the tears—"if you just did that, you have balls the size of a damn elephant's."

"He wouldn't. I know he wouldn't. If you'd pause for two seconds, you'd see that too."

"Says the man—"

"Says his best friend. Says the man who—" He cut off his own thought with the grind of his molars as if biting off the very words and swallowing them back down.

Savannah shook her head in disbelief. How could he have been the same person as the boy she'd grown up with? The boy whose hands shook when buttoning the vest of his prom tux because he was about to meet his date's parents. The boy she had had a crush on, but not a soul knew because she was so afraid he'd find out and laugh at her. How could he have ever been worthy of her love? How could she have missed the signs that when Ryan needed him most, he'd run away? Yet here he was, staying, and fighting for what he thought was right like the Cason she had known.

"You are..." she said and stopped.

"Say it," Cason said through gritted teeth.

"You...How can you have done the things you have done and stand here like you are, telling me off? How the hell do you think you have legs to stand on to even talk to me?" she hissed.

Cason opened his mouth to reply.

"Savannah," Helen admonished as she came around the corner, "this is no time to raise Cason's hackles."

Reality swept in like a cold winter wind, snapping them both awake to their surroundings.

Cason recovered quickly and, putting on his manners, stepped back before excusing himself, leaving Savannah to regain her composure and throw daggers at his backside as he left the kitchen.

Savannah heard a commotion in the other room. She and Cason had been in their own icy world.

Mrs. Devereaux's voice said, "Maybe he's hungry? Are you hungry, little Miles? How about a sausage?"

Theodore whined, "No, Mom, that'll give him gas."

"Well, what, then?"

"Fruit?" Myrna's voice suggested.

"Oh, we can't make decisions for His Majesty-Wagesty," Lucille said. Savannah leaned to watch through the pass-through as Lucille made fish lips at Miles. Her insides still burned from her confrontation with Cason. It had been a long time since they'd gone toe to toe. But it was always there between them; they were like angry magnets drawn to the fight that had perpetually simmered since his return from Afghanistan.

"Just let him decide," Lucille cooed as her pooch shrieked in her face. "Give him the plate."

Theodore put the plate under the dog's nose.

"No, Theodore, he can't eat in my arms. Put it down on the table."

Another crack of thunder, and the lights went out.

"Oh lord," Helen said as Cason headed down the bedroom hallway to the garage. Savannah wondered if he had foreseen needing something from there or if he just needed a break.

"At least it's not pitch-black." Savannah said to her mother, who had not returned to the living room.

"Yet."

The dog barked louder.

Savannah watched her mother come up and take her arm; she blew out a breath as her grip tightened. "It's like nails on the chalkboard. They can't go home in this. And now we can't see. All we can do is hear, and all I can hear is that damn dog," she hissed.

Savannah raised her eyebrows. Helen upheld good Southern sensibilities, and cursing wasn't part of them, unless things were bad. Apparently this, for her mother, was very, very bad.

"It's all right, Mama. We'll think of something."

In the low light, Savannah saw her mother put a smile on before turning and going to her guests. Soon, more light flickered in the living room; Cason was lighting kerosene lanterns from the garage. A thought struck Savannah. She left the darkened kitchen, headed down the hall, and slipped into Cason's room.

As her eyes adjusted, the dresser took shape. Wallet, keys—and pills. Three containers in all. Nearly indistinguishable from each other in the dark. Dark-blue plastic cylinders with labels on them.

Savannah squinted and, picking up each one, tried reading the labels. She tilted them toward the window, but it was no use in the stormy light. There was, she remembered, a flashlight in the bathroom.

Suddenly the barking sounded louder, and then Cason's voice behind her: "Can I help you?"

Savannah jumped. She looked over at him as he shut the bedroom door behind him, the yapping getting quieter again.

"You better be looking for earplugs."

"Surprise, I'm not. Which one of these is your sleeping pills?" she asked, tolerating him in the room with her—she *was* going through his things.

Cason was quiet as he took the container out of her hand and squinted at it. "You realized you need a time-out?"

Biting her tongue, she said instead, "I was thinking that there's a little dog who could use some rest right about now."

Cason turned back to her. "One of these would kill it."

"I know that, dimwit," she said, mentally trading *dimwit* for something stronger. She picked up another bottle from the dresser. "It will have to be cut very small."

He snatched the bottle from her hand and grabbed the third one too. "I'm not helping you with this."

"I didn't ask you to. But my mama cursing a few minutes ago—something I thought impossible for her to do in a social situation—has me concerned."

Cason was quiet for a moment and then said, "Gosh, Savannah, sounds like you do have a heart."

"Don't push it. That and I *will* set fire to the house if that dog doesn't stop yapping soon."

He reached into his pocket and pulled out his military blade.

"Jesus, Cason..." she said, watching him. He was a little too fluid producing the thing. "You always carry that around with you?"

"Even sleep with it." He handed it to her.

"Hmmm, I'll keep that in mind when I make my plans to murder you in your sleep." The slim steel fold blade was warm from his body heat.

"Wise. You should also know that I'm a light sleeper. And the door to this room squeaks."

"A little WD-40 and it sounds like I'm in business." She turned the folded knife over in her hands. "What do I do with this thing?"

"Unless you plan on biting the pills smaller, you'll need that blade."

"I know what this is," she said dryly, wrestling with the folded blade. "But how do I open this thing?"

He took it back and flicked it open.

Savannah tried to not be impressed by such a simplistic lethal skill as opening a fold blade one-handed as if he had done it a thousand times. "Okay, we're halfway there. I still can't see what I'm cutting."

"Right," he said and went to his cot, kneeling to pull out the trunk. He fiddled with the lock and then opened it. It was too dark for Savannah to see into it; he moved too quickly anyway. Shortly, he had what he wanted and had shut the trunk. He turned around with two sticks and cracked them. A low green glow emitted from them.

Savannah looked past him as he returned to standing next to her. "What's in there?"

"Nothing."

"Nothing?" she asked, thinking of his skill with the knife. "You better not have guns in there, Cason. You live with my mama, and there had better not be anything explosive in there either—"

"There isn't. Now, are we going to do this?"

Savannah looked back at him, his sleeves rolled up to his elbows. "Fine," she said, focusing on the immediate issue of silencing the nails on the chalkboard out in the living room, "but since when is it a 'we' decision?"

"Since hearing that your mom actually cursed in the presence of guests. Feels like Armageddon."

Savannah had to agree—glancing out the front window as debris whipped by in the torrential downpour, it looked it.

"Right."

"How small do we want to cut these things?"

She stood next to him, her shoulder brushing his in temporary truce. "Maybe we should pulverize it?"

Cason looked her way. "And what, have him snort it with a hundred-dollar bill?"

Savannah returned his glare. "No need to give me sass, McPherson. I'm not hearing any good ideas from you."

Just then the door opened abruptly, letting in the yaps and howls. "There you are. What are you two doing? Your presence is missed," Helen said, coming in and brusquely looking from them to the pill container in Savannah's hand.

Savannah felt paralyzed, not knowing what to say.

Cason answered for them both in a low voice. "Trying to figure out what dose of my pain pill to give the dog."

Helen looked to Savannah. "Quarter of the pill, an eighth if you can manage it. Hide it in peanut butter." She turned, paused briefly at the door to say loudly enough to be heard in the living room, "And don't delay with those glow sticks!"

As the door shut, Cason said, "Yes, ma'am..."

Savannah turned back to Cason. "Good lord, she didn't even bat an eyelash." Savannah took the blade from Cason and, pushing him aside, said, "I'm much better at detail work than you."

"Fine by me. If you OD that dog, it's on you."

They were silent as she held the pill under the knife's blade. "I know. But you have to give it to the dog."

"Afraid he might bite you?"

"Not really. I'm not sure which end is its mouth."

Cason laughed. An odd sound, one Savannah wasn't sure she had heard in years.

"It's all fur. Shouldn't it have a tail or something?" she added.

"Just go for the end that's making noise."

Savannah cut the pill in half and then half again. "This blade is sharp. I should be able to do an eighth..." she said, concentrating. "There." She picked up a piece of pill the size of a sesame seed. "I'm not sure this thing is going to work. It's so small."

"Worse comes to worse, we can dose him again."

"Right. Now, I hope he likes peanut butter."

"I'll give it. You clean up."

"Deal," she said as he left. With his knife. She hadn't forgotten the trunk under his cot, though. Cason must think her a fool if he thought she'd let the subject go. For all she knew, he kept explosives in there, little keepsakes from his time at war, the cowardly bastard.

A few moments later there was a pause in the barking and conversation between the Devereaux, replaced with the rumble of Cason's voice. The pause only held for a moment.

Savannah knelt in front of the trunk and opened the lid; she let the light of the glow stick Cason had left make everything inside eerily green. The trunk held the crisp, strong smell of laundry detergent. Under the lid she found a water bottle, some food packs with *MRE* written across them, another knife, a rope, and a folded uniform, and under that she saw the edges of a stack of letters bound with twine.

Weapons forgotten, curiosity made her reach for the letters, and as she pulled them up from under the uniform, the fabric fell open a little. It had been folded in what seemed to be precise thirds so that the name badge with *C. McPherson* was visible. Ignoring the bound letters for the moment, she undid the material further to refold it exactly the way it had been before she disturbed it. As it flopped open, she saw that the lower portion of the camouflage shirt was torn away, and the ragged edge was darkly colored, a muddy brown in the green of her glow stick. Looking down into the trunk, she saw the matching desert camouflage pants. The way they were folded, it was obvious that they had seen the same attack as the shirt, displaying blood on the upper left hip. Her fingers went numb. She forced them to work and pick up the pants; she looked at the stains, like dark ink. The pants leg had seen a pair of scissors, as if a medic had cut the pants from its wearer. Realizing that she held Cason's last uniform before he'd been medically discharged brought a wave of confusion crashing down around her.

The day Cason had come to her mama's home from his medical discharge two years before burst forward like lightning from her memory. Fresh off the plane from Germany, he sat on her mama's couch. She remembered his words, as clear as if he'd just spoken them: "He wouldn't be dead if it weren't for me." She felt her insides stiffen. His cheeks had been hollow and dark circles had haunted his eyes as he recounted a clearly well-rehearsed speech about how Ryan was a hero; he then circled back to his involvement in Ryan's death at the end. There would be no investigation because he was just a coward, not a deserter. Apparently, Savannah thought, you could be a real fuck-up in the army and they'd still give you a gun. It was at the end of his speech, about his bald betrayal of Ryan, that her hearing cut out and her blood pressure rose. Right at that very moment, their standing two-year hatred began. He sat there and recounted how Ryan had been a hero when the hillside had erupted in gunfire, but Cason had escaped. He let Ryan be out front and as a result traded Ryan's life for his. It was his fault that her brother was dead; Cason had let him bleed out. The skirmish, he said, had left him with just a nick as he was fleeing. He had been otherwise unscathed.

Now, she couldn't process what she was seeing.

Just a nick?

The door opened. The person paused before closing it again. Savannah was paralyzed. She felt him come farther into the room. He didn't speak; the weight of what she was holding in her hands muted their voices. The reason for their personal battle hung loudly from her fingertips. Everything that had shoved them apart was now exposed, with both of them looking directly at it.

When he did speak, his voice was quiet, choked. "What are you doing?"

The small lantern he'd come in with shed full light onto the uniform. Originally, it had been a sandstone camouflage field uniform, but not any longer. It held large swaths of rust-colored dye. Her mind corrected her: *blood*. Now she could see smears on the shirt front too. As if someone in front of Cason had pushed him away, smearing his handprint across Cason's chest.

Her hands began to shake. "I was—" she said and stopped; she was imagining the horror that the uniform had seen. "Cason..." she whispered.

"Put. It. Away."

She turned to him. "Why did you..." she managed and then choked; the amount of blood didn't add up to his story of his wounds. "This is yours." She heard the accusatory tone in her own voice.

"Put it back." His voice went glacial.

Her mind went to the absurd thought that maybe he had had these fabricated. It was a testament to how deeply she clung to her belief in his betrayal. "How did you even get these? I thought these would have been destroyed at the hospital."

"That's not important. Put it back."

"But it is. Are these real?"

It was clear then that they were; his eyes blazed with something. Defiance? Anger?

"Why didn't you tell me...?" She added quietly, "This isn't the uniform of a man who walked away from my brother, letting him die alone." She felt as if something were siphoning the air from the room as the polarity of her paradigm began to shift. "The pain in your hip isn't from you running away. This is..." she said, bunching the uniform in one hand and smoothing the fabric with her other, "This is the *front*." Everything she'd come to believe of her brother's final moments were gone. In the wake of that emptiness, she felt a vacuum, a cavernous black hole fill her chest. She gasped for real truth to fill it.

"You...you must have nearly died," she added, holding out the uniform as if he didn't know.

"Don't..."

"You lied to me." Her thoughts came in fits and spurts. "What happened, Cason? What *really* happened?" she whispered.

He looked toward the front windows instead of her. "No" was all he said for several heartbeats. He swallowed hard and, looking back at her, added, "This isn't the time." He put down the lantern and stepped toward her—but the uniform was like repellent, and he stopped.

Sound in the room faded as the pressure in her ears from her hammering heart rose; the only competition was the loudly clanging violence that the tattered uniform had seen.

Savannah managed, "All this blood, Cason...How'd you not die?" Savannah's throat constricted as she looked up at him, the dark figure looming above the lantern.

His face was twisted up as if recalling an image, and he shook his head slowly in disbelief. "It's not all mine."

Savannah did choke then; the obvious took hold of her. The other person's blood...It was Ryan's blood. Cason had held him to his chest, not walked away from him.

Her heart tightened with escaping emotion, and hot, hard-fought-against tears swam into her vision.

"Put it away, Savannah."

She moved her shaking arms, trying to fold the stained fabric pooling in her lap. But then she asked, "How could you have let me believe all this time that you left him there to die? What did this?" she asked, fingering the frayed edges of the pant hip. "This...this all happened, and all you have is a nick? I might not be a medic, Cason, but I can see that the body that was in this uniform would not have walked away with just a scratch. And something tells me that this hole is too big for just gunfire."

When he didn't respond, she repeated, "What did this?"

Cason was like stone before reluctantly uttering, "RPG." The acronym for a rocket-propelled grenade fell heavy in the room; it was the only thing either of them said for some time. Cason broke the silence; his voice was harder still. "It hit the ground next to us right after Ryan was shot. Now you know, so put them away."

She tried folding the shirt and pants, but her hands shook too hard as her world crashed down around her. Questions shotgunned out of her mind, "Cason," she said, looking up at him. The meager lamplight couldn't touch his eyes; they were dark, endless pools. She wanted to see his leg, wanted to rewrite the history between them, starting from the moment he sat down on her mother's couch two years ago. She needed the answers to all of it to fill the vacuum of reality that was now widening.

"Why did you lie about what really happened to you?" she asked, adding, "This is not just a little fragment, just a hip injury. It was more than that, wasn't it? It was way worse than that, wasn't it?"

"No, don't, Savannah..." For one sentence, his voice was tender. Then it snapped back to its coldness. "Don't put your goddamn pity on me."

Stung, Savannah stood facing him. "You'd rather I spent the rest of my life hating you and ripping at you than telling me the truth?"

"I'll take your hate any day, Savannah, but I don't want pity. Especially not from you."

"Does my mother know the truth?"

"She put two and two together, Savannah. Just drop it."

She felt like a fool. How could she not have known? And why had her mother not told her what she really suspected? It was all too much. She felt the walls start to close in. "Drop it? Just drop it? Erase the knowledge that my brother didn't die alone? That you didn't step over his dying body and escape when a little shrapnel hit you? Go back to thinking you were a coward? Just go back to hating you? No. This," Savannah said, pointing to the rumpled uniform. "I need to know it all."

Cason stepped back away from her waving his hand through the air as if the memories were being uploaded into his conscious mind and he was trying to fight them back. "No... No. What will that do for you, Savannah? It won't bring him back," he said, his voice rising.

"I know it won't bring him back, but you need to step into my shoes for a second. Everything I've known about his last moments is false. You were there, Cason; I can see it on this uniform—" she said, feeling her voice crack with emotion, knowing that the handprint was her brother's final stamp upon the world.

"Don't do this."

"Just tell me, Cason. Please."

"No," he said, shifting uneasily, his breath uneven.

"Just tell me," she whispered. "That's his handprint, isn't it?" She knew it was but needed to hear it from Cason.

He looked as if he would respond but then stopped wrestling with an internal voice that said not to and obeyed it.

Savannah closed her eyes and felt them overflow, tears trickling down her cheeks. "Tell me," she whispered and put her hand over her eyes.

"No, just leave it. Put it away."

Her hand fell. "You can't be serious."

Ryan had been Savannah's protector, her guardian, filling the role of father and older brother since the day their father died up to the day of his own death, and now her heart ached to be put to rest. To know the possibility that her brother hadn't suffered alone as she had thought, that maybe their best friend had held him in his arms as he exited the world.

"You, of all the people in my life, you would keep this from me? Damn you, tell me now." She pressed one last time.

He turned away from her, looked away for a fidgeting moment, and then turned on his heel back to her. He looked as if he was about to crack with the pressure of the memories she had brought back.

Then he did indeed crack.

Truth gushed from the emotional fissure in the wall of his well-controlled emotions. "What will that do for you, Savi? How will that make your life better, knowing that our two squads were ambushed earlier that day? You already know that Ryan and a team of six went in to retrieve our pinned men. Why do you need to know that he made it out alive only to be shot dead at the door of the Humvee?" His voice rose an octave. "What good will it do, knowing that I was standing in front of him when he was shot and took shrapnel to my leg from an RPG? That I held him, right here, like this," he said, making his hands into fists and holding something invisible in his arms, "as blood poured everywhere. I put my goddamn hand on his shredded neck, Savi—is that what you want to hear? Where does that get you? Will you sleep better at night, knowing that it was a fucking bloodbath?"

Savannah absorbed the violence he painted with his words and then softly answered his question. "I won't sleep better at night. But when I close my eyes, I need the peace of knowing you were there. That you held him. I'll not sleep better envisioning the bloodbath, but that you were there? That gives me a comfort I've not had. You were there, together. You, not some soulless desert, were the last thing he saw before he died. *That.* That is what I needed to hear, Cason. I was strong enough to hear it then, and I deserve to hear—"

"Do you? You think you deserve to hear it? It's not only your brother, Savi. It was me too on that damn hill. It was the worst moment of my life."

"And how was I supposed to know that, when all you've fed me is a lie that you conjured up to make me believe that you'd left Ryan? That you lured your best friend to war and left him there to die to save yourself?" She picked up the shredded uniform again. "I may not deserve to hear it, but you left me with crumbs to put pieces together. I don't know why you did that. But I do know now that there's no way you could have saved him. If I had to guess, the RPG ripped apart your leg, leaving you with only one good side, if that," she said, spreading out the fabric again.

"You don't understand Savannah, I *need* you to hate me."

"Why? No. I won't do it. I don't understand why you need me to hate you. Is it some penance for Ryan's death? You were hit with shrapnel, Cason. What the hell were you supposed to do, pick up my two-hundred-pound brother when you were hurt like that?" The RPG, the bullet that took her brother's life, the new information that Cason had been right there—all of it seemed to shiver in horror and then expand like a python eating a gator. Her mind was hinged open now, seeing him as if for the first time. Seeing everything.

"My god. You did, didn't you? You did put him in the Humvee." She had been wrong about him for two years. He'd been the Cason she'd grown up with the whole time. "Tell me the truth, Cason. Jesus, how can you have lived with a lie like this for so long?"

Cason remained silent.

The truth was stark once it was revealed. She should have known better. She should have known that, because of the type of man Cason was, he would not have left Ryan behind. But the pain over Ryan's loss had been blinding, and her pain had found an outlet: hating Cason. And Cason had seemed to be a willing participant in her grief.

No, she wasn't going to do that for him. It wasn't right.

"Cason..." she said, "You might not be able to tell me the whole truth about that day, but I know enough that I have to apologize for the way I've treated you...You say you need my hate—I don't know why—but I can't participate in whatever that need is about. I'm sorry." She stepped forward.

As she reached for him, he came to life. He stepped back. "Don't touch me," he said; then his lips parted again as if he meant to say something more. The words never came. Instead, he turned from her and slipped out the door and into the darkened hallway. Disappearing like a ghost.

The open door let in ethereal light from the lanterns in the living room.

"Savannah, hon? Is Cason with you? We need that extra lantern —it's hard to see some of these puzzle pieces." Her mother's voice sounded startlingly loud. In Cason's absence, the world tumbled back in on Savannah.

Savannah struggled to process what her mother was asking. Her mind was fat with new information that was tearing her well-constructed world apart. She had thought being at her mother's society tea that day was going to be trying, but now, as she wiped her face dry, she was certain another second there in false company would be unbearable.

"I've got it," she called back and gathered her wits enough to hastily toss the uniform and glow sticks back into the trunk and close the lid. She heard her cell phone ring in the front room.

Another person making demands on her. Savannah closed her eyes and started counting to ten.

"Savannah," her mother called. "Your phone is going off. Please come get that thing and make it be quiet."

Ten.

She picked up the lantern and with great effort put a smile on her face and headed out to the front room. Mrs. Devereaux was commenting on how peaceful her little pooch was being. "He's normally totally frantic with cell phone ringtones too. Takes him a while to calm down, he gets so worked up. It must be your soothing home, Helen, that makes him so at peace," she cooed.

Theodore added, "I think he was just hungry, Mother. That peanut butter was just the trick. Cason sure saved the day." He smiled like a schoolboy at Helen.

Mama's lovely home, Cason's snack, oh, and that eighth of a narcotic. Just that old thing.

Savannah handed the lantern to her mother and went to her purse hanging by the door.

The caller ID said the person on the other end was Phillip Nigel. Savannah gritted her teeth but also realized she rather welcomed the distraction. "Mr. Nigel," Savannah answered as she walked down the hall toward the garage door. "What can I do for you?"

The phone crackled with static, but his nasally tone of annoyance rang clear. "You sound like you really don't know what I'm calling about. Incredible, since we spoke just a little bit ago."

She realized she'd been grinding her teeth as he spoke. She unclenched and answered, "I actually don't. When we spoke, it sounded like we would sit down Monday and go over the rest of the project details. Has something happened, Mr. Nigel, since that conversation?"

He scoffed. "As a matter of fact, yes. No one showed up to work today," he said, sounding triumphant.

"That's right. It's Saturday. Workers won't be back in your home until Monday. Was there something you needed done today?"

"I was under the impression that Knight Interiors worked half days on Saturday."

"Mr. Nigel, we've not once worked on a Saturday—"

"Not for me, but for others."

"Mr. Nigel—"

"I don't feel Knight Interiors is providing me with the level of service I deserve. I'll be canceling this project with you."

Savannah's blood went hot. He'd beaten her to it, but instead of being thrilled, she was enraged. Especially after everything that had just happened, she had wanted to be the one to end things.

"Fine," she said, "are you home now? I'll make a courtesy call, and you can make it final with your signature."

"You sound like you've been waiting for me to come to this conclusion. You're not even going to try to win me back?"

"Are you home or not?"

"Of course I am!"

"I'll be there in ten," Savannah said and headed back down the darkened hall to the living room where her mother and the Devereaux still sat. *No doubt enjoying their hollow, polite conversations about nothing,* she thought caustically.

Savannah felt the fabric of her world tear farther apart.

"You're not going, are you?" Helen asked, getting up.

"I am. Bad news from work that I need to attend to," she said, shouldering her bag.

"Well, where's Cason? He can drive you in his truck."

The thought of him, after everything, hit a raw nerve in her. "How should I know? I'm not his keeper."

"Savannah Rae—" her mother admonished as her daughter stepped out into the storm.

Chapter Five

Savannah was deep in thought as she drove to the Nigel residence. Rain poured like a river from the sky, making streams where just an hour before there had been road. Strong winds rocked her car, and lightning split the sky open in the distance. But it was lost on Savannah.

After everything Cason had really done for her brother, he had let her believe that he'd left his best friend to die. That day he came to their house two years ago, he told her he'd done nothing for Ryan. Her mother cried, and Savannah stood in anger. She told him to get the hell out and to never come back. The rage only built as her mama cried and closed Ryan's room up.

Savannah took care of her mother in those first days, putting her own need to grieve aside. Just one week later, Savannah knew she'd have to earn more money to keep up her mama's house. The lawn had gotten out of control, and bills were starting to stack up in her fog of grief. Only the next time she dropped in on her mama, Cason was there, mowing the lawn. He was there again, fixing her car, and next thing she knew, he was living in Ryan's old room. The anger ground so deep it went into her bones, but she couldn't deny the hope that had returned to her mother's eyes or the way she would be out of bed every day before noon. She had begun to socialize again and to live. She couldn't take that from her mama, so she bit her tongue and poured her energy into her work. If she made enough money, she could pay someone to do all that Cason did.

And now...it was all undone; it was all a lie. What was she even striving for now? In one fell swoop, the driving motivation she had come to know in her life after Ryan's death was kicked out from under her.

The worst part was that this new truth felt right. The lie he had told wasn't the Cason she had grown up with; she had thought that maybe the war had changed the marrow of him. This truth was the Cason she knew, the one who had punched out Bobby Sanders for snapping her bra in middle school, who played high school football with Ryan, who never passed a fight he could break up or failed to help her mama with yard work. It was the Cason who grew up rough taking care of his addict mother until he could leave. He was the kid who, at thirteen, picked up a metal pipe to defend his mother's trailer when her dealer stopped by for an overdue payment.

It was also the Cason that drove back to New Orleans from five hours away to meet Savannah's homecoming date in person because Ryan couldn't make it and asked him to. Mama had said it wasn't necessary, and at the time Savannah knew she heartily agreed. The adolescent face of her date, the football team captain, blanched when the door opened and Cason stood there in his uniform. Later, in the limo with friends, her date kept massaging his hand after the hand-shake and avoided touching her the whole night. Now she knew Cason had put the fear of God and the wrath of Cason into him. He was a protector, a born leader, and through grief she'd ignored what she had known in her heart of hearts. He couldn't have left Ryan to die. The why of it, though, still tugged at her. Why had he said he did?

Now, all this time later, her mind was vivid in conjuring up Ryan's shot and bloody body, but instead of seeing Cason step over him, she saw Ryan ripped and bloody in his arms. With Cason trying to pick him up, trying to carry him to safety. Trying to do the right thing by him because that's who he was.

Tears and the rain blurred her vision. She wiped her tears away just as she flicked the switch to make her wipers rapidly clear the windshield.

Savannah screamed and hit the brakes.

As she slammed on her brakes, the SUV locked up and slid. Uprooted, lying directly across the road, was a massive old oak tree. It appeared to race out toward her hydroplaning vehicle.

Instincts made her yank the wheel to the side. The SUV swerved and spun nose to tailgate.

Her hair whipped out at the centrifugal force of the spin. The steering wheel was vibrating and locked in the turn position. Savannah panicked. She muscled the wheel the other way as the world outside her window blurred even more. The tires caught pavement, and in one moment the entire SUV lurched, then tumbled. Glass shattered into the cabin; metal screamed and crunched under its own momentum. In seconds, the careening vehicle smashed into the massive trunk. As it tumbled up and against the stout gnarled branches, wood, leaves, and water violently mixed with the glass in the cabin.

Savannah's screams were silenced by the airbag blowing her back against her seat. The side bag exploded, slapping her hand from the wheel. The SUV came to a stop. Before Savannah had finished taking her next breath, she screamed again—the car was falling onto its side over ripped limbs. Finally, battered, the vehicle sat silent, save for its still-running motor. Thunderous rain rushed into the smashed vehicle, wetting Savannah's bloodied face and arms.

Savannah, hanging in her seat, tried to look around. Her hair was plastered to her face. She went to part it, but pain shot through her arm. She tried the other one. Better. Pieces of glass were everywhere, parts of the dash had come off, and fragments of the side mirror sat in the crushed passenger seat.

She was sideways. She could see up into the black sky out the shattered driver's side window.

Cold rain splattered her face.

The distinct metallic flavor of blood coated her tongue.

It was painful to draw a breath. Savannah took more self-inventory: she could move everything down to her toes. Groaning, she reached for her seat-belt latch that was digging into her hip. She tried to undo it, but the passenger seat had crushed the center console against the buckle.

Her heart thumped hard in her chest. This couldn't be happening. She couldn't be sideways. Her car...this couldn't be real.

She yanked on the belt. It wouldn't budge. She tried slipping free of the belt, but it had locked tightly in place. Jarring pain shot through her side, and she involuntarily sucked in her breath, which made her hurt even more. With the breath, she recognized the unmistakable smell of gasoline and hot plastic. Looking out the fragmented windshield, she saw what had been her hood. The branches that were jabbing into it had begun to smoke.

This is real. Her mind was tripping over itself to catch up with what her body had just experienced.

Reaching forward, she grabbed the key and tried to turn off the ignition. Part of the steering wheel casing had been ripped off, just above her knee. A thick branch sat wedged just below the ignition switch.

Her mind caught up to her body then as she looked at the branch as if it were the cause of all of the chaos. Panic flooded into her extremities. She'd never been in a car wreck or been in so much pain. It was all so unknown; she felt like a newborn foal fumbling around in a decimated world.

She fought down the panic as fear moved in to take its place. Trapped in her seat, she tried to slide her knee over and knock the branch lodged in the steering wheel column loose.

"Dammit," she said. It was wedged too far against the shaft. Savannah yanked again at her seat belt.

The smoldering gas, wood, and plastic seemed to be sending out more smoke. Savannah reached for anything flat. She grabbed a piece of what had been the housing for the side view mirror and wedged the piece between the crushed console and her seat belt. She shoved hard, and the piece snapped in half.

"Shit," she whispered and then reached for a piece of broken glass. Savannah applied it to the belt. The piece cracked, fracturing into smaller pieces, slivers embedding in her palm.

Tossing the glass aside, she started pulling at the belt again. Her arm screamed, and now so did her cut hand, and all she seemed to be doing was unintentionally making the belt tighter and tighter. "No..."

She saw her purse tucked under the dash of the passenger side.

My phone.

Rain sizzled on the motor, blending steam with the acrid smoke.

The dash had been shoved down in the tumble; she couldn't get her leg out to reach for the bag. Savannah shrugged out from under her shoulder belt and hung sideways, grasping for her purse. The strap was just out of reach.

She cursed, stretching for it, pain tearing up her side. She cried out in pain and closed her eyes, sucking in air through clenched teeth.

Taking shallow panting breaths, she looked toward her out-of-reach purse again.

From her position, she saw there was an actual fire under the hood.

"Oh god," she murmured. Fire she knew. Who hadn't been burned by fire? Fire took oxygen, her oxygen, and created meat-sizzling heat with the help of fuel. Fuel like oil, gas, wood. She was sitting in a human barbecue.

Panic tingled up her arms and seized her mind.

"Help!" she hollered, feeling the heat of that fire and trying not to think of her skin as beginning to sizzle.

The densely wooded stretch to Phillip Nigel's would be deserted in the midst of a storm. Yet she had to do something, anything.

"*Help!*" she screamed clutching at the pain in her side as the flames, fanned by the whipping wind and fed by the engine oil, licked at the storm-darkened sky. "Somebody, help me!"

She yanked at her seat belt again as smoke began to billow up.

"*Help!*" she screamed again.

The vehicle swayed slightly then, and a branch cracked next to her shattered window. A familiar voice called to her, "Savannah!"

"Here!" she gasped, choking on smoke. "I'm trapped—help me!"

Another branch cracked, and Cason's voice carried stronger into the cabin. "Hold on; I'm coming. Everything is smashed."

He appeared over the edge of her window just a few seconds later.

"Cason..." she said, not asking why and how he could be there; she simply reached for him. "Oh my—thank god. Help me. I can't get out. My seat belt..."

His eyes were distant but sharp, as if he were in a different time and place. He moved swiftly. Reaching into the cabin, he grasped her upper arm, stabilizing her. With his other hand, he reached down past her to the ignition.

"It's stuck. There's a branch against it," she said and, feeling the last of her dignity get swallowed by panic and fear, begged, "Please, Cason, help me."

"Here," he said, putting her arms around his neck, "hold on."

She didn't hesitate. She gripped him tightly as he leaned in, bringing with him the smell of crushed foliage. His head was right next to hers. One arm went around her middle.

The fire suddenly billowed higher, throwing heat against them both.

Cason cursed under his breath.

Suddenly she felt his other hand working at her belt: his knife. It took him just a second to cut Savannah loose. The belt fell away, but her legs were still pinned under the steering wheel.

"Ouch," she said, as he tried to pull her directly up.

She heard Cason curse again, having hurt her.

She looked down, her forehead pressing the collar of his shirt against his neck. "Let me go, and I'll crawl out the back."

"No. The fire is getting too hot. Savannah, you need to get out now." His voice got louder, competing with the roar of the engine fire.

"I know, but I can't." She winced as he gave her another pull. "Oh god, Cason, that hurts."

"Okay. I'll...Here." He released her back into the tilted SUV.

Savannah slid down onto the crushed middle console, reached back between the seats, grabbing a rear seat belt for support, and tugged her legs free. Heat chasing her, she crawled over the side of the front passenger seat into the back as Cason tracked her from above. As she reached for the rear window above her, her feet slipped on the wet leather. The SUV rocked on its perch within the branches.

Savannah screamed and grabbed the driver's headrest. Feet dangling, Savannah swung forward, looking for purchase.

Cason swore above her as he caught his balance and reached down. "Hurry, Savannah! This thing is pissing gasoline."

"It's moving!"

"Fuck it. Move your ass, Sparling!" he shouted over the roar and snap of the fire moving toward them from the front.

Heat spewed and snapped forward as glass dug into her bare feet. She caught a foothold and pushed up. She reached up for his hand through the window. Cason closed the gap in a second, his grip a vise around her wrist; still, she screamed as the whole SUV moved, tilting back farther into the branches, threatening to topple once more, onto its roof. Cason slid forward on the crushed side door, his face contorting against the heat. She lost her footing again, and she dangled from Cason's hand. Pain tore up her left side as he yanked her up. She slapped her other hand on the window frame, glass cutting into her palm. Heat scoured the side of her face as the dash melted.

On his knees above her, Cason gripped her by the armpits and lifted her out of the wreckage into his arms. The SUV swayed again.

Cason cursed against her cheek as he lost his balance. He threw his arm out, caught them both.

"Savannah," Cason said, trying to look into her face, "we need to jump off this thing. Can you move?"

She nodded. She tried to say she could barely breathe, her side hurt so bad, but she didn't get a chance as he moved swiftly, wrapping his arm tightly about her middle. Pain exploded through her abdomen, and everything went black.

CASON FELT Savannah go limp in his arms; her head hit his shoulder. Panic pulled on him. The heat at his back felt like the desert, and with her body in his arms, he fought hard against the visions that had been trying to drown him since he had arrived on the scene.

Pushing his demons away, he sent up a prayer, put Savannah over his shoulders, and holding her there, leaped from the SUV into the thick, broken branches of the oak. The flames chased him down to the pavement. He thought of nothing as he hauled Savannah away from the wreckage. Making it to his truck, he yanked the door open and eased her into the passenger seat.

"Savannah," he said, tapping the side of her face, "come on, Savannah, wake up," he said, trying to keep his déjà vu at bay. "Come on, wake up...Look at me, Savi—say something mean, please..." He gave her face a harder tap.

Savannah's eyelids fluttered open, and she croaked, "My side is on fire." She winced, grabbing for it. "I'm on fire."

Relief flooded through him. "You're not. You're fine. You're gonna be fine. Look at me, Sparling," he said, tapping the side of her face again when her eyes closed.

Savannah made a guttural sound.

"Look at me."

Her lids fluttered open, and dark, pain-filled eyes looked back at him.

"You're okay," he said to her, and then, for just a moment, was reckless. He grabbed her up into his arms and slid one hand into her tangled hair, holding her tightly to him. "Thank god."

She groaned and pushed him away. "My side."

"Hang tight," he said and pulled the seat belt across her, gently securing it. In the distance, her SUV went up in an inferno, flickering eerie light on the wet pavement and sizzling in the rain.

"Your cell phone isn't in your pocket by any chance, is it?" he asked her as he started his truck.

She moaned her response, and he kicked himself for not having a phone of his own.

The road back to the house was littered with more branches and high-water spots. He was thankful his truck was sticking to the road despite his loss of visibility in the rain. He worked against the adrenaline pounding in his veins, maneuvering slowly around the bends back toward the hospital. At the intersection leading to the hospital, Cason hydroplaned to a stop. The entire road was underwater. He debated driving through it but, unlike the Humvee he'd driven down the backside of an Afghan mountain, his truck wouldn't make it. Through the slashing rain the lightning illuminated the stop sign at the base of the intersection, which had water partway up the post.

Cason cursed under his breath and took her to the next best option. *At least Mrs. S. will know if an air ambulance is needed.*

The familiarity of that thought had him cringing.

"You still with me?" he asked his silent passenger.

Another groan. Cason pressed on a bit faster. He focused on the road before him and not on the memories that had come to the surface. He'd been right behind her after she left. He'd known which way she was going, which was good because she outpaced him on the road. That had scared him. But not as much as watching her rig go up and over into the tree had. Wanting so desperately to stop watching but being unable to, he saw her tumble toward death, which made his soul break.

After walking in on her with his uniform, the one he'd taken risks to get back and had kept hidden, he had been in the garage trying to rid himself of the images of Ryan pushing him away as his own hand covered the pulsing warm blood that was rushing from the bullet gash in his neck. Watching him fight the loss of blood and feeling his own panic that the war had become real in a way he'd not felt before. That it would gut punch him so hard he could feel his mind shatter in its inability to cope. That moment had been rising up to him again as he paced the garage floor, but Savannah's voice yanked him from that memory when he heard her talk with a client. Then in disbelief, he heard her leave.

Now, he glanced over at her again. *Still breathing. She's not shot. She's going to live. She's just bruised,* he told himself.

He cursed the storm, the flooding, and everything else that stood in his way to the hospital. But Mrs. S. had over thirty years of medical knowledge. He repeated to himself that she'd know if they should risk an air ambulance; she'd know if Savannah was bleeding inside.

Gritting his teeth, he pushed the truck faster over the wet pavement. The visions of a narrow arid mountain trail and himself in the driver's seat of a Humvee swept up. "At least," he mumbled, "I'm going nose first."

Gradually the house came into view, and Cason put his truck in park. He ran to the passenger side and lifted Savannah out of the truck. Rain beat down on them, torrents of water slashing at the grime on their faces and arms. A gash on Savannah's forehead bled into the water, spreading gruesome watery-red rivulets across her cheek and down her neck.

Savannah came to for just a moment to whisper, "I can walk, Cason."

He mumbled, "Not on my watch," and carried her into the house.

Chapter Six

Savannah's eyes fluttered open as the pain in her side shot her awake. "Ow, stop it."

"Stop your fussing, young lady," she heard her mother say, and she felt a gentle tap on her hands as she tried to push Helen away.

Opening her eyes, she recognized the purple stripe of her mother's comforter folded down to her waist in the lantern light. The humid warmth of the non–air-conditioned room settled heavily against her skin, carrying with it the smell of antiseptic and the old vinyl of her mother's blood pressure cuff.

Then she realized she could see her waist, as in, her skin, as in... She moved her head a little. Her red bra was the only thing she was wearing.

"Mama...where's my shirt? Why...oh," she said and closed her eyes as her mother continued her ministrations by wrapping gauze about her middle.

"You remember now? You'll be fine, sweetie—no signs of a concussion or internal bleeding, and your temperature and blood pressure are normal, thank the Lord, but you've cracked a few ribs. The EMT can't get here in the storm. It's a miracle Cason was able to get you back here." Helen was quiet. The low light of the lantern next to Savannah on the side table illuminated her mother's face.

"Mama," she said, getting a hold of her mother's hand, "I'm okay."

Helen's hand shook as she looked up. "Oh, honey, when Cason carried you into the house, I about lost my mind. You looked like you had more than cracked ribs. I've had to bury too many—" she said. Tears rushed to her eyes. "I can't lose you too."

Savannah smiled and held her mother's hand. "Only the good die young, Mama. I'll be around forever."

Helen squeezed her daughter's hand back and smiled, letting the moment pass before wiping her eyes and returning to her task. "Sure, it'll just be you and that dog Miles, living forever."

Savannah laughed and then winced. "Ooooh, ouch, that hurts."

"Hold on while I get this gauze around you a few more times. It'll feel better once I do."

"No, Mama, that hurts. Just leave it. I'm fine."

Helen sighed and looked down Savannah, giving her daughter a break, and touched a spot over her eye. Savannah winced. "What's that?"

"Just a light gash. You were out so I put a liquid stitch in there." Savannah realized then that the side table was an arsenal of medical equipment. Gauze, tweezers, blood pressure cuff, Betadine solution, cotton balls, bandages, liquid suture material...

"Wow, did I need all of that?"

Helen's cool soft fingertips brushed her daughter's temple as she nodded. "Yes, hon. All of it."

"Oh."

"Don't worry about it—you look pale. Just relax and let me finish up," she said, holding up the gauze between her thumb and forefinger.

Savannah made a pained face. "No, Mama. I'm fine. I don't need my ribs bound anymore."

"Savannah, you're not fine. You've been in a car wreck, and if this damn storm would ever cease, you could get to where you need to be, which is a hospital that has better equipment than me." She sighed in exasperation. "But you have nothing life-threatening, so don't worry. Now, sit forward, Savannah Rae, and let me wrap this around you."

"Where is Cason?" she asked, trying to distract her mother.

"He's talking to the police department on the phone now. From the sounds of it, they're going to let your car burn out and retrieve it tomorrow when the storm passes. It's too dangerous to get it now."

"What a mess," she said absently.

Helen shook her head. "What were you thinking, going out in all that? What did that client say to you to make you go out in the middle of a storm?"

Savannah could barely recollect the phone call with Phillip Nigel. It was what had happened before that that she recalled with vivid clarity—everything had changed.

"I was just going off half-cocked, Mama. That dog got me all riled up," she said, telling only part of the truth.

"Speaking of that dog...I gave you one of Cason's pain pills too. And...Myrna and the Devereaux are still here." Helen gave her daughter a look. "They are loving this, would you believe it. Watching Cason bring you in, they about clapped with glee. It was like their own trashy Southern romance, but better because it was real and will make for some good gossip."

The door opened just then, and Cason slipped in. His black shirt and dark slacks hid the dirt that must be there. A long tear at his shoulder exposed scratched skin.

"Cason!" Helen admonished, fumbling at the covers.

"I'm a little underdressed," Savannah mumbled but felt a kind of comfortable familiarity toward him then.

He ignored them both and, moving to the side of the bed, took the wide gauze from Helen and said, "I've got this."

Savannah brought the sheet up over her chest. "I doubt it. You're not squeezing me any more than I'll let Mama. I'm fine, Cason."

"Cason," Helen interjected, "please, she's indecent. Let me get a shirt for her, and then you can try."

"Ma'am, it's fine. I've seen worse," he said, rolling out more of the gauze. "The Devereaux, though, are looking for something in your kitchen."

"Oh!" she said, looking at the door and then back at Savannah. "I'll be right back," she said, leaving and pulling the door shut behind her.

As the door shut, Savannah looked at Cason. "You've seen worse? That means you see half-naked car-wrecked women regularly?" she asked, looking up at him as she inched the sheet higher. She wasn't sure she liked him witnessing her in her current state of being achy all over with just the lace of her bra and a sheet covering her bare breasts. Comfortable familiarity or no. She was starting to feel like the definition of vulnerable.

"Sit up," he said, looking down at his hands as he pulled out a length of the gauze.

"If I won't let my own mother torture me, what makes you think I'll let you?"

"Savannah," he said, sliding onto the bed next to her, "if I have to manhandle you, it's gonna hurt ten times worse."

"I appreciate what you've already done for me, but I have to draw the line—"

Cason caught and held her gaze as he reached forward and pulled the sheet down. "Now, sit up or I shove this gauze under your back."

"Fine," she bit out, feeling fully exposed. Only he never once looked down at her lace-covered breasts but rather kept his eyes averted as if he knew she would be vulnerable and, despite the situation, was trying to be as gentlemanly as possible. As she sat up, she winced.

"And for the record," he said, moving in close to wrap the gauze about her middle, his warm fingers adeptly unrolling it across her back, "when I cop a feel, you'll know."

Savannah hissed through her teeth at the pain.

"Here." He turned his shoulder in toward her. "Rest your shoulder against mine."

She leaned forward and instead rested her forehead against his shoulder; the cool damp of his shirt was juxtaposed with his radiating heat. His body was like a firm wall of earth pressing back, solid and safe.

"Now exhale—I'm going to tighten up."

She let her breath out just as Cason tightened up.

Savannah whimpered, and he said quietly, "Hardest part is over."

"Mmmm..." she said into his shirt. The burnt plastic smell was still there. To distract herself from the pain and the images that were slamming to the front of her mind of hanging in her seat, realizing that she was going to be a human barbecue, she focused on what he'd said. "*When* you do cop a feel, McPherson? Is that what you said?"

He grunted his affirmative, letting his fingers move the roll across her hunched-over front.

"You planning a feel?" she asked, her head still down.

"Maybe," he said, playing along with her.

Savannah's breath hitched as the gauze wound about her broken rib, and she gripped the sheets, "Is that what all this rib wrapping is about?" she said, trying to keep the pain out of her voice.

"Nothing says 'take advantage of me' like a chick who's been tossed around in a fiery SUV."

"True. I don't want to do that again. It was a new experience for me. I'm not sure I enjoyed it."

Cason gave a half laugh. "That would be good. I can see how it wasn't fun."

Savannah thought about him pulling her out that back window of her crushed vehicle and wondered how he had known she was there.

He must had been right behind her. Savannah hissed through her teeth as the feeling of a spear being rammed through her side caught her off guard.

"Hold up, soldier; what you're doing hurts too much now." She gripped the hand that held the gauze.

Cason stopped, his outer hand wrapping gently around her side. "I'm just doing the last tightening up. I need to do this so that the ribs don't move when you breathe deeply. Lean back a bit."

"No."

Cason moved his shoulder forward, pushing her backward into his wide supporting hand, then gently tightened the gauze before tearing it off and securing the end.

Savannah couldn't move—the pain was vacillating between piercing and bone-deep aching. It was all too much. She closed her eyes and just focused on trying to breathe without actually breathing.

"Lean all the way back," he said and softly lay her down against the pillows. He tucked the comforter up under her arms.

Savannah reached out and grabbed his rolled-up shirt sleeve at his elbow. Her teeth gritted as something warm, activated by all the pain, washed through her.

"It'll pass, Savi," Cason said reassuringly above her. "The first ribs you break are the worst."

She just made a noise of acceptance at the back of her throat.

"Actually," he amended, "they are all bad."

"That's not reassuring."

He rolled up the rest of the gauze while she gripped his shirt. She felt his arm move, and the banality of the task was comforting. Or it was the person doing the task who was comforting?

"Distract me. When did you break your ribs?" she asked, her eyes still closed against the pain at her side.

She felt him put the gauze down. "Boot camp. Fell backward off the circuit wall onto my rifle."

"What'd you do?"

"Finished the circuit, then went to the infirmary."

Savannah smiled. She could barely move, much less heft a rifle and run the rest of an obstacle course.

"What?" she heard him ask curiously.

"It's just, I feel like a lazy dog on a summer's porch now."

"Well..." he said, thinking, "I wouldn't compare the two. I just fell down, and you got to joyride in a rig that was out to kill you."

Savannah felt the smile spread across her face; it was nice not to be at odds with him. It was nice that things were the way they had been nearly a decade before. She opened her eyes to find his head turned and him looking absently at the wall next to the bed, inwardly focused.

"Some people would just let me go... after what happened," she hedged, mulling over the thought of him following and what had happened. The thing that changed the personal drive she had in her life.

Cason shifted his weight. "I had something on my mind that I needed to tell you, and when I heard you leave, I just followed," he said without hesitating. His own thoughts seemed to be tracking on a similar vein.

She recalled that he had wanted to say something more. There, at the end, when she'd tried to comfort him—when she needed that connection with him after all he'd recounted—he seemed to want to say something more but then just stalked out.

"What did you want to tell me?"

He watched the wall for just a moment more, then turned to her. His eyes were soft, resigned. Taking his time, he drank in her features, as if memorizing the contours of them. "It's not important now. After everything I told you...Savannah, I promised myself that you would never have to know what I do about how your brother died. I didn't ever want you to know what it was like over there. I went through that hell so that you didn't have to, but I told you anyway. I'm sorry." His resignation visibly turned to disappointment in himself, and he said, "I should have said something different. You shouldn't have to carry this burden too. And you wouldn't have left in this storm if I hadn't admitted what I did," he said, nodding at the storm through the darkened window.

"I'm glad you told me, though. Not glad as in happy and joyful, but there's a relief there, that he was with *you*, his best friend."

He was still, absorbing her words, listening.

"Thank you for finally telling me," she said and then added, "Don't be sorry about it. I can only imagine that it was ten times worse telling me than it was hearing it."

"But it's not something you should have heard. We might not get along, but the least I can do is protect you from that nugget of hell."

"And we don't get along..." she said, feeling the fingers of calming sleep grasping at her as the adrenaline from the afternoon started to fade. Forming words got harder. "Because you made a big fat lie. I've needed to hear truth from your lips a long time. You could have just told me that you wouldn't tell me details. I don't understand why you made up a story that would give me an aneurism."

Savannah's grip loosened, and she absently stroked his arm as if he needed soothing. His forearm was muscular like stacked ropes lined up, connecting to his wrist. It supported his weight as he sat propped over her, accentuating the muscle definition. The same musculature that before had demonstrated pure strength in hefting her out of a burning vehicle that was perched in a tree. *Muscular* and *adept,* her foggy mind supplied for her.

He looked down to her hand on his arm. "Big fat lie?" he said, his tone lightening, but he finished, "It's complicated, Savi. And I don't believe that if I told you not to ask for details that you'd not ask. Have you met yourself?" he asked, looking at her out of the corner of his eye. "You're not one to back down from the things you want."

He gently took her hand off his arm; it was momentarily swallowed up by his before he placed it on the comforter over her belly. There he trapped it under his own and mumbled something under his breath that sounded like "That, and I'm powerless against you."

"What was that? I couldn't hear you." Savannah asked, feeling a warmth cascade down her side, obliterating the pain she felt.

"I'll always be here for you. You know, if you want to toss another car into a tree."

She smiled. "Sure." Her brain was getting foggier, but she had something more to say, something about faults. "But, Cason, you should know that no one but me made me get in my car. No one told me to drive hell-bent for leather, except me. I'm alive because of you."

Her free hand caressed his arm, moving up to the tear at his shoulder, then back down again. The firmness of his stature and the warmth radiating from his body tugged at her; a feeling of safety enveloped her.

His lighter mood tugged at the corners of his mouth then as if he'd discovered her secrets. "How's that pain pill working?"

Savannah felt good. She had the warm body of the man who had pulled her from a fire braced over her. She let herself feel how nice it was that his usually hard voice had softened toward her. She noticed how it shifted to mischievous, and she felt great; he made her feel great. "With all that you've done, I think I love you" tumbled out of her mouth.

"Whoa," he said and gave a low chuckle. "Really? Well, then."

"Mmmmm...you have no idea how well," she said and gazed hazily up at him.

"I have some idea, Savannah." He patted her hand under his. "You should rest now."

"No," she said, trying to restrain him and feebly grabbing at his arm, "don't go. There's so much to talk...about..."

CASON WATCHED as Savannah fought to stay awake, her slender fingers wrapped around his arm in a death grip. His arm still pulsed from where her fingertips had purposefully grazed caringly up it.

As her eyes fluttered shut, he took her hand and splayed its fingers against his palm. He traced each of her fingers with the pad of his thumb, memorizing it, feeling its gentle softness in his own large, rough hand. He didn't want to leave. Being there with her eased a knot of stress that had gotten lodged deep in his gut. He wanted to slip behind her on the bed and gather her up into his arms. There he could keep his ear to her shallow breaths all night. To make sure she didn't slip off this plane of life like her brother had.

Despite what he wanted, he reluctantly slid her warmed palm off of his and onto the comforter; then, with one last look, got up and left.

Chapter Seven

Savannah was stiffly making her way down the hall to the bathroom the next morning. She ran the taps and, taking her rib wrap off, stepped into the shower. She let the lukewarm water turn piping hot, turning her skin red and billowing floral-scented steam around her. She stood for a long time under the therapeutic spray until the water began to cool.

Out of the shower and feeling closer to being alive, she dressed and followed the rich aroma of freshly brewed coffee down the hall and to the kitchen.

Her mother was on the phone in the kitchen. "Thank you, Dr. Lowe," she said before hanging up.

Savannah put her hand to her side and braced herself along the kitchen wall with the other as she asked, "Was that my pediatrician you were just talking to?"

"Oh, good morning, hon! How do you feel?" Helen asked, smiling and taking in her daughter for a moment, spectacles off, before turning back to write something down on a pad, glasses back on.

Savannah squinted out the front window and then back at her mother. "Did you get the license plate of the truck that hit me?"

Helen smiled at her daughter. "No, hon, it was a tree, from what I hear."

Savannah grimaced back at her mother. "I smell coffee..." she said, shuffling further into the kitchen. "What did Dr. Lowe have to say?"

"Oh yes." Helen picked up the pad and held her glasses up as she read from it: "He'd like to see you as soon as is convenient, and he is recommending X-rays at a minimum today. How does your side feel this morning?"

"Mmmmm," Savannah said, pouring a cup of the strong coffee. "It's actually feeling a touch better. It was a fine shade of purple under the wrap, kind of like my arm," she said, lifting her sleeve. "But better. I'll go see my doctor this week and have it checked out, but not much they can do for a rib break. No need to call Dr. Lowe into the office on a Sunday."

"Well, we'll see about that. At least let me give you another once-over—I'm worried I didn't get all that glass out. You probably still have some in your hair too, hon."

"Mama, I'm sure I got them all out in the shower, and it was mostly my hands and feet that got all these little cuts...and the piece that found its way into my bra. But I got it, and I'm fine."

"Savannah, hon, sooner is better for these things, you know."

"Seeing the doctor? I know, Mama, but—" Savannah turned to look at her mother over the rim of her coffee mug. Through the steam, she realized that her mother's usually perfectly coiffed short gray-blond hair was flattened on one side as a testament to her having fallen asleep on the couch. Dark circles had moved in under her eyes overnight, giving her the distinct look of someone on the verge of losing it. Instead of arguing, she said, "Okay, Mama, if that's what you'd like to do. That'll be fine. Did you sleep at all last night? I recall taking up your entire bed."

She smiled up at her daughter. "Yes, honey, don't worry about me. Now, Cason, on the other hand, I do want to talk about. When he left you last night, he seemed particularly disturbed."

Savannah looked down the hall in the direction of his room and then back at her mother. "Is he here?"

"No, he's gone to take care of your car."

Savannah closed her eyes. "Shit."

"Watch your mouth."

"I need to be taking care of that." She put down her mug. "Mama, can I borrow your car? I need to—"

"You need to do nothing, Savannah Rae Sparling. You need to go to the doctor; the rest can wait. Do you hear me?"

Savannah suddenly felt weak and, pulling out the dining chair, sat hard.

Helen was at her side, startled. "Are you okay, hon?"

"Just...just a little dizzy is all," she said, feeling the room right itself.

"Put your head between your knees, and I'll get you a glass of water. Coffee is no good for you right now."

Savannah obeyed, sighing in pain. After a glass of water and some toast, she changed into a spare set of clothes she kept at her mother's house, so they could go to the doctor. She opted for a pair of her mother's flats over the heels she had.

They had gotten all the way to the garage door at the end of the hall before she remembered: "You were going to talk to me about Cason?" she asked.

Helen shook her head. "I forget—we can talk about it another time."

Savannah let it go easily, her mind rushing onward. "Okay," she said, "now we do this doctor thing, and then I need to use your phone and possibly your car for the rest of the day. I doubt my purse and everything in it survived the fire. Once I get credit cards and a new cell on order, I need to go car shopping and—"

"Stop," her mother said, holding up her hand. "You need to sit down again before you fall down. Dr. Lowe can wait for a moment—you're as white as a sheet."

Savannah let her mother guide her into her room and with a grunt of protest as she sat on the edge of the bed said, "I just thought of Phillip Nigel...and work."

"You'll call in sick this week. Dr. Lowe will see to it that you have a doctor's note."

Savannah turned her head toward her mother and cracked an eye at her. "I feel like a stray."

Helen smiled softly, stroking her daughter's short, straight hair. She tucked a piece of it behind her ear. "No, dear, you've just come home for a bit." She waited for a few moments before saying, "Let's get you to Dr. Lowe's."

A half hour later Savannah was treated to a flashback of her own as she stepped into her childhood doctor's office, her mother at her side.

Dr. Lowe was just as she remembered him, only shorter—now that she was taller—and gray haired. He looked fit for his age and still had kind eyes behind wire-rim glasses.

"Savannah! My, how much you've grown—just look at you," he said, beaming; then to her mother, he gave a warm smile and clasped hands with her. "Helen, so wonderful to see you again—just wish it were under better circumstances."

They made small talk as he ushered them into the first exam room, the entire clinic eerily quiet. They were about twenty-four hours early for regular hours.

"I'll let you change, Savannah, and I'll be back in in a bit. Helen, you still remember where the gowns are?"

Helen smiled at him. "I might be retired, but I'm not dead, Martin."

They shared a laugh before he shut the door, and Helen went to the far stark-white cabinet and pulled down a crisp cotton hospital gown decorated with the ubiquitous small pale-green tri-dot pattern.

"Did you see his hand?" Helen whispered to her daughter as she handed her the gown.

Savannah paused midway through removing her pants, thinking about what her mother had said, and then continued undressing. "His hand? No, what was wrong with it?"

"Not what was wrong with it, but what was missing," Helen said with obvious concern.

"Like a finger?" Savannah said and winced, trying to take her shirt off over her head.

"Should have used one of my button-downs," Helen said, helping her daughter get her shirt over and off her head. "No, from his ring finger. Did you really not notice it?"

Savannah looked askance at her mother while she slipped into the hospital gown. "No, is he not wearing his ring? Could mean that he just got a rash or dry skin under it, Mama, and took it off until it heals. That kind of stuff happens."

Helen shook her head and went to the door. "I'll call him back, and look closely at it. It's tanned over; he's not been wearing it for some time, Savannah," she said, exasperated. "It's no wonder you're still single—you don't have an eye for these things!"

After her mother left, Savannah felt mentally exhausted by the exchange. And her mother's mention of being single had spurred a hazy memory of Cason. The night before, he'd been there for her. She remembered him sitting quietly with her as they were laid bare to each other, both raw and needing. All of it swooned into a deep twist in her gut and a tug at her heart.

"That's new," she said to herself. A new feeling not just for Cason but for anyone.

There, sitting in the doctor's office, she had one clear thought: *See Cason again. Just see him.* She needed to see if that feeling from last night returned or if that had been temporary and her misplaced contempt would come floating to the surface again.

. . .

Dr. Lowe came in, and they made small talk again as they moved through the exam. Savannah did notice that Dr. Lowe had no wedding ring and that there was no sign of one having been there recently. Her mother was extremely chatty and bubbly, to the point where Savannah noticed and started paying attention to her over the doctor.

"Now, this head gash will heal nicely. Helen, is this your work?"

Her mother tittered and, smiling, said, "Of course. I've done a number of those over the years."

"How can I forget?" he said warmly back to her. "You were the best. I was so sad to see you go."

Savannah watched her mother's face turn pink. "Well, some of us think that retiring is a good thing. Have you thought more about taking the leap?"

"Not much for me to retire to, sadly." He turned Savannah's chin this way and that.

"I thought you and your wife had made plans?"

"Mama..." Savannah said in warning.

"Oh no, it's okay, Savannah. Your mother and I worked together for decades. You probably noticed my lack of ring. We separated years ago, and the divorce was final two years back."

Savannah realized why the news hadn't reached her mother; it would have been around the time Ryan died. Helen didn't remember a thing from then.

"Oh, I'm so sorry, Martin," Helen said, reaching across her daughter to touch Dr. Lowe's arm.

Savannah snatched her mother's hand up and held it tight. "So, about this gash on my forehead?"

Dr. Lowe went on to explain that it would heal fine save for a small scar, but they had an excellent plastic surgeon in the clinic that he could refer her to; then he sent Savannah down the hall to get the X-ray of her chest.

Savannah paused at the exam room door. Dr. Lowe wasn't

coming, so who was going to run the machine? "Is—oh, I forget her name—Ruby? Is she working?"

Dr. Lowe smiled. "Close—it's Ruth, and no, she's not. I'll be running the machine since we're not technically open today."

Savannah waited at the door for another beat or two, expecting him to follow, and when he didn't she said, "Right, I'll meet you down there."

The X-ray room was chilly and dimly lit. Dr. Lowe came in after a few minutes, whistling. "Great!" he said, as though Savannah had said something to him. "Let's get started, then, shall we?"

He flicked a switch on the machine, went to the operating station, and tapped keys and pushed buttons as he instructed her over his shoulder to lie back on the wide table.

He came over and positioned the overhead device over her chest and a lead blanket over her pelvis.

"It's great seeing your mother. How has she been?"

"Good," Savannah said as he made minute adjustments.

"Oh, good."

There was a long pause, and Savannah felt the silence begin to engulf the room.

Dr. Lowe nodded. "That's good. So, she's doing well then?"

Savannah looked up at him and wanted to smile at his awkward attempt to find out more about her mama. "I would say that she is, yes."

"Great." He nodded again. "I'll just jump behind this wall here and snap a picture, and we'll go from there. All right? Are you comfortable? Good?"

"Yes," she said as he left. "Just fine," she murmured.

BACK IN THE EXAM ROOM, waiting for the results to come in, Savannah and her mother looked at each other.

"You want to tell me what's going on with Dr. Lowe, Mama?"

"Your mother can't inquire after the well-being of her former

employer? I worked with him for over thirty years, Savannah Rae."
She huffed in her chair, looking toward the door.

"Mama, you turned pink when he complimented your handiwork
on my head wound."

"Keep your voice down," she said, turning back to her daughter.
"And why wouldn't I? It's a very prestigious thing to have your work
complimented by a man of his stature. He's much better than I am at
wound dressing, that is for sure."

Savannah watched her mother, and when she turned an even
rosier shade of pink, Savannah smiled and said, "You have a crush on
him."

"Hush!" Helen said, looking wild-eyed at her. "I do not,
Savannah Rae. That is such a crass thing to say."

Savannah laughed but had to stop quickly, wincing. Her mother
finding someone she was interested in was rare. Over the years
Savannah had encouraged her to "put herself out there," but she
rarely did. On the odd occasion when she did, each date ended with a
shoulder shrug and "Dating isn't my cup of tea, Savannah." Now, to
see her show interest in her children's pediatrician, the man she had
worked with, for decades, Savannah felt a mixture of oddity and
entertainment.

"Oh, you are completely crushing on him, Mama. Ow," she
added, putting her hand to her side.

"Serves you right," Helen said, and the door swung open after a
quick knock.

Dr. Lowe was holding the X-ray in his hand. Savannah sat back
up on the exam room table as he flipped the switch to the light box on
the front wall and slipped the X-ray in.

"Looks like we have just one slight fracture on your left side,
here," he said, pointing.

"Slight?" Savannah asked. "Are you sure?"

He adjusted his spectacles and paused, reviewing the black,
white, and gray image of her rib cage once more. "Yes, very. I'd go so

far as to say it's just a hairline fracture. You'll heal nicely and quickly."

"It feels like a rib is jabbing into my lungs." She didn't want to say that she had expected at least three horribly broken ribs stabbing her lungs.

He turned to her. "Well, more than likely you've got some muscle and tissue damage from where the seat belt went across your chest. They could very well be swelling and causing your side discomfort," he said, his tone assured and calming, a tone she realized she'd not heard from anyone for a long while.

"All right, I believe you, Dr. Lowe. Thank you. But," Savannah said, "what I heard from you before, though, is that I need some plastic surgery."

Dr. Lowe smiled and chuckled, making her mother beam up at him. He gave Savannah's knee a pat. "You're right as rain, kid, other than a hairline fracture to your rib and multiple abrasions. You're one lucky champ. And I don't really think you'll need plastic surgery for that head wound—your mother did a great job."

Savannah felt a whoosh of sarcasm sweep through her. "Okay. So does that mean I get a lollipop now?"

"You betcha!" he said and, opening the door to go, added, "I'll let you get your clothes back on and meet you in the lobby with it."

"Martin, I'll walk out with you," Helen said, leaving her daughter to change by herself.

Savannah smiled as the door shut behind her mother. Apparently she thought that a hairline fracture did not warrant shirt assistance, not when there was Dr. Hottie to talk to.

As soon as the thought of Dr. Lowe as a hottie rolled into her mind, Savannah wrinkled her nose. *Maybe not that nickname.*

Alone, her thoughts went to Cason again. Where he was, what he was doing, and if they had gotten her SUV out of the tree. What shade of charred would her things be? He didn't have to tend to her wrecked vehicle, but he was. She remembered what her mama had said a few days ago about him when she'd been watching him at Ms.

Myrna's construction site, that it wasn't what he said that mattered but what he did.

Her mother was pink with delight, talking with the doctor, when Savannah met them in the empty waiting room.

"How much do I owe you?" Savannah asked as she approached them.

Dr. Lowe and her mother were startled out of their conversation. "Oh!" Dr. Lowe said and beamed, handing Savannah a red sucker. "Here you go, champ! I was just saying that today's visit was no charge. It was more of a social call." He gently patted Savannah's back as they made their way to the door.

"Oh, that's nice of you, Dr. Lowe, but I have insurance. We should probably—"

"There's no need. Your mother and I go back a long way. I owe her a bundle," he said and smiled at Helen.

Savannah agreed before it got...weird*er*. "Thank you, Dr. Lowe."

"Yes. It was good to see you, Martin," Helen said and went in for a hug as he stuck out his hand to say goodbye to her. Savannah watched uncomfortably as he pulled his hand back to give her a hug. Except her mother had stopped midway and tried switching to a handshake.

They laughed awkwardly and settled for a handshake. Savannah waved and headed out the door before any other farewell options could be extended toward her.

The day was a bright, sunny, and warm one, as if the storm the day before had never happened. Her mother unlocked the car. "You're not to say a single word, young lady."

Savannah smiled and got in. "I didn't say a thing!"

"I can see it on your face. Not a word, Savannah Rae Sparling."

"Would it be weird if Dr. Lowe was my new dad, but I still called him Dr. Lowe? Or if I called him Dr. Dad?"

"Savannah!"

Savannah laughed and winced again. "Oh, Mama. That was painful."

"Your rib? I should hope so, child. With you tormenting me like this, you deserve it," she said playfully.

Savannah smiled as they set off down the road. "Oh, stop. You're enjoying every minute of it."

"I am not!" she said and giggled as they turned off the main street.

"See!" Savannah said. "Not to mention you're blushing. You have a crush on him, admit it."

"I do not. That is absolutely ridiculous."

"Well, if not a crush, you're happy he's single. Did you find out why?"

"Savannah, I'll not kiss and tell."

Savannah squealed from the passenger seat, "You kissed—"

"That is not what I meant. I meant—Oh, you! Child, you're getting my tongue all tied up, and I can't think straight."

As Helen turned the car into her neighborhood, Savannah said, "I did that? You mean Dr. Lowe—or Maaaaartin—did that."

"Now you're just teasing me," Helen said.

"Yes, and you love it," she said, laughing. "Ow."

As they approached the house, Savannah stopped laughing. The blood drained from her head, and the world she'd experienced the day before came rushing back. She felt dizzy, looking at the charred rubble of her SUV on the back of a flatbed tow truck in front of her mother's house.

Reality fizzled the good mood, and Savannah felt her protective shell roll over her.

"My god," Helen said as they pulled past the truck and up into the driveway.

Savannah got out and stood at the top of the driveway, her palm against the side of her mother's car, holding herself steady. There on display at the curb was the thing that had very nearly become her tomb. Only the metal remained, and the popped and twisted rubber of the tires wrapped around the wheels.

The what-ifs swirled sickeningly in her belly. If it hadn't been for Cason, her mother would have been identifying her mangled remains that day, not sharing a laugh on the way home from the doctor's office. The thought of herself dead and her mother's pain over losing her last child sent Savannah scurrying.

Her mother came up behind her as Savannah finished retching next to the garage and put a hand on her back. "You all right, hon?"

Savannah waved her back. "I'm fine," she wheezed. "Just give me a moment."

The pain in Savannah's side was blinding, and its only blessed side effect was that her brain was clear of any thought. Nothing registered but pain. Not the SUV, not the night before, not anything but the sharp mind-bending pain in her side.

She heard her mother talking with someone behind her, but she couldn't turn to look. She waited until the heaving stopped and then used the hose next to her to wash down the lawn. She caught a bit of the water in her palm and splashed her face.

Blowing out a stiff breath that moved her rib cage as little as possible, Savannah felt the adrenaline rush that further clarified her thoughts as the pain eased. The mental list that she'd put off from that morning gradually came forward, soothing and reassuring in its rational, task-oriented nature. She could deal with this situation, one checkbox at a time.

"Reality is a bitch, isn't she?" Cason's voice came from behind her as she turned off the hose.

"I'd say," Savannah mumbled and turned, wiping her face and hands with the hem of her shirt. Cason's stance was wide; he held folded papers in his hands and a casual look of disdain on his face. A look she'd come to recognize as him, a look that was commonplace between them. She ignored it and the way his fitted gray shirt and jeans made her think of iced tea and football: he looked like home. She said, "Cason, I...I'm not sure that thank you is enough. I think I owe you..." She paused, unsure how to thank a man for saving her life; no words matched the feeling of gratitude. And he wasn't making it easy. She shielded her eyes against the sun to look up at him. "Yes, I owe you, it feels like, my entire life. I owe you my life," she said more clearly. "And thank you for taking care of my car this morning."

"Don't thank me." He looked more than serious as he handed her the paperwork he'd been holding. As if old shadows had renewed their haunt of his soul. "I'm just glad your mom doesn't have to identify your charred body today."

Savannah's mind stumbled over his words, the enormity of the situation still heavy in the pit of her stomach. "And that is why I'm thanking you," she said coldly. "I'm sorry, but I thought things were different between us."

"I don't want your thanks. You should apologize to your mom, though. You almost made her childless."

Savannah realized she had her answer from earlier. He was still an ass. She made for the tow truck. "Where's the driver? I'm sure he needs my insurance information."

"In the house," he said. "You plan on getting that information out of your purse? Because it's a load of ash right now."

Savannah stopped and turned back to him. She felt raw. "Are you trying for Dickhead of the Year? Because if you are, it's working. I think they've got you at runner-up."

"Damn," he said. "I was working for first place."

Shaking her head, she changed directions and walked toward the house. After she gave her insurance company's name and contact information to the tow truck driver, she spent the rest of the day dealing with out-of-office messages and actual persons for the claims adjuster, the credit card companies, the cell phone company, and a locksmith to get into her home, and she arranged for a rental car to be dropped off at her mother's house. Savannah noticed the afternoon sun had intensified as she returned Knight's voice mail from the day before with one of her own regarding the Nigel contract and that she'd be out Monday but back on Tuesday.

The rental was dropped off shortly after that, and Savannah took another call from the claims department.

"All right, Ms. Sparling, we have a claim number for you. You ready for it?"

"Hold on." Savannah's scratch paper was full. She dug through the opened mail on the counter in the kitchen and grabbed an envelope. "Okay. Go."

Savannah wrote the number down and thanked the woman before hanging up. She flipped the envelope over and saw that it was from the army's local liaison office. Savannah dug through the mail and found the letter that went with it. Her heart twisted when she read Ryan's name.

There was an awards ceremony in four weeks to honor him, as well as the other soldiers, the survivors and the fallen, of his and Cason's squads. Those words alone squeezed Savannah's heart, but it was the next sentence that sent her insides spinning.

A particular commendation would be given to one soldier, Cason McPherson.

"Mama," Savannah called. She looked at the envelope again. It was the first she'd seen of it, and it was postmarked a week prior. She picked up the invitation as her mother came out of her room, showered and with a puzzle in one hand and her spectacles in the other. "What's this?"

"Oh, I'm glad you're still here, Savannah," Helen said. "I thought you'd gone. Would you like to have dinner with us? Is Cason still here?"

"I don't know, Mama. What's this?" she said and then rephrased: "Or rather, when were you going to tell me?" The day was unraveling again, the threads of control siphoning through her palm.

"Ah, let's see," she said, putting down her crossword book and taking up the invitation. "Yes, oh." She handed the letter back to her daughter. Picking up her book, she silently went to the living room and switched on the corner lamp and sat in her easy chair.

"Are we not going to talk about this?"

"There's nothing to talk about."

"All right." Savannah put the invitation down, and with the

rental car keys in her hand and claim papers in the other, she simply left. There was one thing that she'd learned from her mother, and it was to walk away from complicated conflict so you didn't act in an unladylike manner. Or say things you would regret.

In the driveway, Cason stopped her and handed her a piece of paper with an address on it.

"This is where your rig is, if you want to make sure the claims guy knows. He won't have to take much of a look at it before he classifies it as a total wreck. Just like your life."

Savannah's lip lifted into sneer. "You know what, McPherson? I wonder why they'd even consider you for a military honor. Though they weren't specific in the invite I just saw—it could be the honor of being a complete asshole." Savannah gave him a biting grin. "Two can play at the game you started. Don't get burned by your own rules."

CASON WATCHED as her rental disappeared down the street. He let his hammering heart slow down. She'd reacted to him as he wanted. That *was* what he wanted, right? For her to punish him, to cut him down to size? He needed it, right?

He had to admit to himself that it was different now, now that she knew he had not left her brother to die. It was harder.

In the house, Cason spotted Helen in the corner doing her crossword, only she didn't have her spectacles on.

"Everything okay?" he ventured as he kicked off his boots.

She looked up and gave him a reassuring smile. "Everything is fine, dear. It's just that I knew I should have told Savannah about her brother's—and your—awards ceremony. I couldn't find the right time to do it. It seems that she whips in and out of here like a whirlwind, and I never have a moment with her."

Cason nodded. "She'll come around," he reassured her. "But I still think you'll have more time with her, ma'am, the less I'm around."

"Oh, nonsense. I could have called her."

He walked over to the couch. "I know today has been a big day for you, and I don't want to add to it, but it's now or never. I'll be moving out soon. Half of the reason she reacted the way she did is that she and I don't get on. The less agitated she is, the better you two will be."

Her eyes were suddenly bright with worry. "No, Cason, you shouldn't feel like you should go. You two and Ryan were so close as kids, I'm sure she'll come around. I—"

He gave her a small smile. "Don't worry. It's my own decision."

"Oh. Well, it's a lot to process," she said and then smiled bravely. "Probably best. You can't stay here with a little old lady forever." She added, "But you can stay as long as you need to find a new place."

"Thank you, ma'am." He stood and picked Helen's phone up off the dining table where Savannah had left it and returned to Helen with it. "I'll plan to be out after the ceremony." Cason handed Helen the phone and said softly, "Call your daughter; talk to her about it. The ceremony—she needs to know that it's hard for you. That's why you didn't tell her."

She tentatively took the phone from him. "I'm not sure she wants to hear from me tonight."

"She is always willing to listen to you. Remember, it's me she can't stand." He turned and headed out of the room, giving her privacy.

He showered off the grime from helping unload Savannah's SUV. It had taken two tow trucks, an army of chainsaws, and a small flatbed crane to get it unhooked from the tree. He had listened to the men all day say how they couldn't believe someone had escaped alive from the wreck. He'd kept quiet during the whole thing, just saying that it was his friend's rig he was helping get out of the tree as a favor.

The hard climbing and other physical labor had his hip pinching. He realized as he picked up the prescription bottle back in his room that the last of his pain pills had been given to Savannah and a small dog. Cason grimaced as he prepared himself for a twisting, sleepless night.

Chapter Eight

It was 8:00 a.m. when Cason found himself sitting in the waiting room of his clinic. His refills had run out; a doctor's visit was required. In his work clothes and work boots, he felt out of place among the much more polished patients waiting that morning. When he had arrived for his appointment, he'd been advised that his doctor had been pulled away on a family emergency, and they were scheduling patients with other doctors. He'd be fit in at some point, but they didn't know when.

He'd asked if the nurse practitioner could just okay the refill. The answer was a resounding no; the doctor had left specific instructions that he be seen before the next refill.

Cason tried memorizing all the magazines on the wall. Then he counted the number of corners in the room—where the walls met, where the front desk met the wall, each angle of each support beam—before pacing to ease the sharp stabbing in his hip that was now making the scar down his thigh ache. It was nearly noon before he was called in. It was another half hour in the exam room, in the exposed exam gown, before the doctor came in.

"Hello, Cason, I'm Dr. George Mathers. So sorry for the wait," he said and reached forward, shaking Cason's hand.

Cason was agitated from the wait and the gnawing pain in his joint. "Sounds like it's a big clusterfuck out there."

Dr. Mathers chuckled as he closed the door. He was tall and thin like a marathon runner, with brown hair and brown eyes and a genuine smile. He pulled a pen from his lab coat and gestured for Cason to sit. "Feel free to sit; from your charts, though, it seems you might prefer standing?"

"I do."

"Okay, let's dive in, shall we? It looks like you need a refill on your meds?"

"Just the pain pills."

"All right, let's have a look at you." Dr. Mathers made small talk as he checked Cason's vitals and overall health. "Looks good. Despite the hip."

"Great, three months' supply is what Dr. Stevens suggested last time." Cason said, reaching for his jeans.

Dr. Mathers nodded. "We're not quite done. Tell me about your hip. Your chart says it's a shrapnel wound from your time in Afghanistan?"

"Affirmative," he said, letting his jeans stay where they were.

Dr. Mathers stood and slid an X-ray film from the packet that was Cason's medical record, put it up on the light box, and flipped the switch. As he did so, Cason realized the man's name was familiar. Who'd been talking about him recently? "I see," he said as Cason's pelvic bone and left femur illuminated. "This little guy is causing the problem." He pointed his pen at a white spot in the joint. He turned back to Cason. "Has Dr. Stevens talked with you about your options?"

Cason thought of his ex-military doctor. "Sir, he just supplies the remedy. We don't discuss much."

"Huh. Well, I'm a surgeon by trade. I run the cosmetic surgery clinic next door. I spent my residency and several years postresidency in the trauma unit at New York General. Since then I switched careers—for my blood pressure's sake," he said, smiling, "and moved down here. Cason, it looks like your initial surgery went well. But you've needed a second, and you've needed it for some time."

"I'm alive. I'm fine."

Dr. Mathers nodded. "Yes, that is a very good thing. But your second surgery is necessary. Did you have one scheduled?"

Cason was quiet for a moment before answering. "I did, but I had a family obligation that required me to leave the hospital." He needed to be a part of the commander's care support team for the Sparlings. Cason still remembered the pulling of the stitches and bandages along his side that day he was supposed to have the second surgery.

The Sparlings. Right—Savannah had mentioned the Matherses to her mother at lunch the other day.

"I see. Why don't we get that scheduled today? The reason I say this, Cason, is that you can take pain meds for the rest of your life, but at some point that shrapnel will dig deep enough that it will finish cutting through your cartilage and will begin etching your bone. These X-rays are from over a year ago, so that piece of metal could already be at your bone."

Cason didn't say that it felt like it. "That's fine. Sir, understand that I nearly lost my leg and men in my unit lost their lives. I don't need another surgery for a tiny piece of metal. It's not *that* painful." He lied. It hurt like hell.

Dr. Mathers clicked his pen and slipped it back into his pocket and sighed. He turned his gaze on Cason. "I see," he said and then added after a pause, "I could tell you that the procedure will be easy. An in-and-out, same-day laparoscopic procedure. I could tell you that we have payment plans if your insurance doesn't cover it—but I'd like to take the couple of minutes we have left to instead tell you about Joy."

Joy? he thought, feeling twitchy standing there with the pain in his hip, with the hours he was missing work, and he wasn't sure skipping breakfast had been smart. This story the doc was starting didn't have a joyful feel to it. His tone sounded damn depressing. Cason just needed his pain meds. He scowled to himself; now he sounded like an addict. Like his mother. That gave him pause, and he forced himself to listen.

"Joy was a girl I met one night in the trauma ward of New York General. She'd been hit twice by bullets from a drive-by. They were bullets from a forty-five caliber that were specially made to shatter upon entry into a body. Lethal. When she came to us, she'd lost her ability to breathe, her organs were shutting down, and at one point we had to paddle her every sixty seconds to keep her heart active. I spent four hours in an initial surgery with her, and then there were surgeries over two more days. We pumped bag after bag of blood into her, and they'd just pour out onto the table.

"What she didn't know was in the next room lay her uncle; she'd been out with him that day. They'd been hit as they came down the steps of his brownstone. I picked every last piece of metal out of her body over those two days. She lived, but her uncle didn't." Dr. Mathers paused, letting her uncle's death have weight and respect in the room.

Cason sighed internally at the familiarity of the story. He knew it. Not this one specifically but it was a war story. Cason knew what Dr. Mathers was getting at and let him finish.

After a moment, he continued, "Joy and I have kept in touch over the years. She's a bright and energetic girl. Patients like that leave an indelible mark on a person. It took her quite some time to recover physically as well as emotionally, and the death of her uncle was the hardest for her. But she did something interesting in her process of healing. She could have easily been enraged or let guilt over her survival weigh her down, but she didn't. She was twelve at the time; by the time she was sixteen, she had organized a dozen rallies against neighborhood gangs. She's twenty-five now and this past year was recruited to the lead gang task force in her ATF region. That was how she found her peace. She had her scars and carried them with her, but she sought peace. My point, Cason, in this rambling story from a retired trauma surgeon is, what will bring you peace, Cason? Is this shrapnel giving you closure and peace to what was—no doubt—a life-altering experience?"

Peace? Closure?

Cason nodded; he knew it was best to nod here. He was very aware of the reason he kept the shrapnel in his joint. Guilt was like a heavy rope around his neck, but it was his. With it, there would be no peace. It was his reminder that he should have died that day on that Afghan hillside. Remove it, and he might forget that fact. Peace was a dangerous thing to want. Without the pain in his hip, he might forget that he made a promise to the best friend who bled out in his arms. And what kind of person would he be if he broke a blood promise?

"Yup. I don't need peace with this," he said, hearing the denial in his own words.

Dr. Mathers nodded. "Okay. But think about it, because I'll only authorize another week's worth of refills with the recommendation to Dr. Stevens that you get surgery. Your case is a simple and easy fix, and you can be back on your feet in just a few days. If it hasn't done too much damage, you should be pain-free once the incision heals."

"I'll think about it. I doubt my insurance will cover anything from a plastic surgeon, though," he said. Feeling the visit was over, he picked up his pants. He didn't like being railroaded either. He knew where the doc was coming from, but wasn't it *his* hip? He should be able to do what he damn liked with it.

"We have financing. I'll send you an estimate of what it all will cost, today."

CASON THOUGHT about his hip for the rest of the day. On his way to get the prescription filled. At work, pouring and skimming concrete. Despite the refill, he'd not taken another pill. He wanted to feel every gouge that piece of shrapnel made in his body. To really feel his guilt.

Surgery, he thought. There was just one penance to pay, just one promise he'd made. Would he really forget, would the guilt let him, if the physical pain were gone?

The pain was his medication; it distracted him from wanting that peace, from fighting with guilt. It kept him from wanting something, someone, he couldn't have.

CASON WORKED OVERTIME that night to complete a private-road project and then, after catching a bite and a beer with the crew, headed back to Helen's. She was still up finishing the last of the day's crosswords...with a man. Cason saw two heads through the front window.

"Hi," Cason said, announcing himself as he closed the door.

Helen turned and looked over her shoulder at him. "Oh, hi, Cason! How was your day? Do you need some dinner?"

"I'm good," he said, looking at the man on the couch, a gray-haired man about Helen's age. He had turned and was smiling at Cason in a fatherly way. His wire-rim glasses made Cason think of a turn-of-the-century doctor—the last century.

"Oh!" Helen said. "Where are my manners? Cason McPherson, this is Dr. Martin Lowe. Martin, this is Cason." She gestured.

Martin came around the couch to shake Cason's outstretched hand.

"Nice to meet you, sir," Cason said, thinking that somehow this was connected with his doctor's visit.

"Likewise! I've heard so much about you from both Helen and Savannah."

Cason felt his eyebrows arch; maybe it wasn't what he'd thought. "I see. Well, I'll just grab a few things and let you two get back to... your date?"

At the mention of a date, both Helen and Martin said, "Oh! No."

"No. It's not that—"

"We are just two friends catching up!"

"Yes," Helen interjected, "I worked with Dr. Lowe for thirty years. He was Savannah's pediatrician. We're just catching up," she said, smiling.

Cason felt relief that he was indeed there to see Helen, but then it was followed by awkwardness. He watched their faces go red. "Ah..."

"Helen," Martin said to her, "it's getting late. I'll let you get your rest." He added, going for his suit jacket, "Cason, very nice to meet you. I'm sure I'll see you again soon."

He waved goodbye to Helen and promised to see her the next day and then headed out the door.

Cason turned back to Helen, she opened her mouth to explain, and Cason just laughed. "It's okay, ma'am; no need to explain. See you in the morning."

Cason lay awake that night, his mind a rat on its wheel: *Holy hell, did Mrs. S. have a date? I gotta get out of here. Move out. Surgery?*

Just before his twisting dreams pulled him under, he thought of Savannah, whether she got a new rig yet, if her ribs felt better, if she could still smell burnt plastic like he could...if she thought he should get the shrapnel out of his hip. She'd have an opinion on it, he was sure.

Chapter Nine

The next morning the surgery was still on his mind, and Cason was up early, to go into the office, he told himself. He rarely did that, but his company's HR person was in at seven, and Cason had questions about his insurance and what it would cover. What little there was of it. That and he needed to get out of the house. He needed a distraction from the significance of removing shrapnel from his body. Every step he took, that sharp gouge reminded him of the war, of the day Ryan died; sometimes it and the New Orleans heat made it hard to remember that he wasn't still overseas.

What if he had no pain?

As he grabbed a granola bar from the cupboard in the kitchen, he acknowledged the most pressing drive for being up early. He needed to see Savannah. The way he'd left things had plowed through all his other thoughts and sat raw in his belly all night, making his hip feel like the metal was etching his thoughts onto his bone. He wasn't sure what he wanted from her or even that he should go over there, but his gut told him it was right. He'd know what it was when he saw her.

He arrived at Savannah's condo, in a modern rectangle of a

building made of scrap wood and steel façade situated at the eighteenth hole of the country club's oak-grove course. Her condo was the second story of the complex. Under the steel awning, he rapped on the door.

When it didn't open after a few minutes, he knocked again and called her name. Cason looked down as he waited. There on her step, damp from morning dew, was a package from her cell company. He bent over, grimaced at his hip, and picked it up just as the muffled padding of footsteps sounded inside.

The door yanked open, slamming against its chain. "What?" she asked.

"Oh," he said, taken aback, looking at her from bare foot to robe to towel on her head.

"Yeah, I'm getting dressed, but nothing you haven't seen before. What do you want?"

Cason knew then, looking at her, that he was kidding himself on why he was there and felt instantly grateful for the bargaining chip he had just picked up. "I've got something to say," he said, holding up her package, "in exchange for your cell."

Her eyes narrowed in irritation. "You can put that back down and leave. I don't need another demeaning lecture this morning on how to be a better person from Mr. Military Hero McPherson, so buzz off."

"I know," he said, believing he had earned that comment.

She looked at him, and there was a brief second when he was optimistic she'd not slam the door in his face.

"Can I come in? I'll be nice," he added for good measure.

After a long pause, she shut the door in his face. He heard the chain being removed, and then the door cracked open. The padding of her footsteps sounded on the polished hardwoods, walking away from the door.

Cason slowly opened the door, feeling the tenuous truce between them, and then closed it behind him. He scanned the room as he took his boots off. The floors were dark polished wood. Huge white leather couches in the middle of the room looked out over the golf course woods. There was a white fur rug on the floor, and on the far side of the room a metal-and-clear-plastic dining set with a whacked-out ruffled white chandelier thing hanging over it. The kitchen was open to his left; a white marble-topped bar ran the length of it. Polished stainless-steel appliances dominated; the rest of the condo was all windows and black-and-white photographs. It was icy cold compared to Savannah's mother's house, which felt like a warm, straight-from-the-oven cookie.

He saw her across the condo go back into the bathroom and begin putting on her makeup; she'd changed into one of her starched white collared shirts that fit her snugly. He felt a tug in his belly when he realized she'd hastily buttoned it, but only halfway. It was untucked over one of her kneelength black skirts. He was definitely interrupting her morning routine, and it felt like just because he was there she wasn't going to alter it one iota. And he didn't blame her; if it were him, he would have already punched himself in the face.

She turned her head to look at him. "You can put that on the counter and go," she said and then turned back to the mirror.

Cason did put the package on the counter, but he wasn't going; he still had something on his mind. Instead, he busied himself. She had a fancy coffeemaker, but it hadn't been programmed to make coffee that morning. He spotted the coffee grounds next to the machine and set to work. As he dumped grounds into the filter and added water, he felt his palms begin to sweat.

What am I doing?

A few moments later, Savannah, her hair wet but her shirt now buttoned and a black knee-length skirt on, came out to the kitchen. She tore open the cell phone box. "You're still here. So, what is it that you wanted to tell me?" She powered the phone on.

Cason wanted to start with an apology but couldn't. "Did you know your mom is dating?" he asked, resting his good hip against the counter and crossing his arms. As he looked at her, he remembered the way they were before he'd been discharged. They'd been friends. Good friends. Maybe even best friends. Being friends, high-fiving good platonic friends wouldn't break the promise. Before he could think better of it, Savannah responded, eyebrows raised as she looked up at him, making his gut do that thing again.

"Are you kidding me?"

"Last night I got back to the house—she was doing the crossword with some guy."

Savannah's warm-chocolate gaze studied his face. He felt himself swallow, as if gulping down words that would get him into hot water of the non-platonic kind.

"I don't believe it." Savannah said, looking at him and trying not to see him in all her polished glass and reflective surfaces. The circles under his eyes had gotten darker; he wore his work jeans and a fitted undershirt beneath his flannel. He was the accent piece to it all, the solidifying point.

"His name was Martin Lowe. He said he knew you."

Savannah's face brightened, and she laughed. "She really did it. She asked him out?"

Cason shrugged a shoulder. "Not sure. He's your doc?"

"Yes, I went to see him for my X-rays. Mama was beside herself, wondering if he was still married. By the time we left, they were both pink with embarrassment and falling on each other. You should have seen the way they said goodbye—it was awkward, to say the least." She put her cell down. "Were they behaving?"

"They didn't look like they'd done much else but the crossword."

Cason and Savannah looked at each other. They spoke at the same time; Cason cursed and Savannah said, "Oh gross." Then she added, "You don't think...She doesn't...?"

Cason shook his head as if to rid himself of the thought. "No."

"But she's a healthy woman. I mean—"

"No."

"Oh god, what if she does? He was my pediatrician!"

"No. No. No. I still live there. No."

That brought a devilish smile to Savannah's face. "You better find a new place fast, McPherson; otherwise you might walk in on some geriatric make-out sesh."

Cason's smile faded as he got serious. "That's one of the things I came here to tell you. I am moving out. I told your mom that I'd be out after the honoring ceremony."

Savannah processed what he'd said; it was out of left field, as if he were confessing to her. Even so, she didn't feel the joy that she would have felt just the Friday before.

"Sure," she said and picked her phone back up; it was like her mind-fidget, grounding her in a task. "I've heard that before."

"I know," he said and then surprised her with "I'm sorry."

Savannah stopped updating her new phone. "I'm sorry?" she asked, looking across the kitchen at him and then added, "Did I hear you right?"

"Yes. That's the other thing."

Savannah let her steel gaze linger on him. "And what exactly are you apologizing for?"

"For Sunday. I'm sorry. I shouldn't have gone at you like I did."

She felt his apology send a wave of unexpected relief through her. She gripped her phone.

"Why did you?"

Cason shook his head. "You're a complicated person for me, Savannah."

Savannah waited for him to continue, and when he didn't, she asked, "You mean, I come with baggage, baggage that's Ryan?"

He took a deep breath. "Something like that, but not in the way that you think." He rushed on. "Sometimes it feels easier to battle with you...but I'd like to be friends instead. Or, I mean, friends again."

Savannah noticed the way he fumbled through his explanation of what he wanted. Even though it felt like that was what he had come there to say, it also seemed as if he were holding back something more he wanted to divulge.

"I see," she said and waited. He regarded her warily as if hopeful but unsure of what her response was to be. It was uncharted territory for Savannah; Cason had been so forthcoming and downright scathing in his opinions with and of her, but now it was as if a switch had been flipped or more like a mask lifted and she was seeing the real Cason for the first time in two years. When he didn't expand on his wanting-to-be-friends comment, she didn't press it. Savannah had an ache in her side and work to get to. She didn't have hours to sit down and try puzzling out the rest of his ambiguous friends comment. "Okay," she said finally, "I have to get ready for work." She left her phone on the counter and a pensive Cason standing in her kitchen and walked back to the bathroom.

Friends again? Her thoughts surged as she waved her hair dryer at her short damp hair with her good arm. *How am I complicated for him but not in the way I think? Is this just friends today, then tomorrow, no? Can I trust him after the whale-size lie he told about him leaving Ryan?*

The smell of coffee started wafting through the condo as the tightening in her chest increased. He was still there...This was all very new. *First, he came to apologize, and now, he has made coffee?* Savannah wasn't sure what to say to him when she finished her hair, so she ducked into her bedroom, slipped her pumps on, and came back out, having bought herself some time to think. Cason had found two to-go mugs and was filling them.

"You're still here," she said, as he glanced up at her when she went to the counter where her cell was. She checked it and saw the scheduler app had finished uploading her data. She added as she checked her schedule, "What else is on your mind, Cason? I have a feeling you're not staying just to make me coffee."

He made an affirmative noise at the back of his throat and finished pouring out the coffee. The comfortable space—like a soft sofa after a long day of standing—between them as kids began to reemerge. "Smells good. You buy the nice stuff."

"No sense in drinking dirt if you're going to have it every day.

Now spill," she said, briefly looking up from the phone as she scrolled through her itinerary for the day.

"Did you say at lunch on Friday that you know Dr. Mathers?"

"Yeah, I'm working his place up in the Heights. Why do you ask?"

Before he could respond, Savannah caught sight of a name in her schedule that made her curse at her phone.

"What?" Cason asked, curiosity drawing him to the space on the other side of the counter from her.

"Phillip Nigel," she said by way of explanation. "Knight scheduled me to meet with him later this morning." Why couldn't he have just vanished from the face of the earth yesterday, while she was recovering?

"That the guy you were going to have sign something on Saturday?"

"Yes. This day just turned into a fat sack of sour milk... *Soc au' lait*," she said with vehemence.

"Yeah, your mom was talking to me about you working for him. He's physically abusive?"

Savannah twisted up her face. "I'm hoping that's just Mama's gossip mill run amok. But for sure he's a grade A piece of work—they'll definitely want to name a hurricane after him. I know every time I work with him I think I should get a voodoo doll of his likeness, then take up sewing."

"Take up sewing?"

"I hear there're lots of pins involved."

Cason understood then and using his thickest Cajun said, "They's strong words, *cher*."

Savannah gave him a quiet laugh. "They is," she answered and then added, "He makes you look like a kind and gentle little boy."

Cason's eyebrows rose in mock hurt. "Sounds like I should take lessons from him."

"Oh, please don't. You're good enough as you are."

"Runner-up for Dickhead of the Year isn't good enough. I'm

trying for first place," he said, bringing up what she had said the day before.

"Ha," Savannah said dryly, "You earned that, and if you want to be friends, you should *not* take lessons from Phillip Nigel."

"Fine," he said and then added, "As my friend, you should take out the hip pin in the voodoo doll you have of *me*."

She laughed and stowed her cell in her work bag on the bar chair. "Sorry, I'm not the one who has that doll. You might want to contact one of your exes for that."

Cason scoffed. "I wish. I haven't slept with anyone in—Anyway, are you taking someone with you to Phillip Nigel's?"

Savannah's attention shot back to him. "No, no, you were about to say?" Savannah asked, propping her chin on her fist looking at him. "You haven't slept with someone in...? Don't be shy, Cason, do divulge. I need blackmail for later when you decide not to be my friend again."

"I'd rather stick to the Phillip Nigel topic."

"And I'd rather have a real unicorn. Spill."

Cason looked at her dryly. "I was just going to say, a while."

"A while as in a year or a week?"

"Yes," he said, and as a smile threatened to break out on his lips, he looked down and screwed the tops onto the to-go mugs.

"That didn't answer my question."

"Exactly," he said, and when he looked up, his features were blank again. He reached across the counter and placed a mug in front of her on the bar. "Are you taking someone with you to Phillip Nigel's?" he repeated.

Savannah took the warm mug. "Nice dodge, McPherson." She added, "I'm not 'taking someone with me' like it's a bar fight, but yes, I am meeting my associate Charlot there. Well, supposedly. As long as she doesn't stay home to work on her chakras."

"Her what?"

Savannah shook her head. "Nothing, never mind."

"What time?"

"Ten. Is that concern I hear in your voice?" she asked, thinking that being friends with Cason could be good if it were all like this moment.

"Sure. I don't like this guy using his tricks on you. Especially if he makes me look nice."

Savannah scoffed. "Heaven forbid I look kindly on you, Cason."

"Exactly. Where would the world be if we got along?" he said, moving toward the door.

"Crashing into chaos, that's where it'd be. I'll keep you as my personal jerk friend. How's that?"

"Thank you," he said, smothering another threatening smile by taking a sip from his mug. He put it on the floor as he slipped his work boots back on.

Savannah watched him and then realized he'd mentioned his hip, which was rare for him, and before that, Dr. Mathers. "You were asking about Dr. Mathers just a bit ago. What are you seeing him for?"

"I didn't say I was seeing him."

"But you did see him," she pressed.

"He subbed for my doc yesterday." He looked at his watch and announced, "Gonna be late. Catch you later, Savi."

"Cason, remember that being friends doesn't mean I'll stop asking questions. I'll figure it out," she said and watched him toast her with her own insulated mug and duck out the door closing it quietly behind him.

She smiled absently toward the closed door, enjoying the feel of having not had to do battle with Cason but actually having had— should she say it?—a pleasant moment with him. What was the world coming to?

Her phone buzzed, and she looked back down, her good mood fading. "Phillip Nigel...this is ridiculous."

Chapter Ten

With a sane client, closing an account should be simple. Knowing Phillip Nigel, Savannah thought as she drove to his house, he'd have to have his say first: about her not showing up Saturday or Monday, about her daring to ask him to pay his remaining balance, about how she clearly didn't recognize his significance in society. Savannah's gut churned as she thought about dealing with his slippery nature and pompous attitude.

She called Charlot to make sure she'd be there.

"Yeah, I'm on my way now."

"Okay, I am too. See you in fifteen."

Charlot giggled over the line and then said, "Yeah, you're not bad yourself" to someone, as sounds of espresso steam and dishware fizzed and clanked in the background.

"Charlot?"

"Hmmm?"

"You really coming, or are you picking up a piece of pastry with that coffee?" Savannah asked.

"Oh yeah, hold on," Charlot said to someone and then spoke into the phone: "What's that, Savannah?"

"Charlot. Nigel project. Are you coming now? We need to be there at ten. If we're late, this entire meeting will escalate from a scrimmage to a war."

"Just getting my coffee now. See you there," Charlot said and then ended the call.

Savannah gritted her teeth and headed toward the Nigel residence. Halfway there, her stomach was in knots, and she was barely doing the speed limit. The car behind her honked, and she pulled over; Savannah wiped the sweat from her brow. Up ahead a mile was where she'd crashed. She couldn't get the car into gear to keep going, so instead hung a U-turn and went the long way.

She was cutting it close with just five minutes to spare when she pulled her rented sedan into the crowded drive. She was still trying to get her hands to stop shaking when she realized the driveway was supposed to be empty. Instead of crowded with contractor trucks. Savannah's nervousness vanished as the present predicament swept in. She tried to keep her frustration out of her voice as she called Charlot. "Why are the contractors here?"

"I'm almost there," Charlot said breezily as if Savannah hadn't spoken, but there was a distinct door chime and the sounds of her walking down a sidewalk.

"Charlot, I don't care if you're almost here. Why are the contractors here?" Savannah repeated.

She heard the other woman sigh. "Because they're working. What's with the intensity this morning? There's no reason for you to meet with him; I can handle the project by myself. And I'm on my way."

Savannah sat silent on the phone. Hoping she was hearing incorrectly.

"Seriously, Savannah. I can handle it."

"You told the contractors to return to work today?" she asked flatly.

She heard Charlot audibly breathe in through her nose then out through her mouth, as if she were performing a meditation of some kind. "Savannah, we've been over this. You need to put more faith in me. I'm constantly fighting an uphill battle with you. Especially on this project, I need you to trust and support me. There was no need for you originally boot me off the project and subsequently have me cancel the contractors just because you were planning to be out. That isn't nourishing my leadership potential."

Savannah counted to ten. Then: "I take it you didn't listen to my entire message."

"Look, I had all these people leaving me messages, and I didn't want outer demands to ruin the spiritual power I had in preparing to show up today. I got the message this weekend that you would be out, yes. And Savannah, that's all I needed to hear—you needed my help, and I honored that. I showed up early and got the contractors here. I'm here for you. After I got things set up, my qi was drained, so I've gone out to get a matcha latte to rejuvenate. It's fine; the client isn't even home."

Savannah wasn't sure how she managed to keep her cell to her ear; she was struck paralyzed by Charlot's awe-inspiring ability to be both incompetent and a design genius.

Not able to take another second, Savannah uttered, "Never mind," just before her thumb severed the connection. A crack sounded in the mansion. Curious, she let the sound draw her out of the car, her bag on her good shoulder. It was plywood stacks hitting the ground—or maybe a gunshot.

She forgot her conversation with Charlot when the doors to the mansion swung open, followed by the emergence of a puce-faced Phillip Nigel. The client was indeed home. He seemed as if the last of his sanity had slipped away sometime in the night, leaving him with hair askew, a ruddy face, and an untucked shirt. He threw his arm out dramatically toward the front gates and shouted, "Get out!"

As if things couldn't get odder—Savannah pulled her sunglasses down, unsure at what she was seeing—Phillip Nigel seemed to have something in his trouser pants making him fidget and slap at his leg. He pushed down his one pants leg with the sole of his other shoe as if it were riding up and needed a tug down.

"What in blue blazes..." Savi said to herself as she made her way around the trucks in the driveway toward the front door and suddenly wound up in a throng of angry workmen storming out of the house.

"That's right! Get out!" shouted Phillip Nigel.

The workmen shook their heads at her as they stormed past, gear in hand. She spotted her general contractor and was about to ask him what had happened, but he cut her off. "We quit," he said as he barged past. Savannah turned to watch their progress out, then looked back to the steps, narrowing her eyes at her delinquent client.

Phillip Nigel spotted her and disappeared back into the house.

Savannah wasn't sure what she was about to walk in on, but it was clear that she needed to get some clarification on what just happened, then get his Johnny Hancock on the cancellation paperwork, and hightail it out of there.

She got to the top step and peered around the corner; there at the end of the long table was Phillip Nigel, pouring himself a tumbler of whiskey with a shaky hand.

Savannah was about to knock on the door jamb when Phillip Nigel said, "As I told the others, Ms. Sparling, get out. This is my private residence." The shake in his hand seemed to also shake his voice. He looked like a man who'd had too much sauce and was chasing his hangover with the hair of the dog.

"Yes, it is. And I'll be on my way as soon as we have—"

"Do you want me to threaten you too, Ms. Sparling?" He whirled around, grasping his tumbler at the rim, his pinky finger extended and the overfilled container sloshing its contents over the sides. "I asked them to get out at gunpoint. Shall I do the same with you?"

Savannah's eyes swept the room. There was no gun in sight, much less anything that could be used as a weapon, save for the bolts of fabric that had yet to be picked up. This cancellation was already living up to the severely low expectations she had had for it.

"Mr. Nigel, did you just threaten me? Shall I call the sheriff, and we can finish our business with him present?"

"I called him when your league of marauders showed up to tear apart my home. Your delinquency this weekend to show up—when I called to cancel my contract with your pitiful firm—I took as acquiescence to my being in the right with all this fiasco. And now you turn up as if nothing has happened. Oh, Ms. Sparling, what a shame you are to your company."

Savannah glared at him as he slurped drunkenly at the rim of his crystal whiskey tumbler. Impatient and frustrated with him and everything else in her life, she snapped open her shoulder bag, drew out the contract form, and marched into the house. She slapped the form on the table and, drawing out a pen, clicked it and handed it to a surprised Phillip Nigel.

"How dare you! Did you not just hear what I sai—"

"Shut up, you dirt-poor gas bag. We're done playing charades about who you are and where you come from, when we both know you and your mama showed up here from Texas just ten years ago with loads of money that you have pissed down the drain since her soul left this mortal coil. Now, do as I ask, and I'll march my pretty little behind right off your property. You don't, and I'll put a lien on your home and take you for everything your sorry butt is worth. Am I clear?"

Phillip Nigel's face was one of shock; then, as if catching himself, he stood up straight, marched toward her at the other end of the table, and slammed his whiskey down. Amber liquid spewed out and over the contract.

Savannah tried not to growl in anger at him.

"You have no right to a lien here. I've been nothing but cooperative. It's you who've been negligent."

"Oh, I can put a lien on this property." Savannah's gaze held his muddy, unfocused one, yet a small chill slithered like a snake up her spine. "Mr. Nigel, Knight Interiors has put new floors, walls, and paper in this house to a point where, if we repossess all the items we've put in this home, your nouveau riche mansion will become unsuitable living space. But we don't do that at Knight; unlike you, we have class. But if we have to put you over our knee and smack what you owe us right out of you, we will. Remember, the contract you signed said any unpaid debts with Knight may result in a property lien until the account is paid in full."

The veins at his temples rose as she spoke, pulsing angrily at her words.

Savannah opened her bag again and retrieved the duplicate she had made that morning.

"Luckily for you I have a copy," she said whipping it out. "Sign it. And cut me a check for your debts owed. Even a quarter of your debts, and I'll trot right on out of here."

As she handed Nigel the bourbon-soaked pen from the table, tires crunched on the driveway outside. More than one vehicle had just pulled into the Nigel drive. Savannah turned toward the door.

"Who is that?! Who is here now?" Startled by his shouting in her face, Savannah didn't see him until it was too late. He barged into her, clipping her with his body as he ran for the door. "Out of my way, woman!"

The force of his hit twisted her back and against the table. The impact to her ribs made her knees give out. Savannah hit the floor, her hand sliding out to catch herself as the other went to her broken and bruised ribs. They felt afire and stole her breath with the pain.

She bit her lip to keep from crying out and shut her eyes against the blinding, stabbing hell.

She barely heard Phillip Nigel holler out the door, "And who are you? What are you doing here? Sheriff, detain—"

"Come now, Mr. Nigel. What's all this fuss about?" she heard the sheriff call back to him before a car door slammed shut.

Another door slammed shut and she heard the sheriff say, "Dunno, she might be inside."

The pain throbbed as Savannah remembered, *Charlot*. If Charlot came near her now, she'd gobble her up and spit her out, then fire her, rehire her, and fire her again just for good measure. She was thinking of all the ways to wreck Charlot, whom she wholeheartedly blamed for the position she was currently in, specifically on the floor, as she attempted to get up. However, that's when she heard another kerfuffle with Phillip Nigel. Savannah looked up, hoping that he would physically block Charlot from entering his home—the only good thought she'd had toward the man since she'd arrived. *No*, she thought, *since I met him.*

"No, you will not enter my home! Sheriff!" Phillip Nigel was yanked out of the doorway.

Savannah made it up to her knees as Cason strode in and scanned the room, dressed in his work attire from the morning, only now his pants and boots were shades of dry and drying concrete. Cason saw her and jogged over to her. He went to squat, thought better of it, and put the knee to his bad leg down. "Are you okay?" he asked as he got to her side. "Your ribs," he murmured, putting his hand over hers at her side. "How'd you get on the floor?"

Savannah was taken aback. She really had been expecting Charlot. To have Cason hovering over her in a protective way had her mind all akimbo. "I—I'm—What are you doing here?"

He ignored her, as Cason was wont to do when he was focused. "How'd you get on the floor, Savi?" he asked gently.

"I..." She focused. "Just...the client...He ran into me as he headed for the door," she said, pointing, as if that were necessary. "I can't be sure it was purposeful or if he's just a drunken idiot."

He held his hand out to her. "Can you stand?"

"Yes, but Cason. What are you doing here? Is this about this morning, when you asked if I was bringing someone with me? Because if it is, you're too late—he's already knocked me on my can."

This put a twinkle of mischief back into his momentarily mutinous green eyes. "I heard it on the police scanner and recognized the address. I'm working close today, so I thought I'd swing by."

She slid her hand into his warm work-roughened one and instantly felt the confidence that having him beside her gave.

"Do me a favor?" she said, gripping his hand tightly with her good side and letting him lift her up off the floor. She took a deep breath and, closing her eyes against the now achy pain in her side, she smoothed out her skirt that had ridden up when she'd fallen. She felt Cason close in front of her.

The concern was back in his voice, "Are you sure you're okay? Maybe I should take you to the hospital or your doc again for another X-ray."

She opened her eyes and looked slightly up at him. He wasn't nearly as towering now that she was in her heels. "I still need a favor before you cart me off anywhere..."

He was quiet, searching her eyes for a moment. Then, like in the silent moments between them many moons ago, she could tell he knew what she was about to say. The smile lit back into his eyes, and he said, "I have a feeling this is going to be one of those favors that might get me in trouble."

"Only if you don't do *exactly* as I tell you."

His eyebrow lifted. "Waiting."

"I need you to beat the tar out of that man," she said, pointing behind him again. "Only make sure that his writing hand is unharmed so that he can still sign the cancellation contract."

That made him smile.

And there it was, the joy in his smile, the way it spread to his green eyes, making them go light green while the gold flecks around his pupils became more pronounced. And the deep tug it made in her belly. The tug that made her forget all the rules she'd made about him and her that morning, and any morning before that moment.

Savannah felt herself smiling back at him, but as soon as she felt the moment, it was gone. The sheriff leaned his head in the front door and called to them, "Ms. Sparling, I presume? Come on out here, if you please; I've got a few questions for you."

She leaned around Cason and said, "Yes, sir, I'll be right out."

Back to Cason she said, "Duty calls," and picked up her bag and slid it gingerly onto her good shoulder, trying not to wince. Cason took it off her shoulder, though, and waved her ahead of him, saying, "I'll help you out."

Seeing him with her polished bag in all his grime, she said, "No, it's okay," and reached for it before wincing. "Oh, wait. I take that back; you can hold it."

"Thanks, and after this, I'm taking you to your doc's place to get your ribs checked."

Cason walked her out. Even though she couldn't feel it, she knew he had his hand hovering over her lower back like a good Southern gentleman would...with a wounded bear. Guide it. Don't touch it.

"I think I just need to get them wrapped back up," she said, gingerly going down the front stairs. "As much as it was a pain to have you do it, it actually helped."

"Did you just volunteer to take your shirt off for me again?"

Savannah paused on the stairs and looked at him with her mouth slightly open and her eyebrows raised. "What did you just say?"

Cason moved past her, nonchalant, "You heard me. Don't delay. Sheriff's waiting and your bag weighs a ton. You got concrete blocks in here?" he asked, lifting the bag and looking at it as if it would have corners poking out to confirm his theory.

She followed him down the stairs toward her car, parked in front of the sheriff's patrol car, Cason's truck, and a just-arrived deputy who was walking toward Phillip Nigel and the sheriff at the sheriff's rear door. "Look," she said, "if it's too heavy for you, you can give it back to me. It's lighter than my purse, I'll have you know."

He arched an eyebrow at her as he looked over his shoulder, saying, "Lighter? What's in your purse? A whole house?"

Savannah felt herself smile as she pulled her shades down from atop her head in the glaring midday sun. "As a matter of fact..." she started, then stopped as they reached her car and the Knight Interiors van pulled into the driveway. The feelings she had toward Charlot were reignited, only this time she wanted the van to spontaneously fall over on its side, trapping her inside, if only for a moment. "Never mind," she said as Cason unceremoniously tossed her bag onto her car's passenger seat.

"Who is that?" Cason asked as Charlot stepped out of the van, her long black hair flowing in a nonexistent breeze and her nearly see-through shirt in a violent shade of pink, making her like a target to Savannah in a landscape of grays, browns, and greens.

"The bane of my existence," Savannah said. The sheriff looked over his shoulder at her, and then he left Phillip Nigel with his deputy at his car and made his way over to them.

"Do me a favor?" Savannah asked Cason, her eyes lasering on Charlot. "Don't let her near me."

"Copy that," he said and strode toward the hot-pink target. "Sheriff," Cason said with a nod as he passed him.

"Mr. McPherson," the sheriff said back. Savannah looked questioningly at the exchange, momentarily distracted. *Do they know each other?*

The sheriff came to a stop in front of Savannah. "All righty then, Ms. Sparling?"

"Yes," she said and shook hands with him. "Savannah Sparling."

"Sheriff Lee. Nice to meet you. Now, Mr. Nigel is three sheets to the wind, so I'm not sure what's really going down here. Something about"—the sheriff took his notepad out and lifted his shades looking at it—"marauders?" then looked back up at her while he tucked his shades into his breast pocket. "They came into his home?"

"They weren't marauders; they were workers who shouldn't have been here since he's a delinquent client. It's all a bit complicated."

"I see, well, I can help you out if there's a dispute here, or will y'all just go your separate ways? I assume the house is clear of all the things belonging to your company? It looked mighty empty just a bit ago."

"We have some fabric that needs removal, at least."

"Right then. So what we'll do is," he said, fiddling around in his chest pocket and pulling out a well-worn business card, "you call me when you plan to come out here to get your fabric, and I'll escort your team on and off the property. I'll need paperwork and such that shows the fabric and whatnot belongs to you. But I think that's our safest bet. He's in no condition to be around others at the moment. I highly recommended that he keep ol' Johnny Walker in the bottle and that he get some shuteye for a few days, get his head straight."

"Thank you." Savannah said, taking his card.

"I'll let you be on your way, but you give me a call, y'hear?"

"Yes, sir."

"All right," he said, then stopped, thinking of something. Waiting, Savannah became aware of the fountain splashing noisily next to them. "Sparling... I thought I knew that name. You related to a Nurse Helen Sparling? She used to work at the pediatric office uptown?"

Savannah smiled. "Yes, that's my mama. Dr. Martin Lowe's office?"

"Yes! Well, I'll be. She was the nicest. My Jimmy would scream like a stuck pig whenever anyone gave him his shots, except for Nurse Helen. It was like she wasn't really giving him a shot, just a little pat on the arm. She's good folk, your mama. Real nice. You give her my regards, will you?"

"I will, Sheriff Lee, I will."

"All right, I'll let you go now..." he said, then thinking better of it, added, "I wasn't going to say anything before, but knowing you're Mrs. Helen's girl, I need to tell you to be safe. I met Mr. McPherson over there," he said, throwing his thumb over his shoulder toward Cason, who was taking Charlot's business card for some reason, "the other day when we were pulling a burnt SUV out of a downed oak tree, and it belonged to one Ms. Savannah Sparling. I assume that's you?"

Savannah's gut churned; she felt as if she were in actual trouble with the law. She could only assume this was what people felt like when their father was about to give them a long lecture or a good scolding.

"Yes, sir, that was my SUV."

"Okay. Now, mind you, I don't know what you were doing out on a road like that in a storm like the one we had, but I do know that my grandmama told me messes come in threes. That's a rule I've found to be true my whole life. You had that one, then this dustup with Mr. Nigel; I take it you won't want a third, so keep your head down, understand?"

"Yes sir," she said, both cursing the small town-ness of New Orleans and marveling at the beauty of it, that the sheriff would make a personal investment in a stranger because he was beholden to her mother. "Thank you," she added.

"Okay, you get on your way now."

She was about to say goodbye and then run for her car, but she and the sheriff both looked back at Charlot when her girly giggle rang out loudly. Cason looked like he was trying to leave, but she grabbed his arm and tossed her hair over her shoulder coyly. Taking the card out of his hand, Charlot wrote something down with a glittering white pen that Savannah recognized as Charlot's personal and only pen she would use.

Sheriff Lee made a scoffing sound and shook his head, moving toward Charlot and Cason, putting his pad back and slipping his own shades on as he did so. Savannah, not wanting to see any more or think about why she felt a jealous rage instead of mild annoyance, made for the driver's seat of her rental.

Savannah got into the driver's seat, started the car, and opened all the windows as the AC blasted on max. The black leather was the same temperature as the surface of the sun, but Savannah's mind was too busy processing what the sheriff had said and if Cason was flirting with Charlot or if that was just Charlot being coy—but why would she be coy with him? She didn't know him. Maybe she knew him? No, this was Charlot: I-just-met-a-man-at-the-coffee-shop-and-we're-soul-mates Charlot. Besides, what did Savi care? She didn't. Not at all.

Savannah reached for her seat belt with her bad arm and acciden-tally grabbed the metal buckle. In the short time the car had sat there, the metal of the belt latch had become a branding iron. "Damn, egg-sucking, rat-faced, asshatted pig-fu—"

She was cut off by Cason's half laugh. He was at her window; he bent down, resting his long-sleeved arms on her inferno of a windowsill. "Are you talking about me?"

She put her head back against the hot headrest, defeated, unsure whether to grasp her side or her burnt hand. "I give up. I need a do over of today."

"What's wrong with getting tossed on the floor with a couple of broken ribs by a psycho client?"

"Nothing, just a typical Tuesday for Savannah Sparling."

Cason gave her a small smile. "The day's not over yet, Savi. Maybe you do need to get those ribs wrapped—I can offer you the McPherson Special, for a fee."

This made Savannah smile halfheartedly. "The McPherson Special? What exactly is that? A body-numbing cocktail? Because that's what I need right now. Make it a double."

"Sure. With a good old-fashioned rib wrapping."

"In your dreams, soldier."

"You have no idea."

"You're right. And I don't want to know," she said with a soft laugh, then deliberately grabbed the fabric of the seat belt and gingerly fastened it using only the plastic part and her elbow.

"Okay, but really, Savi, go see your mom and have her give you another wrap."

She made a face as if she were thinking about it, saying, "Sure, as soon as my schedule frees up."

Cason gave her a knowing look before patting the window frame. "See you later. Stay out of trouble. Or call me before you get into it, so I can be on time."

Savannah put the car in gear and gave him a smile before she slowly pulled away, saying, "I'll see what I can do. Bye."

"See ya."

. . .

THE OFFICE WAS BUSTLING when Savannah entered, and she informed Knight and a few coworkers on the Nigel project of what had happened and requested an additional person to follow up with the sheriff to get Phillip Nigel's signature on the docs and the residual fabric. After retelling the story for the third time, she was feeling drained. She was told to take the rest of the week off to recoup. Savannah insisted she was fine but did agree to take the rest of the day.

As Savannah wrapped up the last few emails and answered the questions of the curious, she made a mental note to buy some wine as therapy. She picked up her things with her good arm and headed out of the office and to the elevator of the ten-story building.

Savannah stepped in, and just as the doors were closing, Charlot slipped in with her.

"No," Savannah said, automatically hitting the door-open button repeatedly, like she had a nervous tic. *God, couldn't she have just gone home to work on her chakras?*

The doors shut.

"Just hear me out, Savi." Charlot's ample bosom heaved as if she'd run up a flight of stairs.

"It's Savannah and always has been, Charlot," she said, ramming the door-open button one last time for good measure; when the elevator began its slow descent, Savannah gave up and turned on Charlot. "I would think it's obvious, Charlot, that you should give me some space. I highly recommend it for your health—"

"You need help Sav—"

"And now you've trapped yourself in a metal box with me," she said ignoring her.

"Trapped is a strong word. I think we should talk about what happened and about that guy who showed up."

"What happened was that you were too busy batting your eyelashes at the barista at your coffee shop to listen to my entire message. The entire message that said he has not paid his invoices and *that* is why we must cancel the contractors. As a result, you left me to clean it up. And the man who showed up is none of your business."

"Oh," she said, letting Savannah's words sink in, "so, he didn't pay his invoices? Oh..."

"Yes, *oh*. It's over now. You're officially off the project, and I'm doing damage control. Or did you not think the contractors would ask to be paid for today? Have you figured out how accounting gets money from a delinquent account to pay them? Or about smoothing out the relationship with those contractors? We'd like to earn back their trust after telling them to show up to the home of an irate client after I first told them not to go. What does that mixed message do for our reputation, Charlot? Nothing good, I can tell you. Now, please stop talking."

"Okay." After a beat, Charlot gained steam again. It was as if she had a negative shield on and only happy words made it through. "But I heard you were assaulted. Now I feel like it's all my fault you were assaulted!"

At the word *assaulted*, Savannah's eye twitched, and she gripped her bag more tightly so as not to use its strap around the other woman's slender throat. "Don't make me into a victim, Charlot—and we have a few more floors to go, so I'd suggest you use the time wisely and be as quiet as a log in the woods."

"Okay," she said, "I'll be quiet about the Nigel thing, but the guy, Cason—how long have you known him?"

"By 'log in the woods,' Charlot, I mean not using your vocal cords. Logs can't talk, and neither should you."

"Is he your boyfriend?"

Savannah began screaming in her head. Aloud she said, "No, Charlot. He is not."

"Oh, good! I asked him out, and then I realized that it might be all too much for you today if he was your boyfriend."

As the elevator doors slid open, Savannah thought of the sheriff's warning about messes coming in threes.

Savannah walked briskly out of the elevator, out of the building, and toward her rental. She scratched "car buying" off her mental list of things to do that day and confirmed "wine drinking."

"So, is that a yes? You're okay with it all?" Charlot hollered from behind her.

Savannah slipped her shades on and murmured, "Yep, definitely three."

Chapter Eleven

Cason eyed the plate of pasta the server set in front of him. He wasn't 100 percent sure why he had agreed to go out with this woman from Savannah's work. She was incredibly easy on the eyes. He was sure her black hair wasn't her real color, but her doe eyes and her wide rack on her tight body made him think that, no matter how bad the date was, it wouldn't be all that bad.

And she seemed nice.

He could use nice, he thought again as he looked across the table at her in the cramped Italian place she'd picked out a couple blocks off of the madhouse that was Bourbon Street. She'd kept on her tight pink shirt from earlier in the day but had exchanged the white jeans for a black skirt that made him wonder if he was in too deep. He was out of practice with all of it, especially for what she was advertising that she wanted later. A poorly placed piece of shrapnel in his hip made sure all his favorite bedroom moves felt like he was screwing with a knife in his joint. He was also no good with small talk, but he was glad to see that Charlot was an expert.

Cason stabbed his fork into his massive dish of spaghetti and meatballs. Charlot said, "It was so brave of you, Cason, to rescue

Savannah like you did. You're a real hero." She gently poked at her green salad.

"Rescue?" he said, before sliding food into his mouth.

"Yes! Today, and you saved me too. Savannah can get a little harsh, if you know what I mean. You must have some strong heroic genes in you. I heard through the grapevine that you're about to be honored at some award ceremony coming up."

He just nodded, food in his mouth. "Mmmmm."

"What was it like over there? Your aura tells me you've seen real pain—"

His hand went up, stopping her, surprised at how quickly she dove into his dark place. "Sorry. Not to be rude—you seem like a nice woman, Charlot—but what do you say that the past stays out of the conversation, and we stick to what we do now?"

Her blue doe eyes got larger. "Oh, my. I know it must be hard for you, absolutely. I'll not say anything more on your time there. When you're ready to talk—"

"You said you work with Savannah? How do you like your job? What do you do?" he asked, moving solidly off the topic of him. His dinner went tasteless in his mouth. *This was a bad idea,* he thought.

She smiled, her lips pursing before she opened them to speak. "So, I'm an interior designer. I work closely with Savannah on all the big projects. I'm that sought-after."

"You're an assistant to Savannah?"

She stabbed at a tomato. "No, Savannah has her own projects, and I have mine. She sometimes needs my input on things. Anyway," she said, waving her fork as if to clear the air with it, "enough about Savannah. When I'm not at work, I'm working this body." She winked. "I do yoga, a pole-dancing cardio class three times a week, and an erotic dance session twice a week. I have an overactive sacral chakra, so I have many outlets for it."

"A sack of what?"

"Sacral chakra. It's my pelvic sexual energy." Her voice purred.

Cason was doubly sure then that he wasn't ready for what she was advertising. He refocused the conversation, praying she'd forget about wanting him to have acrobatic sex with her. "So, you like to work out?"

"Something like that," she said and tucked her chin, smiling up at him through her lashes.

Cason looked down, and then back up when she didn't continue talking. "You okay?" he said. Her expression was frozen in coquettishness.

"I bet *you* like a good workout," she said, leaning forward, letting the scoop neck of her shirt do some work.

Cason kept his eyes averted from the peep show being forced on him. "A good workout? My work is pretty physical. You could say that's my gym—"

"What do you do?" she asked breathlessly.

Cason put the last of his pasta in his mouth, buying time. He looked up at her again and thought of what to say in response that didn't seem sexy. It felt like he could say, "Shovel sewage," and she'd orgasm on the spot. It was too easy. Savannah flickered across his mind. Yes, he preferred the Savannah Sparling method of real debate, the banter and good-natured verbal ass kicking. Cason said, "Concrete," and Charlot started talking again, something about how hot that was and how she bet he was always taking his shirt off. He just thought about Savannah. She'd probably give him hell for taking this particular coworker out, and he supposed that was really why he had done it.

For the rest of the meal, Cason tried to focus on what Charlot was saying and not to think too much about Savannah. Or the fact that she'd been shoved to the ground earlier that day and could probably have stood having someone nearby that night. And he was sitting with Charlot.

The dessert menu came, and Cason was about to politely say he wouldn't be having any. The date *had* been a bad idea. Then he felt Charlot's foot slide up his leg. "Let's get dessert at my place—what do you say?"

Her foot got to his thigh, making his brain stutter. "I—"

"Great, let's go."

Cason paid. He knew it was futile to explain that he would just be dropping her at her home. So he kept silent as he followed her out of the restaurant. He held his truck's door open for her while she talked; he wasn't sure what she was saying. His mind kept going to the metal in his hip. He'd kept the limp out of his step as much as possible, but it was starting to grind.

He smiled at her when she got in. She chattered on as he drove her back to her place. But halfway there, he forgot about his hip when Charlot laid her hand on his inner thigh and squeezed.

Cason looked down and then over at her in surprise.

"Maybe you should drive a little faster. I'm not sure how long I can hold out," she said, sliding her hand higher; then she boldly cupped him.

Cason nearly ran a stop sign.

"Ooh," she said, "you excited too?"

Cason was speechless. He couldn't drive, listen to her, get cupped, and speak all at once. He grabbed her hand and gently set it aside. "Can't do more than one thing at a time when you do that."

She giggled and said, "Okay."

He internally grimaced.

Charlot lived uptown in a small garden apartment complex. They parked, and he helped her out and walked her through the courtyard to her door. "Thank you for a nice night, Charlot."

Charlot looked over her shoulder at him as she unlocked her door and opened it. She gave him a smile that Cason recognized.

"Tsk-tsk, Cason, it sounds like you don't want to come in with me."

"I think it's better that we just—"

Charlot grabbed his shirtfront then and yanked him into her apartment, slamming the door shut behind them.

As soon as the door shut, she dropped her purse and threw herself at him, there in her entryway. As she plowed into him, Cason put back his leg to catch himself, but it was his bad one, and it gave out. They both hit the wall behind him, rattling the acres of photo frames that trailed down the hallway.

Charlot's lips were on his, and her hand went down the front of Cason's pants. As soon as her fingers touched him, it was as if all the stars in the sky exploded. His mind went blank, save for acknowledging the sharp pain in his hip. The feeling of pleasure and pain blended together into a toxic cocktail, and he gave in.

Cason grabbed her narrow hips and yanked her against him, trapping her hand between them. He wove his other hand up into her long ponytail and, wrapping it around his wrist, crushed her mouth to his. As he gave in to the rush of feelings, including pain, the thought of Savannah disapproving wound up from his subconscious.

In a split second, his mind had Savannah in his arms, her lips against his, and he growled with confined pleasure. Cason's chest tightened as he deepened the kiss; he needed more. Physically more.

He slammed Charlot back against the opposite hall wall and pressed his aching body against hers. They gasped for air and found each other's lips again. Cason opened his mouth and devoured Savannah, his eyes closed, seeing her clearly in his mind's eye. She wore a tight shirt as well, and as his hand traveled down to her breast, he felt her respond.

She pulled her hand from his pants and undid the top button of his jeans.

Yes, his mind said. Cason pressed against her harder, desperately wanting to meld his body with hers.

Savannah whined in pain then, but the voice wasn't hers. Neither was it her voice when she pulled back from their kiss and pushed him away, saying, "Ouch."

Cason took a deep breath and opened his eyes, the heat still lingering in his belly. The woman pinned against the wall had wide blue eyes and long black hair.

The realization of what had happened was like ice water down his spine.

"Oh" was all he could say.

"Yeah, that was a little rough for me. Maybe we can go a little softer? Maybe a little couch time?" she said, her lips red and roughed up.

He shook his head to clear it and stepped back. "Sorry...I..."

She gave him a weak smile in her dimly lit hallway. "We can also just watch a movie. I don't actually have dessert. Well, I do, but we're supposed to wear it—whipped cream and fudge sauce."

Cason barely heard her through his own mortification that he'd conjured up Savannah so realistically that he'd nearly had sex with this woman because of it.

"I have to go" was all he managed before striding from the apartment.

CASON SLAMMED his palm against the steering wheel of his truck. "Shit!" Having a one-night stand was one thing; sleeping with someone while imagining she was Savannah was another thing entirely. The warning bells of losing his focus made him squeeze his eyes shut and run through his mental checklist.

Where am I? Not in the mountains.

Where do I feel I am? Nowhere.

What did I see? Savannah. Was she real? He struggled with the question. No, she wasn't. He knew she wasn't. The lines were blurred, though. She had felt real. He had never kissed her, but he knew his imagination had created something spot-on. It had felt —*Jesus*—it had felt good.

He took a deep breath, tried to clear his head. Maybe being without pain pills was having an effect on him.

The part that rubbed salt into it all was the dawning reality that he might not be fully prepared for the hell Savannah would unleash on him after hearing about the night from her coworker. Right after he said he wanted to be friends. Was it okay that he went out with her coworker? He should have asked. *Right?*

Cason cursed again; he had no answers. He started up his truck and drove out into the night. Not back to Savannah's mother's house or to Savannah's house—he just drove. He needed out, needed to get away. His slip of control scared him. If he had a grip on reality only when he was neck-deep in meds, what did that make him? If there was ever a strong reason to leave Savannah's mom's place, he had just found it.

He drove on through the dark until the weeping oak trees of the Heights came into view. As a kid, he used to wander under a mossy grove of oaks behind his mother's trailer, far from the Heights. The streamers of moss had reminded Cason then of green rain, and still did. Silent and stoic, the trees they clung to stood unmoved by human emotion, feelings, or drama. They grounded him, then and now.

Cason pulled off to the side of the road and parked. He sat for a long time intently watching the warm, heavy evening air move the hanging moss, shutting out all other thoughts, as the moss gracefully did a slow dance in the air.

Savannah.

It wasn't her, his mind responded.

He felt the ache tightening his chest again. He had to forget her, despite what every fiber of his being was waking up and yearning for.

The hypnotic lure of the living made him want to forget about Ryan and the promise he'd made. Although, that was the trouble with making promises with the dead, renegotiating or striking a compromise were impossible. Rather, promises with the dead relied on the moral and ethical steel of the living to keep them alive.

In the orange sulfuric light of the street lamps, he noticed the concrete sidewalks had begun to buckle over the tree roots. Behind the thick trees, the houses were stately and silent. They were built in the mid–eighteen hundreds. The homes were variations on a central theme of wrought iron, dark shutters and wrapping porches, each with a rocker and heavy riots of ferns hanging in baskets from the porch beams. They were a piece of New Orleans history and with that honor came the burden of needing endless labor to keep them stately. It was the kind of work that kept mischief at bay and the mind at ease, Cason thought.

As if summoned from his own mind, he noticed the peak of a white for-sale sign around the wide trunk of the oak next to his truck. He leaned over and saw the rest of it; a red sticker at the bottom spelled out *Foreclosure* in white letters. There, right there next to him, was a literal sign, indicating the solution he so desperately needed. He stepped out of his truck and up onto the sidewalk. The sign was in front of the boggy green lawn of a shuttered two-story Victorian. It stood starkly white against the dark night. It was perfect.

He went back to his truck for a piece of paper and pen to write down the phone number.

If he played his cards right, he could be putting sweat equity into the old place by the next month. Optimism infused him, and all residual thoughts of Charlot slipped away.

Chapter Twelve

S avannah thought that if the sun could take just one day off, it should have been that one. Just one day when it could be pitch-black so that the light didn't feel like it was shooting daggers through her eyes and into her brain.

Two ibuprofen were not proving to be enough for her hangover. At least the Malbec imported from Argentina had been worth it.

Savannah's mind was as clear as cotton as she walked into work. She gave appropriate good mornings and waves as she made her way down the hall to her office, which looked out over town. She got her bag onto her desk and tossed her sunglasses down before being overtaken by an overwhelming urge to purge her insides. She left her office, ducked into the corner restroom, and did just that. Recovery was close at hand.

She washed up and walked back to her office down the short open hallway of black-and-gray workstations, which were made cheery with accents of wood, swatches of bright cloth, and splashes of paint. Halfway there, the water cooler beckoned to her like an icy spring-fed pool in the middle of the desert.

She was getting a glass down, the offices to her back, when the distinctive sound of gold bangles behind her made Savannah cringe. "Hey," Charlot drawled and put a hand on her shoulder. Savannah turned to see concern in her blue eyes. "You're at home this week."

Savannah put her glass under the dispenser's nozzle. "No, Charlot, I'm obviously not at home this week. And please get your hand off my shoulder." She gave the offending hand a pointed look.

Charlot pursed her lips in a pity pout. "Of course, Savannah. You must be really hurting from yesterday—both emotionally and physically."

Savannah closed her eyes and asked how it was possible that Charlot could be so incredibly irksome and simultaneously oblivious to it. And she added a prayer for a large dose of patience. "I thought I made it clear yesterday," Savannah said, opening her eyes and lasering them on Charlot, "that you should give me a wide berth, for at least two weeks, so I have time to forget you calling in contractors on a delinquent account." Her pounding headache turned into drilling at her temples.

Charlot sighed. "I know, and I totally was, but then I went out with Cason last night—"

Savannah gritted her teeth. "And you felt the need to tell me all about it," she said, pressing the button for cold water, letting the splashing sound fill the air between them. Wishing it would drown out her words.

"Exactly. Savannah, I think he's madly in love with you."

Savannah choked. "What? Why would you say that? You should get away from me—"

Ignoring her protest, Charlot continued, her bracelets clinking as she waved her hands. "I had a dream about it."

"You had a dream?" Savannah said, feeling her eye twitch.

"Yes, and his aura."

"And his aura?"

"Yes, there's no need to repeat everything I say, Savannah. I'm trying to tell you that your friend is madly in love with you. He told me all about it last night at dinner."

"He told you?" Savannah wasn't 100 percent sure she wasn't hallucinating the conversation.

Charlot sighed. "Yes! We went out to dinner—cute Italian place —and then back to my place for dessert." She wiggled her eyebrows at Savannah. "If you know what I mean."

Savannah felt her jaw go slack; she couldn't figure out how to get her voice to work. She desperately wanted two things to happen: for Charlot to shut up and for her to not stop talking.

"When you said yesterday that he wasn't your boyfriend and you were cool with me seeing him, I couldn't wait. He's super dark in that Greek-tragedy sort of way, and I tried talking with him at dinner about why, and he changed the subject. Which is cool—that kind of thing takes time, right? And I thought I'd talk with you about it today, but then he and I went back to my place, and...I don't think I want to see him anymore."

Savannah tried to make sense of her bouncing logic, grasping hold of only the tail end. *A bad date?*

"Besides clearly not being into me, he's incredibly rough. I like a little soft cuddling and gentle kissing, you know?"

"No."

"Oh, well—" She pointed down. "You're overflowing."

Savannah looked down at her water glass; it was indeed overflowing. She let go of the button as Charlot continued.

"I knew at dinner I could capture him with some good old-fashioned whipped cream and fudge body paint—"

"At a restaurant?"

"No, later—back at home."

"Still." Savannah could not imagine Cason being into such a paperback-romance move.

Charlot seemed to read Savannah's tone as prudish disgust because she asked, "Haven't you ever tried it?"

"No, I don't need to." Savannah looked pointedly around the office, but Charlot didn't seem to take the hint that it was neither the time nor the place for talk of sex games.

"Don't knock it until you try it."

"That's like putting mayo on peaches, Charlot. They're both delicious—doesn't mean one goes with the other."

Charlot shrugged and powered on. "That's closed-minded. Anyway, back to our date," she said. "I got straight to business at my place, and he was still pretty distant. Until we fell back against the wall, and then it was like," she said, looking out over the buzzing personnel of the office, "he came alive."

"Uh-huh" was all Savannah could manage, as she prayed no one could hear them while simultaneously not caring.

"He just slammed me against the wall and grabbed me, my hip and hair."

Savannah felt like she was losing her mind; her heart hammered in her chest as she imagined Cason doing those things. She'd felt those arms around her before and knew exactly what something like that would feel like. It would feel solid, unbreakable, and will bending. She forgot completely that this was not the time nor the place.

Charlot lowered her voice to a conspiratorial whisper. "His kissing, Savannah. I swear I have bruises on my lips because of him. There was this split second when he looked at me, and it was hot. I mean, scorch-the-earth hot. And I thought, *Okay, maybe I can get a little rough with him*. But I didn't, and when I did tell him it was too much, he stopped immediately, a real gentleman. Then it was like he really looked at me, like he realized at that moment that he'd been making out with *me*. I think in his head he was making out with someone else. I mean, he'd been fairly distant the whole night, you know? And he kept asking questions about you, and there's the whole aura thing. And later I had a dream about you two, so I figure he was making out with me but was thinking of you," she said and wiggled her eyebrows again at Savannah.

"That's a leap."

"You would think so. But I have it on good authority he was thinking of you."

"And what authority is that?"

"His lips said a lot of things," she said, making a pained face and gently touching her lips.

"He said..."

"You know, Savannah, you might be good at the whole boss thing, but I know people's spiritual desires. And he craves a strong woman who can be his equal and nourish him through a deep, long-standing relationship of understanding—"

"Okay, I don't want to hear anymore. I have a splitting headache."

Savannah picked up her glass. Cason was maybe thinking of her? Hadn't he just said the morning before that Savannah was too complicated for him? She felt her limbs go pleasantly numb.

"Sure, but just a heads up he was an animal. Way too rough for me." Charlot sighed. "I'm going to call the cute barista guy and go out with him. I think he's more my speed. And, Savannah, I know you have all this rage, and Cason, I think, has some of it too. It's tingeing your auras. You two should hook up. You'd set some bedroom furniture on fire if you did," Charlot said and then made a sad face at Savannah. "You look tired; you should head home. I can take over your projects while you're out." She patted Savannah's shoulder.

Savannah came back to reality long enough to say, "When pigs fly." Taking her sloshing water glass, she headed to her office.

Savannah sat hard on her desk chair. The thought of Cason being rough with her had her breath coming up short. She could use rough.

Savannah closed her eyes. *What am I thinking?*

Cason was not a man she fantasized about. Then she remembered seeing him without his shirt the week before.

No, that didn't count. She didn't know it was him in that moment. There was too much baggage there. She was just out of it because she'd not eaten anything save for a 2006 Malbec the night before.

In the office kitchen, Savannah took a powdery beignet from a bag of them that an adoring client had sent to their office, warmed it up, and poured herself a mug of coffee.

Back at her desk, she settled in and ran through her list of projects; she updated to-dos and cleared her afternoon for the Mathers project. She'd be overseeing the kickoff to their renovation, which meant meeting with the contractor at their home to set schedules and project deadlines.

Thinking of the Matherses, Savannah remembered Cason talking about seeing Dr. Mathers. What a man like Cason would need with a plastic surgeon was beyond her. She had flipped through a few more pages of the project binder when it dawned on her. *His hip.* He was going to fix his hip? That was huge, right? He had lived with it for so long she had thought he would just go on living with it. He was making a change, a big one. Taking care of his hip, leaving her mother's house, and making amends with her? It felt like he was cleaning house—he might actually move out this time. She wasn't sure how she felt about it all. Her finding his uniform and uncovering the truth seemed to have shaken something loose in him. She craved knowing what that change was, talking with him about it.

Her phone rang.

"Hi, Mama," Savannah said.

"Hi, Savannah, dear. You available for lunch?" Helen asked. Her mother's tone seemed serious.

"Is everything okay?"

"Yes, hon. Can you make it or not?"

Savannah was taken aback. "Yes, Mama, I can."

"Okay. Thank you," Helen said and then hung up. She'd hung up before confirming the time or asking Savannah to bring anything. Savannah looked at her watch and realized that noon was just a few minutes away. Grabbing her things, she headed out to her mother's house.

When Savannah arrived, her mother didn't look up from setting plates on the table for just the two of them, and Savannah noticed her hand shaking when she set the fruit salad down.

"BLTs with ambrosia salad and iced tea. My favorite! What's the occasion?"

"Nothing," Helen said briskly before adding, "Wash your hands and come eat."

As she washed up, she decided that Cason had talked to her mother about the Nigel project. That would be too much for her mother just a few short days after the car wreck. God knew that even Savannah was still trying to sort through it all.

"Is there something you want to talk to me about, Mama?"

"What?" Helen's voice came out a squeak as she looked over at her daughter. "Did Cason tell you?"

Savannah realized then that this had nothing to do with her. She felt her forehead crease. "Is everything okay?" she asked again.

Helen clutched her napkins. "I'm sorry, Savannah. I just wanted to have a good lunch, and then afterward we could talk, but I can't seem to get through setting the gosh darned table."

"Mama, it's okay. What's up?" she asked, touching her mother's shoulder, her stomach clenching, waiting for the bad news.

Her mother took a deep breath and said in a rush, "Dr. Lowe and I have been seeing each other for two days now."

Savannah was so relieved that she laughed.

Helen's face went from concern to admonishment. "I'm not so sure what you find funny in that, Savannah."

Savannah shook her head. "No, sorry, Mama. I just thought that you were about to tell me some dreadful news. Seeing Dr. Lowe is nothing compared to what I thought you were going to say."

"Oh, well. Okay."

Savannah grabbed her plate and filled it, suddenly starving. "I'm glad you two are seeing each other. If you want to date, Mama, I'm completely fine with it. Just be sure to wear protection—"

"What?" Helen asked, shocked.

"Mama, if you want to...you know...just be safe."

Helen's face was a mask of horror.

When her mother didn't speak, Savannah felt uncomfortable. "Did you not just say you were dating him?"

Helen blinked rapidly at her daughter. "Yes, but no. But Dr. Lowe—"

"Mama. It's okay if you call him Martin."

Helen pulled out her chair and sat hard. "I was expecting to tell you that he'd been coming over to help with the crosswords. He's very smart, you know, and then to prepare you for the fact that I might invite him to brunch one weekend." She heaved a breath. "But you thought I was some hussy who was sleeping with him in the house of her dead husband!" she exclaimed.

Savannah felt her eyes go wide. "Wow."

"What do you take me for, Savannah Rae?"

"Wow," Savannah said again, watching her mother's face turn red.

Helen stood again, still clutching her napkins. "Is that what people are saying about me around town? That I'm some sort of home-wrecker now that Martin has been seen coming here?"

"Mama, stop. Breathe."

Helen swallowed hard and then, after breathing deeply, nearly hollered, "Well, do they?"

"No, not a soul thinks that, Mama. He's been divorced for years. How about you sit down and tell me what you wanted to tell me about Martin."

"I just did!"

"Okay." Savannah held up her hands, palms out, placating. She chirped, "Crosswords are fun! You say you've seen each other twice now?" She tried hard to rescue the sinking ship of the conversation.

Ignoring her, Helen continued, "And you think we're having sex? Cason lives here! I'm not that kind of woman! Martin's just gotten divorced!"

"Mama, again, he's been divorced for years; you've been widowed for decades. You deserve to be happy in your own home, so if that means loving someone—"

"I'll not have sex with him!"

"That might disappoint him," Savannah mumbled and, changing tactics, sat and started digging into her favorite lunch.

"What?"

"I'm just saying, Mama, that crosswords lead to sex. Everyone knows that. You shouldn't be toying with him like you are unless you're willing to go all the way." She plopped more salad onto her plate.

Helen sat abruptly.

Savannah looked over at her blanching mother and exclaimed, "Oh my god, Mama, I'm kidding!" She put a hand on her shoulder. "You're being very thoughtful in telling me, and I appreciate it, but I also think that you should be happy, and if that means more than crosswords and brunches, I'm okay with it."

Helen was quiet a moment. Something passed across her face, and Savannah realized she was considering what she had said. Finally, her mother asked, "What if he does want s-s-s-s—"

"You'll ask your girlfriends what they think. Not me. That's what you'll do," Savannah said.

"Right..." Helen said, and when Savannah nudged her untouched plate closer to her, she said, "All of this ridiculous talk has me out of sorts. You can have my sandwich. You look dreadful—have you eaten since I saw you last?"

"Honestly?" Savannah asked.

"Oh for Pete's sake, Savannah," Helen said, guessing the rest of her daughter's answer. "I'll make you up a container of leftovers. You need to eat!"

"I'm eating now, Mama. I don't need all your food. You need to feed that dolt Cason, remember?"

"Don't speak of him that way. I know you two are like circling cats, but you can't talk about him that way under my roof, you hear me?"

Saying it, Savannah hadn't felt the usual jab anyway. Her mind was changing about him—to what, she wasn't sure, but she was doubly sure she didn't have the time to look too closely at it. "Yes,

Mama." She added, "Besides, I hear he's moving out for real this time."

"Yes, well. I think his desire to has to do with Dr. Lowe coming over."

"Martin."

"Yes, Martin. He walked in as we were finishing the *Times* puzzle, and I think it was awkward for him," Helen said, scooping a bit of the creamy goodness of the ambrosia salad onto her plate.

"Mama, have you thought that he simply may want a place of his own?"

Helen was quiet as she replaced the spoon and lifted a half BLT sandwich from the platter. "Yes, but I think he's still in recovery. He is making some changes, though. Going to see Dr. Mathers was quite a step."

Savannah's interest was piqued. "I heard about that," she said, stretching the truth.

"Yes, he's finally going to take care of that hip of his, starting today, in fact." Helen looked a little abashed. "I overheard his conversation with the doctor this morning, him agreeing to the surgery." Savannah made a face to encourage her mother to keep going. "Well...the cost of the surgery won't be covered by his insurance. So, I offered that he could stay here as long as he needs to. I think he might take me up on that. This surgery is going to cost him his entire savings, maybe more than that, no doubt." She took a bite of her sandwich.

Savannah had an unusual urge: she had to pay for that surgery. She saw all of Cason's positive momentum like a train, and staying with her mom for longer than he wanted and using his entire savings might derail that train. She couldn't let that happen. It felt weird to think about it. She'd been at his throat for so long that doing something good for him felt oddly new. Though even if they were at each other's throats, she'd still pay for it to make sure he moved out. But this was different; she was doing it because she cared. Knowing

Cason, however, she suspected he'd never allow it. But if it came as an anonymous gift? Maybe.

"When's the surgery?" Savannah said around a mouthful of fruit salad.

"Honey, really. Don't talk with your mouth full, and sit up straight. You're wearing such a beautiful suit. You really look like a lady, but slouching makes you look like you've wilted."

"Don't be peckish, Mama. Just because you talked yourself into your houseguest staying," Savannah said, finishing her mouthful and adding, "when all you want to do is turn this place into a love nest for you and"—she scrunched her nose, teasing her mother— "Maaaaartin."

Before her mother could respond, something clanged out in the garage.

"What was that?" Savannah asked, turning in her seat to look down the hallway.

"Oh, it's just Cason. He's changing the oil in my car. Says he has a list of things he wants to take care of before surgery. He's taken the afternoon off to go to his pre-op appointment at the clinic."

Savannah looked from the hallway back to her mother. "Pre-op? That was fast, right?"

"Faster still is that the surgery is tomorrow morning already. I'll be driving him."

"I mean, these things take time, and how did Dr. Mathers fit him in?"

Helen nodded after taking another bite of her sandwich. She chewed for a bit before washing it down with iced tea. "I was thinking the very same thing. I just hope this Mathers fellow knows what he's doing. Although Martin has nothing but high praise for him as a colleague."

Savannah added, "Judging by the nose and chin of Lucille Devereaux, I'd say he's the best."

They finished lunch in an argument over whether or not Lucille Devereaux had ever had any work done. Savannah could not believe her mother, who'd known Lucille since childhood, couldn't see that she plainly had. Helen smiled as she picked up their plates to take to the kitchen. "Maybe I'll get some work done too, if Cason's surgery turns out well."

"What in the world do you need done, Mama?" Savannah said, carrying their glasses in behind her. "A boob lift?"

Her mother put the dishes in the sink and turned on her. "A lift? Well, I never!" she exclaimed and then waved at her daughter. "Git, shoo, you horrid little girl."

Savannah laughed and said, "I'll tell Cason congrats on removing the pain in his ass and then to get out of your hair."

"Okay, but actually be nice to him, Savannah. I think he's taking this surgery hard. He's acting as if he were off to the hangman."

Chapter Thirteen

S tepping into the garage, Savannah closed the door behind her and looked around the shelving unit down the side of her mother's sedan to the front, where Cason had a knee down, back to her.

He tossed a grease-stained rag to the smooth oil-spotted concrete floor. "Almost done, Mrs. S."

Talking with Charlot earlier *had* made an impression on Savannah. An impression that noticed the way his shirt tightened across his back as he crouched. She noticed how his air of masculinity blended with the roughness of the inside of the garage, tallied it all up, and said, *mine.*

Savannah shook her head, pulling her mind off the delusional seductive path it was headed down. "I hear congratulations are in order; Mama says you're removing the pain in your ass."

"Nope. She's still standing right here."

"Ass."

He looked over his shoulder at her. "You got something on your mind, Savannah?" he asked. Savannah heard the bitterness in his tone and had a hard time not reacting. Spending years allowing herself to just react and not think when it came to him meant taking a moment to calm the angry response that got caught in her throat. The moment of adoring his body passed.

When she didn't respond, he picked up the rag again and pulled oil off his fingers as he stood. "I said, you got something on your mind?"

She had to remind herself of what her mother had just said, that he was acting like he was off to the hangman. He was just touchy about the upcoming surgery.

"Yes—"

"Then spit it out."

"Careful, soldier. I come in peace," she said, holding up her hands, but she heard the answering bite in her own words.

He scoffed, and she could see then in the dark circles under his eyes that pain or worry or both continued to rob him of sleep. "I don't want to talk to you, and I need to finish putting your mom's car back together, so how about you take off and we do this dance some other day."

"What the hell is wrong with you, McPherson? I just want to talk to you about your surgery—"

"And I don't want to talk about it."

"Why?" she asked, feeling her old ire creep back in. He was so good at getting her back up.

"Why do you care, Savannah? You never come around here—why start now?" He shook his head like he knew he shouldn't have said it but couldn't help himself. "Sorry—"

Savannah's insides clenched, and blind with hurt, she verbally punched him back. "Listen asshat, I didn't come here to start a damn pity party with you. But now that I think of it, I think that must be what you really want."

He blew out his breath and looked up at the ceiling, a look Savannah knew well as patience gathering. She tried not to feel good about knowing her verbal hit had landed. The next one was going to be a knockout.

"Let's face it, Cason," she said, resting her hip against the front fender, folding her arms. "It's pity you want—or was that not what you were looking for when you were tongue-deep in Charlot's mouth last night?"

His head slowly came down. His combat-green eyes were angrily guarded, but color rose up his neck. "What are you talking about?"

"Charlot and I had a long chat today at the water cooler. Not one I initiated, mind you, but one that went into detail about the pity screw that she nearly gave you last night. I'm surprised, Cason—I thought you were the 'go all the way' kind of man."

CASON FELT his eyes narrow and the flood of emotion that he thought he'd quelled the night before well up in him. Savannah was rising up to him just like the old days. That wasn't what he wanted now. He wanted things to be different, but his head was all ajumble. "Go all the way?" He needed out of that garage, or he was going to do something he'd regret or do something he really, really needed. "Excuse me," he said and took a step to the side to pass her.

She put her hand out. "No, I have more I want to say—"

Control slithered away from him, and he felt the first whispers of fear make him say, "Fuck you, and get out of my way."

Savannah's eyes went satisfyingly dark. "What'd you just say to me?"

Her demeanor charged his like the first licks of the storm charge the air. He let go of control, gave it over to the one person who could take it from him. "I said, fuck you."

She pushed off the car. "You son of a bitch, why I even thought about helping pay for your surgery I don't even know."

That made him feel incompetent, "Wake up, Savannah. If I needed your money, I'd ask. I want nothing from you," he lied, poking her shirt, feeling both satisfaction and a sense of the deep shit he was about to be in as he left a smudge of grease on the billowy white fabric.

She slapped his hand aside, and he lost the last slippery grip he had on his self-control. In a moment he had her up against the garage wall, his one hand at her shoulder, his other pressing against the softness of her midsection, effectively pinning her.

He pushed his face close to her defiant one. "Don't push me, Savannah. I'll not take a dime from you. Ever."

"Why is that, Case? I'm trying to do something nice for you," she hissed into his face. Her hand went to his at her shoulder and the other to his chest. It was the kitchen all over again. Only this time she grabbed a fistful of his shirtfront and twisted.

Feeling her nails dig into his skin and his shirt go taught across his back was the equivalent of pulling back on a bowstring. "You know to not call me Case, and I want nothing from you. So stop."

"What the hell is wrong with you, McPherson? Why would it be better for Ryan's little sis to hate your guts for the rest of your life? That's what you want, isn't it? That's what all of this crap and being an asshole to me is about, right? You can't bear the thought of being soft with me, letting me in, letting me help you."

He hated how easily they read each other; no matter how much he would try to hide it, she'd find him out.

Defeat crept in.

His hand was hot on her abdomen like a branding iron making his mark; she imagined her hand to his shoulder did the same. Something intangible moved then between them, a shift, a change of feeling.

Savannah could feel his breath on her cheek, feel his racing pulse in his palm at her belly. Its rhythm matching hers, beat for beat. He took up the entire garage in front of her, the world satisfactorily blocked out.

"I need you..." he said quietly, his nose nearly brushing hers. "I need you...to hate me. It's the only thing that gets me up in the morning."

His voice hit a chord within her, the quiet way he delivered it. As if he meant to say *love*, not *hate*. Her love was the only thing that got him up in the morning. The line between love and hate was as clear as mud.

Mentally hearing the word *love* made her look at him again. Really look. His green eyes were intense, and his five o'clock shadow made him broody and rough. He was quietly begging her to see the difference.

Savannah watched as his gaze left her own and traveled down to her lips and up again. She felt the hitch in her breath as he began to close the distance—and then he stopped.

Savannah felt her heart pull in her chest as if it were tethered to Cason.

"What are you doing?" he asked, his lips hovering close to hers, his eyes nearly closed.

"I—I—" she started. "I don't know."

"Good," he said and put his lips to hers.

Savannah groaned as a firestorm of emotion raged in release under this new connection and rattled through her love-starved body.

Cason's hand cradled her face as he pulled her off the garage wall and in close against him. She felt his fingertips brush along her jaw while his other at her hip tightened. As their lips spoke against each other, whispering the bodies' secrets, Savannah felt his fingertips dig into her hip. Through those points, he seemed to be allowing his bald need for her to escape, telling her just how much he wanted her. Cason answered her groan with his own as he opened his mouth to hers, deepening the kiss.

Savannah felt it then as she tasted him and he, her. Her senses were full, feeling him, hearing him, smelling his effort in a clean shirt that had found grease, and now tasting him. The blinding sensory play shattered something buried deep within her. An emotional armor-piercing round. It was a simultaneous feeling of freedom and a yearning that had her grip his shirtfront as if it were a lifesaving line in a lifetime of shipwrecks. Just as her knee came up to touch his hip, the door into the garage swung open.

"Savannah? Cason? Is everything all right in here?" Helen called into the garage.

Savannah gasped and pulled back, and Cason fell back against the car. Once again, Helen had impeccable timing. Her arrival was like a dunk in an ice tank.

"Here, Mama," Savannah said, taking point and walking past Cason, letting him recover. "We were having an argument, and I was just leaving."

Helen tsked disapprovingly at her daughter. "I see. Savannah, leave Cason alone. I need his help with my car, and he can't help if you're badgering him."

Savannah put the back of her hand to her just-been-kissed mouth. "Right. Sorry, Mama. I'll get out of your hair now."

"Now, wait just a moment," Helen said, holding a hand out to stop her daughter. She peered past her and the shelving unit to where Cason leaned back against the car. "Cason, are you all right, hon? You look like someone put you through the ringer."

His hands were in his pockets, and he was trying like hell to think of something other than his mouth on Savannah's or her body molded to his. "Yes, ma'am, just fine," he said. He cleared his throat.

"Good." She looked back at her daughter. "Okay, you can—What's that on your chin and your neck? Is that grease?"

"Goodbye, Mama." Savannah pushed past her mother and was gone.

Chapter Fourteen

Savannah pulled into the circular drive of Dr. Mathers's home. A century-old two story, it was stoically held up by the original columns in the front of the home.

Her blood had almost cooled to normal temperature. Her brain was still rattled, though, and she needed a metaphorical splash of cold water to emotionally cool off. She'd been with her fair share of men, but none had so exquisitely set her on fire as Cason had.

"It's just hormones," she said to herself in the rearview mirror. Then: "Get a grip, Sparling."

Taking a deep breath, Savannah checked once more in the mirror. She had gone home to change her shirt, and now she made one last swipe at the place grease had been on her neck before stepping out onto the circular brick drive and making a note to hire a landscaper for the Mathers renovation. The front siding was losing the fight with the ivy and roses clambering up it and into the eaves. It was a hard thing for folks new to New Orleans to grasp—they didn't realize how fast Mother Nature rose up to take back what she deemed was hers.

The thought of Cason's lips on hers swam up, and she stopped halfway to the door. She straightened her skirt and tucked a lock of hair back behind her ear and then continued to the door.

When Mrs. Mathers invited her in, Savannah found the home cool and inviting. The contractor for the project had already arrived, and with him were several subcontractors. Savannah happily immersed herself in the work, and they spent the afternoon measuring and talking about materials and start dates for each phase.

It was well after five when everyone wrapped up. Savannah and Mrs. Mathers sat in the kitchen as they had for their earlier meetings, glasses of iced tea before them.

"Now, I believe we owe Knight Interiors the deposit check still?"

Savannah pulled out her contract, checked, and agreed. As she watched Mrs. Mathers go to the sideboard for her checkbook, Savannah thought about what she'd admitted to Cason about the money.

He'd be furious with her, but the need to do it for him was even stronger.

"Mrs. Mathers?" Savannah said.

"Yes?" she said, looking up as she sat down with a pen and opened the checkbook.

"I have a favor to ask of you. I'm not sure you'll be able to do it, but I hope you can."

A HALF AN HOUR later and a single check heavier, Savannah left the Matherses' home. Their remodel was shaping up to be perfect, as was her personal agenda. Well, it would be, if she could survive the storm.

She was out on the drive when Mrs. Mathers called from the stoop, "Oh, Ms. Sparling?"

Savannah turned—"Yes?"—and slid her sunglasses up.

Mrs. Mathers approached, a damp paper towel in her hand. "I'm so sorry! I noticed it as you were leaving. You've got black smudges on the back of your skirt here. I'm so sorry—some of our construction zone must have rubbed off on you!" she said, handing Savannah the wipe.

Savannah felt her face turn crimson. "Ah, yes. I must have bumped against something." *Or someone, rather,* her mind supplied, and in an instant she was mentally back in Cason's arms and feeling his fingertips on her backside.

Savannah took the paper towel from Mrs. Mathers and thanked her. How had she even missed that spot? Oh, yes. That mouth had made her mind scatter to the four winds, and she was still collecting the pieces.

"Oh, you're just as pretty as a flower. I couldn't bear thinking that we'd be sending you out with our remodel grime on you."

"That's fine, Mrs. Mathers. It happens all the time. I have a spare set of clothes in the car for just this purpose. Please, it's not your fault. We'll see you again soon. Bye now." She smiled and made her escape.

Blushing furiously, she slid into driver's seat and shoved her keys into the ignition and drove to the end of their drive before stopping and turning in her seat. She craned her neck—there on her rump she saw the mark of Cason's hand. Had Mrs. Mathers realized it was fingerprints and graciously stayed silent? Her heart thumped heavily with an odd sense of pleasure. Flipping her AC to max, she drove away. As she did, she voice-texted her next clients to tell them she'd be running even later.

Chapter Fifteen

The operation room was sterile, the equipment ready. The pre-op appointment the day before had gone well, but it had made Cason no less nervous about going under the knife—or laser, as it were. Memories of his first operation, in Germany, kept surfacing. The smells of antiseptic and blood in particular. Now, the anesthesiologist and Dr. Mathers made small talk with him, helping to ease the last few minutes before they put him under.

"We'll proceed just as we discussed in your pre-op. Any questions?"

"No."

"All right. When you wake up, you'll be a new man." From the look of the man's eyes, Cason could tell Dr. Mathers's face crinkled into a smile under his mask.

The anesthesiologist, a woman Dr. Mathers's age, stood over Cason. "Ready?"

At Cason's nod, she placed the mask over his face and asked him to count backward from one hundred.

Cason knew the drill, and instead of numbers, he thought of

Savannah. Thought of her in the garage, remembered the kiss, the real thing, and then let his mind go perfectly blank.

SAVANNAH CALLED her mom that morning to check in. "Mama. How'd it go? Or is he still in surgery?"

"Yes, he is still in..." There was a long pause, and then her mother said, "Come to think of it, I'm glad you called. I can't pick him up at his scheduled time. Would you do that for me?"

Savannah was sitting in her office, looking out over the city center area. "Why? What are you doing?"

There was a pause before she answered, "It's personal."

Savannah raised her eyebrows.

"You'll need to pick him up. Here's the address."

She played along. "Okay. I'll pick him up, but I still have work to do, so he'll have to come back to my place, so I can work from home."

"You can do that here, hon."

"You don't have Wi-Fi."

"What?"

"Internet."

"I do too."

"That's true. What I meant to say is that you don't have an internet connection that moves faster than a dead mouse."

"That might be true, but—"

"You'll need to come pick him up at my place."

Her mother was quiet, thinking, and then said, "Yes, that's fine. Actually, Myrna can help me drop his truck there, so he can leave when he wants to."

"But I thought you had something personal to go do, Mama—"

"I do, and I have to go now. Bye!"

Savannah looked down at her cell. Her mother was up to something—what it was she had no idea.

. . .

At two o'clock, Savannah showed up to Dr. Mathers's office and checked in with the front desk person, a bright and happy woman who was a decade younger than Savannah.

"Hi!"

"Hi," Savannah responded, "I'm here to pick up Cason McPherson and to check on his bill?"

"Yes..." she said, turning to her computer, and after a few clicks she said, "He's just about ready. You can go back and visit with him—is he your husband?"

Savannah tried not to choke. "No, just a friend."

The woman looked at Savannah for a moment and then asked, "Are you Savannah?"

"Yes." Savannah said, relieved that her mother must have called to give them the heads up.

The young girl smiled. "He's been talking about you nonstop since he woke up." She turned back to her monitor. Savannah had a moment of gratitude that the girl wasn't looking at her, because she could feel her cheeks flushing. "As for his account, it's paid in full. I can't give any more details than that without his permission."

"That's all I needed," Savannah said absently, focused on Cason talking about her. "I'll just wait here until he's ready."

"Are you sure? You can head back now. He's only got a few more minutes until he's ready for discharge."

"That's fine," Savannah said and found a chair next to the exit in the waiting room.

It was as the woman had promised—just a few minutes later, Cason emerged. He had a single crutch under his left arm and an immobilizer on his leg. Dr. Mathers was assisting him.

Savannah stood. Cason reached out for her naturally, and she bore his weight as he adjusted his stance next to her. He smelled of sterile linens and antiseptic. Despite the setting, he looked healthy and rugged. He looked as if he'd spent a week in the woods.

"Hey, babe," he said and kissed her cheek before turning to Dr. Mathers as if he'd done that a million times before.

Savannah kept the surprise she felt to herself and maintained a neutral face as Dr. Mathers spoke. "Now, he's got two days where he needs to stay off of his feet. It's just a tiny incision, and if he can keep relatively immobile, it'll heal faster. We were lucky to get him in when we did; the shrapnel hadn't gotten to the bone just yet, and was small enough that our incision was minimal."

Cason smiled at Dr. Mathers and held his fist up for him to bump.

Dr. Mathers laughed and did.

"Now, wait, babe, till you see this."

Savannah raised her brows at this repeated use of the word *babe*.

Cason switched his weight to his other side, leaning on his crutch instead of Savannah, dug into his pocket, and pulled out a small, clear plastic container with a fragment of metal in it.

"This is what was in me," he said rattling it. "It's part of the RPG. Part of the fucking insurgents who fucking killed your brother and failed to get me," he said, his voice slurring at the ends of the words. Cason wavered on his crutch, his mood clearly darkening. Savannah righted him as he continued. "Those motherfuckers failed—"

"Shhhh," Savannah said softly. Millions of questions piled up in her mind like a mountain. It was obvious that whatever boundaries he held in his daily life were in a shambles from the anesthetic.

He looked at her, his eyes glassy, and touched her face. "Okay, babe. I'll be quiet."

Savannah ignored his calling her babe again and just gave him a reassuring smile. She turned to Dr. Mathers. "And what is he on right now?"

"A light painkiller and the residual anesthetic. He may do and say things that he normally wouldn't because the medication does not allow him to suppress his inhibitions. It's a harmless side effect that happens to a few patients. Especially those wound tight or who put themselves under a great amount of stress and self-control." He pulled out a bottle of pills and gave them to Savannah. "One pill every eight hours as needed. You have enough there for a few days.

His pain tolerance is through the roof compared to yours and mine. Tylenol will be fine for managing aches after these run out. As for the rest of his recovery, we'll see him next week for his post-op. In the meantime, if anything comes up, feel free to call me here or at my home—you have those numbers?"

Savannah smiled. "I do, and I know where you live too—and have to congratulate you on selecting the best interior design team in the state."

"That's right! Great, my wife has spoken very highly of you and your team! Well, bring him over if anything happens, but I assure you, as long as he stays immobile for the next few days, he can be back to work next week Monday."

"That's good, babe," Cason said to Savannah. "I've been arranging to take over the ops department at work—that's a pay bump big time, and it'd be nice to work at a desk. With that, you can cut back your hours at work. It'll be good for us." Putting his hand to her abdomen, he rubbed gently as if caressing his unborn child.

"Okay..." Savannah said, grabbing his hand and taking it off her stomach. Then she said to Dr. Mathers, who had a questioning look on his face, "When will this wear off?"

"In just a few hours, he should be back to his old self."

"Good."

"If you don't mind me asking, are you two—"

"No. Definitely not."

"Are we what?" Cason asked.

Savannah's mind flew. "Going for ice cream," she blurted.

"No ice cream?" he asked. "But you love ice cream."

"Goodbye, Dr. Mathers," she said, and they left him standing in the office foyer with a puzzled look on his face.

CASON WAS A TALL, solidly built man who was able to heft concrete chunks into wheelbarrows and who had the finesse to smooth a patio into a polished work of art. On drugs, he was an unwieldy mass of a man, as Savannah found out back at her condo.

She gripped him as he tried to coordinate his stabilized leg and crutch with his stride to her front steps. Then up them. Savannah had him in a bear hug by the time they made it to the top step, for fear that he'd topple backward down the stairs. Cason occasionally tried to push her off him, saying, "I got it, babe. I got it."

She finally got the front door open and him through it. It was another few minutes before she got him to her bed, only after knocking the nightstand lamp to the floor.

Cason fell back onto the bed and smiled up at her. "Made it."

Savannah was breathing heavily at the exertion and looked around her room for a blanket for him. Her dark-wood and eggplant-toned room, before Cason was in it, had seemed masculine with a touch of feminine in the soft lines and glass lamps. But seeing Cason flopped in the middle of her duvet with the large padded headboard behind him, she saw the room as the equivalent of one giant pink ruffle.

"All right," she said, moving toward the chest at the end of her bed. "Let me get you a blanket."

"Nah, I got it, Savi. I'll just get under the covers. I'm beat, feel like I could sleep forever," he said, making his way to a modified seated position at the edge of the bed.

She looked up from the open trunk and started to reach out her hand to stop him from moving any farther but paused when Cason reached behind his head and pulled his shirt off. He wadded it into a ball and tossed it across the room. It landed softly and slid over the polished dark walnut floor, stopping in front of her double-mirrored closet doors. She looked up from the shirt to his reflection, not sure what to say. Using his good leg and pushing himself up off the bed, he stood unsteady, oblivious to her, paused at the end of the bed, and reached for the button on his jeans.

Savannah's breath stopped, and time stood still. She watched the chiseled features of Cason McPherson, a man who was stoned and

living in an alternate reality where he called her babe and god knew
what else, while he took his pants off. On the one hand, she wanted to
leap up and stop him. Stop him from doing what would embarrass
him when he realized later what he'd done. On the other hand, she
wanted to let him continue on his beautiful train wreck of
undressing.

Cason twisted his wrist, yanking open his fly. Underneath his
jeans were body-molding black boxer briefs. The white square top of
his incision bandage was visible. Cason slipped his thumbs under the
waistband, unaware of the fact that he would momentarily be bare-
assed and caught with his pants around his brace.

"Wait," Savannah said. She leaped up and grabbed his wrists.

"What?" he said, confused.

"You—you're still wearing—" She swallowed hard. She was close
enough to Cason's half-naked body that she could feel his radiating
heat. "You're wearing that," she said, pointing to his leg. A strange
thought struck Savannah then. "They didn't suggest that you wear
sweats or something? Doesn't wearing jeans after your operation
hurt?"

"Nah, can't feel a thing."

"Either way, it's probably best that you keep your pants on," she
said breathlessly, hastily reaching for both sides of his button-
down fly.

Cason was looking down at her hands as Savannah pulled the
two sides together. His breath warmed her cheek and fluttered a few
flyaway hairs. Savannah tried to not see the V of Cason's pelvic
muscles or the line of dark hair that started below his navel and drew
her eyes south, or notice how she could now smell the earthy rich-
ness of him. The sterile smell of the hospital had faded with his
effort to reach her bedside while drugged and with an immobilizer
on his leg. Savannah was about to move her fingers down to the
bottom button when she realized that she would not be able to put
the button into its hole without her fingers touching what lay right
behind it.

"Why the hell did you wear jeans?" she asked, letting go of his fly and stepping back.

His face was still down, but his eyes came up and alighted on hers, a slight smirk spreading across his lips. "You're cute when you're flustered."

"I'm not flustered. I'm—" *Cute?*

Cason moved quickly. He cupped the back of her head as his other hand grasped her hip and brought her in against him. "I love you," he said. His thumb brushed over her eyebrow while his other hand continued to hold her tight. Cason very gently put his lips to hers.

Savannah had been struggling to breathe properly since he'd lost his shirt, but at that moment she lost the function completely. Blood flooded her extremities; her hands gently touched his warm skin as his lips softly pressed a sugar-coated promise against her own. Captured in his embrace and deep in the sea of his strange, gentle love for her, Savannah took several seconds to recover after he pulled back. Cason put his forehead to hers and gave her a smile that melted something chillingly deep within her. It was as if at that very moment he believed she had always been his better half, that they'd been together as lovers and soul mates since the beginning of time. Not two people who, when he returned home from war, had become archene-mies vying for the other's blood.

"Cason," she said, knowing that he wasn't in his right mind, "I think that you should just lie down and s-sleep." She was struggling to keep her mind from exploding with the overwhelming moment they were sharing.

"Sounds good. I'm beat," he said—the moment gone—and flopped back onto the bed, wincing.

"Maybe slower is better," she said, going to the trunk and pulling out a thick blanket to lay over him. She leaned forward and arranged the pillows under his head. As she pulled the decorative ones out from underneath him, she froze. His wide hand had come to rest on the back of her thigh, her inner thigh, and moved up under her skirt.

"Thanks, babe," he said, his eyes already closed.

Savannah looked down, confirming what she could feel: his wrist between her thighs, his hand firmly on the back of her leg just under her rear, his thumb stroking the lower curve of her buttock with a familiarity he shouldn't be able to possess. Her heart jackhammered in her chest; she felt like an audience member watching her life as a play.

She finished pulling the pillows out and tucked in the blanket around him. By the time she got the last corner tucked, his hand had loosened and fallen away from her. Savannah went to the nightstand, picked the fallen lamp off the floor, and replaced it on the table.

Looking at Cason, she saw he was sound asleep, his postoperation slumber taking him deep. Savannah moved back to the bed and sat next to him. She studied his face. Cason was like a puzzle in that moment, one whose pieces were scattered, and as she quickly placed them, she began to see a whole separate picture than the one she'd had of him. But as much as the puzzle came together, there were still so many missing pieces.

Why did he call her babe? Why did he pretend for two years that he'd walked away from her brother on the battlefield? The picture he formed, she thought as she gently touched his cheek with her fingertips, was unclear, but it showed that on some level he felt more than friendship toward her. His lips, too, had attested to that, now more than once.

Savannah got up, refusing to be drawn in by the idea that the curve of his lashes and the sharp arch of his brows and the hard lines of his face somehow all looked right in the midst of all her things. Instead, she left him there to sleep. In the other room, she tried to focus on work.

Chapter Sixteen

Savannah greeted the next morning with a sore back. Couch sleeping was for the birds. She stretched and kicked off her blankets, reaching for her phone on the coffee table. Six on the dot. She lay back again and put her arm over her eyes. The day before had been an experience and a half. It would be interesting, she thought, if Cason remembered any of it.

Her mind played the feeling of Cason's lips on hers over and over, the way he'd pulled her to him, touched her, it had been as if he'd always been intimate with her. That ideal butted heads against the Cason she'd known for two years, the man who, up until recently, had played the bad guy in her life so well.

She remembered the night she found his uniform; he told her then that she was too complicated for him. For some reason he needed her contempt, and she knew it stemmed from his time at war. How she factored into his time at war and what his state the day prior meant, she didn't know, but one thing was plain: Cason had feelings for her. Soft, furry, bunny feelings for her.

The alternate reality and where he had gotten the idea that she was carrying his baby—that was going to get solved that morning.

She looked up from the couch toward her room. The door to the bedroom was shut.

Getting up, she headed into the kitchen. As she reached for the refrigerator door, she remembered that the last time she'd shopped was a week ago. She'd been subsisting on coffee and random bites of food from her mother's house since then. Yanking the door open, prepared to do creative work with her lack of goods, she was taken aback. The entire fridge had been cleaned out; all expired food had been replaced with microwaveable and oven-ready casseroles. Someone had stocked her refrigerator with a week's worth of food. Or a few days' worth, for a hungry man. Included in the lot was a coffee cake, prepped and ready for the oven. *Mama.*

As she waited for the oven, taking in the coffee cake on the counter, she had a thought: her mother might have guessed at a change between her and Cason.

She slipped the cake into the oven and set the timer as the first dribbles of aromatically rich coffee fell. As she got down two mugs, she felt a shimmer of something in her belly. A feeling of apprehension or excitement or both, she couldn't tell.

After adding a touch of milk and sugar to her mug, she picked both mugs up and headed toward her bedroom. She paused outside the door and took a deep breath. "Now or never, Sparling," she whispered and then gently pushed the door open.

Streaks of sunlight cast long beams across the polished floor—and the empty bed. Savannah paused at the door, taking it all in. The sheets and duvet had both been tucked under the mattress—regulation military—despite the duvet's fluffy bulk. She looked around the room. Cason's clothes were gone too. She hurried to the other side of the bed to make sure he hadn't made the bed, gotten dressed, and then collapsed on the other side.

He was nowhere to be found. Savannah left the bedroom, set the mugs on the counter, and headed out her front door. Cason's truck, which had been on the street the day before, was gone.

Back inside, she called her mother, who cheerfully answered, "Well, hello, hon—"

"Is Cason there?" Savannah interjected.

"Cason? No, I thought he was with you."

"No. He and his truck are gone. Mama, he was in a weird state yesterday. I'm not sure he was any better when he left."

"Oh," her mother said and then added, "Hold on. I'll check his room—"

"Just look outside—is his truck there?"

"No, hon, it's not. Just keep your britches on."

Savannah took a deep breath. The morning was not going as planned.

"Ah. Oh," she heard her mother say. "He's gone."

"Okay. Where would he have gone to? Does he have a friend he stays with sometimes? We need to check there."

There was a long line of silence on the phone.

"Mama?"

"Yes?"

"You okay?"

"He's gone."

Savannah closed her eyes and tried to calm her nerves. "I know, Mama. I'm trying to figure out where he would have wandered off to."

"No, hon. I mean, none of his things are in your brother's room. Not a single item," Helen said, and Savannah could hear the closet door open. "Nothing. Not even a note." Both Savannah and her mother were quiet, letting it sink in. Then: "I have to g-g-go."

"Mama, he's not dead." Savannah bluntly stated what they were both fearing. There was no reason for him to be dead, but it was a fear they'd live with always, after Ryan. "I'll find him."

Chapter Seventeen

H e stood, looking. There were those trees again. Tall branches laden with weeping moss. Their tendrils sweeping the ground as a ghostly breeze moved them. Then there was the heat. The scorching heat that had nothing to do with the sun but rather the damp air that settled on your skin and seeped into your bones and turned smells into stench. And inside that rat's nest of a trailer, it was Hades's living room.

His back was against a wall. He'd slipped with Savannah, slipped further than he'd ever thought possible, and now he was running from his mistake. There was no way he'd be able to explain in any rational world what he'd said and done.

He had never thought he would ever again stand where he was at that moment. Never thought that rusted-out trailer would see his effects again. But he wanted family then, wished he could have it. Even if it was riding on the broken potential of a sober parent. Or riding on him standing slightly bent in the filthy, sparse living room, staring at a woman he had once called his mother.

She sat at the hobbled kitchen table, a cigarette hanging from her fingers. "Figured you'd be back," she said, her accent thick and gravelly as the salty mud at the edges of the property.

He put his pack down and pulled out the chair opposite her and sat. "I heard you were looking for me."

She gave him a dry look. "Says who?"

"Let's cut the shit, Georgia."

"It's Peaches, but you should be calling me Mama."

"What do you want?"

Georgia took a long drag on the cigarette, the ash quivering as she did. Her thin arm reached out to the pile of mail on the opposite side of the table. It had spilled over at some point to the other chair and the floor, blocking the kitchenette's door behind her.

She flicked the letter to him. It stuck to the tabletop in front of him.

The army insignia in the upper left corner of it told him what was in it.

"Honors, it says."

Cason squinted at her. He wasn't used to this game. If Georgia had been spreading word around town that she was looking for him, it all came down to getting something from him. Always. But this looked like genuine interest. She'd not done that before.

"Don't look at me like that," she said. "I can read. My son's a goddamn hero. Says so right—"

Cason picked up the letter and tore it in half and then in half again. He flicked the pieces onto the table.

She scoffed and leaned back in her chair. "So, you know you're getting a fancy medal."

"I'm not sure when you learned to read, but it doesn't matter what that says—you're not going. You're not invited."

"Oh, it has my name written across the top. It's honoring my blood. Nancy," she said, throwing a thumb toward the trailer next door, "says so, so I'll be going." There it was. She hadn't magically learned to read after all.

"No. What else do you want?"

She arched her eyebrows. "Aww, now, is that any way to talk to your mama? I raised you up to be a hero—I deserve some respect."

Cason felt his insides twist. "Respect? Maybe you can find some at the bottom of a whiskey bottle."

"Fuck you, you little sack of shit," she hissed. "Who do you think raised you? Who changed your goddamn diapers?" He sat through her rant, her well-rehearsed words washing over and past him. She was like an aging Sunday preacher at the pulpit. Hell and damnation, pay penance for your sins, it's your fault hell happened to you, you should have prayed harder. Or as it translated with Georgia, it was her motherly reminder that he was no good, a little *sack of shit*, she should have given him up when his daddy left, he had dragged her down into the crap of a life she had now, she would have been somebody if he'd never been born. He calculated the length of time she had been without money. The dates of the bills on the table and the length of gray growing out on her orange dye job—they all told him she'd run out of money a long time ago. Again.

He took a good long moment to remember, to never forget who she was, and to kill any speck of hope he had had in her being a real mother to him. She would just be the woman who gave birth to him, and through some miracle he had survived her and he wasn't as fucked up as he could be. There was a limit, though, of how much of her he could take, and he reached it quickly.

"Let's get something straight," he interrupted. "I raised myself, and then you, before I left. I kept the lights on in this shit hole and kept you from killing yourself when you were too deep to know a pistol from a toothbrush. You don't dictate anything in my life. That," he said, pointing to the pieces of the invitation, "is my life. You don't go. You don't show up, and you sure as hell don't get a two-minute speech."

She scoffed and took a drag as she looked at her son. "Fine," she said in a puff of smoke and shrugged. "If I was such a shitty mama who taught you nothing about being a hero, I won't go."

Looking into her eyes right then, he refused to believe, even though he had been told, that the gold-flecked green eyes he had were just like hers. He hoped his were never so bloodshot. "Fine?" He wasn't sure she had actually agreed. She wasn't an agreeable sort of person.

"Yeah, what do you want to hear? Yes, sir?" She gave him a mock salute.

Cason watched her, kept eye contact with her. Waiting.

She lazily took another drag and then balanced the long, arching ash all the way down to crush it into the overflowing ashtray. She stood, her cutoff shorts showing her thin legs and the skin that had begun to wilt under the abuse she inflicted on her body. She opened the small fridge and took out some sweet tea and then got a dirty cup from the sink.

"Want some?"

"No."

She poured. The sound of the tea splashing in the plastic filled the space between them. "You know what would be good in this?"

Cason didn't answer.

"Some good ol' sweet Bourbon County whiskey. Been off the sauce a while now, but every now and again, I get a hankering for it, and it'd be mighty fine in this." She lifted the cup to her lips and took a long drink. "Been sober for a couple months now. Feeling saved by the Lord. But if my little boy doesn't know that, that's okay."

"Don't."

She twisted the plastic cup this way and that, looking into it as if it kept a hidden message. "It's all right you come running back to your mama, and you're too embarrassed of me and don't want me to go to a fancy honoring party. I understand. I do. I really do. It makes me sad. And I just want to be honest like I am at the meetings I go to in town. Honesty is good. So, I'm going to be honest now. I think this sadness could lead me back down the path of sin."

"Then let it. We're done here. I don't know what I was thinking coming here." He stood.

"I see you got that bag; you came for a place to stay. You come to mooch off me, and I ain't got nothing, but you won't let me go to—"

"Fuck this. I'm out."

"Wait, you can stay here with your mama." She put down her cup and rounded the short counter. "You pay the bills and get these cupboards all stocked, you can stay a while. But I'm going to that party, says so on that invite."

Cason felt millions of ghostlike fingers reach, clawing at him. They were guilt, the gnawing gut-wrenching fingers of guilt pulling at him, telling him he should care, that he should stay, that she needed him, that she couldn't do it alone. *Just look at her—she* needs *you. She's your mother; you have to.* He knew he'd shown his hand, and now those fingers would pull him under.

"Forget I came."

"Case, Casey—"

"Don't call me that."

She whined, "Okay, fine, but do you want your own mama to go back to drinking?"

There it was.

He grabbed his pack and shouldered it; there was no way he could have stayed there. He'd sleep in his truck until the papers for his house were finalized. He wasn't sure what he'd been thinking.

No, he knew what he'd wanted: to have family. Somewhere to turn when everything went to shit. But it was pipe dream. It was just him. It always had been, and it was looking like it always would be.

"Go back to drinking. Forget to pay your bills. I'm done. I've been done. Don't show up to the ceremony. If you do, I'll have you removed."

"Now, is that any way to talk to your mama?"

"It's been a long time, if ever, that you've acted like my mama."

Her face went more sour. "Fine. Then you'll pay me to not go. Hundred bucks keeps me from showing up. Five hundred and I'll be out of your life forever."

Cason's blood started sizzling. "I'll not give you a dime."

"Then I'll show up and make a real big stink. I hear there's an open bar too."

He wanted to pay her off. He'd done it in the past. Five hundred would buy him a year. But as much as he didn't care if she used it for drink or not, he wouldn't be the one to buy it for her. Enabling her was just as good as pulling the trigger on the pistol she had once hallucinated was a toothbrush.

"You're not welcome there, and I'll see to it that you don't get access. Don't push this. I know you see this as a hot ticket. It's not. It's an honoring ceremony for my men who paid the ultimate price for our country. Show up drunk, and you disrespect them and their sacrifice."

"Fine. Fifty bucks, I won't go."

"No," he said and toed open the rickety door of her trailer.

"Case, I'll go if you don't give me the money. This is a bargain. It's how you bargain."

He was out of the trailer and stepping over rusted lawn chairs and tires to get to his truck when she hollered to him from the steps, "I'll take whatever you have on you!"

He tossed his rucksack into the backseat of his extended cab.

"That's a good deal!" she yelled.

His hand was on the door when he turned to look at her. She'd gone from aloof to begging within thirty minutes. How much of her was in him? How much of his need to be with Savannah, that yearning, was just a hereditary need for a fix? Looking back at her, her thin arms and legs in unwashed clothes, he thought how every dime she had was going into her own personal abuse. He thought of the ancient house that was soon to be his. No, he was fixing things. He wasn't completely broken. Not yet.

Chapter Eighteen

Days passed. Savannah's search was futile. The construction company receptionist said Cason had called in and extended his time off by a week. He wasn't due back to work until the following week, having taken a full two weeks off, above the doctor's recommended one. Now the first had gone by, and well into the second, Savannah kept hunting him. His coworkers weren't saying where he'd gone either. Savannah worked on her projects and in between those tasks stalked the work sites of Cason's construction company in case he came back early.

Savannah stopped by her mother's house with Chinese takeout. She'd been stopping by daily until the last two days, when work had gotten slammed with new clients. The week had been brutal to her personal time, leaving just enough hours to sleep before working again. She had mockups due and final layouts to approve, which made the time pass and allowed her guilt to pile up, unattended, until it was big enough to take advantage of any quiet moment. Savannah could barely take care of herself, let alone a grown man or her mother, who seemed distracted of late. Savannah knew that the honoring ceremony was weighing on her mind, as Ryan's memory was being dragged out of the shadows and Cason had disappeared into them.

"Hi, Mama!" Savannah called as she swung the front door of her mother's place shut. The record player was on, filling the house with the sounds of seventies rock. It had been a long time, as in well before her brother's death, since the house had heard that old machine.

Savannah put the food down on the table and dropped her bags on the couch as she went to the player. She turned the sound down and hollered again. "Mama?"

The thought that Dr. Lowe could be over passed through her mind, and Savannah quickly decided to grab her bag and leave. Just then her mother came out of her brother's old room, a handkerchief tied about her head and cleaning gloves on her hands.

"Oh, hi! Look what the cat dragged in!" she said, a happy grin on her face.

Savannah was confused. "Hi, Mama, I brought dinner. What are you doing?" She noticed then the boxes in the hall and the bag of trash outside his room. "Did Cason leave a mess?"

Helen looked over her shoulder and then back at Savannah. "No, hon, I'm cleaning out your brother's old room. I think it's about time."

Savannah felt the shock rupture through her, all the way down to her toes. "No."

Helen tilted her head. "Yes, hon. We've lived with his death looming over us for ages. We've not let go."

"No, Mama, he's..." She tried to find the words for the hollow feeling that had taken up residence in her heart suddenly. No, it had always been there. "That's *his* room."

"He's not coming back," Helen said gently.

"I know that," Savannah snapped. "It's just that you didn't say anything. Are you throwing away all his things?"

Helen gestured behind her. "I realized, Savannah, that when Cason left, it felt like Ryan had died all over again. We haven't had closure with his death. I've kept this room as a shrine, hon, and when

Cason moved in, I allowed myself to...I'm not sure, become his mother?"

Her words were muffled—the ringing of panic in Savannah's ears was too loud. "Are you throwing his things out, Mama?" she said again; like a magnet to steel, Savannah was blindly drawn to the boxes and bags in the hall.

"Honey, it's just—" Helen said, reaching for her daughter.

Savannah knocked her hands aside, her panic making her breath come short, and she fell to her knees at the sight of her brother's things.

In the darkened hall, Savannah tore dusty paper towels and scrap paper from the bags. Her hands shook as the world she'd carefully protected herself from came crashing down upon her.

Ryan was gone.

"Hon," she heard from somewhere far away, as if she'd been dunked into the Earth's core and just a single tunnel connected her with the life above.

Old receipts from the last time he'd been home, a childhood sticker collection that had been scribbled on, and scraps of notes she couldn't understand. But to Savannah they were all precious; none could be gotten rid of. Her mother had been its guardian, and now she was burning down the House of Ryan.

"No..." she said. Her world had started in that room; she'd follow Ryan into it, the adoring little sister; it was fitting, then, that it should end there. "These are pieces of him—you can't get rid of him," Savannah said, snatching items out of the garbage. She gathered them into her lap until she couldn't see them through the mist of her tears.

She felt her mother's hand on her shoulder. "I know, sweetheart." She felt her kneel down next to her. "I know."

It was all she needed to hear. After all the years of stepping back, that simple action of hearing that her mother knew broke her. No one knew better than her own mother how she felt.

Savannah let herself cry, let herself feel the pain of Ryan's loss once more, this time on the heels of Cason's absence. She allowed it to rip forward from her subconscious into reality. She had thought it was her mother who lived as if Ryan would walk back into the house after all these years, but it was her too. She let her grief rise up to the surface, and she faced it. Her mother's arms were lovingly tight about her as they both cried for Ryan. For Savannah, it was truly the first time.

THE SMELL of garlic woke Savannah sometime in the middle of the night. She was curled up on Ryan's bed, his pillow clutched in her hands. Letting go, she smoothed out the fabric and felt a lightness in her chest, as if she'd cleared something physically from her body. Eyes swollen, she padded to the bathroom and splashed water on her face. Keeping the light off, she looked in the mirror at the woman in front of her. She was a solid presence, one that had shed years of a haunting memory.

Walking down the hall, Savannah let the water cool her face as it air-dried. In the kitchen, she found Helen microwaving the Chinese food. She turned when she heard Savannah emerge from the hallway. "Oh, hi, hon. Feeling better?"

"Lots," she said and pulled a chair out to sit and watch her mother through the kitchen pass-through. "You?"

Helen nodded as she stirred a box of takeout noodles. "Yes, feels like I just did a spring cleaning on my insides."

Savannah nodded.

"Chinese food was a good idea, dear."

She rested her head on the pass-through counter and looked up at her. "Yeah, seemed like a great idea at the time." Then she looked down at her hands. Then she looked all around her. It was as if she were seeing the entire house and everything in it, including herself, anew. The couches seemed quaint; the pictures on the wall, including the ones of Ryan, seemed fresh. Savannah got up to look closely at a picture of her mother, her brother, and her, taken in the eighties. Her brother sported a yellow polo with a blue popped collar.

His and their mother's hair were styled big. The tightly rolled cuffs on Ryan's pants were the only outward sign of his rebellion against their mother's choice for his outfit. Helen wore a purple dress with boxy shoulder pads, and little Savannah was stuffed into a pink jumper and white Mary Janes.

"I remember he hated those pants—"

"'It's got pleats, Ma!'" her mother mimicked and then laughed.

Savannah smiled and turned to look at her mother. "Exactly...*pleats!*" Savannah looked back at the picture. "I hadn't really realized, but we all were fashionably questionable in this picture."

"No, you two were perfect. And exactly fashionable. Now, come grab a plate and serve yourself. I have some of his army letters I want to show you."

"Oh yeah," Savannah said, remembering that her mother had more than once tried to show them to her.

Her mother got situated in the living room with her plate of steaming noodles and greasy, crunchy citrus chicken and started taking the lids off of old shoeboxes. Inside were neat rows of opened envelopes.

"Do you think that this is what normal people do after a breakdown? Do they eat Chinese and go through their loved one's letters in the middle of the night?" Helen mused.

"If not, they should."

The letters were filed into three shoeboxes, and Savannah chose the one closest to her. Around a bite of egg roll, she asked, "Are these in any order?" The letters in her box looked much less organized than the ones in the other boxes.

"Order?" her mother asked, looking up, a letter in hand. "Look here. This one is from his first deployment to Iraq. He said it was 'hotter than sh—.' Well, now, he did have a foul mouth."

"Especially after boot camp. I thought I'd heard it all, but when he came home, it was as if he were speaking a foreign language. My favorite was when he'd yell at drivers who didn't use their turn signals that they were a bunch of pig fu—"

"Savannah."

"Yes?"

"I remember quite clearly what he said."

Savannah smiled at her mother's disapproving frown. "Those were good times."

Her mother hid her smile and went back to the letter. "Other than—"

"Wait, did you say that these are in order?"

"They should be chronological."

"Oh," Savannah said, looking down into her box. "These all seem to be mixed together." Each letter had a divot in the top and bottom as if it had been bound with twine. She pulled one from the top of the pile. Unfolding it, she didn't recognize the handwriting as Ryan's. "Whose..." she started and then stopped. She recognized this person's penmanship. His calendar was filled with the tight text, but why would he be writing to her mother? Her gaze went to the top; he wasn't. The letter was addressed to Savannah. Cason was writing to *her*.

Confused, Savannah turned the letter box over so that its contents fell in a gush all over the couch.

"Savannah!"

She ignored her mother's admonishment and found another letter addressed to her and another. They had not been posted to her mother's house or to any residence that she'd ever had but instead to an apartment in town. The last apartment Cason had had before being deployed with her brother, as if she'd lived there with him.

Savannah looked up wild-eyed at her mother. "How long have you had these?"

Helen's eyebrows drew together in confusion. "Since he mailed them to me. Must have been years, Savannah; you know that—"

"No," Savannah said, holding up a letter. "*These.*"

Helen leaned forward and squinted. "That has your name on it, but why? And that's not Ryan's handwriting. That's Cason's," she said, confused, and then put the letter she'd been holding down and held her hand out. Savannah kept scanning the envelope. "Hand it over—let me see what this is all about."

Savannah's eyes flew over the tight black lettering that Cason had written...to her. "No," Savannah said as her eyes absorbed his words. They were personal and familiar; they spoke to her as if she were more than just friends with him, as if they were intimately familiar with each other. As soon as she finished one, she picked up another and read. He told her everything: described his time in Afghanistan and the dry, hot weather, and interwoven with his reality was his relationship with her. The letters were a blend of fact and fantasy.

At her third letter in, Savannah looked up at her mother. "You didn't know about these?"

"No. Now, what does he say in them?"

Savannah shook her head and swallowed hard. She knew in earnest then that these had been the letters from Cason's trunk. "I—I don't think I should share these with you. Where did you find them?"

"What do you mean you shouldn't share them with me? What do they say?" Helen said, holding her hand out. "Pass me one of them, Savannah Rae."

"Where did you find these?" Savannah pressed.

"In with your brother's letters. Now, what do they say?"

Savannah looked down at the letters on the couch. She sifted them again, and there was one with a deep crimson corner, nearly purple in color. She cracked it open, the blood-stained corner sticking. In it was a hastily written letter to her that was cut off halfway through. He spoke of Ryan's squad joining up with them and a skirmish that morning that made him want to be home with her more than ever.

Savannah realized then that if this letter was in the pocket of his uniform and not in with his effects, he would have gone to very long lengths to get the uniform back.

She looked down again at all the letters. Letters Cason had

written to her, with letter after letter bearing the same information: the conditions he was in, the nonclassified details of his missions, and wildly, a relationship with her that he had begun to live in at least part of his mind. The anesthetic and pain meds the week before had broken down his barriers and let out his true feelings. As well as a world that he'd successfully hidden until then.

She looked over at her mother. How did she explain their content? "They have personal feelings that I think he might want to keep...that he might want..." she said. "I think that these are for my eyes only."

"Well, then, why did he stick them in with your brother's letters?"

Savannah shook her head. "I assume that he thought we'd not go in there for another decade. By then—"

"We might have forgotten about him," her mother finished.

"Exactly."

Savannah successfully kept her mother from reading any of the letters from Cason for the rest of the night. She locked them in her car and then came back and read through Ryan's field correspondence. Some were emails her mother had printed out; others were old-fashioned airmail.

"Do you know, I think this one would be good to bring with us to the honoring ceremony," Helen said, handing her daughter a copy of an email her brother had sent to her.

Helen took off her spectacles as Savannah read it to herself. "Yeah, it kind of sums up his time there. He seems happy too," she said when she'd finished and handed it back. "But do they have an area where you'll be able to display it?"

"No, I've been asked to share a two-minute talk about Ryan at the event. I think all families have been asked that."

Savannah nodded. "Then it's perfect. It's like Ryan wrote your speech for you. Now all you have to do is figure out what to wear," she said, smiling, and then picked up their plates and headed to the kitchen.

"You know, I still have that purple dress from that photo. Maybe I'll wear—"

"No way, Mama!"

"Oh, come on, maybe a little perm too, to give my hair some boost."

Savannah started laughing at the thought. "Only if you get gold nail polish and wear matching eye shadow."

Savannah heard her mother giggle. "And you? What will you wear? Something to make Cason McPherson forget all his troubles?" Then her mother muttered, "Because he'd better reappear in time for this ceremony."

Savannah nearly dropped the plates in the sink. "What? Why? What?"

"Oh, dear, I might be old, but I'm not blind. You two are sweet on each other. I was hoping some time together after his operation would help, but since that didn't, maybe this gala will push you both in the right direction."

Savannah came around the edge of the counter and stared at her mother. "I—well—I don't see how."

"Sure, dear," Helen said. She hid a yawn and said, "Well, I'm beat. I'm headed to bed. I'll see you in the morning."

"Yeah," Savannah said, still shocked that her mother thought she should wear something scandalous for Cason. "See you in the morning."

Chapter Nineteen

I n the attic, Cason went to the rack of clothes against the exposed eaves. He had been sleeping in the top part of his new house for the past two nights. He shoved the few clothes he had hanging next to the garment bag away and then turned the hanger so that the bag's zipper faced him. He touched the waterproof plastic that the cleaned and pressed uniform hung in. Slowly he bent down, and crouching, he grasped the zipper and slowly brought it up, opening the bag to the dark-blue contents it held.

He pushed the shoulders of the garment bag back to unveil his army dress pants and jacket with his cap; Cason inspected the contents. The shoes were tucked at the bottom, their mirrored finish having gone dull from sitting.

Cason blew out a breath. The last time he'd put the thing on was Ryan's funeral. The ache in his hip returned. It should have been him in that casket that day; he had no one to miss him. His mother would certainly have enjoyed his death much more than his life because of the check she would have received from it.

He touched the buttons and adjusted the bars on the suit coat's left breast. It was from another lifetime, it felt like. A whole other world that he'd stepped out of and was about to step back into. His palms began to sweat. Internally, he grimaced and then prayed she'd be absent from the gala that night. But knowing Savannah Sparling, she'd be there, and she'd hunt him down. She'd want answers. Answers he still wasn't ready to give. He wasn't sure he'd ever be able to give them.

He tucked the uniform back into the garment bag and slung it over his arm and headed down the stairs two at a time. The drive to the country club, where the ceremony was being held, was short, and it was also familiar; the road was on the other side of the swamp from the trailer he'd grown up in. The club had worked gardens and paved paths into the muck, allowing the wealthy of New Orleans a delicate way to interact with the old moss-covered oaks of the area. An area he had frequented as a kid. He was stepping back into more than one world.

The rest of the way there he tried to clear his mind. No matter how painful the memories would be it wouldn't change the course of his life. That had already been done.

He could do this.

AT THE CLUB, one of the event coordinators greeted him and escorted him to the rearmost building. Built sometime in the mid–eighteen hundreds, the building was a three-story brick mansion with a swooping brick balcony wrapped around the main floor; wrought-iron patios jutted from the upper floors. The entrance was a double oak door with wide brick steps that he followed the coordinator up. Into the cool air of the mansion she guided him up a series of inner stairs and then down a palatial hallway to a segment of rooms in the west wing. The wing was designated for the soldiers and their families to get ready in. He was early, and no one else was there. The room the coordinator showed him to smelled of oak and lemon wood polish. It was expansive, with tall ceilings, plush rugs over polished hardwoods, and delicate-looking tables and chairs. A table and long mirror had been set up for Cason; there was water and a copy of the event program. After hanging his things, he went to the wide windows and looked out over the lawn, gardens, and oak grove that skirted the grounds. No one was out there save the event staff completing last-minute tasks.

He returned to the garment bag. His hand rested a moment on the zipper. He thought again to donning his uniform for Ryan's funeral. His leg had been on fire during recovery from his first surgery, and Mrs. S. had looked like she might keel right into the grave after Ryan was lowered in. Then there was Savi...She'd been stoic. Like a beautiful rock statue whose eyes were death lasers pointed straight at him. He had wanted her his whole life, but his need to honor Ryan's last wish was stronger. He'd wavered the last few days, the freshness of Ryan's death—he didn't think it could diminish over time—but was corrected as he held his hand to his garment bag zipper. The pain had been much worse then.

Diving in, he unzipped it and stepped back in time and let himself be reminded of all of it. Cason removed his boots and set to polishing them to a mirror shine once more. It'd be that, then shave. If he took his time, he could stall until it was time to go downstairs. Avoiding everyone, someone, Savannah, altogether.

Chapter Twenty

Cason slipped the last gold button into the top jacket hole and looked up. There, looking back at him, was Sergeant McPherson of the Second Platoon, Battle Company, 173rd Airborne Brigade. He felt a shiver of apprehension sliver down his spine. His dark place was seeping out.

He closed his eyes and took a deep breath.

Where am I? Home.

Where is hell? There, not here.

He opened his eyes and picked up his civilian clothes and hung them in his garment bag. Back at the large windows, he looked out over the grounds again, back and down to the main clubhouse. The sun had started waning in the sky when he arrived, and now it had become dusk, with the ceremony starting in the next hour. The grounds in front of the mansion had been strung with small lights, and they flicked on, illuminating the garden path from the clubhouse up to the mansion. The traffic to the mansion had increased, and now families he recognized from Ryan's funeral were mingling, drinks in hand.

There was a knock on his door, and the voice of the coordinator came through: "Mr. McPherson?"

SAVANNAH ARRIVED at the country club and stepped out into the back lawns, where a New Orleans jazz quartet played on the balcony. She wasn't sure she'd stay the whole event. She loved that Ryan was being honored but hated living in the past. As Savannah looked for her mother, a warm breeze moved the humid air and picked up across the expansive gardens, bringing with it the evening scent of jasmine and freshly turned soil.

Savannah was glad she'd decided to take her mother's advice and wear a gala-appropriate dress, and even more so that she had decided to unlock her opera diamonds. She secretly loved the way they created miniature flames when the light hit the cuff, the cascade of them from her ears, and the solitaire nestled at the base of her neck.

She scanned the crowd and spotted clients and a few of her mother's friends from her social circle. The Devereaux and Ms. Myrna were in the distance, all dressed to the nines. Ms. Myrna was in an icy-turquoise tunic with frosty-white leggings and matching earrings and eye shadow that complemented her dark summer tan. She had found, unsurprisingly, a strapping young man in the crowd and had her hand on his upper arm. Savannah avoided the Devereaux, looking instead for her mother, as Miles the pocket pooch had made an appearance.

Holding her clutch in one hand, Savannah took a glass of champagne from a passing server with the other. The immaculate lawns and sprawling gardens had been decorated with lights. Surveying the crowd, Savannah spotted her mother and her date, Martin. She smiled when she caught their eyes and worked her way toward them.

"Hello!" her mother and Martin said in unison before each embraced her.

"Hi, you two look sharp," Savannah said. Her mother's dress was a maroon top with a matching knee-length skirt of lace over satin. Modest pumps and a bit of mascara and she looked fancier than Savannah had seen her in decades. "That's a great dress, Mama, and Dr. Lowe, I like how your tie matches."

"Thank you, Savannah. You yourself are looking quite fashionable this evening." He smiled warmly behind his wire-rim glasses, his suit looking freshly pressed. There was a maroon orchid at his lapel.

"Oh!" Helen said and dug into her purse, pulling out a folded green ribbon. Savannah noticed Dr. Lowe and her mother wore the same ribbon. "Only the immediate families of the honored have them. Ryan's color is green, and here's yours."

Savannah took it and looked down at her strapless currant-colored silk dress.

"Right," her mother said, "I'm not sure where you'll put that..."

Savannah smiled and sacrificed the folded top edge of her gown. "I'll put it here," she said as she finished pinning, "over my heart."

"This is quite the affair," Dr. Lowe leaned in to say. "It is very nice that your brother and his comrades are being honored this way."

Helen beamed and Savannah said, "Thank you, I think we both agree. Huh, Mama?"

"Yes. It's quite nice." She looked at Savannah. "I haven't seen Cason. Have you?"

Savannah scanned the crowd again. "No, I haven't either. Though I haven't seen much of his or Ryan's units out here. Just the families. Don't worry, he'll be here, and I'm sure he's been fine." She knew it was senseless to tell her mother not to worry.

"I'll worry if I want to. I haven't seen him either, but I heard from Myrna that he is alive and well. She talked with one of the men he works with. Apparently he's lying low, making sure his hip heals. She said the day of his surgery he had an accident that set him back."

Savannah felt her cheeks flush. Oh, he had an accident all right, an emotional equivalent of a ten-car pileup.

Helen continued, "Myrna also said that they've got a place in upper west wing where they are getting ready. They'll stay there until the ceremony begins. It's all highly organized."

"Up in the west wing?" Savannah said, looking at the mansion behind her mother.

"Yes but—Savannah!"

"I'll be right back," she said over her shoulder. She had some emotional rescuing to do.

Chapter Twenty-One

Cason checked the creases in his uniform as he answered the knock. "Come in."

The coordinator poked her head in. "You have family here to see you. May they come in?"

He felt his brow crease and was about to say no when he heard her.

"If you ask him, he'll say no. Thank you for showing me here."

Cason's gut twisted pleasantly as Savannah, smiling at the coordinator, stepped into the room. She thanked the coordinator and, closing the door behind her, leaned back against it. She was wearing red. Deep bloodred. Her lips matched her dress and a ribbon for Ryan was over her left breast. He felt her eyes take him in as well.

"Found you."

"I wasn't hiding."

"Really? I—"

"I don't want to talk about it," he said. He heard the finality in his own words.

"It?" she repeated. "The whole 'after your surgery' part, not the part where we made out in my mother's garage, right? So, let's chat about that kiss we had. It's been a few weeks since then, but I've hardly thought about much since. Actually, no, that's a lie. I thought about finding you. A lot."

"I don't want to talk about that either. Goodbye," he said with less conviction than he had anticipated as his palms became damp.

She stayed against the door as she nodded. Her rod-straight dark-brown bob swayed a little, a piece of it coming out of place. He fought the urge to move across the room and tuck it back. He just wanted to get near the skin at her neck. The skin at her shoulders. The rounded skin above her dress's bustline. Her entire dress seemed to cascade and ripple against her body, leaving nothing to the imagination.

Despite what he said to her, he did want to talk with her. He wanted to know what she thought about the things he said and did with her. Did she think he was crazy? He had scared the shit out of himself—why wasn't she running from him? But he couldn't ask; the questions were all wedged between the fear of opening that Pandora's box and the curiosity about opening that Pandora's box.

She ignored his response anyway, pushed off the door, and walked into the room and over to a small table under the windows. She had the look on her face that said she had a million questions and would systematically get through each one and soon. She absently picked up the small porcelain vase that sat there and placed it back, turning it. Then, as if it weren't quite right, turned it again. She looked up and out the window and broke the silence. "Know what I think?"

"No, and I don't want to talk—"

"I think you're sweet on me, as my mama said."

Cason tried to keep the surprise off his face, despite the fact that her back was still to him. He felt the corner of the Pandora's box lift.

She continued, "I get that coming to this realization only now, after all that has happened, makes me seem not so clever. However, I just wanted you to know that I've discovered your secret: you like me as more than just a friend."

. . .

HE WASN'T TELLING her to get out; he wasn't saying anything. Savannah kept her gaze out the window so as to not spook him now that she had his tenuous attention. Her insides were in knots; it had been weeks since she'd seen him, and now he was there, all tangible and crisp in his uniform. The damn thing was making her knees weak and her clear plan go blurry. "It seems like I should have known after the garage kiss, but I was too self-absorbed. It was new for me not to be able to think or breathe after being kissed. No, it's true," she argued as if Cason had spoken. "No one has made me so completely dimwitted as your kiss did. And before that, you showed up at the Nigel project. At the time, I completely bought your story of hearing it on the police scanner—but really? If I was just a friend, you probably would have called later. Or just asked about it when we saw each other next."

He sighed. "Why are you really here?"

"This is why I'm really here. That and the thing you don't want to talk about."

"I'm nuts. There. Now you should go."

"You're not nuts, but I think—"

She saw him shake his head from out the corner of her eye. "No, no. I don't want to talk about it. You standing there is making my mind go—" He made a sound like television snow and shook his fingertips over his forehead.

Her heart thumped heavily in her chest. *Oh, yes.* This was the right thing. Savannah turned and slid her eyes over to him. "My standing here is causing what?"

"I can't think; you should go."

Savannah leaned back against the windowsill as a pleasant, warm blooming sensation expanded in her chest. "Good, because I had a ridiculously long list of things that I wanted to ask you, and now that I'm here, now that I'm looking at you, looking mighty powerful in all that deep dark blue, I can't remember a single thing I was going to talk with you about."

He held her gaze, as if weighing heavy options.

Savannah pressed on. "And to address your concern, if I really thought you were nuts," she said, "this conversation would be a very different one. I think that you had a moment of truth that scared the crap out of you. That's not nuts—that's called an epiphany. I think, though, that the two things might feel the same." She hurried on while she still had him. "And it didn't scare me, Cason. It made me think that I might like whatever that was that happened to be a reality. It also made me think that this isn't a new thing. I think you've been sweet on me for a long time. Like an illegally long time."

Savannah felt a jubilant victory when Cason smiled. "Illegally long time?" he asked, then apparently got what she was eluding to, because his eyebrows rose, and he said, "Ah."

"It was the time you stuck your hand up my skirt 'accidentally' in high school when helping me down out of the back of Ryan's pickup that gave it away. Don't worry, I liked it," she said and risked an answering smile. Savannah drank him in: his midnight-blue uniform, the rigid gold stripes that ran down the outer edges of his pants legs, disappearing into the tops of his dress boots. The colors, stripes, and bars on his left breast, the gold *V*s on his shoulders, and the medals, commendations, and overseas combat awards made him larger than life. He'd gotten a haircut recently, making him regulation. And looking like an army deity. An army deity that was so utterly human with her, a man who had let her see him so intimately, and yet she had only just realized that she was his weakness. A weakness that he went to long lengths to protect himself from. The why of it still begged to be answered like an itch to be scratched.

"I confess," he started, clasping his hands in front "that my hand up your skirt was not an accident. I think I was deliberately checking for something."

Savannah went with his diversion. "What on earth could you possibly have been checking for back then?"

"Did you just ask what on earth a high school boy could be

checking for up a girl's skirt? You do seem a little less clever than usual."

She gave him a narrow-eyed look, and the corner of his mouth hinted at a smile. "I mean, my skirt was already pretty short."

"Underwear. Kind, color, and coverage. At least two of those markers."

Savannah looked up at the ceiling and then back at him, trying to keep her face as straight as his. "You and Ryan made that up—I always wondered what you two meant by KCC."

He was quiet, his countenance changing back to somber. "I miss him," Cason said then, and the plain admission surprised her.

Savannah nodded. "I do too."

Cason seemed resigned to something then. "You're going to hear about what happened that day in a few minutes. Specifically, what I did."

Savannah nodded. "You *are* the Patriotic Medal of Honor recipient and all."

He shook his head. "I don't like it. I'm not the only one who got us out alive. And I didn't pay the ultimate price."

Savannah folded her arms about her middle, cupping her elbows, and said, "I think I'm ready to hear it."

Cason blew out a breath and took her back to the arid mountains of Afghanistan.

Cason was vivid in his recounting. It was the explanation that she'd wanted two years ago, but in the clarity of time she realized not only would she not have been able to hear it back then but Cason hadn't been able to tell it. Now, though, she had to dab away the tears as the heartbreak of Ryan's death resurfaced.

Cason had held him in the end, had picked him up and put him into the Humvee, then floored it descending the goat trail back down the mountain. The men in his vehicle had suffered casualties; the vehicle that descended after them lost two more, bringing the death toll to nine. Half of their men were lost.

His eyes were on the floor, his knuckles white. He left no detail out, and when he was done, she felt as exhausted as he looked. It felt clearing and heavy. The heavy burden of knowledge had been shared.

The silence that sat comfortably in the room once he finished speaking allowed Savannah to mull over the events and settle on one point. An odd point that made her wonder why, through the violence of the event, that that one detail stuck out to her. She wasn't sure non–spatially adept people would recognize it as significant. But someone must have—someone in the honoring committee or the men in his crew. Cason had driven the men to safety without turning the hippo of a Humvee over on that alpine goat trail. He'd descended the mountain, he said, at full speed.

"I don't remember much after that," Cason finished.

Savannah blinked, opened her mouth, and then closed it. "Did you just say that you drove a vehicle the size of Texas down a goat hill at full speed, backward, while taking fire?"

He swallowed. "Anyone would have done the same in my position."

"No, I...I don't think just anyone would or could. You saved how many men? No, I think you were specifically made for that task, in that moment, and you did it, against unbelievable odds."

"You don't think of the odds when you've got your best friend bleeding to death, and all you can think of is *Faster, or he's gonna die. Drive faster.*" He shook his head. "And I wasn't fast enough, Savi. I'm so sorry. I wasn't fast enough."

Savannah's voice was soft, working around the lump in her throat. "You know as well as I do that he was shot in the neck. He wasn't alive when you put him in the Humvee."

Cason shook his head. "Savannah, what I don't get is, why him? Why not me? Just one step over, and it would have hit me in the chest. I was wearing my vest. He's got you and your mom. Me? I've got shit. Why not me?"

Savannah nodded. She knew that question well. "We weren't friends after you came back, and honestly, I asked that very same

question a lot over the last two years, and I know the answer is that
we don't get to know. You're alive. Ryan's not. Asking why will just
drown you. I've only just figured that out. Mama and I shared a
crying jag to beat all crying jags when we cleaned out his room.
That's when it really hit home for me."

"You cleaned out his room?" he asked quietly.

"Yes, she's going to turn it into a craft room or some such. We
kept a few boxes of his things. You should come by and go through
them, see if there's something you'd like to remember him by, as he
was."

"I...I don't know if I should."

"You should. I know Mama would love you to. If you can't, I get
that too, but the offer will always be there for you. Speaking of homes,
where are you living now, soldier?"

He took a moment to answer. When he did, he was smiling. "You
should consider a career as an investigator."

Savannah gave him an answering smile—she knew catching him
off guard was playing a little dirty, but she had a feeling that after
today she might not see him again if she didn't know where he lived.
And the ceremony was starting in less than an hour. "Questions come
as a package deal with the female DNA."

"Alexander from work kept telling me you were stopping by.
How'd you know where the crew was every day?"

"Me? Oh, I didn't." Savannah nudged the vase again in a fidget
before looking up at him. "Myrna, however, knows the exact location
of every Miner Concrete truck ever put into service. I tell you, she
doesn't miss much. Except your new location. I was a few days away
from putting out a BOLO on your truck. I figured I'd try to find you
here first before lying and telling our friend Sheriff Lee that you'd
robbed me blind."

"He might not believe you."

"I can be pretty convincing. But I'd have a higher success rate
with my actual goal if you'd tell me outright. Like, where do you
live, McPherson?" There was indeed something between them;

he'd all but confirmed it earlier. Why he was holding back on her was just another question, which just made her that much more curious.

"That's my private business."

"You know, McPherson, at some point I'll find out and probably sooner rather than later, since now I want to know why you're hiding your new place from me."

"That's not what I'm hiding."

"I see," she said and sat back, resting on the edge of the sideboard next to the vase, bracing herself with her hands on either side. Something made him take a deep breath and focus on her face.

Curious, she said, "You okay?"

"Don't do that," he said.

"Do what? Ask where you live?"

"No, I mean, what you're doing."

"I'm sitting," she said, looking down and then back up at him. "The table won't break. These tables are reproductions, not actual Civil War heirlooms."

He shook his head. "No."

"Seriously. Not to mention, four-inch heels are hard to just stand around in. I'm giving my feet a break."

"You're distracting."

Savannah felt her eyebrow rise. "By sitting here?"

"No, by...I can see..." He raised both of his eyebrows and made a pointed glance down to her cleavage.

"Ah..." Savannah felt an odd sensation of satisfaction and embarrassment creep color into her cheeks. She slowly straightened up, a slight tug at her rib reminding her that it could hurt again if she wasn't careful. "That wasn't on purpose, I assure you."

Taking a deep breath and checking the length of his cuffs, keeping his eyes averted, he said, "I wasn't sure how much longer I could be a gentleman."

Savannah opened her mouth to respond and then closed it, feeling a smile bloom at the corners of her lips. "You know, if you asked like a gentleman, I'd let you take a good long look at them in this dress."

His eyes still on his cuffs, his face illuminated in a rare, beautiful smile that poured joy like sweet molten honey down through her core.

"I've gotten a good peripheral look."

"There you are, using those sexy big words again. Jesus, Cason. Stop coming on to me. I think it might be illegal for me to do the things I'm thinking of while you're in your dress blues."

He laughed then and laid the full gaze of his penetrating green eyes on hers, and there she saw it, the *yes* in them, the enticement to do exactly what she was thinking. He was thinking of letting her do just what she wanted.

She took a step toward him. "Seems like you might need a hug."

"Something tells me a hug is your cover story."

"It might be. But I'm sticking to it."

She took another step toward him, coming within arm's reach, and noted his eyes on her mouth, and the way her own heart felt like she was in the midst of a marathon.

"I like to start slow, just a hug," she said and moistened her lips.

"You shouldn't do that," he said, his breath catching.

"I can't win with you. Or should I say, lose? Because I'm thinking that we might be on the right track for a win-win situation."

"Not in my uniform."

"Agreed. How fast can you get it off and back on?"

"What are you doing to me?"

"I'm not sure. It feels like you're doing it all to me."

He wiped a hand over his face. "I can't do this."

The line between them snapped. Everything had seemed so right too. Confusion swirled—it wasn't just the uniform. It felt like another stiff arm from him. Frustration surfaced. "Right," Savannah said and nodded. "What exactly are we doing?"

"We're doing nothing." He blew out a breath he seemed to be holding. "I made a promise. I can't—"

There was a knock at the door, and Helen stepped into the room.

"A promise?" Savannah asked, then stepped to Cason's side, feeling reality crash back in around them. "Mama, get out."

Cason cleared his throat and turned around, a small smile on his face.

Savannah felt the moment blow away in the breeze and tried to not let her frustration show.

"Hi, you two." Helen said, ignoring her daughter, "Just checking in—Oh, now, Cason, aren't you handsome? I'm so happy to see you. I was worried, but oh my, just look at you." She stopped and took him in. "Well, I never..."

"Mama, we'll be right out—"

"I've come to rescue Cason. The event coordinators are looking for him, and they're starting to call people to their seats. Savannah?" she said, beckoning for her daughter to come with her.

Cason said, "Thank you, ma'am—"

"We'll be right down," Savannah said tersely, clearly annoyed by what seemed like endless interruptions by her mother.

"No, now, hon. People are waiting, Savannah. Let's go get our seats. It'll be embarrassing if we're late to our seats and keep Martin waiting. Not to mention Cason needs to be downstairs now."

"Will you excuse me?" Cason said and simply stepped out of the room.

"Mama," Savannah said in a low tone, "that wasn't necessary."

"What wasn't? Was I interrupting something? Come on now," she said, and Savannah had the feeling that she knew she was interrupting something—but society waited for no one.

"Mama," Savannah put her fingers to her temples. "I'll meet you at the table. I just need to freshen up."

IN THE BATHROOM in Cason's room, Savannah gently patted her face with wet hands, trying to revive her stuttering mind. The next time she had Cason alone in a room, she was going to lock the door.

Cason had said at the end that he'd made a promise? Had she heard
him right? Was that why he had pulled away? He was in his dress
uniform, and they had just agreed he shouldn't do anything in them.
But why didn't that feel like that was it? The walls between them got
built and taken down so often that she was reminded that this was the
yo-yo she had not wanted to be in. But still, instead of firmly giving
him space, she wanted to do the direct opposite. She wanted to crawl
into the dark places of him and turn on the light.

"God." Savannah sighed and looked at the darkly eye shadowed
woman in red looking back at her in the mirror. "Is this what love
feels like?" If it was, she could see how people confused it with
feeling sick. Her insides were twisted up in knots. She wanted—no,
needed—more time with him.

Helen was waiting for her when she exited Cason's room. She
held out her arm for her daughter. "You won't believe who's here."

Savannah raised a brow at her mother as they made their way
toward the formal ballroom. They entered the cavernous and lavishly
decorated room from behind the stage, through the potted foliage.
Microphone and podium were set; guests streamed in through the
main doors, making their way to their seats at linen-covered circular
tables set with dinnerware and short floral arrangements. Off to the
side, there was an open area where the program stated formal
dancing and refreshments would be later.

Weaving through the tables behind her mother, Savannah
prompted, "Who did you see?"

A coordinator came up to Helen right then and said, "Mrs. Sparling, we have your table here."

"Wow, front and center," Savannah said as they moved through
the starched coverings to the front.

"Yes, we want all our family representatives up front for the ceremony." The woman bustled off, clipboard in hand.

"Have you seen Martin?"

Savannah set her clutch down. "No, but Mama, what were you
saying earlier about seeing someone?"

Helen wasn't paying attention, though. "There he is." She gave a wave, and Martin worked his way from the back bar through the sea of tables and seated guests.

Savannah didn't even care anymore who her mother had seen, but now she was frustrated that her mother was so distractible. "Mama! The suspense is killing me. Who'd you see?"

"Who did I...? Oh yes! Peaches. Of all people."

Savannah's head spun. *Cason's mother.* "Does Cason know she's here?"

"I have no idea. He must, though. She wouldn't know about it otherwise, right?" Helen placed her purse down and gestured to the chair next to her. "Martin, here's your seat."

"Are you sure? This seems like family only," Martin said from behind Savannah.

"Nonsense. You're my date."

"If Cason doesn't know, I need to go tell him now," Savannah said while Martin and her mother negotiated the seats.

Just then the main coordinator, the one who had been carrying a clipboard, took hold of the microphone. "Welcome, everyone! Thank you so much for being here. We will be getting started in the next few minutes, so please take your seats. Thank you!"

"Well, you can't find him now. Just sit down. There's nothing you can do."

"What do you mean just sit down?" Savannah asked her mother, who'd obviously forgotten what Peaches was to Cason and what she could do. She was chaos on two legs; just knowing she was there somewhere seated at a table in the gala, no doubt spreading lies as she slugged down drinks, Savannah could feel the place tilt toward entropy.

"I know gosh darned well what I mean when I say sit down. Don't let that woman get under your skin. There's nothing she can do except harm or embarrass herself. To give her credit is to give her power, Savannah—you know better. Now, would you please put your bottom on that chair?"

Savannah knew deep down her mother had a good point, but the need to defend Cason was strong. She reluctantly complied and slowly sat, scanning the white-clothed tables as she did so. More than half her client list was indeed there, and as the MC spoke into her microphone, Savannah spotted a bad orange dye job at the back of the room.

Savannah was distracted when her mother was asked to go up on stage. She watched as other coordinators ushered the family members of the men up to the stage. She turned her gaze to follow her mother as she took the steps and then looked at the rest of the stage. To her surprise, it was filled. Dark as midnight, blue uniforms formed a line along the stage. The spaces between the men were filling in with the family members of the fallen soldiers.

It had been one thing to see Cason face-to-face in his uniform earlier, but now that he was standing stoically on stage, his stance shoulder width, his chin proud, and his eyes distant, it conjured up an emotional swirl in her belly. There was a seriousness to his nature that made him Sergeant McPherson. The soldier who automatically took point commanding a team of eighteen against the enemy. A man who was determined enough to execute an escape plan while his leg was hemorrhaging blood.

Helen stood next to him. She looked calm; she patted Cason's arm and then smiled down at Savannah and Martin. Savannah smiled back at her and thought for just a moment that Cason's gaze had also flicked to hers. When she looked again, however, his stare was focused into the distance.

"Quite the to-do, don't you think?" Martin leaned over to whisper.

"Yes, it is," she said. "They put a lot of heart into it."

Savannah caught a wave out of the corner of her eye. Myrna's blue crushed-silk sleeve fluttered back and forth. Savannah followed her wave to Cason, who didn't respond, and then to her mother, who smiled, unabashed, and waved back.

"Good evening, ladies and gentlemen. Thank you for coming

tonight to help us honor the brave who are with us still and those who gave their lives for this great country." The MC was back at the mic and reading from her program notes. "With us, to help us pay tribute and present the awards this evening, is General Glisan, commanding officer of the United States Army's ISAF. General Glisan is a four-star general with previous commands including USFORA, JSOC, USCENTCOM, and MNFI—"

Savannah leaned back and whispered to Martin, "Is she speaking in code?"

Martin smiled. "I'm glad I'm not the only one wondering that."

"Sounds like the alphabet, out of order."

"I think it might be translated into: we have a very prestigious guest with us tonight."

Savannah smiled and turned back to the stage as the MC finished, "Please help me in welcoming General Glisan."

As applause rose, Savannah turned in her seat again to try to get another glimpse of the orange-haired woman. At the far rear table, there was no sign of her. Savannah scanned the nearby faces—expectant and watching the approach of the army general—to no avail.

"Thank you and good evening." General Glisan had taken the mic. "I am humbled to be here before you and to stand in front of these brave individuals who risked their lives for God and country. It is a great honor that I have been tasked by our commander in chief, the president of the United States, to present the medals given tonight. Many of you are friends and families who have heard of the events on that fateful day two years ago in enemy territory. For those who have not, please allow me to take a moment to tell you, since this kind of bravery is rare and fortifying to the American soul."

Savannah listened to the general as he recounted the story, as Cason had earlier. She was glad it wasn't the first time she was hearing it because, even though his descriptions were clinical in us-versus-enemy terms, it didn't take a big leap to get a visual on what went down on that rural mountaintop. Her mother, up on stage, dug her Kleenex out from up her sleeve, where she'd had the foresight to stash it, and dabbed her eyes. Savannah's heart ached, wishing she could be up there with her mother to give her a hug, but her mother looked down at her, and Savannah put her hand over her heart and the green ribbon that represented Ryan. Her mother smiled back and covered her own and gave her a watery, knowing smile in return.

Savannah caught sight of Cason as his entire countenance shifted. He hadn't moved, but his body language spoke volumes to her. His face morphed into anger and then rage; he was about to come unglued at the sight of something behind her.

Savannah seemed to be the only one who noticed and turned. And there, being ushered forward along the outer edges of the tables, was Peaches. She stumbled in her heels and stopped, grabbing the coordinator by the arm and lifting her foot unsteadily to check it. Her zebra-print spandex dress rolled up her aging thighs.

Savannah looked back at Cason for some sign that he wanted her to intervene. His gaze was boring into hers, silently begging for help. She stood and put a smile on her face as if she just needed to do something ladylike, like powder her nose or take a phone call. Or take down a fifty-year-old terror. She took the direct route toward Peaches and the coordinator, but they were on the move again. Savannah lifted her dress a little and picked up her pace, rounding the last table as Peaches and coordinator got to the stage steps.

It was too late.

Through the leaves of the potted palm trees lining the stage, Savannah watched as Peaches put her foot on the bottom stair and wobbled. The coordinator attempted to help her, but Peaches shrugged her off. Savannah emerged around the line of potted palms to see Peaches career off the step and into the standing speaker.

Savannah halted, blinking, not believing that this could actually be happening. She watched as Peaches, caught in the cords, tried to extract herself. Standing ankle-deep in the extra speaker wire that had been neatly coiled and stacked out of the way, Peaches turned it instantly into chaos. Her chunky heels caught the cords, and with one hand on the back of the speaker, she tried to kick them off. As she did so, she seemed to bind herself even more tightly into the mass of coils. It was if they had turned to snakes and wound up her legs. Those at the table just beyond the plants openly stared through the gaps at her. The general stopped talking and stepped forward. Savannah didn't have to look at Cason to know he was boiling with rage.

The coordinator attempted to help, and Savannah rushed over and grabbed the coordinator. "Just focus on the program. I'll deal with her. She shouldn't be here—"

"You bet your ass I'm s'pose be here!"

Savannah looked at the stricken coordinator. "*Now.*"

The coordinator spoke into her headset, and the general, who had moved toward the edge of the stage, nodded, going back to the podium.

Savannah looked down at Peaches still trying to extricate herself from the cords. She'd get one heel loose and then the other would get stuck. The general's voice once again filled the room as he described the actions of the first fallen soldier, and then he invited the soldier's family member to speak on his behalf.

Shame crept from Savannah's neckline up into her face. She looked over at Cason; his eyes were looking forward, but the matching flush in his cheeks was unmistakable. She only half noticed the lingering stares on Peaches and then descended onto her like a hawk to a mouse. She grabbed the woman's arm. "Move it," she hissed.

"Now, who the fuck do you think you are? And what the fuck do you think I'm trying to do? I'm not standing here for my goddamn health—my ass belongs on that stage."

Savannah's voice was a low whisper when she said, "Your ass belongs nowhere near this stage." Her grip on the older woman's arm was like a vise, and she pulled her from the cords.

"Ouch," Peaches said with no emotion. "Now, look, I've lost my damn shoe."

Savannah wanted to say that she was about to lose more than a shoe but dug deep for her ladylike manners and said instead, "I'll get your shoe."

She retrieved it as Peaches smoothed her dress out and wavered, waiting.

"Here's your shoe."

Peaches put it on; her muddy eyes casually took in her surroundings as Savannah took her in. Her hair was the color of washed-out peaches and dry as straw with a grow-out that would make a stylist lose sleep. But it wasn't her appearance that made Savannah shudder and want to pitch her out the side door; it was the ramble that she had carried on since falling into the speaker.

"You intend to keep me from my due. And I got a whole lot coming to me," she slurred, getting close enough for Savannah to smell the alcohol on her breath and from her pores. "I got a good-for-nothing son here. I'm the goddamn hero." Her voice seemed to compete with the audio of the woman currently speaking. The woman speaking was the aunt of an infantryman who had manned the fifty-caliber machine gun at the base. He was shot and killed, but not before buying the two squads precious time to push the insurgents back and make their way to the Humvees.

Savannah's gut churned from suppressing her growing temper. Physically tossing her out the door would cause people to look and watch, interrupting the woman at the podium receiving the award for her fallen nephew. Savannah pressed herself to be smarter, even if it was morally questionable.

"Let's go get a bourbon while we wait." Savannah put her hand to Peaches's back to steer her, but Peaches was practiced with brush-offs, and shed Savannah's hand.

The next family member went to the podium when the first left. The exiting woman shook the general's hand and, with her other hand, took the open box the general presented to her: the medal her nephew was being honored with posthumously.

"Actually"—the coordinator who had let Savannah handle Peaches came forward, covering the mic of her headset—"here is better. I—" The coordinator cut herself off when she noticed Savannah's icy stare.

"Hands off me. I'll stay here." Peaches wobbled and gave Savannah a long head-to-toe look. "Who the fuck are you anyway?"

"You don't remember me?"

Peaches scoffed, "No. Should I?" Her stare was cut off by her intoxicated slow blinks.

Savannah shook her head. "I'm no one. Just someone who thinks you should get your due."

It took Peaches a long time to process what she meant, the alcohol making her just as Savannah remembered her, bitter and drunk.

"You being sassy with me?" Then it dawned on her. "You're that Sparling bitch. You not gonna help me, Cason's mama. You gonna keep me from my due. You had better be respecting *me*."

The coordinator's eyebrow rose. "But Sergeant McPherson is receiving one of the highest medals of commendation, the Patriotic Medal of Honor that's—"

Peaches laughed. "Sergeant who? That good-for-nothin' piece of shit of a son I got? Ain't you heard a word I've just said?"

Savannah's eye twitched.

"He ain't getting my award. I got hero blood in me, got wasted on him."

The coordinator looked askance at Savannah. All Savannah could think about was how Cason had survived his own mother. She knew the woman was a drunk who didn't care about Cason unless there was something she wanted from him. But to come to the honoring ceremony in front of hundreds of people was not only desperate even for her but also out of character. She liked to silently trash people, drink, and use drugs within the comforts of her own trailer.

Savannah's voice was arctic. "Are you sure there's no bar, tucked away, for the woman with hero blood in her?"

The coordinator wilted under Savannah's stare. "I—I...Sure. Yes,

I mean. Of course. Fully...stocked?" she said, looking at Peaches and then at Savannah for confirmation.

Peaches's eyes were glassy, but she could hear the doubt. "Nah. Y'all are sassing me. I'll stay right here."

Savannah had misjudged her. The woman was adept at knowing when she was being conned. Years of practice of doing so herself, Savannah supposed.

On stage, the various family members continued to come forward, sharing their stories and then shaking hands with the general before returning to their spots. Savannah barely heard any of it as she swiftly thought of plan B, all while resisting the urge to knock Peaches out and drag her from the place. That was plan Z.

Then Savannah realized that an actual bottle would be more convincing than the thought of one. She looked toward the back bar but caught sight of Martin smiling up at the podium. Savannah glanced toward the podium and was surprised to see her mother there. It was her time already?

"...been hard for my daughter and me to move on from his death. It was as if he'd be home from deployment at any moment. Like the other folks mentioned, it's that constant waiting feeling. Recently, though, we worked though some things and finally got to cleaning up the last of his effects, remembering him as he was and remembering the good times we had. Part of that was going through all the letters and emails that he sent while he was deployed and that I'd kept. My daughter was over, and we went through them. I found this one to share..."

The letters. Now Cason would know she'd found his letters.

Savannah's eyes flew to Cason, watching his reaction gradually unfold. His eyes closed heavily and stayed shut as he went under-water into the depths of his own personal hell. Instead of swimming, he looked as if were allowing himself to simply drown.

Savannah ached for him.

Helen was saying, "'The weather here is hot again today. Starting to like all the heat—hundred and twenty feels nice. Kind of reminds me of home. Keeps the joints limber, and the sun's been good for my tan. We mostly are doing PT and drills while we wait for orders. I was thinking, Mom, when you send another box of cookies can you send smokes too? Kidding.'" Helen looked up smiling. "He wasn't kidding." Then she read on: "'Saw my first sandstorm today. It was wicked sweet. Came in like the thunderstorms we got as kids, only instead of water, it's sand, and it comes at you sideways. I'm still finding sand in places...'"

Savannah got lost in her brother's letter, watching her mother read it aloud. Finally, Helen finished the letter from Ryan and, wiping a tear from the corner of her eye, turned and smiled at the general. Savannah watched as her mother received the medal on Ryan's behalf. A camera flash went off, and Helen was back next to Cason. She patted his arm again.

The coordinator handed Savannah a tissue with a soft smile. She realized then that a single tear had made its way down her cheek without her knowing it. She wiped it away and came back to the reality that was still next to her. She said to the woman, "May I speak to you?"

They stepped to the side, toward the rear hallway, away from the stage and Peaches. Peaches watched them for a second but then turned back to the stage, putting a hand out to steady herself.

"Let me explain," Savannah said quietly to the coordinator. "Peaches is not to get onto the stage. It's not Cason McPherson's wish to have her here."

"I'm sorry, but she's listed as his mother, and we didn't get any indication from Sergeant McPherson that she should not be invited, let alone not speak."

"You need to trust me—"

"I'm sorry. I didn't ask before, but who are you?"

"Savannah Sparling, Ryan Sparling's sister and Cason's—Sergeant McPherson's—good friend."

"I'm sorry, but you're not—"

"She's clearly drunk," Savannah said, desperate. "Do you want someone who's intoxicated on stage?"

"Oh, but..."

Savannah thought she was continuing to protest, so she said, "I want to talk to your supervisor. Now." But then Savannah noticed the woman was pointing to the stage.

Savannah turned to find Peaches headed up the stairs; a coordinator in all black was at the top ready to guide her to the podium.

All eyes were on Peaches.

Savannah looked at her mother, who held a confused expression on her face as Peaches got to the top step.

"Stop her," Savannah turned and hissed at the coordinator.

The coordinator's eyes got wide. Her hand went to her headset. "S-stop her?"

Savannah went for the stage. As Savannah rushed toward Peaches, she heard the coordinator say more firmly, "Stop. Her."

"Hey, y'all! Great party, huh?" blasted out of the speakers.

Savannah almost tripped over her own feet with mortification—she was too late. Peaches was at the podium.

At the stairs, Savannah saw Cason break his disciplined stance. It wasn't the lunge that Savannah had feared he'd make, but he took one step forward.

The head coordinator put her hand on Peaches's arm; her voice was low, but Peaches was loud and clear: "What? You tell that bitch I'm not going nowhere. There's no mistake. I'm—"

Savannah reached up and yanked her from the stage.

Helen, seizing the moment, stepped back to the suddenly vacated podium. She wore a cool and practiced surprise on her face.

Savannah dragged Peaches down the stairs; her grip on the older woman's upper arm was firm enough to leave bruises.

Her mother said behind her, "Well, now! That was a bit exciting, wasn't it? I'm sorry, I must have missed my cue to come up here again. You see, I'm Cason's mama too." She turned and looked over her shoulder at Cason, smiling. Cason's foot moved back into parade rest. She nodded and turned back to the mic, and Savannah felt a bloom of relief at her mama's quick thinking. "Well, technically, I'm just Ryan's mama, but Cason and he were inseparable since they were kids. His daddy and mama are"—Helen's gaze discreetly went to the woman being hoisted down the stairs and away from the stage —"gone, so I'll speak on their behalf."

As the rhythm of the ceremony returned to its previous pace, the general's face went back to active listening instead of open curiosity, and the murmur of the crowd died back down to quiet.

Peaches, though, was far from done. She seemed to come alive in all the physical chaos and surprised Savannah with her arm twist. She flung off Savannah and with claws out went for her, saying, "You fu—"

Savannah grabbed a handful of her gown and lifted the hem, swiftly sidestepping the intoxicated woman. Peaches stumbled past her, and Savannah used her forward momentum to propel her by the arm out the door. But as chaos would have it, her feet caught, and she toppled forward in a ball of angry cursing. Savannah watched her hit the carpet behind the potted palms just as Martin came around the edge of greenery.

"Can I—Oh my," he said as Peaches, her dress riding up again, grabbed her heel and threw it at Savannah.

Savannah dodged it and said to Martin and the coordinators who were gathering, "Let's get her outside."

Chapter Twenty-Two

It was starting to add up that he'd rather be hit with RPG shrapnel again *and* be stabbed than be on stage at that moment. So blinding was Cason's rage at his mother that he had barely noticed the switching of women at the podium. It was Helen's smile, chocolate-chip-cookie warm, when he finally saw it, that brought him back. He'd stepped forward, he realized. He stepped back. He reminded himself where he was.

New Orleans. Awards gala.

Is it bad? Yeah.

Could it be worse? Hell yes. Breathe.

Savannah.

He caught glimpse of her and Mrs. S.'s boyfriend dragging Peaches from the crowded ceremony. He realized then that people were clapping. He saw his cue and stepped forward. The blood pounding in his veins quieted enough for him to hear the general say, "On behalf of the United States Army and the president of the United States, we bestow upon you the Patriotic Medal of Honor, due to your distinguished actions of heroism at the risk of your life, above and beyond the call of duty while serving..." Cason waited at the end of the recounting of his actions that day two years ago. The general placed the medal around the collar of Cason's uniform and secured it.

As the general rounded to his front, Cason snapped to, putting his fingertips to his brow as the general saluted him in turn and then shook Cason's hand in camaraderie. "Well done, son. Well done."

"Thank you, sir."

The rest was a blur. He stepped back, and applause came up, and a few minutes later they were all gathering to be escorted offstage. Dinner would commence and then dancing and festivities. Cason noticed none of it. He was of one mind, one focus.

Helen put her hand on his sleeve. "You all right, hon?"

"Sorry, ma'am, I have to take care of something," he said and strode swiftly offstage and out the side doors that Peaches had been escorted out earlier.

Cason looked both ways and didn't see Peaches or Dr. Lowe and Savannah. He moved down the side of the building to the front steps. Looking over the expanse of lawn, he saw them. He took the steps two at a time.

They had gotten over the main lawn and to the stone path leading to the clubhouse and front gates. Only Peaches had gotten hold of the old-fashioned lamppost at the start of the path, and she appeared to be refusing to let go.

Chapter Twenty-Three

"Martin, that hand," Savannah said, trying to grasp Peaches's other hand.

As Martin grabbed, Peaches tried to bite him. "Now, ma'am, if you'd just listen to reason—Ouch! Please do not bite me!"

"Y'all are messing with fire. I fought off more than the likes of you."

Savannah looked around for more help and instead saw a human inferno coming toward them. The elegant lighting cast Cason's uniformed figure as a hallowed army menace, come to dole out punishment.

Savannah cursed.

Martin stilled and looked at Savannah. "What is it?" Then he followed her gaze.

Peaches pulled out of their grip and, staggering backward, flipped them both off. "Can't hold me down, ass—"

"Georgia McPherson." Cason's voice was commanding.

Startled by the name, Peaches looked past Savannah and Martin at her incoming son.

Cason strode up and came to a halt next to Savannah. Peaches stumbled backward again.

"I told you not to come. You'll leave now."

Peaches recovered. "Aww, honey, Mama just wants to have some fun." Going docile, she looked down and picked imaginary lint off her zebra-print dress.

Savannah felt her lip curl.

Cason kept his voice low. "I've already told you. You've never been a mother to me, Georgia."

The mood changes in Peaches could cause whiplash. "My name's Peaches, you little shit."

"You're Georgia. That's the name on my birth certificate. That's all you are to me."

Helen had caught up with them and piped up. "Now, let's not make a scene. Come on, Peaches, Martin and I will run you home."

Martin murmured his agreement and gently tried to coax her down the path with them.

Ignoring them, Peaches squinted up at Cason. He stepped forward, imposing. "I suggest you take up the last good offer to come to you and go with them."

"You think you're big shit, don't you? Standing there all high and mighty. You think that uniform you got on scares me? It don't, and you know what else? You ain't no son of mine; you don't do *me* any honor. You stole from me; all that crap you did over in the war you learned from me. I raised you, and this is how you treat me? You think that shiny medal around your neck means a damn thing without me? It don't. I'm the one they should—"

"Stop." Savannah had heard enough. She put up her hand to Peaches. "Just stop, Peaches. Don't do yourself or him any more disservice by disgracing his actions."

"It's fine," Cason said. "She's leaving." He had not taken his eyes off Peaches.

The sneer on Peaches's face had Savannah's gut twisting with ire for the woman who called herself Cason's mama. Who had put herself before her own son and gone so far as to try and rip every last good thing from him. Including on the one night he needed every good thing in his life more than any other.

Cason voiced his warning. "Think very carefully, Georgia."

Peaches turned her sneer to Savannah. "You're fuckin' him, aren't you?" Her eyes were alight, watching Savannah's reaction.

Savannah flattened her lips while her palm itched to slap the smug manipulative face right off the woman. She heard a low rumble of warning from Cason as Helen and Martin murmured objections behind her.

Peaches smiled as if she'd won the lottery. It made something small, yet consequential, snap within Savannah.

Savannah looked down and stepped closer to Peaches, then looked up and into her murky eyes, mimicking the older woman's smile—only she kept her eyes cold. "Why, yes, Mrs. McPherson. I am. And he's *good*." Savannah dragged out the syllable, watching the smile fade from Peaches's face. "I'd bet your trailer he didn't get that from you, seeing as you couldn't keep his daddy around. And speaking of your bragging, you keep talking as if there were myriad"— she took a moment to pause and enunciate—"*myriad* means a lot— things Cason has learned from you, but really we all know that lying on a couch in filth-stained pants with a booze bottle in your hand is all you did. So how about you take your greed-sniffing, foul-mouthed, hooch-soaked, responsibility-dodging, ignorant self out of here before I break you."

Peaches's eyes went wide, and Savannah could almost see her cat claws come out. "You worthless wh—"

Cason grabbed Peaches's upper arm and shoved her toward Helen and Martin. "Gone. Get her gone. Or so help me god…"

Helen said, "Yes. That's enough, Peaches."

Savannah was glad to have her gone but felt a bit robbed of the physical altercation cussing Peaches out had seemed to guarantee.

Peaches let herself be taken down the path back toward the clubhouse. She spat over her shoulder at Savannah once they were some distance away.

"Hateful woman," Savannah murmured.

She looked over at Cason. He was not doing well.

His hands moved open and then closed. His jaw was working overtime. Suddenly, he turned to his right and walked from the lamplit path into the deeply shadowed wood. The evening mist had begun to rise, and it softly moved out from the oak grove, where the green moss hung down in lacy fingers. As Savannah watched him head into the mist and trees behind it, she saw him pull his medal off as if it were choking him.

"Cason?" She followed him from the path and into the woods, moving branches out of the way as she went. She saw him several strides ahead, working the buttons of his uniform coat. "Are you okay?" she called, only he turned a sharp right and she lost him in the darkness. Savannah stopped and got her bearings. Her heels were sinking into the soft, damp ground, and the sparse shrubs under the closed canopy pulled at her dress.

"Cason?" she asked into the darkness. Her eyes began to adjust, and the narrow path emerged between the wide trunks of the oak trees and shrubbery. She slipped her heels off and walked deeper in. The grove floor was spongy; twigs snapped underfoot while moss brushed across her shoulders and cheeks. Savannah got to where Cason had turned and found him in a narrow clearing. He was a dark shadow in the midst of a stand of wide, swarthy old oaks. Their sprawling branches were low slung and painted green, with fern tips jutting out like spears.

His coat lay over a low, gnarled branch, along with his medal. He stood in the clearing, undoing his tie while unbuttoning his white collared shirt. He gave up halfway and tore the shirt open then yanked his undone tie off, the tip snapping as it came out from under his collar.

"Are you okay?" It felt like a stupid question, but she couldn't think of anything smarter to say.

"No. It's fucking hot."

Savannah felt the cool of the evening on her skin. "I think that if you calm—"

"I'm trying," he said over his shoulder. He reached back and pulled off his undershirt. "You should go," he said, his breath becoming labored.

"Actually, I think I should stay. It doesn't seem like you should be alone right now."

"I'm not alone." He tapped the side of his head as he paced. "I feel like I'm about to go nuts with everything in my head." His skin began to take on a sheen in the moonlight.

"Fine. Let's go nuts together." She stepped toward him. "How can I help?"

He paused. "Doesn't work that way. You should go. You of all people shouldn't be near me when I get like this."

"Like what? Having a flashback?"

He was silent, looking in her direction for some time, and then: "Call it whatever you want."

"Is it better for me or for you if I go?"

Another pause. "I can't think right now, Savannah. You must have read the letters. You remember what happened after my surgery. My flashbacks aren't always that nice. And in case you haven't noticed, you have a prominent role in them, so what do you think?"

"I think...I think right now, to blur the lines between reality and fiction might be okay. You were unknowingly what I needed for two years. I can be here for you now. This doesn't scare me off."

"I wasn't sparring with you for your health. If you're real, you should give me some space. I have to breathe. I have to think."

Savannah wasn't sure what was happening, but she could feel Cason's focus becoming lost. "It feels like maybe I should stay..."

"Go. It's getting too hot out here. Sand is starting to kick up."

Savannah looked around. The mist was rising, but there was no sand. "Cason..." she said, cautiously taking a step toward him.

"Have you seen Ryan?" he asked, rubbing his hands over his face, and then groaned, "No, that's not right."

"No, it's not, he's—"

His groan became one of sheer pain, and he gripped his leg and went down to his knees, cried out, and fell back.

Savannah felt herself go pale. It was as if Cason had been shot. The shock ricocheted through her, and she just stared at him; the agony he was feeling was so palpable that she felt it herself. Her heart, responding to him, picked up its pace, and she instinctively looked over her shoulder. There was no one there, save them. In the shadowy light, she felt pulled into his nightmare.

Savannah shoved it back aside and in a single moment of clarity dropped her shoes and lifted her dress's hem and took a step toward him. "Cason? Can you hear me?"

He spoke through gritted teeth. "Savannah, we're taking fire. You gotta go. Get out of my head. I need to think."

She took a stabilizing breath and left her critical mind, which was panicking, and instead opened her heart, for once letting it take the lead.

"You've got it twisted up, soldier," she said softly by his side. "You're home with me. Not in the desert."

"Bullshit. Get out of my head! We're taking fire!" he shouted then and rolled onto his stomach. "Humvees..." he said, looking around.

Savannah took another step and was next to him again. She crouched down. "I'm going to touch you, Cason, on the cheek. I'm right here. Come back home. You're not in the desert."

Gently, she touched the back of her hand to his cheek. His clean-shaven face was damp with sweat, but his skin was cool, clammy. Cason reeled back, and his tenor changed. "Get out, Savannah. I don't know where I am. If you're real, you need to—"

"Be reckless, yes." And moving with him, she guided him onto his back, and in the stunned silence, she swiftly kissed him. Fingers splayed on his sweat-slickened chest, head down and lips to his, she let her mind clear, focused on his body, on the frantic way it moved under hers and then stilled.

Savannah felt the reluctant acquiescence in his lips' response. She settled for that meager acceptance and relaxed onto him, let the heat she'd felt in the garage weeks before swirl in her memory and pour like silken threads through her palms and into him.

Savannah reached down and hiked her dress up just enough to bring her knee up next to him, and her other leg pressed down firmly between his uniformed thighs. She felt his hands land on her waist before sliding down to her hips where they gripped tightly. He pulled her in against him as if on instinct, but as soon as he did, he pushed her away again. "No, Savannah. This isn't the time. I need to think. There's—"

"Don't think. Just trust me. Let your mind go and follow me, Cason." Her lips gently brushed his, teasing his mind toward her. She pressed down against his questioning grip with her hips and rocked like a lullaby against his body before pressing her pelvis against his. "Let go and give me control," she whispered. She kissed his lips, then gingerly tasted the dry softness of them with the tip of her tongue, asking permission to delve deeper. Cason responded, parting his own, letting her in, and gradually followed her lead. She slid her hand up and over his shoulder feeling the sweat begin to evaporate as his body temperature returned to normal. Her thumb traced his cheekbone and then moved up and into his hairline. Cason's grip became tight again on her hips, and he pulled her down in against him.

He whispered, breathless, against her cheek, "I'm going to die here."

"No, baby. You're home, with me. This is real," she hushed against his ear and then lovingly tugged it with her teeth before dragging her mouth sensuously down along his neck.

Savannah felt Cason's hand search up her back before weaving up into her short, thick hair and gripping tightly he pulled. The tug to her roots was like a trigger for Savannah, one that told her Cason had grasped her towline and was ready to be dragged to safety.

Responding on instinct, Savannah bit down hard on his shoulder before kissing it tenderly as if in apology.

She felt the desert fall away then; she felt the rumble in his chest and heard a submissive groan escape his lips. He was all hers. Feeling that power infuse her body, Savannah moved languidly over him, savoring his rescue and what surely would be his resuscitation. She brought her knee up from between his thighs and settled it down on the other side of him, straddling his prone and assenting body. She whispered against his freshly shaven neck to the flat planes of his now warmed cheeks, "Come with me."

Cason trailed his fingertips down from her hips, across her thighs, and to the hem of her dress. He gathered the fabric in his palms while chasing her mouth with his. They pulled and pushed at each other, making real the heat he'd imagined. His hands, having found the edge of her dress, slid under and against her bare skin.

Savannah sucked her breath in as his fingers, splayed wide, searched up the backs of her naked thighs to her rear. There they gripped, spread her apart, and pulled her down hard in against him. It was Savannah's turn to groan. Cason's need was thick and proud, just on the other side of his uniform's zipper.

"We better get these pants off of you."

"Savannah—"

"Shut up." She drove her hand down between them and undid his fly, releasing him.

"Savannah, it's too much. I need to think. I can't think like this."

"The time for thinking is gone. If you trust me, follow my lead." She led with her body, slipped her hand over him, wrapped her fingers firmly around him, and pulsed gently.

Cason's chin fell back, and a guttural moan escaped his lips. His fingertips dug into her hips, pressing her down as he arched up, crushing her hand between them. Barely keeping her own thoughts clear, Savannah felt him climb onboard her life raft.

Pressing up against the iron grip he had on her hips, Savannah put her lips to his and slipped herself onto his rock-hard erection.

For a moment, just a brief moment, the air quieted around them, and the connection between them stilled all the night's creatures. The vacuum of *why* in Savannah's life came crushing down as the answer, *this*, rushed in. The resuscitation that Cason needed was finally in his arms, and he gripped it tightly.

Slowly, as if moving across winter ice, Savannah shifted, taking him deep within her and then sliding glacially up again. Cason's breath came in raggedly and rasped out as his arms tightened around her, pressing her against him.

The intimate feel of him deep within her made Savannah gasp, and her body pleaded for more as emotion rolled like a warm tide through her limbs and torso, pushing the air out of her lungs.

Savannah heard her own sexual cry soak into the mist that had thickened around them, building a protective, sound-dampening cocoon. She needed more from him, wanted more, and building up, she began to ride Cason harder. He responded, giving way to her. She felt his hands over her body. Savannah's mouth tasted the salt of his skin, smelled the spice of his aftershave and the primal draw of his natural raw male musk. She drew her teeth over his strong jaw and sank her lips onto his mouth once more. She tasted his throaty moaning and felt his erection deepen within her, its tip tapping against the soul-shattering point that sent an earthquake shiver cracking through her body.

She pressed her palm to the earth and rode him even harder. He gripped her back and pushed himself up against her body. Pumping firm and deep, the pressure built low in the apex of her thighs. Warmth swirled out from where Cason and she connected. She felt his breath on her neck before he growled, and her own voice cried out as release careened through her. It shattered, blinding her with its blissful haze. She felt Cason's breath expel in a full-body contraction just before his own throaty call answered hers. Liquid warmth ran, pulsating thought her veins, sending her up to giddy heights as his thick erection had her climax again. Sliding her pelvis against his, she felt her body quake once more in a final tickling orgasm before she succumbed to the shelter of his arms.

THEY LAY like that for some time, Savannah upon Cason, Cason's arms around the still-dressed but skirt-lifted Savannah. Savannah's mind was blank, quiet, and satisfied. She felt a peace that seemed to emanate from Cason beneath her. The coolness of the breeze tickled along her bare thighs and shoulders.

Cason smoothed the hair back from her forehead. "Did you...?"

"Yes."

"Huh."

Savannah looked up at him, resting her chin on his chest. He was looking straight up at the canopy of the oak trees.

"I think I was trying to go nuts before this, though."

"You tried."

He looked down at her. "Was this real?"

That question surprised her; her smiled stayed, but her brow creased. "Real? Was it that good, that you have to question whether it was real or not? It certainly was like a dream, though..."

His hand caressed her back as she listened to his heartbeat. It thumped slow and steady under her ear, the smell of crushed grass and sweat imprinted on Savannah's memory. Those woods, the thick oaks and haunting Spanish moss, would be time machine right back to that moment any time she saw them again.

Savannah took a deep breath and memorized it before moving. The urgent need to pee became more important than her need to stay glued to Cason's front. She came up on one arm and kissed him quickly. "I'll be right back—nature calls."

Cason's gaze was sad, as if she were going to leave him forever.

"I swear, I'll be quick," she said.

He said goodbye as she made her way to the woods and ducked behind the first girthy oak. The leaves cracked under her feet as she squatted and wished for a moment that she'd brought her shoes and then also wished for running water and facilities. Savannah smiled as she thought of him under her, how everything had changed now between them. How they'd become one person and pulling him from his nightmare had been the most risky and stupid thing she'd ever done. But it had been worth it. The sex—even as crazy and confusing as it was—was amazing, soul satisfying, and powerful.

She finished and waded through the mist and back to him. Only, he was gone. The grass was flattened where they'd made love, looking like a black felt blanket in the low-lying mist. She searched and found his shirts and medal were absent from their perch on the branch.

Savannah kept her optimism up she hadn't been gone that long, and called his name as she gathered her shoes up. Maybe he had to pee too? She waited and called his name and then waited some more. Eventually she picked her way through the shadowy cluster of trees back to the trail, and with each step her optimism began to fade. Maybe he had gotten lost? Maybe he was still in some sort of fugue state? Maybe Cason's cold detachment had resurfaced once again... No, she reassured herself, there was a good explanation. No one could walk away from what had just happened between them with just a *goodbye*.

She came out of the grove just up from where she'd left the path and felt exposed. As if her fresh roll in the hay was like a beacon of light blinking over her head. She debated on heading back to the festivities or going home. The valet did have her key, making a quick escape possible. But he needed a tip, and that required her purse.

Savannah's eyes caught a figure entering the lower hallway of the rear mansion where the music from the dancing was happening. The figure was Cason.

A deep disappointment feathered through her veins at the reality that she might have had a one-night stand with Cason in the country club's bushes. It was soon followed up by defeat. She'd given Cason McPherson everything she had, and that was all she was willing to give. She slipped her shoes on and using her fingers combed out her hair and adjusted her dress as she made her way back to the mansion on the blessedly empty path.

Chapter Twenty-Four

Cason's mind tripped over itself as he rehung his uniform. The room that he'd dressed in earlier was just as he'd left it, but he'd returned to it a completely different man. He had experienced a complete loss of control of his mind. The rage, the desert, making love to Savannah...He'd never been so far gone before. It scared the piss out of him. He could actually feel her straddling him, her taking him deep into her and fucking his mind blank.

He held the wreathed star of his medal in his palm, shifting it this way and that with his thumb, the blue of the ribbon hanging over his fingers and the golden-bronzed Roman soldier in the star's center catching the light. He secured it back into the wide black velvet box they'd left in his room. He zipped up the garment bag after tucking the box in next to the shoes at the bottom. The pants he'd have to dry clean. He thought of Savannah. Was she down at the gala? Could he face her after what he'd imagined they'd done? After all she'd helped him with and the moment they'd shared earlier there in his dressing room, he still had to leave her. He had to get his head straight. Leaving her was a jerk thing to do, he thought as he shouldered his bag, but he needed the space. Otherwise he'd do what he was yearning for, and that was to touch her again.

Cason slipped out the door and down the brightly lit hall toward the exit. The dancing and music were in full swing downstairs. The music filtered through the walls and serenaded him out the lower side door and into the night. The lights didn't reach that side, and he continued to skirt them as much as possible as he headed for the clubhouse and main gates beyond.

He was well out of sight as he passed by the street lamp where he had gone into the grove of oaks; his feet stopped there. Cason closed his eyes and felt her on him again, felt a real kind of intimacy with Savannah, and then opened his eyes and continued to the parking lot. Never had one of his hallucinations been that vivid.

Cason waited for the valet to bring his truck around.

"Not up for all the dancing, I take it?" The second valet made small talk. He seemed to be half Cason's age, with braces.

"Not much."

"Yeah, you're, like, the first person to leave."

Cason nodded and hoped his truck would arrive that second.

"Well, not the first. There was a hot lady who left first."

Cason didn't think anything of it until the boy added, "Smokin' hot in an emo kind of way, ya know."

"Emo?" Cason asked, not knowing why he was asking.

"Yeah, like, dark eye makeup and moody," he said, nodding as if that cleared things up. "Oh, here's your truck," the kid said as Cason's truck came to a stop and the first valet jumped out.

As they put his things in the passenger side, he felt curiosity gnawing at him. He tipped them and asked, "What kind of car did she drive?"

"Who?" the first valet asked.

"A white shiny SUV. Good tipper too," the second valet said with a full, glinting smile.

Cason nodded and handed him a little more.

Was it real? Cason thought again of Savannah as he drove out of the lot.

He remembered how she'd left his dream, going behind a tree with the excuse to pee. He'd left then. Grabbing his things and wishing the dream hadn't ended. He felt the usual confusion that came with the flashbacks, and he shook his head in disappointment; he shouldn't have let his mind get that far. But he'd had an evening full of triggers.

Out on the road, he left it all behind. He drove back to his house in the Heights, to his new rundown, beat-to-hell house that he called home. As he pulled into the drive, the headlights swept the front of the house, revealing the peeling paint, sagging front porch, and weeds that were taking the foundation back. He killed the engine and turned off the lights.

There in the dark something about the moment with Savannah worked forward in his broken mind. Making love this time to Savannah in his mind had been different. He could still feel the fabric of her dress under his fingertips; the smell of her was so vivid it was alarming. Yet it wasn't those things that started to ring like an alarm bell in his brain; rather, it was that every other time he'd been with her in his dreams they always were the same fantasy, and he was always the one in control. That night he had been anything but.

The realization swamped him. It was clear then, clear like he had not let it be before: Savannah had actually followed him into the oak trees. She'd been as real as the sun rising in the east every morning.

"Fuck." Cason slammed the heel of his hand against the steering wheel and then covered his face with his hands and lay his forehead down.

The promise he'd made was shattered.

He sat in the silence of his truck for a long while. The night moved past him as he let what happened—actually happened—wash over him. Eventually something moved past the embarrassment, disappointment in himself, and guilt over breaking a blood promise.

It was the reckless feeling that things couldn't get any worse.
Cason backed out of the drive.

Chapter Twenty-Five

Savannah tossed her clutch onto the counter; it slid down the length of the granite. She kicked off her heels and pulled a bottle of wine off the wine rack.

The cork came out with a pop, and Savannah reached up while taking a swig from the bottle and got down a wide-mouthed wine glass. She indelicately filled it, letting the wine splash wildly out of the bowl.

She picked it up and drained it. She gasped when she swallowed the last drop. She refilled her glass modestly and then left the bottle on the counter and turned, looking at her posh apartment. Everything was as it should be. Hard paired with soft, the couch's firmness with the lambskin throw, the clear modern coffee table and the art deco white paper chandelier over the glass dining table. The accent pillows, the art on the wall—all of it, down to the dark walnut tone of the hardwood, had been handpicked by her. The entirety of her life was in control. Except for one moment in the woods. One moment when she pulled Cason back into the land of the living, only to have him walk away from her.

Getting her clutch without having to make small talk with

anyone was thankfully easy since her mother and Martin, as well as most of the other guests, were busy finishing dessert or dancing. Her hands had begun to shake as she pulled into her parking spot back at home, and only now, as the last warm swallows of her wine settled, did the shaking stop.

Had she made love to Cason McPherson as if he were the last man on earth? And had the experience been so earth-shattering that it had obliterated the good-sex bar she'd set? Yes. And any one she could ever imagine? Yes, that too.

She took a sip of wine.

Now what the hell was she supposed to do? She'd used up every last ounce of energy by stepping into the nightmare of a man who'd literally witnessed hell and making love to him as if he were the last good thing on earth.

She sighed and put her wine glass down. It wasn't helping. What she really needed was a six-foot-plus man, built for power and speed and given the smarts to outwit her to walk into her apartment and finish what they'd started.

Savannah sneered down at her wine for making her wish for ridiculous things. Leaving the kitchen, she bent down to pick up her heels as a solid knock sounded on her door.

And then the door opened.

Chapter Twenty-Six

Cason had taken the steps two at a time and knocked before he gave himself a moment to think. When she didn't respond, he simply did what his instincts told him and tried the knob. It gave, and the door swung in.

There, heels in hand, was Savannah. Tall, regal in bloodred, the hem of her dress pooling about her feet. He couldn't remember stepping into the room or flicking the door shut behind him. The only thing he could recognize was the need to feel her against him again. To embrace the realism of the entire thing.

"No, please come on in—" Her voice was sassy, and then his hand was holding the back of her head, and his lips were on hers before she could finish what she was saying. Hand in her hair, he gripped tightly, pulling her head back so that she was looking up at him; he broke the kiss as he walked her back against the kitchen counter. "It took me a while to realize that what we did in the oak grove wasn't just in my head."

He felt the fight in her veins swirl into something else; the hardness of her face softened, and the woman he couldn't control himself around came out. Then that smile, the one that illuminated her eyes as if fire and mischief were all she had planned and he was the intended recipient. He put his lips to hers once more. "Savannah," he murmured there.

He felt her respond, felt her mouth open to his, pulling him in, letting him drown there. He felt her hand as it slid down his scarred hip and felt her thumb dig in. Cason pulled back and hissed through his teeth. He looked down at her; her eyes—those gold-flaked chocolate pools—held heat.

"Feel that?"

"Hard not to."

"Good." She went up on her tiptoes and nipped at his chin. "I want you to be really clear about where you are right now and who you're with."

"Savannah..."

"Good, we have the who down. Now, where are you?"

"Right where I need to be." Cason hissed again. "Do that again and, Savannah, this is going to get physical."

There was that smile again spreading across her face. "Excellent."

Her arm went around his neck, surprisingly firm while pulling him to her lips; softly once more she poured words, emotion, and something physically needing into him. Savannah Sparling, one-woman wrecking ball, was showing him tenderness, softness, and yearning. Cason closed his eyes and sunk into it, let himself go—then there it was, her thumb on his incision again, pushing pain, cathartic, mind-clearing pain. It was memories and trauma. It was heat, warmth, and penetrating reality to have her thumb there. All of it juxtaposed with the softness of her lips, the soft swell of her breasts against his chest, and the welcoming warmth of her citrus-scented skin.

She said, "We'll say 'George Washington' when we want this to end, at any time, got it?"

"And what exactly are we going to do here that requires a safe word?"

"Having sex the way I think we really want to. The way where you're right here and present the whole time. You did say that if I did this again, things were going to get physical." She applied pressure to his hip once more.

Cason growled and hefted her up onto the countertop behind her and spread her legs. "Good to know what we're getting into." Keeping his grip in her hair, he yanked her head back again as his other brought the hem of her dress up and slipped his hand underneath. The backs of his fingers touched the warmth at the apex of her thighs, and Savannah groaned. Cason's teeth scraped down the ridges of her exposed throat over the threaded diamond and down to the top of her dress. Then he let go of her hair and found the zipper at her back and tore it along its track.

He heard Savannah's laugh whisper along the edge of his ear as she leaned forward, her own slender fingers finding the lower edge of his shirt. With more force than he would have thought her capable of, she yanked it up and, as he raised his arms, off of him. He felt something smile deep inside and felt it flex; there would be a sparring of a different kind between Savannah and him. One that he wasn't so sure wasn't pure destiny.

She yanked his fly open before he could get a grip on her, and as the crimson dress slipped off the rounded shelf of breasts her strapless lace bra made, her foot came up and shoved him back. Surprised, he stumbled and came up against the refrigerator. His gaze went happily dark as she slid off the counter; the red of her dress slithered and rippled over her hips as it succumbed to gravity and cascaded to the floor.

Cason swallowed and felt the depth of the situation he was in fully impact him. The erotic juxtaposition of her naked flesh, its creamy hue against the dark of her short hair and black lace bra, with the flashing of the gems on her wide bracelet and the matching ones at her ears and throat, had his other-self pressing tight against its confines. It was the wrestling feeling of seeing all of her, yet not enough.

He recovered and came at her, his hands itching to slide against the milk of her skin. Only she had other plans. Savannah ducked away from him and, stepping backward, toward the living room, she reached her hand back to undo her strapless bra. She reached her other hand out and crooked her finger at him.

He felt an eyebrow tick up. "Oh, I'm coming for you. Savannah, that bra's mine to take off."

Her smile curved across her face. "Not if I get it first."

Cason only needed two large steps to be up against her. Reaching down, he grasped her thighs and spread them apart, lifting her up and against him. He heard her breath catch, and before her arm could come around his neck, he tossed her back onto the boxy white couch, there in the open-air living room. She landed with a soft thump and a laugh that licked at the air.

"Stay," he said, pointing at her while he kicked his boots off.

"I don't think so." She wriggled back into a sitting position.

Cason left his pants on and went back to the woman getting away with something he wanted. "I say so," he said and, putting his knee down on the cushion, reached for her. He grabbed an ankle and pulled her toward him at the opposite end of the couch.

"I don't see how you'll be able to get it off, soldier"—she put her foot to his chest and pushed him back, freeing her ankle—"if I don't want you to."

"I expect to hear a safe word if that's a no."

"Oh, we're far from anything like that—"

Cason reached down and, holding around her knee, yanked her toward him. With his other hand, he grasped her thigh and flipped her over. She squealed into the sofa cushion as he put one hand on her lower back and with the other flicked the bra open. He came down against her back then, feeling the naked length of her under him. The soft round of her buttocks pressed against his fly and her warm silky skin against his bare chest.

She tried to reach back, but he grabbed her wrists and stretched her arms out over her head. He rocked his pelvis against her rounded backside and felt her whimper in pleasure under him. She turned her head then, looking at him over her shoulder; he bent down and kissed her face. Again, gently, against her cheek, and as her dark eyes closed, he kissed their lids, and then buried his face into her dark hair and breathed her in. Citrus, flowers, and something more of her, something that was only Savannah, something only her body made, and that something made him ache.

He gave her a fraction of space as she tried turning over. Hands still overhead, she twisted under him, losing her bra. Cason drank her in. Watched as her legs spread and her eyes closed, and he felt her test the binds his hands had her in. He felt his mind scatter his thoughts like a wind over sand. Cason visually scoured Savannah's curves, how they were wide at her hips before diving in at her waist and curving back out again over her breasts and shoulders. Her full, luscious breasts. He put his mouth down to her begging lips and let go of her wrists with one hand. He lowered himself against her and drank in the feel of her soft, smooth, palm-filling breast. Caressing it gently, letting his thumb rub over her areola, and enjoying the pleasant reaction it elicited from her as his hand tightened, Cason rocked his pelvis against hers.

Her stray hand dragged itself down his back, her nails making his skin go taught as she scraped. Her fingers ducked over his side and slipped between them; he made room for their quest. She found the outer flap of his button fly. Cason opened his mouth and deepened their kiss, slipping his tongue into her mouth, warning her what he was planning to do now that he was released.

Breaking the kiss, Cason knelt back and hooked his thumbs over the edge of his jeans and pushed them down. He made to go back to her, but Savannah's foot came up yet again and pushed back against his shoulder, her head shaking no. "All of it," she said.

He slid a leg off the couch; it was now or never. He stood over her with his eyes on her and her eyes on the top of his now-visible scar. He shoved his pants fully off and stepped out of them. She sat up and her hand went to the place above his knee where the scar started. He closed his eyes. He felt her slender fingers touch the scar tissue there, an odd sensation of not feeling her touch and feeling it, as some of his nerve endings still worked. She wound her way up to the thickest part of it, where skin tissue was nearly absent, where the shiny part of it rippled up to where the metal had shot into his hip joint. Her touch seemed to lift, but the shooting nerve endings said differently; she was working her way up. She gently splayed her fingers over the top of the scar and caressed his unmarred skin up to his waist as her other cupped him between the legs.

He felt the pleasurable rumbling moan she pulled from him, felt his head fall back as she took him entirely into her mouth. He sunk deep into the feel of her warm mouth.

Then his eyes snapped open when Savannah dragged her nails from the base of his scar up to the top where his hip surgery had been. He looked down, the broken nerves were lighting a firestorm on his thigh just as it swirled into an erotic combination with the sensual tug of Savannah's mouth on his shaft.

Cason gasped, his hand going to the back of her head; he felt the small daggers in his thigh blending with the cathartic pleasure Savannah was rendering within him. There was no pity there, only the eye-opening salve of her seeing his RPG scar, the thing that gave him the Patriotic Medal of Honor, the thing that ripped his life apart, and there was Savannah pouring herself into that wound. Ripping it open as she sewed it shut like no one else could.

"Savannah," he whispered down to her. She looked up at him, and he had to close his eyes. "Stop, or this is going to be over fast."

Instead she took him deeper and let her teeth drag along his most sensitive of skin, then gave the tip a gentle nip. His head snapped down as he yanked her head back; her lips twisted wryly back up at him. Slowly he watched as she gently touched the tip of his erection with the tip of her tongue. He felt the floodgates of emotion break. He grabbed her and tossed her back onto the couch, followed her down, and molded himself against her.

· · ·

Savannah groaned and arched, letting Cason lie along her legs; commanding a man so powerful had her head swimming. That he could be so raw with her had her body begging to be satiated by him. He kept his gaze steady while hers flickered with emotion that racked her body. She felt his wide hand slip up the back of her thigh as his breath whispered in her ear, "Please."

Her knees slowly spread wide, and Cason took the invitation and slipped himself deep within her. She felt his hand grab the cushion of the armrest as he pushed within her. To feel him plunge so deeply had, for the second time that night, left her clutching him to her.

Cason rocked their connection, thrusting the swirling emotion that had begun to build the second he walked in the door into a grasping need. The feeling was exquisite, made more so by the need to move, to chase, to be chased. Savannah felt emotion build within her; she reached up and slid off the couch.

Cason gave chase.

As Savannah slithered onto the floor, he followed, shoving the acrylic coffee table aside; it toppled with a clatter. The faux glass apples hit the white sheepskin rug and rolled out in chaos. Savannah and Cason separated as she army-crawled for the dining table. Only she didn't get very far before Cason was on her again.

His broad hand grabbed her knee as she looked over her shoulder, giving him a wolfish smile. "Game on."

Twisting just enough, she put her other foot to his chest and shoved, using his body like a brick wall, propelling herself forward. Cason's eyes were clear with the hunger of an unfed animal having found its prey. She rolled onto her back, and he lost his grip on her knee. Cason growled as Savannah escaped, slithering through the fur toward the dining area only to have his full body come down on her backside, pinning her to the softness beneath her.

"Going somewhere?" he whispered into her ear.

Pinned under him and between his elbows, Savannah sunk into the feel of giving over total control. Starting with the needed connection he gave her. Slipping his knee behind her thigh, he spread her legs wide and guided himself back into her confines.

There, connected, she surrendered to him. Let him press his pelvis against her rump and love her hard. The sweat built on their skin, slickening their bodies half with exertion and half with unraveling pent-up sexual need. She'd never wanted someone so badly as him; to yearn for him was a primal reaction, one that opened her animal senses. She felt his skin slide against hers, smelled the exertion in his sweat: salty, earthy, as if he'd worked hard in the field all day—or was delving into the forbidden shadows, hand in hand with her.

She reached back and pulled his head forward as she moved back onto all fours. Still moving close to her back, Cason settled his cheek next to hers while bracing their lovemaking with his palm to the fur floor.

Hearing his breath beg her body to release him, she felt her own breath catch in response. She slowed his pace and sat, yearning once more to move, to delay the finale, to play as long as possible in the chase. Pushing him back onto his haunches, she pressed her back against his chest and put a hand back to cradle his head next to hers; she twisted, putting her lips to his. Just as her lips touched his and before his arms could slide up her thighs and wrap around her middle, she pushed off.

He'd guessed her plan and seized her ankle. Savannah turned and kicked his grip off.

Cason just shook his head at her and smiled with a low rumble in his chest when she lost his grip, making him charge again.

She was up against the table when Cason captured her. He grabbed her thigh and flipped her back onto the dining table.

Savannah felt the thrill of his fading restraint. His holds were becoming stronger and more forceful. It felt like dancing on the edge of a cliff.

Savannah's hand struck out for balance, hitting the table runner, shoving the fabric and decorative candlesticks off the opposite edge. They too clattered over the dark hardwoods. He pushed her knees wide and bent, returning the favor from earlier. The glass-topped dining table was cold against her skin, but she didn't feel it when Cason's mouth sunk down onto her. His tongue played, tasting and teasing her pleasure. Her head lolled as the warm honey feel of his temptations swirled and built within her.

Cason was back in control, taking them once again to the pinnacle where she'd shudder and beg things of him that she would otherwise never do. He was stripping down each of her personal walls and in their place building something stronger.

His mouth teased and suckled a low, begging mew from her. His hand gripped her hip and pressed her down as his tongue found the center point of her womanhood and, assisted by his fingers, slid up into her. With his mouth and fingers between her thighs, Savannah cried out, her knees fell open, and she tried to arch up into him. She was completely and utterly his. He pushed up into her, wide fingers moving with practiced restraint against the sensitive flesh just within her. She greedily reached down and grabbed a hold of his hair and let out a muffled scream while biting her lip and pressing him harder.

Only he pressed back, and instead of plunging his fingers deeper and faster like she was begging for, he slipped his hand up over her breast, releasing her hip, and came up over her. The table groaned under the weight of their bodies.

As he climbed up her body, Savannah opened her eyes, feeling as if she were going to combust if he didn't touch her again. She watched, paralyzed from being so close to complete bliss—she watched the wrecked demon who had taken over Cason's body as he came over her. His eyes were keen and focused on her own; they watched as hers took him in. Took in the power play of his musculature under his skin, as his shoulders, wide, knotted like rope, released, and he lowered himself onto her mouth. There, Cason's scent and her own mixed, further sealing what their bodies were doing.

Savannah wrapped her legs around his hips and arched. He plunged in deep, rocking over and over. Heat bloomed once again between her legs, and unable to get enough of him, she dragged her nails up his back. Cason's voice rumbled in his chest, whispering a cry out against the skin of her nipple. Savannah responded as he took her nipple into his mouth and suckled hard. The singing sensation radiated out into her chest and pulled a penetrating yearning from between her legs, begging sweet mercy that the chase be finally over. To let her mind and body find the summit of the mountain they were climbing.

Reaching overhead, Savannah knocked the end dining chair out of the way, and with help from Cason's pushing thrusts he slid them down the table. Connected, they poured off the end of the table and fell to the wood floor with a thump, Cason's body above hers. He pushed her down and tucked his pelvis in, once more pushing deep within her. He was slow, stopping when she got close, and put his mouth to hers. On an elbow, he used his other hand to grip her hip and keep her still as he delved within her.

Savannah blew out a throaty breath. "Please, oh god, please, Cason. Yes, this. Yes, harder."

Coming up against the wall, he pulled her up with him into a crouch and then to standing. He settled her there with her legs wound around him, wiped the hair off her sweating forehead, and kissed her hard on the mouth. "Beg."

"Please..." she whispered.

"More," he said, and moving his palm down the back of her thigh to her rear, he grasped and pulled, gently separating her. He rocked his pelvis forward, knocking himself deep within her.

Her head fell back against the wall, and she cried out. "Cason, I need you. Please..." she said and put her mouth to his and tucked her heels tightly into his buttocks, pressing him on.

She felt him growl and lift her up off the wall; the picture frames slid crashing to the floor. They moved down the hall and into her bedroom. There, he dropped onto the bed with enough force to slide the mattress sideways. The duvet bunched, and Savannah grabbed a hold of it as Cason connected them once again.

His eyes locked on hers as he reignited their purpose. Savannah's breath caught as the molten honey moved this time with purpose; the mountaintop was rapidly coming.

"Savannah," he whispered, his face mixing anguish and pleasure and something darkly satisfying, "it's always been you."

Pleasure built, swirling deep in her belly, suddenly spreading out to her limbs...the pleasant suffocation of climax. Savannah heard herself cry out. She heard her voice begging Cason not to stop, never to stop.

Warmth poured throughout her, and Savannah rode the aftershocks, letting him ride them with her. He thrust until Savannah couldn't take the blinding euphoria anymore, and her cries turned into uncontrollable laughter. Cason's own growling call answered her joyous ones and warmth filled her insides as he orgasmed within her.

A SMALL SMILE tugged at Cason's lips; his fingers memorized the contours of Savannah's chin and forehead while they lay naked on her tossed bed. Cason barely registered that it was still dark outside and that they'd trashed her apartment.

"Hi," she whispered.

"Hi," he whispered back. He kissed her softly, letting his lips linger before gently pulling back and letting his gaze rest upon her again. Letting the smile of hers become a photograph in his memory. He put his head back down on the white of her pillow and pulled her in close, curling himself against her backside. Arm around her, he slowly disengaged.

Chapter Twenty-Seven

Savannah stared down into the trash bin. She lived alone and knew every corner of her apartment, every corner of her now-empty—looking as if it had been burglarized—apartment. She'd given Cason thirty minutes after she woke up to come back. Another thirty as she brushed her teeth and freshened her hair, assuming the whole time he had just left to get coffee, breakfast, hell, a mani-pedi. An hour later, she decided to get her hands busy or she would use them to choke him when he came back.

As she was about to dump the broken shards of her picture frames into the trash, she noticed a crushed piece of paper in the refuse. She put the dust bin on the counter and dug it out. Smoothing it, Savannah recognized Cason's handwriting with her Mont Blanc pen from her clutch.

Savannah. The ink was blotted at the comma after her name as if the pen had stayed there for some time while its writer struggled for the right words. *I'm sorry. Sorry that we can't have more of this. I made a promise. I wish I could explain. It means we can't be together, like we were last night, again. Goodbye. I know you're going to rage when you read this, but please trust me now. This is for,* the pen drifted a bit, then: *Fuck.*

Savannah could only imagine that it was then that he crushed the whole thing and trashed it.

He'd made a promise that he'd broken with her...Savannah's mind went dark. He said that before...Was he with someone else maybe? This loving her and leaving her was becoming a habit of his.

She closed her eyes and tried to stave off the feeling of going entirely insane, and couldn't. He was right—she was going to rage. She needed to be face-to-face with him, and *now.*

Where was he living?

Pages of Cason McPhersons came up when she searched online for him, but the search engine was clever enough to pair the name with her computer's current location, so the first few were actually relevant to her Cason. They were all newspaper links to the awards ceremony or mention of him and the place he worked. She narrowed the search by adding their parish name. The first result made her heart leap; she hadn't even thought to look there.

Savannah clicked on the parish home listing and discovered that Cason McPherson had recently purchased a home in the Heights for a little under a hundred thousand dollars, out of foreclosure. He had paid in cash. Savannah clicked the address and was taken to the maps page, where the directions, address, and aerial footage of Cason's home were. She sent the link to her phone and, grabbing her clutch, left.

Chapter Twenty-Eight

The flap and squeak of bats in the upper rafters of the old Victorian woke Cason. Dawn had just broken on the horizon, and the small residents were returning home. He lay on the cot listening to them, their flap and rustle echoing in the empty upper floor. It was a game between them and him, where they kept their entrance. He would find it, eventually. Most likely, he thought, during the next storm.

He was lucky he'd gotten the house cheaply. The bank had wanted the foreclosure off its books, and he'd walked away with the house and enough left over to start the deep remodel it needed. His surgery would have put a financial crimp in getting supplies for the remodel, but someone had come through. They had said that a fund for vets had paid for it when he'd called to clarify why his bill said zero dollars owed, but he knew better. When Savannah Sparling sunk her teeth into something, she didn't let go until she got it.

He admired that about her. His mind slipped back to her as it had done relentlessly the past few hours.

Cason sighed and sat up on his cot. Making love to her over and over hadn't honored the promise he'd made. He had buried many things that he needed—wanted—over the years in order to fulfill his duty to his country and, later, that promise to his best friend.

He got up and stretched and put his shirt and jeans on, before padding downstairs and into the torn-apart kitchen. A hot plate and coffee machine were the only appliances. Both were as old as sin.

Cason flipped the switch on the coffeemaker and thought of the good coffee Savannah had. The morning that he'd gone by her place after her wreck, he should have told her about the promise. Should have told her when he was at her place again after surgery, and last night before the honoring gala. She'd have understood a blood promise to her brother, his best friend and brother in arms. It all had gone sideways, he thought again, when she'd found the uniform. He should have gotten rid of it, but there was so much from that time that he was only now starting to process. Staying loyal to Ryan had in some part made his death more bearable. He was doing something for him, keeping a request that he'd uttered with his last breath. Only the guilt threatened to swallow him alive now that he was away from Savannah and could think clearly. The night before wasn't what Ryan had wanted.

The warm smell of coffee filled the air as he looked out the large glazed window and over his wild yard, now becoming slowly lit with the rising sun. The way he knew it was lighting Savannah's east-facing windows that morning. The way it surely illuminated the carnage she and he had caused in her apartment, chasing joy. He felt his heart beat heavily in his chest as he thought of her then, felt her again under his fingers. Felt her open to him, felt himself become one body with her.

He pushed her out of his mind and instead focused on his broken-down home and what he was going to do first. It was his new path. To build something that was his, only his, and it would only get emotionally complicated if he had to tear the whole thing down.

Back at the coffeemaker, Cason rinsed out his mug from the day prior and poured in fresh coffee. The longer he stayed away from Savannah, the better. She'd forget, he'd forget, and eventually it would all be water under the bridge. Just a hiccup in time. Nothing more than a passing fancy.

Cason tried to think of another cliché to describe what he knew deep down was more than that, but he couldn't. The reality was that one furniture-breaking night with Savannah Sparling had opened something deeply consequential within him.

The morning birds had taken up in song when Cason shoved open the side shed's doors and pulled the table saw out again. The soft crisp smell of pine filled the air. Fresh lumber had been delivered during the week and sat stacked neatly at the back of the shed. It was too early to begin cutting. Instead, he went to work measuring the timber for the wall frame that would replace the existing rotten one in the kitchen. The doorway would be widened. Back inside, he immersed himself in measuring the details in the kitchen; with those numbers, he went out and made pencil ticks on the wood. Once it was late enough to start the saw, he would have everything laid out.

Cason was halfway through the first frame when the hairs on the back of his neck went up. He paused with one hand on the two-by-four perched on the construction sawhorses and looked up. The road seemed empty, save for the few neighbors' parked cars that had been there all night.

Rarely was his gut instinct wrong, so he waited, listening and watching. The massive trees lining the street were easy cover for anyone watching him. The feeling got stronger, and slowly he let go of the wood and began to walk toward the house.

She stepped forward then. Cason stopped; his heart began hammering in his chest again. He was in deep shit.

Savannah had a cursory smile on her face as she walked up the overgrown drive in her flats. She pushed her sunglasses up atop her head and said, "I figured sneaking up on a war vet was far from a bright idea."

He just watched her approach; he felt like the target of a heat-seeking missile. There was nothing he could say that would ease the situation, nothing he could do that would make what was about to happen any better.

Savannah continued to his silence, "Well, a good morning to you too, Cason. Why, yes, this is a great, even beautiful, morning, I agree." Her smile went predatory and then faded.

"Good morning," he managed.

"I'd say that you left me warm and naked in bed to go get breakfast and come back and then forgot, but I read the letter you threw away. I found it while I was throwing away shards of the stuff we smashed while you were screwing me."

"I see."

"Do you?"

He changed tactics. "How'd you find this place?"

"That's your response? How'd I find you?"

"Savannah..."

"Not really what I was hoping to hear. I found you by an internet search; parish records are now online."

"Ah."

"You were right in your letter by the way, the part where you said I'd rage. I am raging. But you look like you're waiting for me to bludgeon you to death. That's not what I was hoping for. I was hoping that you'd tell me to get the hell off your property. That way I could tell you that you'd have to make me; then I'd be justified in calling you a cocksucker. You'd get mad that I called you that and come for me; then I could say later to the police that I was afraid that you were about to attack me, and that was why I maced you."

Cason felt the smirk slide onto his face despite his effort to keep it away. "I have a feeling this is how restraining orders get started."

Savannah was quiet, quiet long enough that Cason felt the air begin to chill. Surprisingly, he didn't welcome it this time; he had to say something. Anything he said, though, he was afraid would come out as begging. He wanted to walk forward and touch her face. Despite her anger, he had the overwhelming urge to kiss her softly like he had earlier that morning. To let every promise he'd ever made to anyone but her float away on the wind.

Instead, he turned and went into the house. Savannah followed. "Why, yes, Cason, I do want to come in. Why, yes, I'd love some coffee. And yes, there's much to discuss," she said in a singsong behind him. He recognized that tone—it was the one that was tempering her wrath.

"Coffee?" he said, gesturing to the coffeemaker.

Savannah stepped over pieces of wood, picked up the carafe, and looked around. "Mug?"

"Just the one," he said, pointing to his, which was visible through the window, outside on his waiting table saw.

She looked at him a long time. "Okay..." She put the carafe back with a *thunk*. "Why'd you screw me and then leave me? Why'd you write a letter saying that you made a promise to someone and that's why you couldn't stay? Are you married? Why did you think *we* were married with a child on the way at the doctor's office, and why did you write a year's worth of letters to me and never once tell me about them? And those are just the beginning. I've got loads more questions."

"Ryan."

This unexpected response gave Savannah pause. "What?"

"Ryan is who the promise was to. I'm not married."

"Oh. You guys were together? Together-together?" she said and sat down hard.

Cason felt the situation slide sideways. "*What?* No, that's not— Wait, really? After last night... you think?"

"Cason, truth with you is like trying to grab a greased pig. I think I've figured things out, and then away you slip. I'm just covering all bases."

"Right."

Savannah looked up at him, her eyes dark with suppressed rage. "This is the part where you fill in the gaps in my knowledge, so we're on the same page. I'll help get you started: I want to know why you fucked me last night and—"

Cason felt his emotions rising to meet hers. "I didn't *fuck* you, Savannah. You're not...It's not like that."

"Then what is it, Cason?"

"Savannah, I can't—"

"Why?" she said, standing again.

Cason felt his control slip then, completely. Leaving him wild and exposed. "Because I'm completely in love with you. I've loved you longer than you've known I existed."

Savannah's arms fell to her sides. "What?" she asked softly.

Cason continued, "I made a promise to your brother when he was bleeding all over the place after he was shot in Afghanistan. I said I wouldn't get involved with you, and when he died, I promised I'd look out for you like he would have. But I'm not him. You were always more than just a friend to me; you'll never be a sister to me. You'll always be more. Always. But I can't—We can't happen. I made a promise. I broke it last night. It feels wrong to do it again."

Savannah stood staring at him; her mind, from the look in her eyes, was working at high speed. "But," she said, "why would he make you promise something like that? Why then?"

Cason knew the time was up. He reached into his back pocket and pulled out his wallet. Flipping it open, he pulled out a tattered photograph from a hidden pocket behind his cards. He handed her the photo.

Savannah looked down at her high school senior portrait. Cason said, "I carried that with me overseas. My first deployment I started talking to you, that photograph, because things were shit. But talking to you made them better. I got flack for it, so I started saying that you were my girl. That's about the time I started writing the letters to you."

The edges were tattered, and the image was soiled, but it was clearly signed across the back in her childish handwriting: *To my main man, Cason.* Then at the bottom in her loopy cursive, *Love, Savannah.*

But it was the three dates added to it, in his handwriting, that piqued her interest. "These dates, what are they?"

Cason opened his mouth and then shut it again. Then he said, "First date, engagement, and wedding."

"Ours?"

He tapped the side of his head. "Just up here, so I'd remember."

"I don't understand..."

Cason sighed. "My first squad was tight. The guys all had girls, and all I had was your picture. They saw the photo one day, and I just said you were my girl. As our time went by, the guys all came back from R&R engaged. It seemed harmless then." He sighed and crossed his arms. "We were assigned to a special ops team in the remote foothills in the north. When we were up there, nothing happened for weeks. Then one day four guys with AKs came over the ridge on a suicide mission. It was over quick, but the gunner next to me caught a bullet with his face. It was the first time I'd seen someone I knew die. I knew him, and one second he was there, and the next he was on the ground, dead."

Savannah let the quiet fill the room. Cason, she could feel, was far from done.

"It was a low-casualty scenario, but it scared the piss out of me. That's when I wrote to you; that's when you became real to me. It started out as some careless thing, and then it turned into something I needed. You became a real part of me, Savannah, and I don't expect you to return even a fraction of those feelings in real life, but you can do us a favor and not say I fucked you."

Savannah nodded but said, "You call a lady after you've been with her; you definitely don't totally disappear. If you cared for me—"

He held up his hand. "Stop. I do care for you. I also know that your brother died, and my last words to him were that I would promise to stay away from you and care for your mom. I don't have the ability to patty-cake shit. I just left. I didn't see another way."

"Again, why would you promise Ryan to stay away from me? And I'm sure he didn't mean for you to not care for me."

"Love you," he said. "I don't care for you, Savannah; I love you. Period."

Savannah nodded. It was a lot for her to take in, and it was far from what she'd gone there expecting. "But why would he ask that of you?"

"I'd gotten used to taking your picture out with my other squad, and when Ryan's unit joined up with us, I didn't stop. He came into the bunk area and got ahold of your photo. We were all hyped up on adrenaline, and he put two and two together and raged." Cason shrugged. "I'd have done the same thing if I had been him. He remembered us as kids."

"He remembered your reputation as a bad boy."

"It wasn't a reputation. I tapped anything on two legs because I didn't think myself worthy of you. The first second I saw you, I wanted to be with you. Only you. My life was hell with my mother; I knew I had zero chances of you noticing me the same way I noticed you. Perfect Savannah Sparling, with her good grades, nice family, and a mom who gave a crap."

Savannah gave him a small smile. "So, pretending started early for you."

"It happens when you have no control over the life you're stuck in."

"But then you went from the frying pan and into the fire."

"You could say that." He took a deep breath and then continued. "Your brother and I didn't patch things up until he was bleeding all over the place. I promised him as I..." he said and stopped.

Savannah watched the darkness of that memory cast Cason's eyes to slate. She felt the grief of Ryan's final moments churn in her gut and ache in her own heart.

"I promised him that I would not touch you, like he wanted. I promised him I'd look after you. I also promised God that he could have my life for Ryan's—but that didn't happen."

The weight of their conversation made Savannah sit on the window seat again and look down at the dusty floor; the hardwoods had been lovingly laid at some point. Time had roughened them and beaten them, but they still held the promise of beauty. A promise that could be realized with some hard-earned sweat equity.

She looked back up to find Cason's gaze on her. "Now what do we do?" he asked quietly.

She gave him a soft smile and let Ryan's memory rest. "Are you planning on refinishing these hardwoods?"

He looked down and then back to her. "That's the plan."

"Good, because they're beautiful. You can't see it now, because they've been roughed up and tattered from years of wear. But they'll shine again." She looked around the inside of the rundown old home. The bones were solid, and the house still held the glory it had been built with, but it was only visible by those with the eye for it. "This house is a really good investment. Both monetarily and...and personally. I can see now that you need this, Cason." Standing, hands in her pockets, she added, "I also see that you've made a promise you won't be able to keep. Not because you're not strong enough to keep it, but because you made it about me. Your promise to keep your hands off me is assuming that I didn't like having your hands on me. I'm not an impressionable teen any more. I know exactly what I want, and it's you, hands-on. You can't make a promise on my behalf without me. It does make sense, though, why you lied to me when you got back about leaving my brother to die. It's how you felt, not what you really did. And in a way it was easier for you to keep your promise to my brother if I hated you. It was smart."

"Not smart enough, apparently." He pulled over a work bucket, flipped it, and sat, resting his elbows on his knees.

"Your heart wasn't in it."

The corner of his mouth tugged up. "True."

"I'd like to at least be friends, Cason."

He shook his head. "I can't, Savannah. I either have you and break a promise to your brother or you're out of the picture. It is better for me if you're completely out of the picture."

"I see."

"Do you?"

"I see that the promise you made to him means a lot to you. But I don't think you're meeting the intent of the promise. Which I'm sure was not to cause me pain."

"It shouldn't have gotten this far. I'm sorry for that—"

"I don't like sorry. You haven't just stepped on my toe, Cason. You've made me feel things that I thought were plainly broken inside me. Being with you the way we were last night made me happy, something I didn't realize I'd been missing. Something that I now see as a purpose in my life. I need happy. I need you."

Cason rubbed his hands over his face, "Savannah...Please stop. I can't be with you, and I feel the same way. You're," he said and sighed, "crushing me."

"Cason," she said, pulling his gaze up to hers with his name. "Ryan was my brother. The blood that ran through his veins runs through mine. You've made a blood promise to him, and as his own flesh and blood, I ask that you break it and make me one instead. One that will fulfill, I think, the intent of the original."

Cason held her gaze. "And what's that?"

"That you care for me. That's it." She paused and amended, "No, I need more. I need you to love me...both in spirit and in action, Cason McPherson." She blew out a breath and pulled her sunglasses off her head, adding, "I'll be around this weekend—call me and let me know what you decide. Or stop by. If I don't hear from you, I'll be back. You know how I am, Cason—I won't let this go. Not unless I'm convinced otherwise. So you might have to move again if you want to be rid of me." She smiled at him but didn't feel the humor; she let the smile slide away as she turned and walked out the open kitchen door. She left the tattered photo of herself on the windowsill of the kitchen. She wasn't sure if Cason could see her racing pulse or the shake of her hand. She'd never done anything like that in her life, been so bare with someone. It was both refreshing and frightening. He could very easily let her go with just a message on her voice mail saying that he had chosen his original promise. She hoped he would see that the two promises were, at the core, the same promise.

The sun had risen higher and begun to warm the air and evaporate the dew off the wild landscape of Cason's lawn. She hadn't lied about the house being perfect for him. It was in every aspect. She pulled the keys from her pocket as she made her way down the driveway.

Savannah heard Cason's boots on the stairs and then the crunch of gravel under feet behind her.

"Savannah, wait."

She stopped, turning around.

Cason had his hands in his pockets. "I'm not sure about this. I want to say yes."

"What's holding you back?"

"I think you know."

She nodded; she did know. Her brother was gone, and he had died in Cason's arms. "I can't compete with his memory…"

"Will you do something with me?"

She looked at him, wary. "Yes."

"I'll be right back." He turned and headed up the sagging porch steps and into the house. He was only gone a few minutes before he came bounding back down the stairs, the house door slamming shut behind him. Only it didn't shut; it bounced off the hinges and swung open again. Cason swore under his breath and more calmly went back up the stairs to shut the door properly. Savannah watched him tuck what looked like a flask into his back pocket as he did so.

He came back down the stairs with his keys in one hand. "Get in." He nodded toward his truck

"Okay…" she said and rounded its front, getting in the passenger side. She got her seat belt on as he clicked his in and started up the truck. "Where are we going?"

"You'll see."

"Do I need to change? Because I was planning on homicide—I'm not really dressed for the public."

"Nope, you're fine in your homicidal getup."

Savannah tried to get more information out of him as they drove but soon stopped. She knew where they were going. "Cason..."

As if reading her thoughts, he said, "This is what I need, Savannah."

She swallowed and then nodded. She rarely visited her brother's grave, but the few times she did, the roads leading to it felt as if that was the only place they went.

"Okay."

SAVANNAH TRAILED behind Cason as he headed toward Ryan's grave. His headstone was in the old part of the historic cemetery. Large marble angels and towering headstones reflected the age when, even in death, prosperity was meant to be celebrated. Now, though, far from those times, sat Ryan's grave, next to his father's and grandfather's. The Sparlings had flashed their wealth two centuries prior and purchased a section of the cemetery. Ryan would always be with family. Savannah's eyes ran over the graves as she followed Cason, remembering grandparents and her own father.

Crouching down next to Cason, she automatically swiped her fingers across Ryan's headstone, clearing it of the odd leaf and piece of grass. She let the pads of her fingers be caught by the etched wording.

Ryan Mathew Sparling
Brother | Son | Hero

Cason apparently had his own ritual. He knelt down, taking the flask from his rear pocket. "Hey, buddy. Brought your sister today." Cason poured a sip of the contents of his flask into the grass next to Ryan's grave and capped it.

Savannah gave a soft laugh. "Now I know why it always smells like bourbon here."

He gave her a sly smile and returned to Ryan's headstone. "We usually make small talk, but today I figure I'll just jump in. Something tells me he might already know why we're here."

"You talk to him?" Savannah asked.

"Yeah," he said, his mouth going up in a sardonic smile, "it's kind of not a problem for me."

Savannah nodded. "Right...I see how it wouldn't be."

She took a deep breath and settled into the grass.

Cason looked over at her. "You okay?"

"Yeah, it's just weird for me. I have to wrap my head around talking aloud to him. I usually just sit and look at his grave and feel angry with you. So this is new for me..." Savannah looked at Cason, then touched the edge of the stone.

Cason jumped right in. "Ry, I broke the promise I made you." He blew out a breath, and his voice went soft. "I remember the moment I made it. I know that earlier I told you to fuck off, but I meant what I said there at the end. I'll take care of her, but I don't know how to do it without being in love with her. I tried, but it fell apart."

Savannah had been watching him, watching the way he was loyal to her brother even after Ryan's death. Honoring a promise to him because that's who he was, to the marrow. She knew now what needed to happen. "It wasn't a promise you two could make alone," Savannah said under her breath. She put a hand on Cason's back, giving him a soft smile. Then she looked down at the headstone and, taking Cason's lead, said, "Ryan, we came here for your blessing. I've asked Cason to stop running from me and give this thing between us a chance. The promise he's trying to honor with you is hurting me. I know that's not what you intended, so as your sister, I've asked him to add an amendment to your promise—"

"Amendment?"

"Yes, I had some time to think about it on the way here." She glanced at Cason. "Like the Constitution has amendments? Get with

it, McPherson." She gave him a playful smile before resuming her
talk with Ryan's headstone. "As I was saying, with the amendment,
he's to fulfill your promise with the original intent I think you had,
which was to not cause me pain. But to care for me with love, both in
spirit and in action."

"I love her. It'll be easy. I never got to tell you that I loved her
from the day I set eyes on her. I'm sorry you found out the way you
did. I wish I had the chance to explain before you got hit..."

They sat crouched in companionable silence, letting their words
sink into the soil and into the ether.

After a long while, Savannah said, "That was a lot of weight to
have carried with you. To fight with your best friend and never make
amends. I see now why you and I fought so well when I thought
you'd left him to die."

He looked at her out of the corner of his eye. "There was something in that sparring, wasn't there?"

"Yeah, it was cathartic. Well, until I found your uniform."

"Savannah?"

"Hmmm?" she said, looking at him then.

"I love you." He brought his hand up to her cheek and pulled her
in, his lips sealing the vow. "It feels so good to tell you."

Savannah's eyes closed as she savored the warm, strong hand on
her cheek and kissing him again, the soft discipline of his lips on
hers. It was those lips that had given him away. Those lips in the
garage, weeks ago, that had shed light on what she'd truly meant
to him.

She wrapped her arms around his shoulders and maneuvered
into his lap as he sat back. He gathered her up and deepened the kiss
before gently pulling away and resting his forehead against hers.

"Okay," he said, "I can do it. I accept your amendment."

"I think Ryan does too. I feel like he's sulky about it but generally
okay."

"Makes sense. He did get to punch me in the face for it."

Savannah leaned back to look him in the eye. "What?"

"When he found your picture, he asked if it was a joke. I said no; he threw the punch."

"I. Wow. I had no idea. Wow. Sorry he punched you. Seems silly..."

"Not at the time. Not in the middle of war. We all had things that would set us off. He thought I'd been with you in high school."

"Oh, now I see why. You would have broken the bro code."

"Yeah, and you sixteen, me nineteen."

"Fast-forward to me at college, you enlisted. He should have laughed his ass off. I think at that time I was going through my 'date all the boys I can before I graduate' phase."

Cason's smile went stern. "By date you mean study with at the library?"

Savannah smiled widely. "Absolutely. If by library you mean my apartment after they bought me dinner."

"I don't want to know this."

"Fair enough. If it makes you feel better, the last guy I went out with was a year ago, and he asked me not to call him again by the end of the date."

This got Cason to crack a smile. "He actually asked you not to call him? What the hell did you do?"

"I may have replied to a few emails while on the date, and I may have ordered his dinner and drink for him because he seemed like he was hesitating. In my defense, it was right in the middle of my trying for my current position, a huge promotion. I shouldn't have attempted a social life."

"Yeah, I remember that. I missed you then, but when you did come by, it made up for the weeks without you. Man, you were intense."

Savannah smiled to herself and tucked her head into his neck. "I don't really want to admit it, but that may have been why I came by. You were so good to spar with. But I think I like this better. Something fuzzy and warm about being close to you like this."

"You can say it."

"Say what?"

"That you love me too."

"Yes, I can."

Cason waited a beat and then said, "Waiting..."

"I've heard that good things come to those who wait."

Cason laughed softly and held her tighter. "I love you."

BACK AT THE HOUSE, Savannah held Cason's hand as they walked up the steps. "I meant what I said about this place being good for you. I'm a little jealous that you have time for a personal renno. I've always wanted to restore a home from bones to furnishings."

"Help me with it."

She looked over at him as he shouldered the door shut behind them. She waited until his slate-green eyes were on hers. "Really? I'm not sure I know how to not overdo things, Cason. You should think about it before you say yes—"

"Yes. I need the help. Especially now that I'm not trying to forget you," he said and then added, "Want me to give you the tour?"

"Absolutely, but, Cason—"

"Savannah." He reached over to her, pulling her in close to him, invading the businesslike space she'd established. "I know you, forward and back. Let's do this. I know you've already eyed my floors, and its hot knowing you see the same things I do. So, again, let's do this."

"Okay. But do you mind if I go back to my place, so I can grab my things? I want to take measurements now so that tomorrow I can get drawings started."

Cason's smile was radiant. "I feel like we started a company together."

"I'm just getting my measuring tape and pad. And camera."

"Still feels like it. And no, you can't leave until I've given you the tour."

He watched Savannah's face while she mulled it over, and then she gave in. "Okay, but can I borrow your measuring tape?" she asked, looking over her shoulder toward the demolished kitchen counter.

"I'm going to change the subject on you."

"Okay," she said absently, spotting the yellow measuring tape on the counter.

Cason straightened up. "Thank you for paying for my op."

She looked back up at him. "What? Oh. I don't know what you're talking about. Is that your measuring tape?" She wriggled in his grip.

"Savannah," he started. "Vet Relief Fund was creative, but I know you."

She shrugged. "Not really sure what you're talking about. Will you give me the tour?"

"You're not off the hook, Savannah. I know you paid for it, and somehow I'll pay you back."

She gave up and turned back to him and put her arms around his neck. "Please don't pay me back. What little guilt I had over being a complete ass to you for the past two years was assuaged when I paid for your op. So if you pay me back, I'm fairly sure that guilt will return too."

He bent down and kissed the end of her nose. "It *has* been pretty useful having the shrapnel out of my hip joint."

She smiled, feeling like a pug with a never-ending kibble bowl. "I bet it has. All that hip action, unencumbered?"

He took a step toward her, pushing her back into the living room. "I feel like I should show you my gratitude with another demonstration of how easy it is to move my hip now."

"After the house tour?"

He took another step and another until she was backed into the living room, coming up against tattered wallpaper.

"This is the living room."

Savannah swallowed as he came up against her. "I noticed."

"Upstairs is the second floor."

"Really?"

"Yup."

"Can I see it?"

"Later."

"I have a feeling that later I won't have much brain function."

"True."

Cason kissed her neck and then dragged his teeth along her shoulder, making Savannah groan with pleasure.

"I'm not sure I'll get used to making you do that."

"I don't want you to."

Cason pressed his hard-on against her and put his mouth to hers again. "Screw the house tour."

"That sounds like the right kind of tour," she said as his hand found the hem of her shirt and slipped under and up to cup her breast. His fingers tucked over the edge of her bra, and he ran the backs of his fingers against her nipple. "Oh no, please. Now."

His voice was hoarse as he said, "Is it no, or please, or now?"

"Yes," she said, pulling his shirt up over his head and off.

Tossing it aside, Cason undid the button of her jeans as she slipped her own shirt off. Their mouths found each other again as her clothes hit the floor.

"Never in a million years did I ever think that I'd find aged wallpaper so erotic," Savannah said as she helped Cason unzip his fly.

As she pulled down his briefs, releasing him, Cason gave a throaty sigh and pressed up against her again.

"Please." Her voice was muffled as she begged against his throat. She went up onto her tiptoes before lifting a leg up to his hip.

Gripping both her thighs, Cason lifted her up against his waist. He pressed her back and, bracing a knee against the wall, slipped into her.

They both gasped for air and rode the wave of pleasure that being joined at the hip again brought. Begging whispers intertwined with the rhythmic sounds of skin against skin and the thump of them both against the wall, echoing in the empty house.

Cason's grip held her firmly as he rocked his pelvis in against her, and Savannah gripped him harder still until his thrusts sparked the first waves of body shuddering delight. Savannah's breath caught as the tickling pull of orgasm swallowed her body, making her limbs clutch Cason hard. Flooded with orgasmic relief, holding each other, they shuddered in release. Cason's growl of orgasm matched Savannah's cry of pleasure as they slid to the floor.

Breathing heavily and warm with laughter, they held each other in embrace; Savannah's legs wrapped around Cason's waist as he held her, still firm inside her. Their voices were soft, muted, as they spoke against each other's skin.

"I love you."

"I love you too."

Chapter Twenty-Nine

The morning dust swept up and swirled around, drying his mouth and nose. The desert was hot and dry. The distinct taste of blood and the pain in his thigh had Cason looking down at himself. He'd been hit. *Ryan...*He reached for his buddy; Ryan was faceup was on the ground, his eyes like glass.

"No..." Cason tried to move back, to get his legs out from underneath his dead friend. Blood was everywhere. He came up against the Humvee, the heat becoming even more suffocating. He couldn't breathe. The sun. It was too bright.

"No," he said again and, twisting away, felt something sting his cheek. His fingers clawed at fabric, the desert pressing down, burying him.

"Cason!" He heard his name being shouted. He had to leave.

The sting came again to his cheek, and the desert faded into purple sheets and a woman straddling him.

"Cason," she said over him as he twisted back to her; her cropped black hair made her look just like Savannah.

Savannah.

"Shit," Cason said and closed his eyes, pressing his fingers against them.

"Where are you right now?"

"Purple sheets," he murmured.

"Good. Who am I?"

"Hot."

She gave a soft laugh above him.

"Name, please."

Everything was rushing back to him now. Savannah, her bed, every night for a week. The house in the Heights was almost ready for a bed. "Savannah."

"Where are you?"

"Your place. A week now."

He felt her kiss him softly on the jaw. Her softness made him want to bury himself in her forever, to crawl in and never crawl out. Especially after dreams like he'd just had.

"I told you not to have that beer," she said, quietly admonishing. "Makes your dreams more vivid."

He grunted.

"Where were you? Humvee again?"

"Yup."

She kissed his cheek. "Look at me."

Slowly he took his fingers off his eyes and let his gaze come to rest on her naked form. Her eyes had gone hazelnut in color, they were so light that morning. "I love you," he said.

As he said it, he watched the way her smile stretched across her mouth, her long, sensual smile like a cat stretching from a long slumber.

He waited for it, the words that were balm to his soul.

She made him wait; kissing him softly on the mouth, she shyly looked up at him.

"I love you too."

. . .

THE COFFEE WAS READY, and Cason slipped on his boots. Savannah, looking at her phone, absently handed him his to-go mug. He took it and placed it on the floor next to him. As she walked back into the kitchen, he asked, "What do you have on your agenda? Can you do lunch today?"

Savannah's skirt was a loose, folded thing that he hadn't seen before, with a matching purple shirt that she'd tucked in. She looked relaxed, happy even. Something he hadn't seen in an epically long time. Something warm moved deep in his belly, something that said, *I did that.*

"Mm-hmmm." Her thumb flicked through her emails.

Cason waited for a more concrete answer, shoving his other boot on. He stood, and when she still didn't respond, he walked over to her, plucked her phone from her hand, and dropped it on the counter. Pushing against her, he backed her over to the far kitchen counter.

"Cason, I—"

He lifted her up and spread her legs, wedging himself firmly between them, grateful for the loose skirt. He grabbed a handful of her hair and pushed her mouth to his. He let his other hand come up and gently caress her through her flimsy shirt over her lace-covered breast, up her neck, and to her chin, where he finally broke the kiss.

"I realized that being in a relationship with you means sharing you with your work. So you'll excuse me if I don't play nice. I don't like sharing."

She gave him a lazy smile. "Did you have a question?"

"Yes. Will you have lunch with me today?"

She pondered his question, pretending to hem and haw about it before smiling at him. "Only if you promise me a shrimp po-boy and fabric samples at the Heights house."

He nuzzled her neck. "I was hoping you'd say that."

She leaned back and looked at him. "You want to look at fabric samples?"

"You say, 'fabric samples,' but I hear, 'sex in the kitchen, sex in the living room, sex on the stairs, sex in the attic, sex—'"

"Splinters. Splinters. Splinters. Splinters."

He gave her a knowing look. "I'll hold you."

"I might have to make it a long lunch then."

He kissed her hard and, gripping her bottom, lifted her up and off the counter, letting her slide down him the few inches to the ground.

"Mmmm, remind me to ignore you more often—I like your way of getting my attention."

He smiled and gave her cell back. "Don't tell anyone. It's a patented move."

She laughed as he headed for the door. She looked down at her phone and then called, "Hold up. I might be late for lunch."

Cason paused and turned back to her, resting his palm on the open door as she said, "Looks like I have the—Oh." Her face fell. "The damn contract addendum for canceling the Nigel project was never officially signed in ink when they did the fabric pickup with the sheriff's escort. Looks like they want me to sit in on the signing."

"You're not going to his place, are you?"

"No. He'll be at the offices. I'll leave right after, should be at your place at twelve thirty."

"Okay. If you're a second late, I'm coming for you."

She smiled. "I know. I'll even text you when I'm finished...Oh!" She made a face of faux shock. "That's right, you don't have a cell phone yet."

He squinted at her. "Twelve thirty."

"Bye!" she said, laughing, as he closed the door.

THE MORNING, Savannah realized as she drove, was a beautiful one. The heat had broken, and a drenching rain had taken most of the humidity out of the air overnight. Everything was clean and fresh. She rolled her window down, and despite the whipping it gave her hair, she left it down and put her hand out and let it ride the wind all the way to work.

"Good morning," she said, smiling at her coworkers as she made her way toward her office past early-morning staffers and tables of fabric, wood, and color samples. Charlot was walking out of the staff room with her green tea in a fire-engine-red mug.

"Savannah!" Charlot exclaimed.

Savannah smiled. Even seeing Charlot for the first time in a week couldn't touch her good mood that morning. "Why, good morning, Charlot. I hope your yoga retreat last week was good. No, I have no open projects for you to take on. Yes, I saw your latest drawings for the Mathers updates. You may go now." Savannah noticed that even after a yoga retreat, Charlot still wore hot-pink nails, chic tattered jeans, and heels.

Charlot ignored her comment and got caught up staring at something surrounding Savannah. "Look at your aura! Bright with sexual energy."

Savannah rolled her eyes and put her things down in her office, only a little surprised that Charlot would see that she'd had amazing, soul-satisfying sex recently. It *was* one of Charlot's talents. Charlot followed her into her office and made mmm-ing noises with a knowing smirk.

"Charlot, what I have done and with whom are to remain solidly in my personal life. Now, is there something you need from me, other than a good, long look at my aura? Which I assume you can do not right here but out of my office, say, from the other side of the building?"

"Fine," Charlot said and wagged her finger at Savannah. "But from the color of your aura and—" Charlot stepped up and wrapped her fingers around Savannah's wrist and closed her eyes.

Savannah stood there looking at Charlot's fingers around her wrist and then at Charlot. She felt that somehow she must have changed over the past few weeks because she felt downright tolerant of the woman taking her pulse and the cloying vanilla-and-patchouli scent that came with her.

Charlot's eyes popped open. "You did it, didn't you?"

The way Charlot looked as if she knew exactly what Savannah had done and with whom made Savannah ask, "Did what?"

"Burnt some furniture with that guy who's your friend, Cason. Just like I said you would too!"

Savannah's eyebrows went all the way up to her hairline with surprise. "I said nothing of the kind."

"Recently too," Charlot said with a girly smile. "I can see it!"

"Charlot—"

"It's written all over your face. Well, at least for those of us who can read stuff like that." She let Savannah go. "So, how was it? He's rough, huh?"

Savannah wasn't sure why she was entertaining the notion of answering, but she did. "Let's just say I'm redoing my entire apartment."

Charlot put her hands in prayer to her lips. "I knew it! I knew there wouldn't be an unscorched surface in your place!" she gushed. "Tell me everything!"

Savannah reached the end of her entertainment. "No. Now, goodbye, Charlot. I have to prep for the Nigel meeting."

Charlot made a gurgling sound as if she'd just seen something disgusting by the side of the road. "Phillip Nigel. I can feel my aura darkening at his name."

"Then you might want to take off before I open the contract documents. It's about to get downright pitch-black in here."

"True," Charlot said and, as she left, added, "But I still want to hear about all this furniture that got broken!"

Savannah sat down and waved her out with a cursory smile on her face and murmured, "Not in your life."

.   .   .

THE MORNING SLID BY, and as noon approached, Savannah pulled out the contract documents for the Nigel project and reviewed them. At ten till, she headed downstairs to the meeting room on the first floor, where they planned to have Phillip Nigel sign the last documents. As Savannah approached, she saw that the legal and accounts receivable department reps were there, as she had asked. There was no way Phillip Nigel was leaving there without signing and giving at least a portion of the amount he owed. Liens had already been issued. The rest was just a formality.

Savannah walked in and smiled at the two people on the other side, Phillip Nigel and his legal representative, a dowdy man with an overzealous side part. The latter was reviewing the final page of the contract cancellation document. Phillip, however, looked pleasantly calm, which gave Savannah an off-putting feeling.

She had the thought again about a cat batting mice around just for the fun of it. She got the feeling that for Phillip Nigel, all was going according to plan.

On the other side of the table from Phillip Nigel's legal representative, Knight's attorney, a man she'd met a few times over the years, he was jovial and quick with a joke but sat silent and serious observing Phillip Nigel and cohort. Her accounts department rep, Karen, had her usual polite smile but kept looking at Savannah and Knight's attorney as if she were nervous. Savannah took her seat across from Phillip Nigel, creating an opposing flank of her personnel against Phillip Nigel and his legal representative. The ground-floor conference room held a media center at the far end of the room, and the glass-and-wood conference table was surrounded by plush leather rolling chairs. A small tray with a coffee carafe and water pitcher, mugs, and cups anchored the table. Savannah noticed no one had taken the tray up on its offerings.

"Hello, everyone," Savannah said. "Let's get things started." People shuffled papers, and her attorney flipped open his portfolio. It was business and business only in that room; it was as if they could feel the—Savannah was loath to say it even to herself—negative energy Phillip Nigel was emitting. Savannah continued, "Phillip Nigel, you and your legal representatives have received a copy of our cancellation addendum. Do you have any questions for us?"

Phillip's head came up as if he were sniffing the air, and he looked over at his representative. "Reginald?"

Reginald looked up. "Yes, that is, no, we have no questions." He passed the document over to Phillip, who had his own pen at the ready and signed without comment.

He passed the signed document across the table and as he replaced the cap on his pen, stood and said, "I believe we are done here." It was then that Savannah smelled the heavy cleansing odor of Listerine from Phillip Nigel. Savannah tried not to gag.

She looked at Karen and nodded.

Karen spoke up. "There's an outstanding check that we'll need to collect from you today, Mr. Nigel."

"Yes, fine. Reginald?"

His representative withdrew an envelope and passed it over. "It's for the full outstanding amount."

Savannah felt surprise raise her brow despite her desire to keep a poker face.

"Good day," Phillip said and, with his representative in tow, left the offices.

Savannah watched his progress down the hall and out the building's doors.

She turned back to her coworkers. "Did he just give, freely, a check for the balance that we've been hounding him for since this whole thing started? That was odd, wasn't it?"

"I'd say that was the simplest funds request that I've ever gotten from a nonpayment," Karen said as she gathered her things. "We'll see if it there are funds in the account next. You'd be surprised how many checks we get that bounce. It's less common these days, but not too long ago after the hurricane, we had a month where not one check we collected had the funds to back it up."

"Right," Savannah said and, looking out the door, knew that with Phillip Nigel, this could be the new game of cat and mouse.

She checked her watch and saw she had fifteen minutes left and decided to surprise Cason by showing up early at the Heights house.

She smiled to herself as she shouldered her bag and left the conference room. Cason would be surprised down to his dusty work boots to see her there before him. He was still military in so many ways; if he said he'd be somewhere at a certain time, he'd be there. Even if the zombie apocalypse erupted, Cason McPherson would be on time. Dead bodies on the hood, but on time.

She let thoughts of Phillip Nigel float away—he was a problem for another day. She headed out of the conference room and smiled. Thinking of Cason did that to her. Feeling the buoyant happiness, she was raising her hand to wave goodbye to the receptionist when a woman with peach-colored hair and cutoff shorts much too young for her aged body came rushing in through the main double doors.

Peaches.

Her raggedy red shirt was stained, and her hands and nose were flushed.

Savannah's brain gave pause. Savannah hadn't thought she would ever see her again after the honoring gala, much less that she knew where Savannah worked. It took her just a moment to recover, for her back to get up, and for the memories from the gala come rushing in and place her firmly in the "hostile persons" category.

Peaches was headed for the receptionist when she caught sight of Savannah and came at her.

"Get out," Savannah said, staring the other woman down, and pointed back toward the front doors.

"Savi—"

"It's Savannah, and you need to leave."

"I can't, it's Case. He's all beat up. He's bad, real bad. We gotta go to the hospital."

Savannah narrowed her eyes at the older woman. She slid her phone out—no missed calls. Though he didn't have a cell...

"He's hurt real bad, an accident. Don't know if he's going to make it. You gotta rush."

"Is he beat up or in an accident? And why are *you* here telling me this?" Her brain refused to acknowledge anything Peaches was saying as truth.

Peaches's eyes darted left before she responded, "I am still his emergency contact, and they called me. I hitched a ride here because I knew you'd want to know."

"Hold on a second, that doesn't—"

"He lost lots of blood, they said. They weren't sure if he's gonna make it. But they said I had to find you. He was asking for you before he passed out."

The minute possibility of truth in her words had Savanna saying, "Fine. Which hospital was it?"

"He's at the general hospital. Hurry now."

Savannah's gut felt off. She picked up the pace, and Peaches followed her out the front doors. Savannah turned and stopped her. "I'll go alone. Thank you for telling me."

"I ain't got no ride. I need to go with you."

"No, you don't. And don't come to the hospital."

Peaches ground her back teeth just before spitting on the sidewalk next to Savannah's feet. "Fine."

Savannah let her lip lift in a sneer at Peaches, who was giving her an equal stare back. The woman was disgusting, making Savannah think, not for the first time, that Cason had to have been adopted.

She walked toward her car on the other side of the small treed lot while keeping a keen eye on Peaches. When Savannah got to her car, Peaches walked back into the building. Savannah unlocked her SUV, tossed her things in the back, and climbed into the driver's seat. She unlocked her cell to call the hospital, but just then Phillip Nigel slid into the backseat, pistol in hand, made himself comfortable, and said, "Drive me home, Ms. Sparling."

Savannah took one look at him and felt her stomach plummet to the asphalt under her car. "No."

"Then I'll shoot you, dear." His boggy-brown eyes glared at her while the car filled with the scent of the mouthwash he'd baptized himself in.

Movement caught Savannah's eye; she looked up to see Peaches making her way across the parking lot. The car was ringing with the quiet as Savannah waited, paralyzed, with the gun on her, for the moment to get exponentially worse.

"Why are you doing this?"

"My dear," he said, breathing harder than was necessary, as if he were excited about something that was going to happen, "this is destiny. Since the moment you set your witchy shoes upon my doorstep."

Peaches slid in then, biting the corner of her lip and her eyes alight with the look of a dog joining a pack on a hunt to kill.

"And how exactly do you fit in?" Savannah asked, trying to keep the fear from shaking her voice.

"He and I come to an agreement after my shithead son had some words with Phillip here, and he come 'round looking for me, knowing I was looking for him. I'm going to set Case straight, and you, bitch, are going to do it for me."

"Rather, Ms. Sparling, it's much more complicated than just family drama. She, unfortunately," he said, nodding toward Peaches in the passenger seat, "is simply a means to an end."

"Fuck you," Peaches said over her shoulder and then turned in her seat to look at Phillip. "Where's my money?"

"Turn around, you trollop," he said, waving the gun in her direction. "You'll get your money, when we get to my home. Drive, Ms. Sparling."

Savannah put her seat belt on, and at the buckle, her hand shook too hard, making her miss the clip.

"Problem, Ms. Sparling?"

Savannah took a deep breath. There was more than just one problem in her car. If she leaped out, she'd be shot. If she didn't do as he said, she'd be dead. Life had gotten so blissful; she should have remembered Sheriff Lee's warning about messes coming in threes. Her grip on the steering wheel made her knuckles white as she drove out of the parking lot and down the street. She wanted to put on her hazards, to honk her horn, to get into an accident—anything to draw attention to the homicidal situation she was in. But every move she wanted to make, she felt unsure if it would it work. It was easy in the movies for actors to save themselves; there was no real danger. The fear of dying was palpable for her, freezing her, icing her joints against anything that would go against the person pointing the gun at her.

The thought of taking her hands off the wheel made her stomach clench in fear. Instead, she ground her teeth and drove to his palatial mansion. Secluded mansion. Gated, secluded mansion.

"Why, exactly, are we going to your home, Phillip?" she asked, hearing the quiver in her voice. "Your business with Knight Interiors is over."

"My business with them is over. With you, it's far from over. You promised me perfection. You said I could call you whenever I liked, and you also made me believe that I could hold you personally accountable for all that happened. Now I'm doing that. I'm holding you accountable. Marauders entered my home, assaulted my privacy, and laid me bare. Your playtime at my expense is over."

"I don't think this is holding me accountable, Mr. Nigel. You have a gun pointed at me; you're holding me hostage."

A shot rang out in the cabin. Savannah jumped and her mind skittered. Gunpowder filled Savannah's nose with its acrid smoke; the blindingly loud crack of the pistol had temporarily deafened her. Had she been shot? What had happened?

Emotion crashed through her, and she felt tears well up into her eyes. As her hearing returned, she heard screaming, and her mind realized she was in oncoming traffic. Savannah yanked the wheel back, her heart thundering like hooves on derby day.

Peaches was screaming.

Savannah risked a glance at Phillip, as he appeared to have been hollering since he pulled the trigger on his pistol. He shouted over Peaches's screaming, "You will not treat me like an imbecile any longer! I am holding a gun. You will respect me or the next shot I fire will be into your gut, you hell-mouthed woman!"

Peaches kept screaming, and Savannah's mouth went dry. The added adrenaline made her hands shake violently on the steering wheel. Her whole body begged to run.

"Do shut your mouth, Mrs. McPherson! Or I'll reconsider our bargain."

Peaches had braced herself in her seat and instead of screaming started whimpering. "I don't want to die today." She looked over at Savannah. "You're gonna die. Not me, I got hero blood in me," she said more to herself than anyone else.

The lane Phillip lived off of came into view, and Savannah's limbs were like lead when she tried to turn onto it. She took each turn wide and quickly, as her foot had difficulty moving to the brake. The next turn they drove past the private security gates of the Nigel residence.

"Up to the front, Ms. Sparling, my dear, and then park. Don't mind the two men I've hired to watch the front door. They may look like delinquents, and while they are—"

Peaches interrupted, turning to Savannah, having regained her fragile arrogance again. "They're my girlfriend's kids. Heard about how you treated me at my time of honoring and don't take too kindly to that."

Savannah felt her lip curl up as she drove up to the apex of the circular drive. Her mouth responded before her brain could stop it. "You mean they're getting paid too."

Peaches lifted her hand in a threat. "Shut your whore mouth, or I'll shut it for you."

Savannah slowed down and stopped at the front door. The home was as it had been the last time they were there, though the Porta-Potty was gone, as were the contract workers. Instead, standing like despicable sentries on either side of the double front entrance were the hired muscle Peaches had found, scrappy and dull looking from their years of belligerence and drug use.

"Out," Phillip Nigel commanded.

Savannah managed to get her door open. She slid from the driver's seat and surveyed the two delinquents who had come partway down the stairs, eyeing her. She took in the enormous erotic fountain behind her and calculated the possibility of survival if she ducked behind it. Fear took her again. Even though it was only a half acre of flat lawn from there to the front gates, there was not a single shrub to hide behind. She needed a sure thing. She needed help.

Peaches got out, slammed the passenger door, and swaggered over the drive and to the front of the mansion as if it were hers. "No one in or out, y'hear?" she said to the two ratty men, one in a torn green hoodie and the other in a black shirt that had a middle finger boldly displayed in white across its front.

"Please, Mrs. McPherson," Phillip Nigel said, his gun pointed at Savannah, "they've already been instructed and paid on that very point. You two, move the vehicle out of sight and then back to your posts." Then to Savannah: "Inside, Ms. Sparling. I have very limited time for this affair."

The men bit the air in front of Savannah as she walked by. The hair on the back of her neck went up, and the feeling of dread finally settled like a stone in her belly. This was very likely a day she was not going to survive. With Phillip, gun in hand, and two hired drug addicts with weapons, her odds plummeted to zero.

She'd need the pistol from Phillip's hand. As soon as the thought entered her mind, fear chased it away. Wrestling the pistol from Phillip's hand was the best way to get shot dead.

Savannah stepped into the AC-cooled mansion, which was set well below the comfortable temperature of seventy-two degrees. It was hovering somewhere south of sixty. The smell of a just-laid plastic drop cloth and the cloying scent of mouthwash tinged the edges of his ice mansion.

Phillip slammed the door shut behind her. Peaches strode past the windows, looking out, as she said, "Why you got this place colder than a witch's tit? Damn freezing in here."

"It's the temperature that keeps the mind alive. Something you are sublimely lacking, I'm afraid," he said under his breath to a half-listening Peaches, and then to Savannah said, "Let's get to it, shall we? Take a long look at what you've done to my home."

Savannah looked again. The protective sheeting had been taken down, the cardboard and all hardwood protection removed. The new drywall was still raw, and the bolt of fabric, the indigo-with-paisley pattern they had gone round and round on, was lying on the bare floor of the sitting room in which it was supposed to have been hung. Its length had been sliced with a hacking hand. The drywall had the same hacked hatch marks.

Flakes of drywall and its white powder were everywhere. Pieces of the blue fabric, shreds of it, littered the floor. And next to the main working table taking up the cavernous front room was a midcentury wood chair on a freshly unfolded plastic sheet. The only clean spot in the entire space.

Again Savannah's mouth bypassed her brain and asked, "What did you do?"

"What did I do? What *I* did?" he said. His voice soared, and he came at her, his gun's eye on her chest. "*You* did this."

Dread swelled up, making her mouth go dry again, as if a mouthful of flour had been shoved into it. She saw something in Phillip Nigel she hadn't seen before. She saw the Phillip Nigel behind closed doors. The one he hid from the public, the one he tried to cover with drink and perfectly pressed polo shirts. Instead she saw the monster he really was, the one who hid his dark desires from public view. The menacing feline who had caught a baby bird and brought it home to torture in play before killing for his fun.

Despite knowing he'd done it, she tried to get him to see reason anyway. To get him to see what he was doing. "Mr. Nigel, if someone did this, you should file a grievance with Knight Interiors, not hold me hostage and threaten me."

"You did this, Ms. Sparling. When you refused to cooperate with me. When you demanded that I pay for shoddy workmanship. When you came into my home and said that I did not own it and baldly claimed I had no rights—"

"I'm sorry you—"

"Don't interrupt me when I am speaking!"

Savannah clamped her mouth shut.

His eyes narrowed into bloodshot slits. "Good girl. Do as you're told. I'd like to say that this has a happy ending in it for you, dear. That if this time you do exactly as I say, all will be forgiven. But you've crossed me too many times. I waited for days for you to show up with that paperwork. Only you didn't because you never had any intention of bringing it to me. You made a fool of me! You had your filth lie to me, to my face! Then, just now, you brought me before a committee of filth to humiliate me more, but I conceded, knowing I'd bring justice to you. Now, Ms. Sparling, I have the upper hand. No amount of trash talk and lies about being in accidents...How dare you think I'm such an imbecile that I'd believe such rubbish! Mother, forgive me for my language," he said, looking up and then back down at her. "You double-crossing whore."

At this Peaches laughed. "Damn straight. Whore."

Savannah took a deep breath, trying to keep her heart from hammering right out of her chest.

"No, you are out of chances with me, Ms. Sparling. I'm going to watch as you get your due punishment. Of course, if asked, I'll say I haven't seen you since our tête-à-tête earlier today."

Savannah's gut churned, and she looked again at the closed door, then to the gun in Phillip Nigel's hand.

"Ah-ah-ah, Ms. Sparling. I'll shoot you dead if you run from me or defy me. Not to mention, dear, that cowardice does not suit you either. Take your due like a good girl."

The world crashed down upon Savannah—it was either do as he asked or be shot to death. The options crumpled her insides.

"Restrain her," he said to Peaches. "Once you are secured, I will get started on the first of your offenses, your promises..."

Chapter Thirty

Cason looked at his watch. It was 12:30 on the dot, and Savannah wasn't at the house yet. It wasn't only the time that made him get in his truck; something in his gut told him to. With the po-boys in the paper bag next to him, he headed to her work.

Once there, he asked the receptionist to page Savannah.

The young woman didn't smile; she looked concerned when she said, "Oh, she was pulled away to the hospital by a family emergency."

Cason's gut sank. "When?" he asked, thinking that something bad had happened to Mrs. S., then added, "Did they say what happened?"

"No, she didn't. I just overheard the woman telling Savannah that someone had been hurt."

Cason's interest was piqued at the mention of another woman. "Someone came in to get her?"

"Yes, an older woman."

Cason was relieved that Mrs. S. was okay. But then confused;

who would have been in an accident making Mrs. S. come get her
and not call? "Did you hear anything else?"

The girl shook her head. "No. I'm sorry."

"The older woman," he said, not sure why he needed clarity on
Mrs. S.'s being there but feeling like he should dig deeper. "She was
shorter," he said, putting his hand up higher than the bar height
reception counter, "with gray hair?"

The receptionist shook her head. "No, the older woman was
taller, thin with orangey-colored hair, and..." She looked unsure of
whether to say something or not but apparently decided to. "She
looked a little rough. I thought maybe it was an acquaintance or
something?"

This time his gut clenched, hearing the description of his mother.
Then he hoped he was wrong, and he asked, "Did you hear her
name? Peaches?"

The receptionist just shrugged. "I'm sorry I can't be of more help.
Maybe try the general hospital?"

Cason felt sure it was Peaches who had been there, and he was
sure his mother wasn't there to escort Savannah to the hospital. He
could only imagine what she really wanted from Savannah—it would
be payment for her standing up to Peaches at the gala, no doubt.
Though this seemed like more work than Peaches was normally
willing to actually do. She'd talk about doing vengeful things but was
a coward when it came to acting on them. More than once she swore
to track down and kill his father, but never had. She hadn't even
managed to sober up for a day. Peaches on a vendetta would definitely not be alone, nor in charge.

Someone called his name and turned to see the woman he had
almost slept with come sauntering up. He immediately wanted to
disappear from her and find Savannah.

"Oh my gosh, Cason! What a coincidence—Savannah and I were
just talking about you this morning!" Charlot said, smiling; then after
she looked at him, her face crashed. "Oh no, your aura is all off. What
happened?"

"Excuse me, I have to go," he said.

"Wait," said the receptionist, "if you're Cason, then who's in the hospital?"

Cason turned back to the receptionist; she'd just confirmed that it was Peaches. No one else would come looking for Savannah using him as bait. "I'm not sure. Excuse me, I have somewhere I need to be."

Charlot got caught up and asked the receptionist, "Who said Cason was in the hospital?"

"This woman who came to get Savannah. There was a family emergency."

"Wow," Charlot said, sounding concerned. "This is the cause of your aura shift. What a derailment of the positive energy that we just had with the Nigel project."

Cason paused at the door and turned back to Charlot. "Nigel? Is that Savannah's horror client, Phillip Nigel?"

"Well, we don't use those kinds of words to outline our clients' characteristics—"

"Yes," the receptionist said to him.

It was a leap, thinking his mother and the Nigel man could be connected. Phillip Nigel and his mother made for an odd pair, and it could just be a coincidence, but if his years taking enemy fire had taught him anything, it was that ignored coincidences had negative consequences, sometimes fatal ones. "What time did the Nigel project meeting get over?"

Charlot shrugged as the receptionist answered, "Just before the woman came in. Savannah was leaving the meeting and coming down here when she came in."

Cason's gut twisted as the possibility of Phillip Nigel finding Peaches. She had made a spectacle at the gala, and attracting bad people was her only talent in life. Though how she had gotten as far as she did at the gala niggled at the back of his mind.

"Thank you," Cason said absently and left. He swung through the parking lot, looking for Savannah's car. He drove slowly, not wanting to accidentally miss it. Nothing. As he reached the lot's exit, he saw something on the ground catching the light. He jumped from his truck—her phone, lying shimmering white on the hot black asphalt.

He tossed her cell on the passenger seat of his truck and gunned it out of the parking lot, his rear tires chirping as he hung a hard right out onto the main drag. He'd already threatened the man once, something he didn't tell Savannah, the day Phillip had knocked her to the ground. He'd watched Savannah's car drive out, and then, once the sheriff and his deputy left, Cason had swung back in. The man had not been expecting the firm grip on his shoulder when he'd answered the door or the even harder words Cason said to him. He wanted to make it crystal clear that if he thought he'd gotten away with his little trick of being clumsy as an excuse in hitting Savannah, the next chat they'd have would be with Cason's fists.

He would drive by his mother's trailer first and then go pay Phillip Nigel another visit. After that, he'd call Sheriff Lee.

SAVANNAH WASN'T in the hot stink of his mother's trailer, and neither was his mother. Cason slid into the driver's seat again and slammed his truck door shut. His tires peeled out on the brown clay as he swung out of her lot.

It took him longer than he wanted to, to double back to Phillip Nigel's mansion. There, set at the back of the property, was the mansion. It still gave him the creeps, despite its opulence. His gaze crested the splashing fountain—he didn't want to look too long at it—and up to the front doors, where two deadbeats stood like sentries. Cason knew to the bone then that Savannah was there. The two looked to be his mother's ilk.

Feeling the onset of battle turn his brain into high gear, Cason didn't slow as he reached the drive's arch in front of the fountain; he had a plan. Right at the apex, Cason hit the brakes, sliding the truck to a stop. He stepped out in a cloud of quartz gravel dust, the po-boy bag in hand. He watched the two men. The one with the green hoodie had something heavy in his front sweater pocket and the other, in a black T-shirt with the finger emblazoned in white on the front, reached behind him. Cason saw only red, enemy combatants.

They came down the stairs as he rounded the front of the truck.

Cason raised the bag and shaded his eyes with his other hand as he said in his thickest New Orleans drawl, "Got dem here po' boys for a Nigel Phillip, or is it Phillip Nigel? Hell, wha'dat receipt say?" He patted his pockets as he kept walking.

"Hold up now; we didn't order nothing," the one in green said, coming off the bottom stair. "Get going, or you're gonna get trouble."

Cason kept walking. "I know it's here somewhere..."

"Hey, fucker. Did you hear what we just said to you? Get the fuck out of here."

"No, I swear on my mama's grave I got the right place now." Cason was within arm's reach of the men.

The man with a finger on his shirt pulled a pistol out from behind him.

Cason felt the desert sand of war pour into his veins. "Wrong move, buddy." Cason clocked Finger Shirt with his fist. The man's head knocked to the side, sending him to his knees in a daze. The man's hand went slack on the pistol grip and Cason kicked the pistol from him. His black gaze swept back to Hoodie, and—

What Hoodie lacked in brain power, he made up in speed. Cason felt the solidity of the man's fist as it landed on his jaw. The rattling pound woke the rest of the anger that he fought daily to keep in check.

Deadly calm, Cason took two steps back and placed the po-boy bag on the ground, tested his jaw, and readied for his attacker.

Hoodie bounced on his toes as if he were a boxer in the ring and, seeing Cason, arms down waiting, charged. The man roared as he tucked his head for a tackle, and Cason let him. In the last second, Cason sidestepped him, shoving him as he passed. Hoodie was tossed forward to the ground. He hit and rolled over onto his back; immediately his hand went to his front pocket but got stuck there. Hoodie's movements were frantic as he shoved himself backward away from Cason and his truck in desperation to get whatever it was out of his pocket.

Cason moved in on him. "Whatever you have in there won't stop me."

The hilt of a forty-five glinted. Cason was on him as he aimed, and kicked the man's hand wide. Before he could take aim again, Cason had Hoodie's arm down, pinning it to the ground under his knee. The man's other fist swung. He punched Cason in the shoulder and again in the ribs. Cason blocked the man's next hit with his elbow, then slammed his fist into his face. Cason followed that punch with another and another before pulling the man's pinned arm out. He stood, yanked the man onto his side and twisted his wrist, making him drop the gun. Boot to shoulder, Cason slammed the man the rest of the way face down into the gravel. The man screamed—then Cason felt an arm slide around his neck.

The man's arm was thin but firm as a noose on his esophagus, making his breath come up short. The man dragged Cason backward; Cason's boot heels caught, digging trenches in the driveway as Cason tried to get his feet under him.

Cason's hands went to the arm around his throat and tried pulling. The two men wrestled, grappling for dominance and, for Cason, air. His legs began to feel heavy; he swung back, trying to hit the man in the face. His punches glanced off the man's shoulder. It was like boxing backward. Finally, Cason let his weight fight for him; he went suddenly and completely limp.

The man cursed as Cason's deadweight yanked him forward. Cason landed on his knees, but was there for only a moment. As the man fell over him, Cason was up and rising with the man over his shoulder. Cason pitched the lighter man with a grunting heft.

The man hit the drive in a satisfying explosion of dust. As he rolled over, he spotted his lost pistol; Cason's kick had landed it nearby. Moving with desperation, the scrawny man scrambled toward it. Cason stepped forward and kicked the pistol under his truck.

He pointed at him. "Stay down."

A shot rang out, and heat singed his shoulder. Cason's gaze swung to the man in the hoodie, sitting on the gravel behind him; his broken wrist was shaking under the weight of the forty-five.

"Your next one should be here," Cason said, putting his finger to his forehead as he moved in on him, "or you should put that down."

"Fuck you, man!" Hoodie's shaking finger pulled the trigger again; its shot was wide. The next shot Cason felt wing his pants leg.

Cason was on him then and grasped the top of the hot pistol barrel, ripping it out of the man's hand. He turned back to where Finger was under the truck, reaching for the kicked pistol.

Cason shot the man in the knee. As his hollers of pain echoed off the front of the mansion, Cason popped the magazine and chambered round. They clattered and pinged against the rocks at his feet. Then he pulled the forty-five in two, tossing the slide and grip into the fountain next him.

Not recognizing when he'd been beat, the man in the hoodie got up and, holding his injured wrist, charged Cason. Cason felt a primal growl escape his throat when, in the last second, he stepped wide. Like a bowling ball down a lane, the man barreled into the front fender of Cason's truck. Cason was quick. He grabbed the man as he bounced off it; holding a fistful of hair, he rammed the man's face into the truck until bloodied; he blacked out. Cason let him go and moved in on the last man. He'd had enough of the brawling bullshit. He heard the man in the hoodie fall to the ground behind him as he rounded the front of his truck.

Halfway under it was the first man attempting to retrieve his pistol. Cason bent over and pulled him out from under his truck by his shot leg. Blood and sand swirled in the air; those scents alone were strong enough to cover the man's screams. Cason's hip pain came back like a ghost, matching the one now at his shoulder. He felt the real sensation of blood dripping down his arm.

The man in the finger shirt shouted and kicked at Cason. Cason's steel-toed boot met the man's jaw in a vicious kick, sending him to lights out.

Cason stepped over his body and moved in on the mansion with purpose.

Chapter Thirty-One

Savannah pulled against the Knight Interior personalized duct tape that had bound her wrists and ankles in the midcentury Scan dining chair. Even in kidnapping, Phillip Nigel strove for elegance. Pistol muzzle pressed against her forehead, Savannah had easily been subdued for Peaches to tape her down.

Savannah's nose itched. Torture upon torture.

Peaches was pacing the wide room now, the pack-dog look back on her face, as Phillip stood at the table in front of Savannah, pouring two healthy glasses of whiskey.

"First, Ms. Sparling. You lied to me about those fabric samples," Phillip said.

Peaches made for the first glass as soon as he finished pouring. She slung it back as Phillip frowned at her. Then, to Savannah, after taking a healthy slug of his own drink, he said, "You lied to my face. Here in my own home. Does this look perfect to you, Ms. Sparling? Hmmm, does it look up to the standard you promised me?" He waited a beat and then turned his annoyed gaze to Peaches. "Really, woman. Must your entire sex be so intellectually retarded?"

Savannah tested her restraints again. She wasn't sure what was about to happen, but it seemed that they'd practiced something and Peaches had just missed her cue. For that Savannah felt a microscopic, if fleeting, feeling of relief.

Peaches stopped circling. "What the hell did you just say?"

"Really, Mrs. McPherson. We discussed that, for each of her offenses, you'd mark her with your blade."

She staggered over. "You mean cut her. This ain't no crayon. I'm going to cut her."

Phillip closed his eyes as the veins at his temple rose and his face turned puce. His eyes shot open. "Cut her! *Cut her!*"

Peaches pointed the box cutter at Phillip. "Yell at me again, motherfucker."

Phillip roared and, snatching the blade from Peaches, swung wildly at Savannah. Savannah felt the shriek in her throat and rocked the chair away from him. The blade was low and swiped up her arm. She felt its tug along her skin before the pain.

Phillip swung around and threw the blade at Peaches. "There! You imbecile, that's how you do it!" He pulled frantically at his pants pocket, pulled out a bottle of hand sanitizer, and applied it liberally to his hands, filling the air with the scent of a different kind of alcohol.

Steeling her nerves, Savannah looked down to see the wound. Fiery pain blazed up her arm, making the wound pulse with her heartbeat. Savannah barely processed that now there was a severed edge of duct tape at her wrist.

"Don't need to throw no damned knives at me—"

A pistol shot from outside carried into the well-insulated home and froze Phillip and Peaches. Then, in a frantic movement, Peaches ran for the box cutter that had slid across the floor, and Phillip lunged for his pistol on the table and moved cautiously toward the front window.

"Who do you think it is?" Peaches said, moving toward Phillip, her box cutter out.

"You are the epitome of ignorance, woman. How should I know? Most likely it is your kin playing games with the fountain again."

Savannah swallowed down the pain and tested the duct tape. Phillip and Peaches argued as they moved to the window, drowning out the first cracking tear of Savannah's duct tape. Putting more muscle behind it, she strained her wrist upward, and the rest of the tape tore along the straight line she realized the box cutter had started.

Watching them watch out the front window, Savannah quietly worked the edge of the tape on the other wrist while blood dripped from the slice on her arm.

"I don't see nothing."

Phillip pulled the sheer curtain back a crack.

Peaches cursed. "What the hell is he doin' here?"

Phillip turned and hurried to the front door and bolted it.

The microscopic feeling of relief grew. The only person who would make Peaches curse in fear was her son. And it was well past 12:30 p.m. The crumpled feeling of defeat on her insides began to shift. If that person was indeed Cason, there was hope that she would not end this day wrapped in a plastic sheet. Or at least she wouldn't be the only one in it; she could have peace of mind knowing that if she died, Phillip Nigel would too. And she'd watch from the afterlife as his rear got sucked down into Satan's den.

Phillip turned to Savannah. Seeing her hands loose, he shouted, "No! You will put your hands back!"

Peaches turned from the window and came at her with the box cutter out.

Savannah growled through the tape on her mouth.

CASON KNEW the best way in was not necessarily the front door. Passing the first narrow window on the side of the house, he chanced a glance in. Savannah was bound and gagged in a chair in the middle of the room. Black rage roiled through him. He suppressed the urge to barge in and kill everyone, including his mother. The two men had been armed but not as crazy as Nigel and, Cason was sure, his mother. That kind of insanity added an element to a fight. He needed a better look into the room.

The mansion seemed to go on forever before ending in a patio that had a side servants' entrance. Cason slipped in and found a large commercial kitchen, empty save for a pile of used takeout boxes sitting in the sink as if they were dishes. Past the stainless counter-tops, dual gas ranges, and hanging pots and pans, Cason paused at the entry to the rest of the house. He slowly pushed open the kitchen door. It was a straight shot past the guest bathroom and into the living room. He could see that his mother held a box cutter in her hand.

Cason turned back to the kitchen. He needed a distraction. A loud and fiery one.

Chapter Thirty-Two

Phillip shouted at Peaches, "Tape her back up!"

Peaches came at Savannah, the box cutter pointed at her. Savannah watched her sunken eyes and not the cutter. "Sit still," she said.

Peaches was within reach then.

The older woman looked down, warily, at Savannah's hands and back up. Banking on having a healthier reaction time than Peaches, Savannah lunged for the cutter as Peaches flinched. Savannah tore it from the older woman's hand. Peaches screeched and made to grab it back, but Savannah was quicker, slicing the blade through the air at Peaches.

Phillip roared, "Dammit! Must I do every—" A noise from the back of the house echoed, cutting Phillip off midsentence. A low whirring sound like a microwave running emanated from the kitchen.

"Go investigate that sound," Phillip said to Peaches.

"I ain't going back there."

"Mrs. McPherson, what in god's name good are you if you do not do what I tell you? I am paying you, Mrs. McPherson. Go back there, now!"

"Hell no. For all I know, this could be a trap!"

Savannah moved slowly, slicing at her ankle restraints while they hollered at each other again.

Phillip raised his pistol at Peaches. "You go back there, right this instant!"

"You pointing that thing at me—"

A muffled boom stopped them.

The muffle was followed by a full-out explosion. The windows shook, and the blast of sound was followed by the pounding pressure of fiery air. Bits blew forward from the rear hall and out like burnt confetti.

Suppressing her shock and using the borrowed time, Savannah sliced the rest of her ankle restraint, freeing herself, and ripped the duct tape from her mouth. She looked up just as Cason charged out of the smoky shadows like a defensive end bursting out the gates of Hade's mansion.

Phillip was startled and swung his pistol toward him. He fired, and Peaches shrieked.

Savannah gasped, feeling her insides clench, but Cason did not slow. He was knocking Phillip's gun hand to the side and slamming his fist into his jaw. Phillip stumbled back, his drink-saturated blood allowing him to take the hit.

Smoke began to billow into the room in earnest then, filling it with the smell of spent propane and burning chemicals. Savannah could hear the cracks of fire.

Peaches made for Cason's back, arm raised. Savannah lunged out of the chair and grabbed a fistful of Peaches's box-dyed orange hair and yanked her back. Cason's gaze met hers, and for a moment they spoke to each other. The darkness in his eyes made her shiver, a darkness that said he'd gladly face down more than a loaded pistol for her. She hoped he saw that she'd have his back so that he wouldn't need to.

Hand in Peaches's hair, Savannah used it like a handle to yank her back and off balance, then swung her wide. Finding the woman was much lighter than she had expected, Savannah hurtled Peaches a good distance in a flail of arms and legs. She let go and sent the older woman rolling across the floor. Still holding the box cutter, Savannah moved in on Peaches. She scrambled backward as Savannah felt the last of her fear skitter out the back door.

"I didn't want to do it. He made me do it," Peaches whined as Savannah stalked her.

"I don't give a damn. Get up," she said down to the pathetic woman now cringing with fear against the side wall leading to the sitting room.

Holding her palm out to stop Savannah, Peaches started to get up. "Don't hurt me. I didn't do nothing. He made me," she said again, her eyes on the box cutter.

"I heard this saying recently, and I think it fits you. Fits everything you've ever said: If I believed your bullshit, I'd buy it by the ton," Savannah said as she towered over her.

Peaches sneered, showing Savannah that her cowering was an act. She made her way to standing and spat on the floor. "You gonna stand there and talk me to death, or you gonna actually do something with that blade, bitch? If I had it, I'd cut up your sass mouth so no man would ever want you. All you'd be good for then is being cunt for him to stick his dick into—"

Savannah jabbed Peaches hard in the nose with her closed fist around the box cutter.

Peaches's hands flew to her face as her eyes went wide with surprise. She brought her hands down as blood ran over her upper lip and coated her fingertips.

"I don't need to use this blade to make you bleed." Savannah said glaring at the bloodied older woman, begging her to entice her into a good whupping, when the snap and crackle of fire caught her attention. Looking back toward the staircase, she saw them crack and peel up under the heat of a fire moving out from the kitchen area.

"Holy sh—" Savannah murmured, realizing the accelerant that Cason must have used to create the explosion was more than just an aerosol can in the microwave. It looked like a propane stove was feeding it at a pace like a mouse moving toward cheese.

Movement caught the corner of her eye in the far sitting room. Savannah spun to see Peaches at the far window.

"Stop!" Savannah said, running after the woman. Peaches didn't hesitate and yanked the window wide open. Savannah covered her face with arm as air whistled past, feeding the hungry blaze. The house, closed up, had bought them time. Opening it and feeding the fire precious oxygen was like feeding a starving giant—it couldn't get enough. It raised the fire's pace to that of a hare in a dog race.

Peaches had the screen off and was already diving out when the flames, now roaring, licked sideways toward the window. Savannah stumbled back to the front wall. The heat of the inferno blasted forward as it consumed the stairs. Sparks spit out ahead of it, planting smaller smoldering fires it would eat as it progressed.

Across the room, she saw Cason stalking a fleeing Phillip Nigel across the front room. Scrabbling over the slippery plastic sheeting, Phillip Nigel tried to reach his knocked-away pistol. Savannah stepped toward them, her heart lurching. Phillip grasped it as Cason reached him. Pistol in his hands, Phillip Nigel rolled over, taking aim. Cason, a blank determination on his face, kicked it as the pistol went off. The pistol flew toward the front door.

The fire's fingers crackled and snapped, scarring the stair balcony with black. Potent, thick wood and plaster smoke billowed farther into the room. The gunshots seemed to have had no effect on Cason. It was as if the weapons were harmless air pistols shooting fluffy clouds.

Phillip looked panicked as he fumbled backward from Cason and came up against the front wall.

"No need for all this violence, son. Let's talk—"

Savannah wrestled with wanting to intervene and wanting to stay out of a fight Cason was easily handling. It was the simultaneous and opposite need to protect Cason from himself by protecting Phillip Nigel that she did not want to do.

Cason didn't respond to the older man's request to talk it out. He simply closed the distance and crouched next to him. He put a heavy hand on his chest. Phillip screamed as if burned and tried to shove Cason's hand off him. Cason bypassed the older man's clawing and slid his hand up to his neck, firmly covering his Adam's apple. Phillip Nigel's hands clasped Cason's choking one and Savannah watched, darkly curious. Until Cason put a knee down on Phillip Nigel's sternum and leaned forward.

The light was completely gone from Cason's eyes; it was as if he'd finally come face-to-face with every one of his demons. Every demon that had held him down, pulled the trigger on his best friend, and attempted to take the last thing he loved in this world.

Phillip clawed at Cason's hand.

Over the roar of the fire, Savannah called to him, "Cason." Then watched as her voice fell on deaf ears. Watched as those demons wrapped their arms around him, dragging him back into their hell, making him a warrior and killer again.

Cason didn't respond to her. Phillip's mouth opened and closed like a gasping fish's as his legs tried to push himself out from under the pressure.

Savannah moved in. "Cason!" she shouted as Phillip's red face turned a deeper color in the fire's eerie flicker. "Cason!"

His eyes snapped up to hers.

"Stop."

He looked down at his hand and then back to her. For a long, blood-oozing moment, Savannah couldn't breathe while he decided whether or not he was too far gone to let Phillip Nigel live.

"Let him go," Savannah added.

Cason obeyed then. He lifted his knee and slowly let his grip loosen. He paused as if deeply questioning letting Phillip go. Savannah slowly moved toward him; as she got closer, she heard him say through the roar and snap of the house fire, "Touch her, talk to her, or harm her—I will come for you. I will finish what was started here. If you think of her, think of her as the woman who saved your life—now there's a blood debt on you. One I'll call in whenever I want to—pray to God I don't have a bad day."

Phillip Nigel's hand massaged his throat as he hoarsely gasped for air. His other fumbled with his pocket. Cason grasped that wrist and held it up; Phillip was tightly gripping a bottle of sanitizer. Disgust scrunched Cason's features, and he flicked Phillip's wrist away.

"Nod if you understand what I just said to you."

Phillip Nigel sneered at his death dealer but reluctantly nodded.

In an odd move, Cason reached down to Phillip's ankle and lifted his pants leg. It revealed what he must have known to be there: an ankle holster. He removed the hidden pistol, a derringer, and stood. He tucked the gun into the back of his pants before leaving his repulsive prey and went to Savannah.

The house was on fire and she'd nearly died, but Savannah didn't give a damn. She needed the feel of Cason, solid and solidifying in her arms. He came up against her—she felt his need to touch her, just as strong as hers—and Savannah put her arms around him as his own wrapped around her, squeezing her tightly. Against her hair he said, "This whole place is a fucking inferno. We need to get out."

She nodded and felt the odd sensation to laugh. No shit the house was ablaze.

She leaned back and looked up at him, about to tell him that she loved him before dragging them both from the place. But the blood at his shoulder, staining his plaid crimson, had her stopping, and the gut-clenching fear returned. Her fingers went to his shoulder. She pulled apart the fabric, revealing the torn flesh.

Her head went light. "And you're bleeding—"

Heat still pressed at them, the cracks becoming louder as the fire claimed the rear of the room, snapping the wood framing.

Savannah's fingers were wet with blood. "Oh my..."

"It's fine. Let's go."

Her own blood she could handle, but staring at his open wound made the crackle of the burning house go quiet. The smoke stuck in her throat. All she knew was Cason's injury. Thinking it was from Phillip Nigel, hate bloomed in her belly. She looked over to where he had lain on the ground, and her body plunged into an icy chill. He was gone. She leaned past Cason and saw him then, a stone's throw away behind Cason, a gun in hand.

"What—" Cason started to ask when she stiffened. Savannah's hand simply reacted; it moved of its own accord, needing no input from her brain for directions on what to do next. It traveled to the small of Cason's back, and as Phillip's gun hand rose to the two of them, she yanked the pistol out from the waist of his jeans. Phillip's shot whizzed past Savannah's ear. Yet her own thumb moved like a slug over hot summer asphalt to reach the derringer's hammer and press it down. She felt Cason curl around her then, and like that defensive end, he went for the tackle and pushed against her. She felt her feet come up off the ground, and she gripped Cason with her other arm. She saw Phillip's eyes close as she finally wrenched the hammer down, and he shot again at their moving bodies. It was there, as Savannah was airborne, that the antiquated pistol finally primed and she felt life freeze-frame. She watched Phillip's face screw up. Watched once more as he took final aim. Watched frame after frame, the way it all chugged by, slowing until it was fully paused. There in the silence was the feel of the derringer's hard narrow metal of a trigger pressed against the crook of her finger and there, halted in time over her pistol's post, was the dark eye of Phillip's gun. Savannah pressed play.

The derringer's explosive shot sounded, competing with the sounds of the fire. Cason finished tackling her sideways just as the rear ceiling fell, bringing part of the second story down. They hit the floor and slid, colliding into the front wall.

Curled up against the sparks and flying debris, Cason cursed and looked down at Savannah. "Are you hit?"

Wide-eyed, she shook her head. "I don't know, but he had a gun pointed at you!"

Cason turned. "He's down. I think you hit him, or he was hit with a beam. Let's go!"

Savannah pulled her shirt up over her nose and mouth and tried the front window as the entire place filled with caustic smoke. The window slid open easily and they knocked the screen out. The sounds of wailing sirens wafted in.

Savannah made to fling her leg out the window, but Cason stopped her. "Hold up."

He peered over the edge, and a bullet shattered the window above him. Cason cursed as they ducked back down.

"I see you, fucker!" a man outside shouted.

Cason cursed again as Savannah asked, "Who the hell?"

"Someone I should have killed."

Savannah remembered the two men outside from earlier. They both ducked as the rest of the window exploded in a rain of glass.

There was shouting outside. "We need to get the hell out of here, man!" another man shouted.

"That asshole shot me! I'm gonna kill him."

Cason looked down at Savannah. "Get down low and stay there." Savannah flattened against the floor as the room took more gunfire. Cason put a hand to her shoulder. "Where's the pistol?"

Savannah realized then that her hands were empty. Surrounding them were burning embers and roof debris. "I don't know. I must have lost it when we hit the ground."

"Okay. Can you breathe okay down here?"

She nodded; then the voices outside came again. "Get back, man! The place is on fire!"

The man's voice was closer when he shouted back, "Not until I see his dead face!"

Cason shucked off his plaid shirt. He wrapped it around his nose and mouth, looking like a Desert Storm warrior; he stood up from his crouch next to the window and into the billowing smoke. It was two long excruciating heartbeats for Savannah as she watched him waiting for the opportunity he was looking for. Cason reached suddenly out the window and, yanking a man back into the room, tossed him against a burning support beam. The man hollered, and Cason moved in on the pistol that had come in with him.

"I'm on fire!" the man shouted.

Cason struck him solidly in the jaw as he rolled off the beam. Cason slid the pistol he had confiscated across the hot hardwoods to Savannah. She caught it and, using two hands, pointed it at the window.

Smoke and sparks swirled. The man, hobbling to his bloody leg, hollered and swung at Cason. Cason dodged and punched down, nailing the wound on the man's knee. The man doubled over in pain as Cason brought his fist up. He connected with his chin, snapping the wounded man's head back.

Cason watched him stiffen with the knockout. He fell back toward the fire. Cason coldly left him there and, crouching under the smoke, went back to Savannah.

The second half of the upper story threw burning debris down. A sizzling support beam cracked and fell in the distance, throwing sparks and heat up into the giant campfire.

Next to Savannah, Cason gently took the gun from her hands and gestured for her to continue to stay down. He went to the window in a crouch before chancing a glance over the sill. As he did, bullets whined into the house.

Savannah stifled a shriek at the sound so close to her face and hit the floor again. Cason waited three beats, then shot out the window.

Two more pops from his pistol and Cason was back next to her, his eyes watering. "Out!" he said. There was a shudder and a bone-deep cracking from the home. Fear illuminated his eyes, and he didn't wait for her. Cason lifted Savannah and tossed her out the window as the first floor collapsed.

Chapter Thirty-Three

Embers flew, and the heat was set on high. He seriously cursed himself for leaving the stoves on and cursed Phillip Nigel for having such a huge fucking propane tank.

Cason crouched, still in the house, as his nose and eyebrow hairs started to feel as if they were singing off. He came up and took a deep breath of cool, clean air from the window, and then he moved. He had watched his mother slip like an eel from the place long before. That left Nigel. He needed to get that man out of the house; his number wasn't up until Cason said so. Leaping over debris and side-stepping licking flames, he moved through the collapsed house as it attempted to consume him. Until he was hit from behind.

Unprepared for it, Cason went down, skidding on burning debris. Turning over, he saw the man he'd knocked into the flames coming at him.

Cason's lungs burned with the last of the clean air.

"I'm gonna kill you!" the man shouted, his voice contorted through the heat waves. Limping and with his finger shirt wrapped over his nose and mouth, the man went around a chair that was turning into a briquette and pulled a knife. Cason let him move in. As he did, the man leaped, knife out. Cason turned, kicking out. His boot tip nailed the smaller man in the head. The kick hit the man's head sideways and crumpled him. He landed on a low pile of burning debris. Cason yanked him up and prepared to toss him out a window. Only he elbowed Cason's face. The hit landed hard, making him gasp automatically for air.

Hot smoke filled Cason's airway through the plaid shirt and took him to his knees. As he hit the floor, he was struck again from behind. He went all the way down, and panic clawed at his mind, irrationally making him want to rip the fabric off his mouth. His lungs struggled for oxygen.

Putting his face into the floor, he felt the pain in his hip again, felt the ripping up his thigh as the RPG went off next to him. He felt the desert sand under his fingers and knew the door to his Humvee—and escape—was within reach. The sick feeling of Ryan's death was fresh in him. He turned over and saw the face of the insurgent who had put the bullet through Ryan's neck.

The man came at him, and letting all thoughts go, ignoring the burning, the heat of the desert, and any thought of death, Cason welcomed him into his arms.

Cason was up, slapping the knife aside; with his other hand, he snatched the back of the man's neck. He tried to turn out of Cason's grip, but Cason moved with him. They wrestled for the upper hand. And Cason slipped his arm around, put the crook of his elbow against the man's Adam's apple, and squeezed. Light dimmed at the edges of his own vision, and Cason simply closed his eyes, holding his breath. He could send Ryan's killer into the afterlife with his eyes closed and without oxygen in his lungs. It would be as easy as dying.

Cason's arm slipped from the insurgent's neck as his strength slipped against the man's attempt to get away. Cason fought to hold tight. The man struggled as the heat of the desert grew, and despite the crackle and dull roar of the whipping sand burning his skin, Cason heard Savannah's voice call his name.

In an instant, the desert retreated, and he was in a house on fire, killing a man who was trying to kill him. His eyes snapped open, and through their watery haze, he saw Phillip Nigel was trying to leave.

Cason felt his hand at the back of man's head; just one forceful snap, and he'd be lights out for eternity. He'd done it before; he could do it again.

Cason tightened his grip. Savannah called to him again.

He felt that tug deep in his belly, the tether she used to pull him to her. Before Cason could decide, the man slumped in his arms, and weak from the lack of oxygen, Cason collapsed with him to the floor.

Cason mentally cursed and rolled off the man. He tried to get his body to move further, but it wouldn't. It needed air. Cason put his face against the floor and, ignoring the acrid heat attempting to light his plaid face-guard on fire—and subsequently him—breathed in.

Coughing, elbows bare and burning, and eyes watering, Cason army-crawled forward. His head felt hollow, and his body pulsed with the pump of his struggling heart as he moved toward the door. The upper story roared as the inferno dug its fingers into the roof, making the entire structure groan. The windows exploded.

Cason rounded the last of the debris; with his elbows and boot toes, he pushed himself forward again and again. He reached Nigel by the door. Shirt over his nose, coughing and sputtering, Nigel was trying to open the door without touching the branding iron of a knob.

Cason grabbed him just as the entire house shuddered. He ripped the plaid shirt off his mouth and put it to the knob and twisted as the rest of the windows blew out and the roof—a wild firestorm—came hurtling down.

Chapter Thirty-Four

Savannah wrestled with the emergency crew members trying to hold her back. She had to get Cason.

Suddenly, the house roared out of the earth and, in a billowing firestorm, imploded.

In her head, Savannah started screaming. Cason was still in there. In that moment, when everyone was startled by the crash, Savannah broke free and streaked through the vehicles. With her shirt, she shielded her face from the heat of the dying house. Rounding the last ambulance, she fell to her knees in front of Cason's silver truck. Smoke billowed up, water arched out of hoses onto the debris—and being pulled back toward the EMTs was Cason.

Blackened with smoke, he was swarmed with medics shoving oxygen onto his face. It took four of them to wrangle him back. Cason kept pulling at his oxygen mask and saying something. Each time, someone pulled his hand away and replaced the mask.

Behind him, Phillip Nigel was being assisted, a gurney next to him and a field IV being prepped.

Savannah pushed to her feet and propelled herself forward, relief making her knees go watery. Cason was hefted onto a gurney, and firefighters wrestled with him to keep him down. She heard him call her name.

"I'm here. I'm here." She rushed to his side, picked up his hand, and held it tightly. He smelled of acrid smoke, singed hair, and his hand was burning hot, as if he had a raging fever.

He looked up at her and smiled as the paramedic pulled his other hand up and swabbed his skin, prepping it for an IV.

The EMTs moved like hornets out of a disturbed nest. Radios crackled, and in seconds two EMTs had Cason in an ambulance, Savannah with him. The rear doors barely closed before they were in motion. Cason closed his eyes.

The younger EMT behind Savannah gently shoved her toward Cason's head and told her, "Keep him awake." They placed cool packs under his armpits. While someone cut his shirt off, Savannah gave his face a gentle tap. "Wake up, soldier. I'm gonna need to see your eyes. Open up, baby. Look at me." She devolved into pleading as the EKG bleeped horrible, slowing sounds.

"Cason." Savannah gave his face a harder slap. "Come on back to me." Staring at the line that had just gone flat on the monitor, she felt her head start to spin. Her stomach sank, and the paramedics pushed her back and slapped large stickers with electric nodes connected to it to his bare chest. At their command, she let go of him.

She swallowed bile down and watched as they tried to restart his heart. They gave him a shot. Waited and then shocked him again.

They shouted forward to the driver, and Savannah felt the ambulance pick up speed.

"Come on," Savannah whispered.

The older EMT cursed, and they charged the paddles again.

That's when it hit Savannah. There, right there, Cason had left her. He'd traded his life for hers.

Emotional sickness swamped her; she couldn't breathe as tears came up and choked her. Then something she hadn't been prepared for attacked her: anger. Anger at the sheer unfairness of life, and anger that, before they could finish what they had started, he had quit on her. As soon as he saw her, he felt fine about leaving her.

"Goddamn bastard." Leaning close to his face, she said, "Wake the hell up right now, McPherson. I'm not done with you. I have plans with you. I made goddamn plans, and if you die, you're going to mess things up like a hurricane on game day. So wake your damn self up."

The older EMT across from her, reached his hand out to her, "Ma'am, I'm sorry, but—"

"Fuck you," she said. Feeling the last vestiges of control leave, she shoved him, looked back to Cason, and said, "Wake up."

When he didn't, she slapped him hard across the face. His oxygen mask was knocked to the side, and she shouted, "Wake up!" and hit him again.

The younger EMT at Cason's feet frantically grabbed her arm as it came back. Savannah made a fist and angrily glared at the younger man as she yanked her arm out of his grip. Savannah's fist accidentally cracked across Cason's jaw.

"Ow."

Savannah shouted at the EMT, "Get off of me!"

The truck went silent as the driver shouted, "Here!" and hit the brakes.

Savannah fell forward, and the EMTs paused for only a moment at the single syllable Cason had uttered. They were shocked back into action. One straddled Cason, to keep working on him as the rear doors popped open and his gurney was ejected out of the truck and hustled through the ER doors.

Chapter Thirty-Five

At the general hospital, Savannah cleaned up and had her cuts tended to and her arm bandaged then sat next to Cason in the ER as he argued with a nurse—a tall fair haired man in worn scrubs and currently sporting an expression of waning patience—about letting him go.

"I'm fine. Really. The oxygen really helped—" he said, a coughing jag cutting him off. "Really, I'll be fine."

"Sir, your burns need to be looked at and cleaned. Minimum you need to be here for twenty-four hours, seeing as you left us for a bit while being transported."

"Right. Well, my burns are fine. I'll keep them clean."

"Sir—"

Savannah interjected, "I'm afraid it's a lost cause. He's stubborn, but fortunately he's an expert in wounds. I think the sutures for the gunshot wound on his shoulder are the only injury he wouldn't try to treat himself, and that's only because he doesn't have a needle and thread."

The ER nurse sighed and looked from Savannah to Cason. "Fine. But he needs round-the-clock supervision. Will you do that?"

"I will. I'm prepared to do that until this knot in my gut goes away—maybe in a year or so?"

The nurse smiled. "Twenty-four hours is fine. We'll send you home with a few things. Now, Sheriff Lee is in the waiting area. He wants to see you both before you leave. I'll send him over."

"We've already given our statements," Savannah said.

The nurse shrugged. Savannah thanked him and then turned to Cason as the nurse left, leaving the green hospital curtain around the bed open.

"You're nuts," she said as he maneuvered to the edge of the bed.

"Now you tell me."

Savannah smirked and put a hand to his warm chest; his skin was still red from the heat. Soot marks ran along his arms and neck. A few clean spots pointed out where his cuts were, where his skin had been swabbed. He looked up at her as she asked quietly, "Are you sure you're okay?"

He took her hand in his and looked down as he interlaced his fingers with hers, then looked back up. "My level of all right is directly related to how alive you are."

She gave his hand a squeeze. "Me too."

Sheriff Lee meandered in then. "Mr. McPherson, Ms. Sparling..."

"Sheriff." Cason stood to shake his hand and then immediately sat back down.

"There are a few things I need to share with you. Once Mr. Nigel is out of surgery, we'll be placing him under arrest. The other woman there, you said, was your mother?"

"Unfortunately."

"I see. Well, we tracked her down. She was in bad shape—real shiners blooming from a broken nose—but she's corroborating your version of events. As such, she'll have to be arrested for her part in all this."

"Good."

Sheriff Lee's brows rose.

"Prison will be the right place for her to sober up."

"I see," he said again and then: "We have recovered the body of one of the men who assisted Mr. Nigel and your mother. The medical examiner is classifying it as suffocation from the fire. The other man we were able to track down—his wrist was broken, as was his face. He lost some blood but is going to live. He'll also be going to prison. His rap sheet is longer than my arm. Having said that, I still don't want you two going too far for the next while. There is a curious case of a bullet hole in the dead man that might need explaining. If I need more information, I'll need to know where to find you."

"You know where I live," Cason said.

Savannah was about to agree, ready to put the entire day behind them, but then realized what Cason had said. "What?" she said, turning her gaze to Cason, who had shaken out his blackened plaid and was preparing to put it on.

Sheriff Lee continued, "I do, and I'm still not sure on why you bought that rundown old thing."

Savannah's gaze went to Sheriff Lee and then back to Cason. "How long has *he* known you bought that place? Specifically, did he know before I did?"

Sheriff Lee pointed between the two of them and said, "I'll let y'all sort this one out." He touched his forehead in salute to Cason before leaving, a grin on his face.

Cason pulled Savannah in close. "Have I mentioned how much I love you?"

Savannah smiled and molded herself to his half-naked sooty front. "I love you too, but you're not off the hook that easily."

Savannah's phone rang then. It was mingled among the things retrieved from Cason's truck. Sadly, the po-boys, Savannah was told, had been run over multiple times.

Cason smiled at the sound of her ring tone. "Saved."

Savannah kept one hand on Cason as she reached for her phone on the small stainless-steel instrument table next to Cason's bed. She sighed when she saw the caller ID.

Cason saw it too. "Answer it. She'll worry if you don't." He gave her hand a squeeze. "And act normal."

"Act...what?" she said and, swiping the screen to answer, said cheerily, "Hi, Mama."

Cason's eyes crinkled at their edges as he smirked. "Now she'll know something's up," he whispered.

Savannah rolled her eyes as her mother spoke. "Yes, we're fine. Brunch tomorrow?" she asked. She looking questioningly at Cason, who just shrugged. "Sure, wait, will the Devereaux be there? No? Great, we'll see you tomorrow then. What can we bring?"

Chapter Thirty-Six

Savannah stepped out of her brand new pearlescent white SUV and adjusted her billowy shirt and jean shorts. She bumped the door shut with her hip and then pulled a paper bag of groceries and pastries from the back as Cason, flowers in hand, slid from the passenger seat. They met at the front of the car.

Savannah smiled and took his arm. "Ready?"

"I was just going to ask you that. Can you make it past thirty minutes?"

"With you? I think I could stay all day. I even turned the ringer on my cell off."

Cason raised his eyebrows as they headed up the stairs. "Miss Savannah...what have I done to you?"

She smiled at him and brushed his lips with a kiss when they paused outside the door. "Loved me like no one else could."

He smiled back at her. "We have a brunch to go to. Stop talking dirty and kissing me."

She laughed as the door opened to Myrna in a fire-engine-red tunic and matching lips. "I thought I heard someone out here! Well, now, Cason, get an eyeful of you. Is that a smile on that dark, handsome face of yours? Come in! Stop wasting time, you two. Your mother, Martin, and I have been waiting for you."

Savannah looked down at her watch as she stepped inside, and the rich smells of strong black coffee, fried bacon, and baking buttermilk biscuits embraced them. "Hi, Mama," she called to the kitchen; then to Myrna, she said, "We're not late, are we? Mama said ten."

"Oh no," Helen said, coming to get the groceries from Savannah, "Myrna has been waiting for you two to arrive so she can ooh and ah over you."

"Hi, Cason, Savannah," Martin said warmly, shaking Cason's hand and then Savannah's. He held Savannah's hand a little longer, placing his other on top. "So good to see you so happy."

Savannah was surprised by the sudden lump in her throat. "Oh, thanks. It, uh, feels good too."

In the living room Helen had laid out an impressive spread that included ambrosia salad—not really a breakfast item in her mama's book. Savannah's stomach gurgled happily, although she was also suspicious, and she excused herself to help her mother. She turned back at the entrance to the kitchen and saw that Myrna's hand had found Cason's arm. He smirked at Savannah, his eyes exuding that playful green mischief he saved for special occasions, and she wagged her finger at him before quietly laughing and slipping into the kitchen.

"Mama, there's ambrosia salad on the table—"

"Thank you, honey, for bringing the extra champagne and beignets!" Helen took the bags from Savannah and said, "It's been a while since I've had a Café du Monde beignet."

Savannah's eyes narrowed curiously at her mother's dodging of the ambrosia salad query. She pressed, "You never make ambrosia salad unless you're bribing me."

"Marshmallows should never be in anything called a salad."

"Exactly, and the last time you made it for me, you said you were planning on seeing Martin full-time. So, what's your news this time? Getting married? I hope it's not a shotgun wedding."

Helen had been moving beignets from the bakery bag to a platter. When Savannah said that, a beignet slipped from her fingers and landed with a puff of powdered sugar on the plate. "I—"

Savannah gave her mother a sideways hug and a peck on the cheek. "I'm only kidding, Mama. But I'm on to you. You have an announcement to make."

"Well, I—Martin and I are waiting to announce it together to you."

"To me? Cason and Ms. Myrna already know?"

"Savannah, now just hold your horses. Don't go rushing off like Christmas morning and tearing open all the presents before everyone is out of bed."

"Oh, Mama, that was just one time."

"You still have it in you, so just hold your horses and wait."

"All right," Savannah said and let her mother go, curious on what the ambrosia bait could mean. It felt right, though, her mother and Martin. Whatever the two were going to announce, Savannah was happy for her. Not to mention that, with guests there too, it must be happy news.

"Now that you mention relationships," her mother said, going to the sink, "when were you going to tell me that you and Cason are seeing each other?"

"Today, actually. We haven't been together all that long."

"Well, at the gala, you made it seem like it had been much longer. Or I assumed that because, well, because of what you said."

Savannah watched as her mother's cheeks turned rosy. "From what I said...?"

"Yes, well, when Peaches was making all that noise, and you cut her off, saying that, well, you and Cason had...been, well—She was very vulgar about it. But you confirmed it."

The light dawned for Savannah. She remembered hissing back at Peaches, saying that she had been with Cason and that he was good. She had bet Peaches's trailer on it...Savannah felt her matching blush. "That was just something I said to bite back at her, Mama. We—"

"Hey," Cason said, coming into the room, "can I help get things— Am I interrupting something?"

"No, hon. Will you take these out to the table for me?"

He leaned past Savannah to grab the platter from her mother. "You two are...red in the face...Ah, you just told her."

More than you realize. Savannah turned to him. "She kinda figured it out."

Cason nodded. "I'm sorry, ma'am. I really wanted to ask you before you found out—"

"You do not need my mama's—"

Helen pulled out champagne from the grocery bag. "Cason, honey, I'm happy for you both. You don't need my blessing to date my daughter. Savannah makes her own mind up about these things. I'm just happy she's found someone who makes her smile the way she is today. But you have my permission anyway."

"Thank you, Mrs. S."

"Now, if you can do something about her wearing shorts to my occasions, I'd be in your debt."

Helen poured the mimosas as Savannah and Cason helped set the table and chatted with Martin and Myrna.

"I hear you and Mama have an announcement?" Savannah prodded Martin at the table.

Martin adjusted uncomfortably in his chair. "Yes, well, your mom thought we should wait—"

"Oh, now," Myrna said, waving a hand at Savannah, "don't be going around your mama to find out what she has planned today. Why don't we find out more about you two?" She wiggled her eyebrows at Savannah as she pointed between Savannah and Cason, who was seated at the end of the table, across from Myrna. "He's dynamite, right?"

Savannah had swiped a marshmallow out of the ambrosia dish and now she paused with it halfway to her mouth. She wasn't sure what Myrna was implying, but if her natural ability to slide into the carnal was any indication, she was directly asking if Cason was good in bed. Which made Savannah think about that morning and how untouched the bed had been. But the shower, the shower was pure ecstasy, with water splashing and hips meeting hips.

Cason leaned back in the dining chair and put his hands behind his head, clearly enjoying the thoughts going through Savannah's mind. She hoped he was the only one who could read them. Since he was there. With her. In that shower.

"Dynamite?" Savannah questioned, playing dumb. "In the, um, kitchen? Oh yes, he's quite good. I've never been much in the kitchen department, just get down to business really—scorching things."

No one seemed to know if she was speaking literally or metaphorically. Myrna just about bounced out of her seat, and Cason's brow rose as if to ask, *Really?* Martin looked relieved at the change Helen's arrival brought. He stood, patting his forehead with his unfolded linen napkin as she sat across from him.

"Savannah, hon, why are you standing there like that? Have a seat. It's awkward having you hover over the table. And, Cason, hon, why are you looking at her like that? What'd I miss?"

Myrna happily supplied, "We were just talking about Cason's 'cooking' skills. Turns out—"

"Oh, Cason's a wonderful cook!"

Myrna gaped at Helen and then at Cason as Savannah jumped in. "No, yes, he is, but Myrna was...She was asking about...She was asking if Cason..."

All eyes were on Savannah then. "I. Well. Oh hell, for the record, yes, Cason is literally a good cook. Yes, Myrna, he's also a very caring and dedicated lover."

At her mother's cough and Myrna's giggle, Savannah rushed on. "But I think we're here for something else." Finally plopping the marshmallow into her mouth, Savannah sat between Cason and her mother and said, "What did you want to tell us?"

"Yes, well," she said, digesting for a moment what Savannah had just divulged; she then continued, "We might as well have it all in the open. So, in the spirit of Savannah's blunt announcements: Martin and I have decided to move in together here at the house, so Savannah, hon, be sure to call before you come over because Martin is retiring and is also a caring, dedicated lover."

Savannah spluttered next to her; Cason choked and then laughed. He leaned back in his chair and held up a hand to her mother. Helen looked at his hand and then delicately gave it a high five. "Nicely done, Mrs. S."

"Well, now, Martin," Myrna cooed to a stunned and flushing Martin. Myrna grabbed his bicep and gave it a squeeze. "Well done indeed."

"Mama..." Savannah groaned in embarrassment and looked at her mother for a long moment, trying to decide what to say. Her mother was the epitome of tact and grace, but she realized her mother had finally taken a page from Savannah's book. Thinking of her mother going about her announcement in a way that Savannah might, she smiled. "I'm happy for you. And yes, I'll call before dropping in." Helen laughed and then turned in her seat and hugged her daughter. "Love you, Mama, and I'm so happy for you."

"Thank you, hon. And it warms the cockles of my heart to see a smile on that beautiful face of yours."

She leaned back, put a warm hand to her daughter's face, and brushing her cheek, said to Cason, "Now, Cason, if this face does anything other than smile, I'll be the one administering a pill wrapped in peanut butter. Are we clear?"

Cason became serious and leaned forward. "Yes, ma'am. Crystal."

"Good, now let's join hands in grace."

WELL AFTER GRACE and after the last of the dishes were washed, dried, and put away, Savannah took Cason's hand and led him down the hall, and into the garage, and out the garage door, and into the backyard. There was a tall oak tree in the corner. She pulled him down next to her under it.

Small insects hovered about, and the smell of freshly cut grass clung to the clean warm breeze. Holding hands, Cason and Savannah lay under that oak tree for some time, gazing through the green canopy up into the blue beyond it.

Savannah felt the goodness of the moment seep into her bones and settle down deep into her soul. "I love you, Cason McPherson." She turned her head to look at his profile against the backyard.

"I love you too, Savannah Sparling."

She looked back up into the canopy. "I was just thinking of all the things that we've been through in the last few years, and I think that from here on out it's going to be clear sailing. Our future is going to be as calm and blue as these skies."

He raised up on his elbow and looked down at her, a lazy smile illuminating his features. He gave her a slow kiss and then said, "Even if it's not, we know we'll get through it just fine. We've been through this—we can take on anything together."

"Let's not get hit by RPGs or trapped in cars or house fires again, though."

"Agreed."

"And Cason?"

"Yes?"

"Do you believe in fate?"

"Yes."

"Me too."

Savannah smiled up at him, her hand gently tracing the edge of his jaw. His eyes closed against her touch. Her thumb tapped the front of his chin, and his eyes slowly opened. Cason leaned down again and whispered against her lips. "I believe in you and me more than anything else, though. You're my one and only, Savannah, the other half of my soul."

"And you're mine."

Epilogue

O ver the next months, the weather cooled. Savannah gave up her condo in town. She rented it to Charlot and charged an astronomical cleaning deposit. Evenings at the old Victorian found Cason and Savannah working together to bring new life to the grand old dame. They argued over the which finish to use on the flooring, dark or light, which tub should be purchased for the rear bath, and what type of stove should be installed in the refurbished kitchen.

Cason got to decide the stove, since he pointed out to Savannah that the only use she had for it was to reheat her mother's dishes. The rest of the decisions they made together, their choices bonding them further to each other and to their home.

Savannah didn't think that she could be so happy, that through all the darkness this kind of light could be waiting for her and Cason on the other side. Simple things became pleasures she looked forward to, like sitting next to Cason on the living room couch, his shoulder touching hers as they debated the merits of where to hang the TV for the best football viewing advantage from the kitchen.

Months glided joyously by, the weather cooled, and one day

Savannah picked up groceries at the supermarket, the Christmas decorations were out.

Christmas morning arrived, and the Victorian was swathed in greenery. A towering Christmas tree took up an entire corner of the wide living room, and on the front door a wreath of Spanish moss and holly hung under a massive garland. No more than a handful of times did Savannah smirk when she looked at it, the Spanish moss reminding her of the moment in the country club woods with Cason.

That morning, as Savannah lay in Cason's arms in their newly refinished bedroom, the curtains letting in watery morning light, she whispered, "I'm so glad we finished up in time for today."

Cason kissed the top of her head, his arm around her. "You know we'll never be done, right?"

"We're done for now, though. The extension can wait a year. And the new roof can be put off until spring."

"Siding?"

"Spring."

"Two-car garage with man cave?"

"Hmmmm, never."

He squeezed her and tickled her sides in response.

Savannah squeaked, "Okay! Okay! The spring," she said and, smiling, looked up at his morning stubbled face; the crinkles at the corners of his eyes and mouth had rarely faded since they made their promise to love each other months ago.

He leaned forward and kissed her. "Thank you for acquiescing."

"Mmmm, you're welcome," she said, savoring his kiss. "Now, I think we have to get up before my mother and Martin find us still in bed."

Cason pulled her in tighter. "That'd be fine by me."

Savannah laughed. "Okay. Then when they arrive, you can entertain them while I cook."

Cason groaned and buried his head into the crook of her neck. "And have your mother find out just how lousy of a cook you are?

Never." He reluctantly threw the sheets back. "Last one to the shower makes the coffee."

WITH THEMSELVES SHOWERED and the baked goods in the oven, filling the house with the buttery smells of dough and cinnamon, Cason and Savannah opened their stocking gifts before Helen and Martin arrived for brunch.

"It's hard to believe that this is our first Christmas together," Savannah said, digging into her deep-green stocking.

As Cason tore open the wrapping on a pack of razor replacement heads, he said, "That's because it's not."

"I know. We've spent a lot of Christmases together, just not together-together. In-this-house together. Oh." She pulled a small black box from the toe of the stocking.

The room went quiet, save for the crackle of the fireplace and the soft hum of Nat King Cole singing low and deep through the room's speakers. Cason slid off the plush sectional and put a knee down on the Persian rug.

"Savannah Sparling," he said, sliding her hands holding the box into his, "we have spent a lot of Christmases together—we've spent over two decades in each other's lives—but this Christmas I want to be different. This Christmas I want to spend with you as my fiancée. I love you, Savannah, more than life itself, and I can't imagine a life without you at my side, as my love, my partner, and my wife." His hands trembled slightly around hers. "Will you marry me?"

The tears that had brimmed in her eyes as soon as he'd gotten to one knee overflowed and coursed down Savannah's cheeks. "I—"

"Will you spend the rest of your life with me as my wife?" Cason asked, his own eyes going misty with emotion.

"Yes," she said breathlessly and leaned forward, wrapping her arms around him. "Yes. Always, yes."

Cason pulled her down to the floor with him and hugged her tightly. "I love you."

"I love you too."

He leaned back and kissed her gently. "Aren't you going to open it?" he said, nodding at the velvet box in her hand.

"I suppose I should, right?" She added with a grin, "Maybe I should have waited to give my answer until I saw it? And there's something just as important in your stocking too—you should dig it out."

Cason's brows drew together. "You got me a ring too?" he asked, pulling his stocking over to where they sat on the floor.

"No, silly—Oh," Savannah said as she opened the ring box. Displayed against the black velvet pillow was a diamond the size of her pinkie nail. It was framed with intricate threads of platinum lace studded with smaller diamonds. "My god, Cason," she said, trying not to watch as he pulled a bracelet box from his stocking.

"Do you like it?" he asked as she slipped it on.

"Like it? I love it. Is this antique?"

Cason nodded as he opened his box. "Yeah, good guess—"

Savannah looked over at him. Her heart had started to pound as he'd cracked open the box, and at his face, frozen in a gasp, she whispered, "You okay?"

She felt the weight of the ring on her finger, and for a wild moment she thought he might ask for it back and walk from the room. The thing in the box was a true life-changing gift.

Cason's hands began to shake in earnest. "Please tell me this isn't a joke," he said, pulling the plastic pee stick from the box and letting the wrapping fall to the floor. "Savannah..."

She studied his face. "Are you happy?"

"Only if this is real," he whispered back. "Please tell me this is real. Does this really say pregnant? You're pregnant?"

Relief and happiness spread through her. "Oh, it's real. We're having a baby."

Cason reached forward and gently cradled her face. "Really?"

"Really."

"Holy...shit." He hugged her again. "I think my chest is going to explode, I'm so happy. I never thought I could be so happy," he said gruffly into her hair.

"Are you crying too?" she asked softly.

"No. My eyes always water like this when I'm happy," he said, keeping his face hidden.

Savannah laughed and pulled back, grasped Cason's face between her hands, and kissed him hard. "I love you," she said and wiped her thumbs over his damp smiling cheeks.

"I love you too. How did I get to be the luckiest man alive?"

"Fate," Savannah said, kissing him again. "Fate and serendipity."

Acknowledgments

I come from a family and married into a family of active-duty personnel and honored veterans of the armed forces. Both my grandfathers and great-uncles fought in WWII. My grandmother would tell me stories about standing on her back porch on O'ahu the day Pearl Harbor was bombed. She spoke of the fighter planes flying so close that she could see the pilots' faces. Being in proximity to war has given me no more than just a peek behind a very dark curtain. But those times at my grandmother's knee and those times sitting with friends who served, hearing them talk about evacuating US citizens from Rwanda or carrying a bleeding comrade for two miles back to base only to discover the man had already died, showed me not only the difficulty of war but also how resilient humanity is. I'd like to thank all those friends and family members for those stories; they've made an indelible impression on me.

I'd also like to thank my fans. I know this is not the sequel to *The Legend of Lady MacLaoch*, but as Cason is a war vet like Rowan, I hope you concede and see this as a fun distraction until the sequel arrives.

Thanks also go to my wonderful editor, Kristin Thiel, and her sidekick editor Laura Garwood who made this into the editing gold you have in your hands now. Thanks also go to Annie Small (*The Small Book Blog*, http://small-book.blogspot.com/) for all her unflagging encouragement and reads and rereads and reading the rereads of this manuscript—you, Annie, are the Queen of ALL! I'd also like to thank the host of childcare goddesses we've employed since my son was born; without them, this final version would not have been possible. Ayn Generes, thank you for your infusion of the NOLA culture into me—I still look for small baby Jesuses in cake. Any butchering of the New Orleans locations and culture is all my fault. Last, but certainly not least, thank you to my husband for, simply, everything.

Author Bio

Becky Banks is a bestselling and award-winning indie author from an old Hawai'i family, who currently lives in Portland, Oregon, with her husband and two children. Becky likes to craft dark romances that stem from her past and require love to see her characters through. When she's not crafting love stories, she's packing lunches for her little ones and breaking up *Minecraft* fights.

Visit Becky Banks online at beckybanksbooks.com and follow her on social media for updates on new releases and more.

f facebook.com/beckybanksbooks

instagram.com/authorbeckybanks

a amazon.com/author/beckybanks

g goodreads.com/beckybanks

BB bookbub.com/profile/becky-banks

Also by Becky Banks

Clan MacLaoch Curse Series

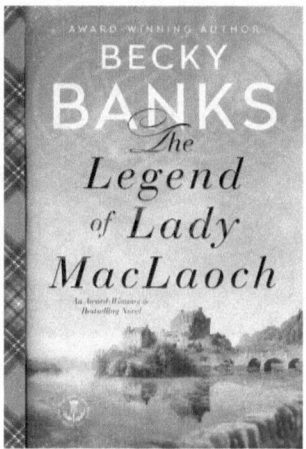

The Legend of Lady MacLaoch. *Book 1 of the Clan MacLaoch Curse Series.*

Centuries ago a vengeful curse buried itself deep into the history of the MacLaoch clan and became a legendary tale told by all those not cursed by its words.

In present-day Scotland, the laird and chief of the MacLaoch clan is an ex-Royal Air Force fighter pilot who has been past the gates of hell and returned a changed man. Rowan MacLaoch does battle with wartime memories and a family curse that threaten to consume him—unaware that his life and that of the history of the clan will be changed forever by the arrival of an American woman.

Cole Baker, a feisty recent graduate of a master's program, stumbles upon the ancient curse while researching her bloodlines. Moved by the history of the MacLaoch clan and the mystery of its chief, she digs into the legend that had been anything but quiet for centuries.

On their quest for answers, Cole and Rowan travel to places they have never before been and become witnesses to things they have never before fathomed. The legend—one started with blood—will end with more shed as its creator finally exacts her justice.

Book 2 of the Clan MacLaoch curse series, The Legend of the Viking.

In this second book of the Clan MacLaoch Curse series, we see our favorite characters, Rowan and Cole, return in their most passionate selves yet. Coming off the loss of the Gathering and the thought-to-be-extinguished MacLaoch curse, Rowan finally has a chance at his happily ever after. That is, until everything that he loves is put at risk, sparking events, that once set in motion, will not be stopped—except by love.

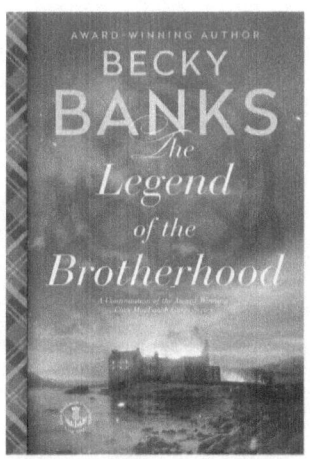

Coming soon. Book 3 of the Clan MacLaoch curse series, The Legend of the Brotherhood.

In this third book of the clan MacLaoch curse series, Cole's two worlds collide when her brother TJ stops by Castle Laoch for a surprise visit. His presence upsets more than the status quo at Castle Laoch; Rowan struggles to find a solution to the bankruptcy proceedings, which are starting to look like the end for the MacLaoch clan. Cole and Rowan - fresh off the battle on the cairn knoll - are bonded even more profoundly as they move to save the castle from bankruptcy and a villainous bankman set on a generation's old revenge. While Cole and Rowan's love is secure for eternity, the struggle for the ancestral MacLaoch home hangs in the balance. Can Rowan's determination, the Baker kids' ingenuity, and residual Viking power from Ormr Minorisson save the castle and clan from ruin?

Romantic Suspense Titles

Flux. *Can one notorious hacker protect the women she's saved before her dark past finds her?*

Vega Flux, a notorious hacker whose single mission in life is to protect the weak from online trolls, crashes up against an impenetrable powerhouse of a man who wants nothing more than to slip the dark shroud off her persona and protect her from her torments.

In this smoldering high-stakes game of defense and one-upmanship, Vega takes a bet she knows she shouldn't and starts the largest hack she's ever attempted, against the only worthy opponent she's ever known, tech billionaire and ex-NFL tight end, Hoyt Kaho'okalakupua. Master of his domain, Hoyt, welcomes the chance to flex his power in a true challenge. With the stakes dangerously high, and his heart on the line, he enters a game with a woman he wants it all from. There's only one fatal flaw: Hoyt and Vega are following different instructions to the same game. He's a law-abiding billionaire, and the world Vega lives in breaks every rule.

Dark passions ignite in this fast-paced thrill ride from award-winning indie author and Maui girl, Becky Healani Banks. As the torments of Vega's past breach her defenses, she reaches for the one man who is uniquely capable of providing the shelter she seeks. And in that process, she touches a power she's never known, real-life love.

Forged. *First loves, dark pasts, and fast cars collide in this high-octane thrill ride.*

Managing editor of a Manhattan fashion rag, Eva Rodgers, couldn't believe she would ever step back into her old life, but the day her father called with his diagnosis, she had little choice. Returning home, and to the past she left behind, Eva signs up as editor-in-chief of the struggling Portland magazine, *Rose City Review*. There in the drizzling Portland metro Eva still holds firm to the New York city values that defined her time there: compromise on nothing. When her European auto, one luxury she missed in the walking and hired car world of Manhattan, needs fixing, she doesn't compromise. Even when the best European auto mechanic her assistant finds turns out to be an ex with a vendetta, Eva doesn't flinch.

Nathaniel Vellanova can't believe what the fuck just showed up at his garage. He'd gotten his life together, buried his dark past, and definitely put Eva Rogers in his rearview mirror. Right?

But fuck him if she wasn't standing right there in the pouring rain needing his help. He'd do it—help her out—just this once then forget all about her. Again.

In this dark and suspenseful story of broken first loves, readers will ride the smoldering heat of high-octane fast cars, glitzy club fashion, and tainted love and ask themselves, are first loves the only love?

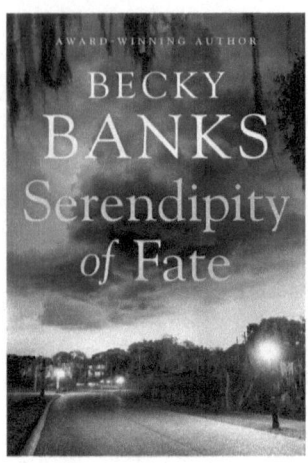

Serendipity of Fate. *Enemies to lovers romance. One war, one blood promise, and the love to save it all.*

It has been two years since Cason McPherson watched his best friend, Ryan Sparling, die in his arms. Now, with a blood promise tied to his heart, shrapnel in his hip, and a war behind him, he's focused on building a useful civilian life in his hometown of New Orleans. Living with Ryan's mother, a widow and retired nurse, he gives back the protection and care his best friend wanted. Only Ryan's sister, a woman whose well-worn picture got him through the darkest parts of the war, does not see it that way.

Savannah Sparling has spent the last five years building her career and life to the exacting expectations needed to achieve partner at Knight Interiors. And nothing could derail them except for the one person from her past who returned home a changed man. Cason McPherson and her brother Ryan had been her entire world once, but now she no longer recognizes him with his caustic attitude and effort to turn every conversation into a verbal sparring match. When a potential client, one large enough to secure her place as partner, requests her as lead designer, Savannah sets a plan for her final career move and Cason's eviction.

In a series of unstoppable events, Savannah's carefully laid plans backfire, and an unfathomable truth is revealed. In the aftermath, Cason and Savannah find that the only people strong enough to save them from themselves are each other. But will either one of them accept the help—and the love—that is offered?

Future Series

Coming soon.

Set one-hundred years into a dystopian future, this socio-political romantic thriller takes place in the sprawling catacombs of The Peoples Republic of Portland. In a world that has been punished by the misdeeds of mankind, one writer sets out to answer one simple question: What would happen if everyone had hope again? Absorbed onto a misfit team of ex-war machine operators, junior journalist Wendy Wilson, moves quickly to adapt or die while trying to save the city she loves and maybe, just maybe, change the hearts and minds of even the most blood-thirsty among them.

Be sure to visit beckybanksbooks.com and sign up for the author newsletter. Newsletter recipients are the first to get book release news and giveaway alerts.

Preview: Forged

First loves, dark pasts and fast cars collide in this high-octane thrill ride.

Managing editor of a Manhattan fashion rag, Eva Rodgers, couldn't believe she would ever step back into her old life, but the day her father called with his diagnosis, she had little choice. Returning home, and to the past she left behind, Eva signs up as editor-in-chief of the struggling Portland magazine, *Rose City Review*. There in the drizzling Portland metro Eva still holds firm  to the New York city values that defined her time there: compromise on nothing. When her European auto, one luxury she missed in the walking and hired car world of Manhattan, needs fixing, she doesn't compromise. Even when the best European auto mechanic her assistant finds turns out to be an ex with a vendetta, Eva doesn't flinch.

Nathaniel Vellanova can't believe what the fuck just showed up at his garage. He'd gotten his life together, buried his dark past, and definitely put Eva Rogers in his rearview mirror. Right?

But fuck him if she wasn't standing right there in the pouring rain needing his help. He'd do it—help her out—just this once then forget all about her. Again.

In this dark and suspenseful story of broken first loves, readers will ride the smoldering heat of high-octane fast cars, glitzy club fashion, and tainted love and ask themselves, are first loves the only love?

Turn the page to start reading a sample of Nate and Eva's story in *Forged*.

Forged: Chapter 1

The memories flicker by like the frames of an old film. Unfocused and dark at the edges. A punch to his gut, to his face. The wall behind him in the yellowing kitchen seems to punch him as well. It slams against his back and smacks his head to the tabletop as the fist from his father throws it there. He's seven.

By ten he learns to dodge the fists, to know when tension in the apartment would erupt. Eleven, he has one foot out the door, has found a second life, a best friend. Twelve, he has already left home to live with his aunt. Twelve slides into fifteen and fifteen into freedom.

Freedom? It was never free.

The memories of that final day came unbidden, as they always did—and slippery. That day he was twenty-seven and holding the phone to his ear, listening to a foreign sound. His father's sobs echoed over the line; they begged him home. To please come, it was his mother... These sobs, from the man who met every sobering morning with a toast of his golden can of Olympia and every sunset with his fist in his wife's face.

Could the son have known then? He'd always ask himself that. Was there any way to know what his father had in store for him when he returned home, for his mother, for the man who was his father? The scars on his skin and the wounds within that had yet even to scar told him not to go, but he had unfinished business with the old man. He'd go, and maybe this time it would be different.

Nate opened the door to the dark apartment he'd once called home. It was after work, the sun had gone down, his boots were slick with the rain he had just come in from. They slipped on the linoleum floor. A smell rose up and enshrouded his body like a cloak. It clung to his nose and at the back of his throat, a tangy, rusty tincture of blood. Warm, as if it were being pulsed from the veins of a being. Automatically he reached for the light behind him, his stomach clenching, his mind telling him no. No. NO!

That was when the memory got slick. Even now his mind recoiled, and the details of that night faded back into the black mist.

Eva, he thought to distract himself. *Where are you now, Eva?* Her name rolled around in his mouth softly, whispered to no one. An entirely different set of emotions consumed him as his parents faded away once more. She was seven when he was ten, and she was there for him every time he showed up with a black eye or a new burn. She'd shown him his first fast car, and later he taught her how to fix them, to make them go faster. At sixteen she rocked his world in a way he would never recover from.

The years had passed like lightning after that day, each one spent with Eva more mind blowing than the next. But as everything in his life tended to do, that too would come to an end.

The pain, now cathartic, motivated, consumed him. His dark past closed up shop and faded away, leaving him with his future. *His* future, where he was in control.

Forged: Chapter 2

The rain hammered down on the windshield as Jenny and I made our way to our recently discovered import garage. I had been relieved to find a BMW mechanic that wasn't too drunk or too deaf to hear that I just wanted the oil changed, not a forty-minute hollering hand-gesture session about how he wanted to replace my brakes. I'd bought the ten-year-old German sedan used and she was perfect—aside from needing regular repairs, which was like Jenny's alpaca yarn, costing me a mint.

Though my car was going to reap the rewards and I would come to blissfully claim at least partial credit for the mechanic find, Jenny and her precious Peugeot were technically the sole heroes in the discovery. On Monday, I'd been in my office ostensibly reviewing the recent shoot for July's cover, but really wallowing in the current state of my life. I knocked the old-school desk light to motivate it to work and thought of the fashion rag—particularly the office—I'd left in New York City. That office had been wide and luxurious—plush gray carpeting and dark paneling, furniture handpicked from a sleek and modern designer catalog—and I'd bitten and clawed my way to that corner palace thirty-four floors into the Manhattan sky in just seven years. Now I felt like I was perpetually crouching low under the Portland, Oregon, cloud cover. My fourth-floor office's midcentury décor had nothing to do with design resurgence; rather, it simply hadn't been touched since Mad Men's inspiration had been reality. On top of that, I had chosen this new life and had a magazine to run, which included advertisers and subscribers who didn't care what my current office looked like. In other words, I had made my own worn-out bed, and I was having to work hard just to sleep in it.

Jenny, my *Rose City Review* assistant and sometimes guest writer, came waltzing in that morning and flopped down on one of the chairs in the semicircle in the middle of the office. "You would not believe what I found," she said smugly.

"What's that?" I bit on Jenny's bait.

"So, you know how I've been on this trek to find the best import repair shop in the city, right?"

"Please tell me that your ancient Peugeot has found one," I said with a laugh and returned to my work, editing pen in hand looking at the next issue's cover choices.

"I did...and they do all years of BMWs and the mechanics are H-O-T."

I glanced at her out of the corner of my eye. "So, you asked one of them out with your oil change? Bold." I said then held up a cover option. "Does her skin tone seem abnormally red to you in this one?"

"No and no. I'll probably work up the gumption, though. This one guy is totally my type."

I gave her a distracted smile, the model on that cover was definitely too red.

"The head mechanic actually owns the place and he's not really hot per se, but he has that air about him that I thought would be perfect for you."

"Perfect for me, huh," I repeated. "And what's that?" I asked as I put down the cover art.

"Unavailable, uninterested, sort of dark—with a past, you know?

But I imagine that with him you sort of feel like you could take over the world."

I arched a brow at her. "Quite the brief first encounter." I looked back down. "If you're right, you just described *complex* to a T, my friend."

Jenny laughed, like a chiming bell tower, loud and ringing. "Yes! That's totally it. Anyway—didn't you say your door has a leak?"

I had dropped my car off the next afternoon, leaving the keys with their front desk woman, who wore something in the shade similar to safety orange and was the same age as my father, and not a single luscious or brooding mechanic was in sight. There were four work bays, from which noise screeched, and a parking lot full of average Euro cars, except for two. They were a little red family car and a black two-door monster. Though I was unsure of its heritage from a distance, however the black monster screamed: *fast*. Something I once knew a lot about.

Now, through the sheeting rain, from the comfort of the dry interior of Jenny's car, I saw the watery glow of my car idling, parking lights on, directly in front of us, beside the main office. I hoped the water seal on the rear door was indeed fixed; otherwise, my baby was now officially a fishbowl.

"Wanna borrow my umbrella?" Jenny asked.

"No, I'm good—I'll just run inside. I have to say"—my hand on the door handle—"I'm impressed already that they have the car running. I bet the heater's on too. We'll see after I get the bill if I'm still appreciating the attention to detail. See you tomorrow and thanks for the ri—"

Jenny grabbed my arm. "Omigod."

"Wha-?" I said, leaning to the side, trying to see what had made her gasp but at that moment only my car and its exhaust and lights were visible through the sheet of water on the windshield. Then the wipers cleared away the water, and I noticed what had made her gasp.

He stood tall in slate-colored work pants and an open rough-hewn jacket with the company logo embroidered over his heart. Leaning against the building under the scalloped awning, he smoked a cigarette like it was the last one he'd ever have. His features were shadowed under the awning, but it could have been pitch-black and I'd still have known who he was. And he was looking straight into the car—and into my eyes.

"Lord..." I said like an oath under my breath.

"I know, right?" Jenny said, misinterpreting me.

"Wish me luck," I whispered to her and to no one and got out of the car.

Nathaniel Vellanova pushed away from the wall and in one smooth movement opened the massive umbrella that had been leaning next to him and strode toward me.

Behind me I heard Jenny reverse out the driveway, leaving me to my past.

***

Continue reading *Forged* ebook or paperback at Amazon.com.